Voden fled through the dark forest. All around him he could hear the soft, insistent rustling made by his pursuers. Their eyes were big with greed, their fangs and claws twitching with desire.

He looked up and saw two ravens circling. "Come out of yourself," they croaked. The hot breath of two wolves played over his face. "Come out of yourself," they growled.

Still he fled, toward a clearing where a darkhooded figure waited. The hood fell back and he saw a face, half of it beautiful, half rotted with decay.

The figure raised a long, wickedly gleaming knife. The knife slashed downward and he screamed with the shock of pain....

Ace Books by Dennis Schmidt

TWILIGHT OF THE GODS: THE FIRST NAME
SATORI
KENSHO
WAY-FARER

Twilight of The Gods:
The First Name

DENNIS SCHMIDT

Fowler's Books
Buy - Sell - Trade
323 N. Euclid
Fullerton 92632
or
2634 W. Orangethorpe
Fullerton, 92634

ACE FANTASY BOOKS
NEW YORK

TWILIGHT OF THE GODS:
THE FIRST NAME

An Ace Fantasy Book/published by arrangement with
the author

PRINTING HISTORY
Ace Original/February 1985

ISBN: 0-441-23929-3

Ace Fantasy Books are published by The Berkley Publishing Group,
200 Madison Avenue, New York, New York 10016.
PRINTED IN THE UNITED STATES OF AMERICA

This book is dedicated to
Freyja.

CONTENTS

THE VIGRID

I

Two men lay just behind the crest of the ridge, hidden by the jumbled rocks and twisted scrub that crowned it. One was dark and slender, narrow of face, with an aquiline nose, thin harsh lips, and liquid black eyes. His hair was the same midnight hue as the long robe that covered his body.

The other was a complete contrast. His huge, muscular form was covered with a filthy beige robe that reached to just below his knees. Blond hair, bleached almost white on top, hung past his shoulders in several braids. A braided beard and mustache, equally blond, covered most of his face. Two cold blue eyes stared from a light-skinned face that was peeling and sunburned. The nose was broken and twisted to the left. Full, sensual lips, dry and badly cracked, could barely be seen in the midst of his beard and mustache.

For long minutes the two lay there, unmoving except for their eyes, which took in everything, cataloging, counting, and evaluating. Satisfied, their eyes met in mutual agreement and slowly, cautiously, the men lowered their heads and began to crawl backward down the slope. Once certain they were well below the line of sight of those on the other side of the ridge, they scuttled quickly to the bottom of a narrow ravine, where a group of men awaited their return.

Surt's black eyes sparkled in response to the greedy smile that curved Borr's lips. "This is what we've been waiting for, Skullcracker," he declared. His strange southern accent and soft deep voice were a murmur barely discernible above the constant hot sigh of the west wind that scoured the barren hills. "This one will make us all rich men."

Borr nodded his blond head and grunted agreement. "Huh. Rich, yes, but there's something strange about this caravan. It's not like the others we've seen. Those guards, for instance, and that big wagon. And that one who rides alone, that one in

3

black. I couldn't quite make out his face no matter how hard
I tried. Strange."

"Strange indeed," Surt responded. "Some of those who lead
the beasts wear the garb of far-off Kara Khitai. The panniers
on their animals look heavy with treasure. In the days of the
First Dark Empire such a thing was not unusual. Now it's rare
for the Yellow Robes to journey to Muspellheim.

"The wagon is stranger yet. It's painted with the designs
and curtained with the rich fabrics of dawn-lit Prin. Who knows
what fabulous wealth lies within? Fabulous it must be, for those
who guard it wear the livery and badges of An, the eldest Son
of Muspell. Their kind do not ordinarily guard caravans. Whatever treasure the wagon carries must be bound for An himself.

"Strangest indeed is the black one who rides alone. He's a
wizard, Borr, and from the looks of him, a powerful one. The
caravan is rich, my Aesir friend. Rich beyond our wildest
imaginings, and it's also very well guarded."

Borr frowned. "A wizard, eh? Why a wizard to guard a
caravan, even one this big and rich?"

Surt shrugged. "I don't know." He looked craftily at the
Aesir. "Surely the presence of a mere wizard doesn't frighten
you? Wizards can die, Skullcracker, just like ordinary men."

The blond man shook his head and growled. "I've not studied the Dark Art as you have, Surt, but I fear neither it nor
those who practice it. I meet wizards and their foul evil the
way I meet all enemies—with cold steel in my hand. There's
no room for fear in the heart of an Aesir warrior. Our fates are
rune-carved by the Nornir at our births. There's no escape. So
no true Aesir cowers at home in fear. We stride forth to meet
our dooms with singing hearts and blood-drenched weapons."

Surt nodded and smiled. Ah, my fine Aesir fool, he thought.
I knew you wouldn't disappoint me. You and your pale-haired
friends are so big, so brave, so stupid. Oh, yes, you fear
nothing. So we'll attack the caravan and many of your men
will die. Then, when the treasure's won and your followers
are few, when you think it's over and you're safe at last, then,
in the dark of the night, while you lie rolled in your blankets,
dreaming of luxury and wealth, I and my jackals will slit your
throats! Yes! And *all* the treasure will be mine! *All* of it! All
the gold and jewels that weigh down the panniers the beasts
carry! Plus whatever incredible wealth lies within the wagon
from Prin!

Yes! And one more thing. A shiver of expectation coursed through his body. One more thing. One thing more valuable than all the rest. He'd caught only the briefest glimpse of it, but that had been enough. For years he'd slaved in harsh apprenticeship to old Shubur. In all that time the wizened little bastard had refused to teach him anything more powerful than the most menial spells of the Kishpu sorcery. He'd had to steal anything else and puzzle it out on his own, but if he could get possession of the thing he'd just seen, he knew he could summon and control vast power! His hands curled into grasping claws just thinking of how he would clutch it. He lowered his head to hide the lustful light he knew burned in his dark eyes.

Borr turned from Surt to look at the thirty men who stood in a silent, waiting group. Most were Aesir, tall, thick, and blond, with wild, shaggy hair like his own. The rest, ten in all, resembled Surt. Like their dark leader, they were condemned criminals who'd somehow escaped the wrath of the Sons of Muspell and now roamed the Great Route between the Oasis of Kath and the Great Wall, preying on the caravans that traveled it. A scruffy lot of murderers and thieves, they made Borr uncomfortable. Not that he feared them. One Aesir was worth ten such in a fight. It was just that they were skulking killers, throat-slitters making a foul living, rather than battle-glad heroes seeking glory. No matter. They were useful allies here in the Twisted Lands. They knew the territory, and this was a big, well-protected caravan. They were valuable extra blades. Still, he reminded himself, it would never do to turn one's back on them.

He knew the worth of his own men. Karldred, the best ax—next to his own—in all of Asaheim; Nial, a swordsman without equal; Thidrandi, Torhall, Ingvar, Haakon, Skirnir, Lodur, all of them hardened Aesir warriors one could stand back-to-back with against any odds. They knew the wolf work, the raven's game.

Borr grunted again and nodded. "I say we take them. How say the rest of you?" Their grins and growls were answer enough. Borr smiled and looked at Surt. "My wolves are eager to pull down the prey and begin the blade feast."

Surt's eyes gleamed darkly. "My friends are ready too. When and where shall we strike?"

"Hmm. They're well armed and alert. Ordinarily I'd think one of these ravines would be the ideal spot, but not this time.

They'd be ready, and the odds are too close. Hmm, I wonder." For a moment he was silent, his blue eyes half closed as he calculated and planned.

"Surt, do you remember that spot on the Vigrid?"

The dark man frowned. "The salt flat? Where the two ravines parallel the trail?"

"Just so. What if we divided our men and put half in each ravine? When they drew abreast, one half would attack. Once the first group had them fully engaged, the second could launch a surprise attack from the rear."

Surt nodded. "Yes. They'll be less wary on the plain. We'll surprise them twice, once from the flank, once from behind."

"If we move out now we'll get to the Vigrid before them," Borr said. "We can travel all night and take up positions at dawn. They should reach us late in the afternoon. The trail runs almost north–south there, so we can launch our first attack from the west to keep the sun in their eyes. That will put the wind right in their faces too."

He paused for a moment, looking speculatively at Surt. "Have you magic to cloak our odor so their horses won't smell us and give the alarm, and to hide the second group from even their sharpest lookouts?" The dark man smiled slightly and nodded twice. "Good," Borr grunted. "Then you'll be in the other ravine and lead the second attack." He looked around at the raiders, meeting nods of agreement. "All right, then. Let's ride. We've a long hot day and night ahead of us."

"With great wealth waiting," added Surt softly. They all chuckled grimly in response.

The Vigrid had once been a shallow seabed. Now it was a vast plain of dried, salty mud, its cracked, ravine-riddled surface lifeless and deadly. A full fifty miles wide and nearly as long, it shimmered in the heat of the southern sun. Nothing moved or stirred anywhere, except the occasional dust-devils whipped up by the ever-blowing west wind.

Haruum hated riding point. Out here in this endless flatness he felt totally exposed, one man with emptiness all around him. He looked back over his shoulder at the caravan that stretched out behind him to reassure himself that indeed it still followed; that he was not, in fact, alone in the midst of this stinking Vigrid. As he turned forward again, the low afternoon sun glared in his eyes and momentarily blinded him. By the Sons!

he silently cursed. The damned thing was brighter now than it had been at midday.

His vision cleared at the same instant the arrow took him in the throat. With a gurgling cry of astonishment he flung his arms wide and pitched from his horse.

The raiders poured from the ravine, howling with bloodlust. Amid a clash of steel and a screaming of horses, they collided with the guards. Borr was the first to draw blood, his one-handed battle-ax shattering first the shield, then the skull of one of the defenders. With a shriek of victory raised to Sigfod, God of Battle, he whirled his horse and launched himself at another enemy. An arrow thudded home in the luckless animal's neck, and it stumbled, going down on its knees and throwing Borr forward. He dove, curled into a ball, and sprang upright even as he hit the ground. Blocking a sword sweep from a mounted warrior with his shield, he chopped at the man's leg and neatly severed it just above the knee. Blood sprayed out in a red fountain as the man tumbled backward off his horse. Borr found himself covered with another's gore. He howled triumph once more and spun about, looking for other prey.

At that moment Surt, leading the second group of attackers, struck, and suddenly everything was a whirling, slashing madness. Borr turned just in time to see two guards on foot rush at him, long battle spears in hand. Quickly he thrust his one-handed ax in his belt, dropped his shield, and unslung his two-handed battle-ax, Deathbringer, from his back. Brushing aside one of the spears as though it were a mere stick, he drove the guard to his knees with a mighty blow that split him from the top of his head to the middle of his chest. The other man struck out with his weapon, and even though Borr twisted quickly to the side, the blade slashed his shoulder. He stepped back, blocking a second thrust. Then with a roar and a leap he was on the man, ax shattering spear first, chest second.

The battle raged on. Borr saw three men close on Ingvar and cut him down. Lodur, kicked senseless by a horse, was skewered on a spear. Two of Surt's black cutthroats went down, one missing an arm, the other spilling his life from a gaping wound in his stomach. More and more died as the wolf-work progressed.

Stepping back from the headless corpse of the man he had just felled, Borr felt a prickling of the hairs on the back of his neck. He looked up to see strange dark clouds growing on the southern horizon. What in the name of the gods? he wondered. Then it hit him. The wizard! Of course. The bastard was summoning something to his aid. Perhaps some demon!

Before he could turn to search, Surt was by his side. His dark eyes were wide with fear and pain. One arm hung limp, blood running down it in a red stream. With his other hand he clutched at his side where another red stain was growing, oozing through his fingers. "Skullcracker," he gasped, "the wizard's summoning something! We've got to stop him!"

"Then use your damn magic, man!" Borr snarled angrily, looking for a new enemy to kill.

"Not strong enough," Surt panted, his face twisted with pain. "I'm wounded. And he's very powerful!"

The Aesir grinned wolfishly and spat on the ground. "Magic! Bah! Give me cold steel any day!" He turned and bellowed to Skirnir, who stood nearby. "Raven-friend," he called, pointing to where the wizard stood, arms outstretched, hands clawlike, compelling, demanding. "The wizard! To me!" Not waiting to see if Skirnir followed, not needing to, he sprinted toward the black-robed man.

Four guards saw them and rushed to intercept. Borr's great ax swung up from the ground, catching one in the crotch, tumbling his steaming guts to the ground. Skirnir engaged the other two, his eyes blazing, bloody foam flecking his lips as the battle madness came on him. Borr realized the man was dying, but also knew he would probably take both guards with him to the Hall of the Gods.

One last enemy stood between Borr and the wizard. The man was huge, blacker even than Surt, with massive legs and arms like the branches of an oak. He swung a sword nearly as long as Borr's ax and handled it as though it weighed nothing. Skullcracker smiled. Here was a warrior indeed! This was the kind of fight the skalds sang of!

The swordsman swung from overhead, a powerful blow meant to split Borr in two. The Aesir met the blade with the head of his ax. His own blow went low, aiming at the knees of his opponent. The huge guard jumped back lightly, his face split by a grin. "Well met, shaggy one," he thundered. "I am Jormungand, the Serpent, and I am your death!" His voice had the same soft deep quality as Surt's, but with a slight hissing overtone, as if the man were indeed some kind of giant black serpent.

"My death's not rune-written on your sword, black one. I'm Borr Skullcracker, and I'll soon crack yours!" He swept his ax in a great arc, directed at Jormungand's ribs. The sword met the ax in a ringing shower of sparks. Again the sword flew toward Borr, and again he blocked, countering with a mighty blow at the head of his adversary. Sword and ax clashed again.

As Borr slashed, parried, and countered, a dread began to grow in his heart. This was no ordinary warrior. Under any circumstances he was a fair match, but Borr bled from several wounds and felt the growing exhaustion of no less than six previous battles. The giant Jormungand seemed fresh and woundless. Plus there was the problem of the wizard. If all Borr had had to do was fight the black giant, he was confident he could eventually overcome the man. But every second he wasted in combat brought whatever the wizard was summoning that much closer. He didn't have much time left, and he knew it.

Damn! he cursed silently. Jormungand blocks or avoids everything I throw at him. The man's a superb warrior! Skald material indeed! The grim cloud that writhed toward them from the southern horizon was closer now, and the black guard knew it. His smile widened slightly as he stepped back from a swing of Deathbringer.

Only a long shot can win now, Borr realized. Well, then, cast it all on one chance. It makes no difference anyway. What's written in the runes is written, and all a man's striving cannot change it. With a silent prayer to Sigfod he swept up the great ax as though to make another head attack. Bringing it forward in a whistling arc, he let go of the haft as it reached throat level. Jormungand, who had stepped back to avoid the blow, was startled by the unexpected maneuver. He tried to block, but was not successful. The ax struck him on the left side of his head, spraying gouts of blood and flesh and sending his ear flying. He staggered and fell.

With a howl of victory Borr sprang forward over the sprawled body of the guard. With his right hand he clawed his smaller ax from his belt. The wizard was only a few yards off.

Suddenly Borr's whole body was afire, heat searing him, his robe bursting into flame. With a roar of anguish he rolled around on the ground, putting out the blaze. The cursed wizard is Warded, he realized. I can't reach the unholy bastard! He glanced up at the cloud, now much closer, and felt a sickness.

It seemed something alive now, not just a mere cloud. Something alive and blackly evil, twisting, writing, seeking, and hungry.

Borr shivered and stood. He looked wildly around for any of his raiders. All were still engaged. None had their bows to hand, having dropped them after the first fusillade that had opened the battle. Bows were of no value in close quarters, and the fighting was now hand-to-hand.

Cold steel could stop a wizard, he knew, and even a fire Ward could not keep it out. The distance was overlong for a good throw. The man was no fool. Yet Borr knew he had no choice. With a murmured plea to Sigfod to carry his ax like the wind and let it create the raven feast, he pulled back his arm and hurled.

The ax flew true and buried its blade in the chest of the wizard. The black-robed man staggered and went to one knee, dying, but not yet finished. Borr pulled the long dagger from his belt and threw himself forward. The Ward was still in place, but it had weakened. The heat seared his flesh and he cursed, but his momentum carried him through. His hair smoking, he sprinted for the wizard. Reaching the kneeling man, whose arms were still outstretched, hands still summoning, demanding, Borr slashed his throat with a sweep of his blade. The wizard slowly toppled backward. As he hit the ground a great roll of thunder cracked overhead, throwing Borr to his knees. Lightning ripped the sky, stabbing the billowing black cloud that had almost reached them. Blinded and deafened, Borr pitched forward onto his face as the world exploded around him.

By the time he came to, the sun was balanced on the horizon. Thidrandi knelt over him, a waterskin in his hands. Borr felt thirst in a sudden wave. Licking his dry, cracked lips, he raised himself on one elbow and drank.

Slowly he came to a sitting position. Every part of his body hurt horribly. The mingled smell of his own blood, sweat, and burnt hair was enough to sicken him. There were worse smells in the air. A disemboweled man lay nearby, reeking of shit and half-digested food. It was one of Surt's.

He looked around. Five of his Aesir were still on their feet. Two of Surt's men were rifling the bodies of the dead for valuables. Every other form lay still and unmoving. The stench of death was heavy.

Carefully noting the locations of all his aches and pains, he stood. He stepped to the dead wizard and picked up his knife. Black blood stained the blade. Grabbing the haft of his one-handed ax, he pulled it free of the man's chest. It, too, was caked with black gouts of gore. He thrust both into his belt and walked slowly over to where Jormungand lay, the left side of his head a mass of drying blood. The great ax lay a few feet beyond him. Borr picked it up and then, resting the head on the ground, he leaned against the haft and stared down at the huge black guard. The skalds will sing of you, Serpent, he promised silently. You were the best I ever fought. I hope your gods feast you well, wherever you have gone.

Turning from Jormungand, his eyes fell on the great wagon that stood silently in the midst of the carnage, the two horses that had pulled it dead in their traces. He caught Thidrandi's eye and pointed. Together, weapons ready, they approached the wagon.

The others, seeing Borr's destination, joined him. In a half circle they finally stood and stared, wondering what great treasure lay within, treasure for which they had spilled so much blood. The chests on the horses had already yielded heavy chains and necklaces, arm and finger rings of gold and silver, some plain, others encrusted with shimmering jewels. One chest held nothing but jewels, several as large as a man's fist. With so much of value carried by mere beasts, what incredible wealth must be within such a conveyance?

Borr set Deathbringer on the ground and pulled his one-handed ax from his belt. Weapon ready in his right hand, he stepped forward and reached out with his left. Carefully his fingers gathered the rich cloth of the wagon's cover. With a sudden mighty pull he ripped it away.

None had known quite what to expect, but what met their eyes was beyond the wildest imagining. The wagon held one thing, and one thing only.

Seated in the center, wrapped in many-hued veils, surrounded by gold-stitched pillows, was a woman. Only her eyes were visible behind the veils, and they stared at Borr with a frightened but calculating light.

For a moment they all stood rooted to the spot in utter astonishment. Then Borr broke the frozen tableau with a bellow of rage. His ax flashed in a sudden arc, smashing into the floor of the wagon, almost splitting it in two. "This," he roared, clenching his fists and shouting at the darkening sky, "this is what we played the raven's game for! This is the great treasure, guarded by so many lives, that we did the wolf-work for! By the gods, I. . . ." His rage was so great, he couldn't find words to express it.

He laughed, a great bellow that was anything but mirthful. "By damn, then! If this is what I bled for, then this is what I'll enjoy!" With a snarl he stepped forward and grabbed the woman by the arm. He pulled her off the wagon and began ripping the veils from her. The body he exposed brought a murmur of awe from everyone. It was faultless. A light brown in color, with high, firm, full breasts, a thin waist, and wide, sensual hips, it even drew a grunt of surprise from Borr.

He threw the woman to the ground, his eyes meeting hers again. There was no longer any fear there. Instead . . . instead Borr could swear he detected a look of triumph in their dark depths. For the first time he noticed the woman's face, as naked now as her body. His breath caught in his throat. She was unlike any woman he had ever seen, strange and beautiful at the same time. Her eyes were black and almond-shaped. Her nose was thin and slightly arched. Her mouth, full and incredibly sensuous.

Despite his battle-weariness and the ache of strained muscles and fresh wounds, the Aesir warrior found himself aroused. By the gods, he thought hotly, this is a woman! He ripped the tattered, blood-stained robe from his body and fumbled with his belt, his hands unexpectedly clumsy with eagerness. Dropping his breeches and stepping out of them, he untied his breechclout with shaking fingers. Naked at last, he threw himself on her with a deep growl of desire.

Her arms went around him, her fingernails digging into his back. Her mouth rose hungrily to meet his in a deep and passionate kiss. Almost losing control, he felt a fire growing in his loins. She gripped him tightly, her body moving with his in a natural harmony he had never felt with another woman. The fire and pressure grew rapidly, incredibly. Without warning, long before he expected it, he arched in a mixture of ecstasy and agony and poured himself into her in a sudden, burning flood. Instantly she responded, moaning and thrashing in her own orgasm.

He paused for a moment, stunned and delighted. But before

he could withdraw and roll off, the woman began to move beneath him, expertly bringing him back to life and rekindling his excitement. They moved together again, more slowly now, each knowing the other better, each trying to wring every drop of pleasure from every movement. Their cries were simultaneous this time, as well as louder and more intense.

Borr found himself staring in wonder into those dark eyes, lighted as his own were by the slowly dying fire of incredible pleasure. The Aesir heard one of the men standing in the awed and silent circle murmur, "A treasure indeed." Before he knew quite what he was doing, Borr was on his feet, legs spread, standing over the woman. *"My* treasure," he growled hoarsely. "By right of Warleader, I claim the woman as my first portion." Several of the others muttered, but they all stepped back. Borr glared around the circle, daring anyone to challenge him. Their eyes dropped one by one. Triumphant, the blond Aesir warrior looked down at his prize. She met his gaze squarely, the light of victory unmistakable in her glance.

With a curse to cover his confusion, Borr stepped back and reached down to retrieve his breechclout from the ground. He put it back on as the rest of the raiders wordlessly watched. Not bothering with his breeches, he thrust his dagger through the strip of leather that held the clout in place. He picked up his small ax and looked around the circle. "Well," he growled, "what are you all standing around for? There's looting to be finished." At once the other men turned away and began to move about the scene of the battle, checking every body, both friend and enemy, for signs of life or things of value.

For several moments Borr watched them go. Then he reached down and picked up the woman's torn garments. He threw them to her, silent, not letting his eyes meet hers. With a grunt he stalked off to see what had happened to his warriors. He could feel her gaze on him as he left. The knowledge that she watched made him both uncomfortable and excited.

By the light of a fire kindled with wood from the wagon, they finished the final tally and bound each other's wounds. Of the more than thirty who had attacked, only eight were still walking. Three more, including Surt, were badly wounded. So badly, Borr doubted they could survive more than a day of traveling. They would have to be abandoned. Raiders could not afford to carry those unable to ride swiftly. The Great Route was patrolled, and by tomorrow evening at the latest they knew a patrol coming from the south would pass this way. They would have to be far from the scene of the attack by then.

Of loot, they had more than they could carry. The eight would have to leave behind all but the best. There were just enough horses, twelve in all. Nine to be ridden, three to carry water, food and booty. By right of Warleader, Borr had claimed two; one to carry himself and food, the other to carry the woman and loot.

One of the black cutthroats approached Borr's fire and squatted down. He gestured out into the darkness. "Surt wants to talk to you." Borr nodded and rose stiffly, favoring his wounded side. He picked a piece of wood from the fire and, using it as a torch, limped to where Surt lay.

He looked down at the slender man. Surt was no longer black. His face was a sickly gray. A thin trickle of blood leaked from the corner of his mouth, his breathing was shallow, and at first Borr thought he was unconscious. Then the pain-filled eyes opened wide, and Borr knelt.

"As rich as I said, eh, Skullcracker?" Surt muttered, his voice strained and weak.

"As rich as you said, yes."

"Good." Surt paused, gathering his strength. "We'll leave at sunrise. The sooner we get away from here, the better."

Borr was silent for a moment. The steady sighing of the hot west wind filled the night.

Surt's gaze became sharper. *"We* leave in the morning, Borr."

"You're finished, Surt. Gut wound. You'll die in half a day. Might not even make it to morning. Only slow us down. We've got to move fast now."

"No." The wounded man's voice was surprisingly strong in denial. "I'll make it. You can't leave me."

The blond man shrugged. "I'm leaving two of my own. I'm not taking anyone who can't ride and ride hard. A lot of us became raven food on this raid. We gained great treasure and much honor, but the price was high, and we can't afford to lose what we've gained because of a few men wounded beyond hope. That's the way the game goes. You'd leave me behind in the same circumstances. That's the risk we take when we play at the wolf-work."

"Don't leave me! I'm wounded, but I can keep up!"

Borr snorted and stood. "You're dying." He turned to leave.

"No!"

"Good-bye, Surt," Borr said without turning. "We go in the morning. You stay. Unless," he added with a sneer, "you've magic enough to heal yourself by then." The Aesir began to limp away, leaving Surt and the dark behind as he headed for the fire and the living.

"*No!*" The tone of Surt's voice froze Borr in his tracks. He spun around and could just make out the form of the slender man, raised on one elbow, his other arm thrust out toward him, the fingers moving in a strange pattern.

"Take me or take my curse," Surt panted, his voice shaking with pain and emotion. "Take me, or I'll take you and all your spawn and all your people! Take me or die, Aesir!"

The hairs on the back of Borr's neck rose in response to the black man's dread words. Something shrugged in the night. Borr shivered involuntarily. Is the little man's power that great? he wondered briefly. Then he took hold of himself and spat contemptuously at the dark. "You're dead, Surt, and even if you had enough life left in you to make your curse stick, I don't fear it or you. I am Aesir." With a growl he turned once more and stalked back to the fire.

In the morning they rode out, passing Surt's body. The man was still alive, but too weak to curse or even speak. His glittering eyes, filled with insane hatred, followed Borr and his little party long after they had left the pillaged caravan behind.

DARK EMPIRE

II

ALL through the blistering day Surt lay as one dead. Yet, strangely, the birds of prey that began to drop from the sky to squabble over the corpses gave his body and that of the giant Jormungand a wide berth. As the sun neared the western horizon Surt's eyelids quivered once or twice and then opened to reveal two glittering black eyes.

Slowly, painfully, Surt began to drag himself across the deserted battlefield. He paused for a few moments as he reached the body of Jormungand, stretching out his shaking hand to touch the still form. Nodding his head, satisfied by what his touch told him, he withdrew his hand and began to crawl once more.

The Dragon was high in the sky, his barbed tail stinging the southern horizon, by the time Surt reached his objective. A dim glow to the east foretold the coming of the moon. The dark man reached out and cautiously touched the dead wizard. He pulled his hand back quickly and cowered down, pressing himself tightly to the ground. When nothing happened after several moments, he reached out more boldly and pulled himself close to the rigid corpse. The wizard was lying on his back, felled by the force of Borr's throat-slashing blow. Carefully Surt felt his way across the still chest.

Ah! There! He had it! With a whimper of joy and terror, his hand closed over the talisman the wizard had worn around his neck.

Surt had seen it the instant he first noticed the man from behind the ridge where he and Borr had scouted the caravan. Wizard or no wizard, the man had been a fool to wear the talisman on the outside of his robe where anyone might see. Perhaps he hadn't realized its true value, or perhaps he was so confident of his own power that he'd become reckless and arrogant. In any case, when Surt had spotted the dull gray talisman, he knew it to be hammered from a piece of virgin sky iron and set with a raw, uncut ruby of exceptional size.

He'd immediately realized it was by far the greatest treasure in the whole caravan, though it did not look at all valuable.

Clutching the talisman to his chest, he began the chant he'd discovered long ago while sneaking a look at one of old Shubur's books. He'd been apprenticed to the wizard until Shubur had caught him stealing spells and turned him out into the streets of Maqam Nifl.

He was weak, and he stumbled over some of the words, slurred others. Nevertheless, the power of the talisman was so great he could feel the force building. Suddenly Surt knew the night was listening.

Momentarily terrified by what he had summoned, unsure he could control it, he had to swallow several times before he was able to speak. Finally, gathering his fast-failing strength, his voice a hoarse whisper, he croaked, "Oh, mighty Nergal, King of Aralu, Lord of Hosts, I call on you and beg your aid." There was a silent acknowledgment from the emptiness around him. Emboldened by the response, he continued. "My enemies have grievously wounded me, lord. I am weak and dying. I cannot offer you the usual sacrifices, nor have I the strength or knowledge to chant the usual rituals. But I killed many men yesterday, and each I dedicated to you as he fell. Accept them, lord, and hear my plea."

A wave of weakness washed over him, and he nearly blacked out. He fought it, panting with the effort, trying to concentrate his thoughts and keep his mind clear. So weak, he moaned inwardly, so weak for such a task. He swallowed twice, but there was no moisture in his mouth, and his throat felt like dust.

He began again. "Lord, I have no father. What is a man without a father? Lord, I have no mother. What is a man without a mother? Lord, I have no brother, no sister. What is a man without a brother, without a sister? Lord, I have no teacher, no master, no city, no home. What is a man without a teacher, a master, a city, a home? Lord, I have nothing. I am nothing.

"Lord, be my father. Be my mother. Be my brother and my sister. Be my teacher, master, city, home. Lord, be my everything. I would be your servant. Mend me and make me whole. I would be your servant."

The darkness threatened to overwhelm him once more. He fought it, doggedly, hopelessly, with the last of his rapidly draining strength and life. It's up to Nergal now, he thought dimly. He either accepts my plea or rejects it. I either live or die.

An unspoken command came from out of the night. Shaking from both terror and exhaustion, he did as he was told. Slowly he pulled himself over on top of the dead wizard until he was lying on the man. Then he lowered his mouth to the gaping grin of the corpse and kissed it, sealing the hole with his own lips.

He felt the dead wizard begin to melt away beneath him. At the same time a bitter fluid passed from the corpse's mouth to his own. He swallowed, half gagging, knowing he no longer had any choice. As the fluid burned down his throat and into his stomach, a strange icy warmth began to spread throughout his body. With it came a return of strength. Greedily now he sucked at the dead man's mouth.

The corpse shriveled away to nothing, a mere bag of skin and bones wrapped in a filthy black robe. Sated, a sense of dark power coursing through his veins, Surt sat up and stared into the night. There in the blackness was a deeper blackness. He bowed his head to it. "Lord," he murmured, "you are my father. You are my mother. You are my brother and my sister. You are my teacher, my master, my city, my home. You are everything. I am your servant, your slave." A grim agreement filled his mind. Then came a command, one that made him blanch and tremble. "Y-yes, m-my lord," he replied, his voice breaking as he said the words. "I . . . I understand and will obey." Abruptly the dark within the dark was gone, and Surt knew he was alone among many corpses.

For several moments he sat absolutely still, trying to control the shaking of his hands and the turmoil in his mind. Lord Nergal exacts a high price for his favors, he thought.

As he sat, the moon rose and cast a pale light over the battlefield. Everywhere Surt looked, bodies lay twisted in the unnatural sprawl of death. Alone, he mused. Alone among the dead. They have all gone to seven-walled Aralu, flung unprepared to the nether shore of the man-devouring river Hubur. Wailing and weeping, they have come to the first of the seven gates and called to Neti, the gatekeeper. Through the seven gates he has taken them, stripping them of their worldly possessions, until at last they have stood naked before the throne of Nergal and Ereshkigal, the king and queen of the land of the dead. Then Ereshkigal has fixed them with her eye of death and hung their bodies from stakes. All, all have passed that way. He shivered.

Not quite all, he reminded himself. He stood, full of strength and determination. The talisman went around his neck and inside his robe.

A few quick strides and he was beside Jormungand. He gazed down at the still form of the giant warrior. "As I am Nergal's servant, so shall you be mine. Neti has not yet let you pass the first gate and enter the realm of Aralu. I have need of the bite of your blade and the might of your arm. So I summon you back from the nether shore of Hubur. I summon you back to the living. Rise, Serpent. Rise and serve Surt, the Black One." Pulling the talisman from his robe, he leaned over and touched it to the forehead, eyes, ear, mouth, and heart of the motionless body. Then he kissed Jormungand, letting some of the bitter fluid that filled him flow between the cold lips.

The big man's eyes opened slowly and he looked about, dismayed. Surt sat back and laughed wildly at his confusion. He stood and shook his fists at the rising moon. "Aesir dogs!" he howled. "Borr Skullcracker! Surt lives! You shall know his revenge! All, all, all will die!"

Jormungand sat up and stared at the man who had called him from the dusty, cold shores of dread Aralu. In the dark, something unbearable snickered nastily.

The patrol from Der came clattering up late the next morning. Only two survivors of the massacre could be found, both camel drivers who claimed to hail from Kish. Most of the treasure the caravan had carried had been taken by the raiders. The rest the patrol stuffed into their saddlebags. Then, giving the survivors a packet of food and a water bag apiece, they rode off in pursuit of Borr and his men.

The two stayed in Der only long enough to change their clothes and their identities. A gold bracelet from the treasure left behind by Borr bought them both mounts and a place in a caravan heading south from Der by the Eastern Route to Uruk. From there it would be an easy journey to Maqam Nifl, at the southern end of the Niflsea.

They kept themselves aloof from the rest of the caravan, eating, sitting, and sleeping by their own fire. Jormungand watched as Surt sat, his legs crossed, his hands cautiously cupping the strange talisman so that no one not directly looking over his shoulder could see it. For over an hour now the Black One had been staring at the talisman. His breath was slow and regular, his body relaxed. Only his eyes seemed awake as they focused intently on the piece of virgin sky iron with the uncut ruby dully glowing from its center.

When Surt finally looked up, he found Jormungand's eyes on his. "Why," the huge warrior asked, his voice soft and hissing, "do you stare so at that thing? Every night it's the same. Stare and stare and stare, for hours on end."

Surt cocked his head to one side and gave the giant an appraising glance. He nodded briefly as if he had reached a decision, then looked around the area. They were alone. He motioned Jormungand closer.

"The talisman is a focusing device," he began in a low voice. "It's made of the metal and the stone sacred to Lord Nergal. It allows me to concentrate on a single point so that I can gather my power. It also serves as a trigger for my imagination. It constantly reminds me of Nergal and helps me picture him clearly.

"Concentration and imagination. Those are two of the most important capacities a wizard can develop. Without the ability to concentrate, to fix the mind on a single idea, magic is impossible. Equally, without the ability to imagine, to call things up into the mind and picture them in precise detail, nothing can be accomplished. If I am to become more than a mere Kishpu sorcerer, I must strengthen both these faculties. The talisman helps to train me."

"Then you would become a wizard?"

"Have I any choice?" Surt responded bitterly. "I'd rather lie on a bed of silk and have a soft woman stroke my brow and satisfy my body. I'd rather sit in a tavern and drink heady wines and sing bawdy songs. I'd rather eat the finest foods and dress in costly robes." He gestured toward the saddle bags that lay on the other side of the fire. "There's enough gold there to last us both a lifetime.

"But when Borr abandoned me on the Vigrid and I lay dying, I did a thing." His gaze was bleak and empty. He sighed deeply. "A man will do anything to stay alive. I'd seen the talisman around the wizard's neck. I knew how powerful it was. By strange chance, I even knew how to use it."

He looked up at Jormungand, his eyes haunted. "I feared death so much . . . so much . . . Ah, so I did a thing. A dread thing. I called on Lord Nergal. I used the words I had stolen from old Shubur so long ago. I begged for my life and pledged my service as payment." Surt's voice was flat and emotionless, but his hands trembled slightly. "And he came. In the dark he came and commanded me. I . . . I lived."

For long minutes the two of them sat in silence. The west wind blew their fire and sent twisted flickerings dancing across their faces. They heard an occasional murmur of conversation from the other fire at the opposite end of the camp. "Now I serve Nergal, and to serve Nergal, I must become a wizard."

Surt's face turned hard and a vicious smile curled his lips. "I will become a wizard, Serpent. I will. A mighty wizard. Then those who have hounded me all my life will learn to fear me. They will shake in terror at my revenge. I will smash and destroy my enemies. Every. One. Of. Them."

Jormungand noticed that the closer they came to Uruk, the longer and more intense Surt's practice sessions with the talisman became. The slender man began to fast, allowing nothing but bread and wine to pass his lips. He grew quieter and more withdrawn with every mile and seemed nervous and worried, almost frightened. He's preparing himself for something, the giant warrior realized. Something unpleasant and dangerous. Not knowing quite what to expect, Jormungand made the only kind of preparation he understood. He sharpened his sword.

It wasn't until they were within the strong walls of Uruk that Surt revealed what the future held. They found a tiny room in a slovenly third-class inn near the northern gate. Sitting in its dim, musty drinking room, which was nearly empty because of the early hour, they sipped a sour wine. Surt stared morosely at the bloodred liquid and spoke so softly, Jormungand had to lean forward across the stained tabletop to catch his words.

"Four qualities must a wizard possess," he began, his voice a singsong drone as though he were repeating something memorized long ago. "And the first of these is intelligence, illuminated by long and careful study. Many things must be known and known perfectly. Powers and potions. Spells and incantations. A wrong measure, a wrong word, and the demons will drag him down to endless torment.

"The second of these is fearlessness. Dire and dreadful are the beings he will call and try to control. If he quails before their hideous aspect, he is doomed to eternal agony in the realm of Kur. He must always have the strength and courage never to falter, never to stop. Once he has put his foot on the left-hand path, there is no turning back.

"The third of these is unbendable will. No obstacle, no

hardship can ever be great enough to stop the strength of his desire. He must be ready to force the entire universe, the heavens above, the earth, the waters below, the gods, the demons, everything, to do his bidding.

"The fourth of these is an incorruptible discretion. Power, wealth, fame, love, all must be as dust to him. He must keep his silence, his counsel, at any cost.

"To know, to dare, to will, to keep silent. These are the four qualities a wizard must cultivate." Surt sighed and smiled wanly at Jormungand. "That's what Shubur taught me. Not exactly the easiest list of things to accomplish, and I'm far from adept at any of them."

He shook his head. "Far from adept. Perhaps Nergal will take that into account. Perhaps.

"Ah, Serpent, it's time I told you. We're not going on to Maqam Nifl right away. We have a little detour to make."

"A detour? Is that what's been making you so nervous the past couple of days, Surt?"

Surt laughed in surprise. "Has it shown that much? So much for my self-control! I'm not as far along as I hoped! Yes, Serpent, that is what has made me so nervous. A simple little detour."

"To where?"

"To the Temple of Cuthah."

Jormungand stared in stunned amazement at the slight man who sat across from him. His mouth worked, trying to form words. Finally he found his voice and managed to gasp, "To Cuthah?"

Surt nodded slowly. "To Cuthah, the temple of Nergal."

"But . . . but . . . it doesn't exist anymore! It was destroyed years ago, before my father was even born. The Sons of Muspell smashed it and the cult of Nergal."

The little man held up his hand. "I know. The temple is a ruin. But the altar still exists, unharmed. It has been guarded through the years by the few priests who survived the massacre, and by forces greater than mere priests.

"Nergal commanded me to go there and dedicate myself to him. The ritual on the Vigrid was only temporary. We . . . we must go, Serpent. Nergal commands it. If . . . if we don't he will come for us. And to fall alive into the hands of the lord . . ." He shuddered.

Jormungand's shudder matched Surt's. His massive hands shook slightly as he wrapped them around the mug of cheap wine. He lifted it to his lips and took a deep draught. By the time he lowered it, he was back in control of his emotions. "So," he said quietly, "we go to Cuthah."

"We go to Cuthah," Surt agreed. "I have some things to buy, so we go tomorrow."

"Tomorrow. Then tonight I'll drink as much wine as possible and enjoy as many women as possible." He looked grimly at Surt. "It's probably the last chance I'll ever have to do either."

To the west of Uruk, stretching north and south for about a hundred miles, lay the misty waters of the Niflsea. Halfway up the eastern shore, just to the north and west of Uruk, a long, narrow peninsula thrust out into the sea and pointed, like an accusing finger, at the smoking bulk of Mount Hela. At the very tip of the peninsula, amidst a jumble of mighty rocks that fell precipitously into the sullen, swirling waters, stood the remains of the Temple of Cuthah, once the center of the ancient cult of Nergal.

In the days of the First Dark Empire, the worshipers of Nergal were a numerous and mighty host. Common soldiers and far-famed generals offered sacrifices on his altar in hopes of gaining victory, for Nergal was the bloodred God of War, the Lord of Hosts. Others came as well, wrapped about and hidden in cowls of deathlike black. Their sacrifices were dark and dreadful, for they worshiped the other aspect of Nergal, as lord of the dead and king of Aralu.

The vast destruction that attended the fall of the First Dark Empire barely affected Cuthah. Most of Nergal's priests and followers died in the chaos, but the temple itself, squat and reeking of evil, remained untouched at the tip of its rocky peninsula.

Slowly, as civilization returned to the land of Muspellheim with the rise of the Second Dark Empire, worshipers reappeared at Cuthah, and the cult grew powerful once more. Too powerful. The Sons of Muspell, the seven rulers of the Dark Empire, feared the strength of the Dark Lord's hosts. Deciding to act swiftly before their power became unopposable, the Sons struck. The temples of Nergal in the cities of Larsa, Ashur, and Isin were attacked and destroyed. Priests and devotees were slaughtered wherever they were found. Finally a mighty army besieged Cuthah itself. For a full month a desperate battle raged, a battle of both red-stained blades and darkest magic. Many souls were sent screaming to Aralu and the Kur.

Eventually the forces of the Sons of Muspell breached the walls of the temple and swarmed within. They massacred everyone they could find in the outer courtyards, then turned the main sanctuary into a gigantic pyre for those they drove and trapped inside. The only living things they left behind were the jackals and the vultures.

The shattered ruins still crouched in grim isolation. Ordinary people gave the whole area a wide berth, for an aura of ancient evil and unspeakable horror still clung to it. In Uruk it was whispered that strange lights and hideous odors had been noticed about the place from time to time. Rumor had it that the cult of Nergal had not been utterly destroyed but driven underground. No one cared to investigate too closely.

Surt and Jormungand reached the ruins just before sunset on the first day of the new year, when light and dark ruled the heavens evenly. To the people of Muspellheim the year began with the autumnal equinox, and the day began at sunset. The dark always preceded the light.

The night of this particular day, when light and dark were equal but dark was gaining the upper hand, was divided into three watches of four hours each. Every hour was dedicated to one of the seven denizens of Aralu. The first watch started off with the hour of Nergal. The second watch ended with his hour. The rite Surt had come to perform had to take place between the two hours of Nergal. Thus it would last eight hours.

The setting sun gleamed a sickly red through the vast cloud of smoke that poured from Mount Hela. Cautiously the two men approached the tumbled rocks that once had been the wall surrounding the temple. The arch over the main, southern gate had long since fallen, strewing the entrance with shattered stone and rubbish. A fat serpent raised its evil head and hissed viciously at them as they approached, then slid slowly into a deep crack at the base of the crumbled wall.

Jormungand's sword was out and his senses alert. "I don't like this place, Surt," he muttered. "It stinks of death. And worse." Surt gave him an icy glance and silently motioned him to follow.

Past the gate was a rubble-strewn courtyard. Here and there in the gathering dark a skull or bone gleamed whitely. At the other end of the courtyard was another opening, its arch also broken and the walls around it scarred by the heat of ancient flames. They passed through it carefully and entered a second, larger courtyard.

In the center of the open space loomed the ruins of the temple proper. Once seven towers had soared over the squat shape of the sanctuary of the god. Now they lay in heaps. The walls had once been profusely carved with horrid reliefs of demons and monsters. The army of the Sons had smashed the vile murals so that only a few leering faces were still recognizable. Even those were enough to make Jormungand sick with fear. He tried to imagine how ghastly it must have appeared in its heyday, but his courage and imagination failed him. Just as well, he thought with a shudder.

Slowly, reluctantly, the two of them crossed the open space and entered the smoke-blackened entrance of the sanctuary. Strange things chittered in the dark of the long passageway.

At the other end they came into a large room. It was open to the night air, the vaulted ceiling long ago having collapsed. Charred timbers could be seen in some of the corners.

In the center of the room was something that made Jormungand's blood run cold. A gigantic rectangular bloodred stone squatted there like some evil, living thing. Unnameable stains covered its surface, the grim remainders of aeons of grisly sacrifices performed upon its pitted top. Long before humanity had walked the earth, strange, shambling half-men had danced around it in ghastly rites. Since men had inhabited Muspellheim, this stone had been a thing of worship and horror. The entire temple had been built around it, for this was nothing less than the altar of Nergal. Jormungand closed his eyes and shook his head. When he opened his eyes again, he refused to look at the altar. The power of the thing was too great, and he feared it more than anything he had ever encountered in his life.

For a moment Surt stood and stared at the altar. Then he stepped forward. He cleared a place in front of the massive stone and began to draw a circle, nine feet in diameter, in the dust. He used a wand of cypress, cut from a tree that grew in a graveyard. Nergal was lord of the dead, and cypress was sacred to him.

Inside the first circle Surt drew a second smaller one. Then off to one side he inscribed another circle inside a triangle. Jormungand was placed there with a strict injunction not to move from the spot. Then Surt wrote powerful words along the sides of the triangle.

Returning to the double circle, Surt opened it at one point and placed a brazier on a tripod inside the inner circle. He dragged within it a black goat they had carried all the way from Uruk. The goat was bound with cords made from the hair of dead women.

Stepping within the circles himself, he carefully closed them. Concentrating as hard as was possible, he began to scratch names of fell power in the space between the two circles. As he wrote he chanted them aloud. "Namtillaku," he intoned, "he who restores to life, guard me. Agaku, he who restores life to the dead, guard me. Suhgurim, he who grants petitions, guard me. Suhrim, he who destroys all his enemies, guard me. Zahgurim, he who shatters all his enemies as if in battle, guard me."

The incantations and inscriptions finished, Surt paused to catch his breath. He peered carefully at the circles, making sure they were perfect. They served two purposes: They concentrated the energy he sought to release in the ritual, and they protected him against the things he was trying to call up. Any break in the line and the energy would dissipate or the demons break in and drag him screaming to the Kur.

Jormungand stood silently within his circle and triangle combination, his eyes wide. He had been placed there, Surt told him, as protection from the forces that would be loosed as the ritual continued. But there was another reason, which Surt had not revealed. It would be easier to summon up the dread creatures the Black One sought to invoke if there was a corporeal body for them to inhabit while they were there. If Surt did everything properly, when the things departed, they would leave Jormungand's body behind. If he made a slip . . .

Timing his actions precisely, Surt lit a fire in the brazier. As the blaze leapt up he threw a handful of powder into it. "Hellebore root," he chanted, "for my Lord Nergal, God of War, Lord of Hosts. May it smell sweet to him so that he may approach." He took another handful of a different powder and cast it into the flames. "Euphorbia, O lord. May it smell sweet to the nose of the mighty warrior." Strange black-red clots followed. "Dried blood from those slain in battle, lord. May it smell as sweet to you as the reek of war."

Surt changed his rhythm and tone now. His speech slowed and his voice became deep and sepulchral. From a black pouch he drew a powder and flung it into the fire. "Asafetida," he intoned, "for my Lord Nergal, lord of the dead, king of Aralu.

May the smell of death be sweet in his nostrils so that he may approach." Slowly, rhythmically, he added henbane and the powdered brains of a black cat to the strangely colored and writhing flames. Finally with a flourish he scattered a few grains of pure sulphur, sacred to Nergal both as Lord of Hosts and as lord of the dead.

A thick, acrid smoke rose from the brazier and hung heavily in the air, surrounding Surt and Jormungand and cutting them off from the ruins of the temple. Within its sphere the altar shone weirdly, illuminated by the twisting flames of the fire. It's as if the temple were whole again, Surt thought as he gazed around in wonder. The light reflects and is diffused by the smoke. It almost seems as if Cuthah never had been destroyed.

He brought himself back to the task at hand. No time to waste, he reminded himself. Everything must happen exactly on time and in sequence. One misstep . . . He shuddered to think of it. Reaching down, he grasped the goat by its horns. "Nergal," he cried, "Lord of lords, master of masters, hear your servant." Pulling an iron knife from his belt, he stabbed the goat lightly, drawing a trickle of blood that dripped down its side and into the dust at his feet. Surt could feel the animal, fearful and in pain, struggle. Good, he thought, good. The power begins to build.

He stabbed the animal again, drawing more blood. He could feel a force gathering, a force generated by his own mind and by the agony of the goat. He concentrated on Nergal, trying to picture him in his imagination. Come, lord, come.

The tension within the circle began to mount as Surt stabbed the black goat again and again. The creature was struggling wildly now, rolling its eyes in terror. Death hung heavy and close in the air.

Surt began to work himself into a frenzy with the rhythm of his chanting and his stabbing of the goat. He felt the pressure build in intensity. The hair on the back of his neck rose. He broke out into a cold sweat and his heart beat wildly.

Suddenly, with a cry he slashed the knife across the goat's throat and the gore spurted out in a gush. He thrust the squirming dying animal high above his head so that the blood poured down over him. He lapped at it with his tongue.

With a mighty heave he flung the goat up and onto the altar. There was a flash of brilliant light. Surt staggered back, momentarily blinded. As his vision cleared he looked toward Jormungand.

The man was gone! In his place stood an incredibly beautiful woman with a body so voluptuous, it took away Surt's breath. The small man knew instantly who it was. "Lilith," he rasped, his voice choked with lust.

She smiled lasciviously at him and opened her loose robe. "Surt, my lover, come to me," she whispered, her voice an invitation to endless orgasm. Surt took a step toward her. Then another. He was at the very edge of the inner circle. He raised his foot to step forward, forward to unimaginable pleasure, forward to the love and desire he had always been denied.

With a sudden cry he threw himself backward. "No!" he screamed. "No! I called Lord Nergal, not Lilith! Only Lord Nergal will I deal with!" He shuddered, realizing how close he had been to destruction. The shape within the triangle shifted and became a hideous demon who laughed and disappeared in a flash.

In the monster's place stood a man dressed in rich robes. Surt knew him at once. He was fair to look on. His fingers sparkled with jewels, and golden chains hung about his neck. He was Hegal, he who brought abundance to men. "Surt, my son," Hegal said, "come to me. I would give you wealth unimaginable. Gold and jewels. Land and palaces. All the riches of the world."

Surt laughed. "Begone, demon! I will speak with Nergal and Nergal only!"

Two more came, promising him fame and power. He scorned them and demanded to speak with Lord Nergal.

At last a darkness filled the triangle, and Surt knew his master had arrived. He prostrated himself on the ground and heaped dust on his head. He bit the earth and filled his mouth with dust. Then he spoke to the lord. "Nergal, lord, master, I am as nothing before you. I am your servant, your slave. Do with me as you will. I have obeyed your command. I have performed this rite of dedication. Accept me as once you did on the Vigrid. Give me strength. Give me power. Give me the qualities I need to be a great wizard. I beseech you, lord."

In his head he heard a swift command. He stood bolt upright and stared at the darkness. He took a step forward and another command came. He took another step.

He stopped. His whole body was trembling. I must go to Nergal, a voice within him screamed. He has called me. I must go.

No, no, no, no, another voice howled madly. You cannot

leave the circle. If you do, you will be destroyed. Nergal is the lord of the dead. This is his temple. He will drag you down to Aralu and hang your body from a stake.

His mind was a turmoil, spinning, swirling, careening down an endless dark tunnel. Can't think, he whimpered into emptiness. Must think. Go to Nergal. No, no, no. Go. Death. Go. Destruction. Go. Can't leave the circle.

He shook and swayed with exhaustion. How long had the rite gone on? What hour of the night was it? End it all. He lifted a weary foot to step across the inner circle, then held it in the air as the two parts of his mind fought.

In the distance of time he heard another voice, a voice he remembered. "To know, to dare, to will, to keep silent." *Come.* The command rippled through his mind, confusing him, making it impossible to concentrate.

Concentrate. Yes. He had to concentrate. He withdrew his foot, set it down within the circle. Concentrate. His hand crept up to the talisman that hung outside his robe. His fingers curled around it. Slowly, painfully, he grasped it and lifted it up in front of his eyes. He stared at it, trying to focus his attention on it. *Come to me.* No. *Come.* No.

Abruptly, like a drowning man breaking the surface he never thought he could reach, his mind snapped into lucidity. "No!" he cried out loud. "No!"

The darkness within the triangle laughed mightily, the peals of its evil hilarity shaking the ground and rattling the few pillars of the temple that still stood. You are worthy to serve me, came the thought into his head. I accept your offering.

Surt staggered backward as if a sudden pressure had been removed. With a surprised cry he sat down, his legs buckling with weakness.

There was a final roar of laughter, and the darkness was gone. Surt found himself looking at the blinking visage of Jormungand.

The weariness washed up over him then. But as he fell into the soft blackness of exhaustion, he smiled. I have won, he thought. I have won.

And lost, added a small voice in the darkness.

ASAHEIM

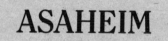

III

~~~~

IT was fall when Borr and his men finally rode into Asgard. The trees that dotted the plains in little groves were bright yellow, with an occasional splash of red. Buri Axhand himself greeted them at the gates, a wide grin on his face as he saw that his son led the returning heroes.

The feasting was long and drunken. In the middle of it Borr stood, swaying, and declared that he was taking to wife the woman he had won in the raid. Her name was Vestla and, he boasted, she had been raised in the Floating World of Prin. There she had learned the one thousand and one ways to please a man. Mistress of her craft, she had been much sought after and finally had been purchased for an incredible sum by the eldest Son of Muspell, the ancient An, to help rekindle his flickering passions. Now the decadent old wizard would have to buy another for his couch, Borr crowed, for he, Borr Skull-cracker, had stolen her from the very caravan that had been carrying her to Muspellheim. She had pleased him, and he had given her the name Ravenhair. She would make, he said, a wife worthy of an Aesir chieftain.

Buri wasn't pleased, for he would rather have had his son marry the daughter of one of his Aesir allies to strengthen political ties with blood bonds. Or perhaps he could even have arranged to marry him to Gullveig of the Vanir by way of establishing a truce with the people of Vanaheim. Someday soon, he knew, such a truce would be essential. The Jotun were just across the river Iving, and there were more of them every day.

Yet he knew he could not deny the wishes of a hero such as his son, especially not when he had brought home so many heavy chains and arm rings of glimmering gold! So he hid his disappointment behind a smile and decided to make the best of it.

*   *   *

That spring, on the seventh day of the ninth month after Borr had raped her on the Vigrid, Vestla Ravenhair gave birth to a son. The child was strong and clean-limbed, with hair the color of his father's and eyes as deep and dark as his mother's. Buri proudly acted as Namefastener and called his first grandchild Voden. The rest of his names he would have to earn in true Aesir fashion.

In Voden's third year, during the coldest winter in memory, a sister was born. They did everything in their power to keep the hall warm, but despite their efforts the baby caught a chill and died before they could even Namefasten her. The ground was frozen so hard, they had to wait until spring to bury the tiny body.

Three years later, in the summer of Voden's sixth year, a brother arrived and was Namefastened Vethur. Large and robust, his birthing badly drained Vestla. Fortunately, she recovered quickly, and the child grew rapidly and prospered. Voden stood for hours at the side of the baby's cradle, staring in fascination at the fluffy white down that covered his head. "Vovo" was the second name Vethur learned.

It was in the late spring of Voden's tenth year that a man painfully limped his way across Bifrosti's Ford, accompanied by a young boy and a small girl. Behind him, a few minutes too late, came a very angry Jotun war party. The Aesir guarding the ford drove them off and brought the refugees to Asgard.

The man who slowly and painfully twisted his way up the Warrior's Hall to stand in front of Buri brought murmurs of wonder from all those seated on the benches along the walls. From his waist up, Volund was the biggest man any of them had ever seen. His chest and shoulders were massive, corded with muscle. His arms were easily as large around as most men's legs, and the biceps bulged amazingly with every motion. His neck was thick and muscular.

His head was huge and shaggy, and his face was of such strong character that few cared to meet the man's piercing glance. The eyes themselves were of a strange gray none among the Aesir had ever seen before. The man's complexion was the palest of pale, his hair the color of fire. A flat, broad nose was set above a tight-lipped, determined mouth that seemed clamped shut against pain. The corners of the mouth turned down slightly, giving him the aspect of one who had known and survived soul-rending sorrows.

From the waist down, the red-haired man was still impressive, but sadly so. His legs, though strongly built, were crippled, forcing him to move with an awkward, shuffling, rolling limp. Such a magnificent structure on such wretched foundations, Buri thought as the man stopped in front of him, inclined his head slightly, and raised his hand in a salute of greeting.

"Hail, Aesir." The voice was deep and vital, yet quivering with fatigue, pain, and grief. Buri motioned and had a bench brought so that the other might sit.

"Well met, stranger," Buri replied as the man lowered his bulk gratefully onto the bench. "Who are you and why are you here?"

"I am Volund," he said proudly, bringing his body erect, shoulders back, chest thrust out. "Volund the Smith. Greatest smith in all of Yggdrasil. Even the Dverg wonder at my creations."

Buri nodded. He'd never heard of the man before, but the Dverg were master smiths, so someone they admired must indeed be good. "Well met again, Volund. A master smith is always welcome in Asaheim." He paused. "What of my second question?"

Volund sighed. "Aye, aye, I will answer. Only my throat is so dry . . ." Buri grinned and motioned for a horn of ale to be brought the man. Volund drank deep. He gave a satisfied sigh, then drank again. "Ahhh, ahhh. Never did I think to taste good beer again! The piss the Jotun brew isn't fit for dogs!" He settled back, his eyes brooding.

"My story, yes, my story. Not pretty, but one you must hear, O Aesir, for what I have to tell affects all of you." He paused, aware of the interest his first words had created. The hall was silent, waiting for him to begin again.

"Aye, affects you deeply. For the Jotun are on the move once more!" Cries of concern and anger ran through the hall. The Jotun! Everyone there knew what that meant, and no one liked it.

The Jotun were a strange people. Some thirty years ago, when Buri had been a young warrior, they had suddenly appeared out of the endless grasslands that stretched northward from the Iving all the way to the Icerealm. They came from the northeast in great swarms, riding in brightly colored wagons, driving huge herds of cattle, sheep, horses, and dogs. They had settled in the area bounded on the west by the Amsvartnir Sea, on the south by the rivers Iving and Sid, and on the east by a range of steep, rugged hills then known only as "the hills where Urd's Spring hides."

Shorter than the Aesir, the Jotun were a brown-skinned folk, with dark hair and brown eyes. Their noses were large and hooked like the beaks of eagles. Astride their horses, on which they virtually lived, they seemed giants, swift as the wind itself. They fought on horseback, firing their short, curved bows with deadly accuracy, or plying their crescent-shaped blades with a skill that made even the Aesir respectful. Night held no terrors for them, and they often attacked then, earning the epithet of Darkriders or Nightriders.

They worshipped Nerthus, the Earth Mother. She accompanied them everywhere they went, drawn in her own wagon by four bulls with golden horns. Nerthus made the grass grow, the cows calve, the sheep lamb, the mares drop sound foals, and the bitches produce large litters of fat, delicious puppies. Enemy warriors captured alive were sacrificed to her in her sacred grove, hung on her sacred tree.

The Jotun also worshiped Gymir, the Sky Father, ruler of the wind, storms, and rain. Gymir was a grim god and liked his sacrifices—young maidens snatched in raids—burned alive on huge bonfires so that they might ascend to him in a column of smoke.

The Jotun claimed to be descended from Ymir, who had been created by Nerthus and Gymir when the two deities mated in a storm so violent that earth and sky blended into each other. When the storm clouds parted and Gymir's Eye looked down on Nerthus once more, there stood Ymir, fully formed, his feet firmly planted on his mother, his head yearning skyward toward his father. Every night while Ymir slept one of his legs fathered a child upon the other. Soon he created the entire first generation of the Jotun.

Originally the Sons of Ymir, as they called themselves, lived in scattered, isolated groups. Eventually a mighty warrior named Thrudgelmir was able to unite them and become the first Warlord of the Jotun Horde. As the years passed, four more Thrudgelmirs followed the first, each claiming and winning the title created by their ancestor. The Jotun became a mighty and numerous people.

But Yggdrasil changed, and the grasslands the herds fed on dried up and turned to sandy wasteland. The fifth Thrudgelmir sent his second son, Narfir, to seek new grazing grounds. After a long, perilous journey to the southwest of his homeland, Narfir gazed with mingled awe and joy at the vast sweep of green that lay to the north of the Iving. He returned to his people with jubilation, and soon the entire Horde, led by the sixth Thrudgelmir, set off.

Buri remembered the time when they had first appeared, howling out of the night, bringing fire, destruction, and grisly death. Some of the Aesir had still been living to the north of the Iving then. The Sons of Ymir swept them away and flung the remnants south.

The major battle had been fought at the ford across the Iving. There Bifrosti held the enemy at bay while the tribes of the Aesir gathered. The valiant guardian of the ford and all his men perished, but not before they piled the Jotun dead up before themselves in great mounds. Ever since that gallant defense, which had bought the Aesir needed time, the ford had been known as Bifrosti's Ford.

Buri had fought in that war. Though young, he commanded the right wing of the Aesir host. They met the Sons of Ymir just south of the Iving on the Himinborg Plain. The left of their line was anchored on the tumbled rocks of the Himinborg itself. When the Jotun struck their line, the center pretended to break and retreat. Howling their victory, the horsemen pursued. Then Buri struck, falling on them from the east, smashing into their strung-out line like an avalanche of iron. From the west the Aesir archers, hidden amid the rocks of the Himinborg, bent their long bows of yew and let fly a hissing storm of arrows.

Trapped, stunned, confused, and dying in huge numbers, the Sons of Ymir panicked and fled in a disorderly mob back across the Iving. The Aesir followed, killing all before them. One group split off to the west and were finally driven beyond the Amsvartnir Sea. Another group fled to the northeast. Buri pursued and overtook them, pinning them with their backs to the hills and the Iving.

There he wrought great slaughter and earned great glory. Wading through the gore of dying men, he came face-to-face with Thrudgelmir, Warlord of the Jotun Horde. In single combat the two fought, the rest of the battle halting to watch. The fight was long and bloody. Buri's life flowed from more than a dozen wounds when he finally struck Thrudgelmir down with a mighty blow from his hand. Thus he earned his name, Axhand. In honor of the battle the hills that silently watched were thereafter known as the Bones of Ymir.

Of all the Jotun leaders only one escaped the disaster: Bergelmir, second son of Thrudgelmir. He fled with the remnants of his people and the wagon of Nerthus.

Slowly over the past decade the Sons of Ymir had begun to filter back southward. They came quietly, seemingly peacefully. On the shore of the Amsvartnir Sea they built a city of wagons and called it Utgard. On a point of land thrusting far out into the sea, in a grove at its very tip, they placed the wagon of Nerthus and proclaimed the place holy.

Quiet and peaceful or not, the number of Jotun north of the Iving continued to grow. Buri had watched their increasing herds and population with uneasy eyes. But he had been too busy fighting a series of minor skirmishes with the Vanir to the south to do anything about it.

Now he looked down at Volund. The man sat, occasionally sipping at the ale in his drinking horn, his gaze vague, his face masked with the quiet of private reverie, while he waited for the Aesir to quiet down so he might continue. Buri dreaded to hear what the man had to say but knew he had no choice. If the Jotun were indeed on the move again, it was something they would all have to know about.

He raised his hand for quiet and then nodded to Volund to continue. Volund sighed hugely and began.

"I lived to the north and west of the Amsvartnir Sea. There the Great Western Forest falls back to form a rich plain, watered by icy, frothing streams that tumble from the Icerealm itself. Once my people were a mighty host." He shrugged sadly. "But the ice advanced and . . ." His voice trailed off.

Volund shook himself back into the present. "Such is the will of the gods," he said harshly, ending the matter. "A wife named Jord I had. A good woman. And three children. I was known far and wide for the excellence of my craft. My swords were desired by all men, for the metal sang when they struck, and they always struck true. From gold and silver I fashioned cunning rings and necklaces and brooches. The height of my craft was the blade I made for myself, which I called Neckbiter, and the ring I crafted for my wife.

"Bergelmir, the Jotun, heard of my skill and came to buy both the sword and the ring. He offered cattle, horses, sheep, dogs, even gold and silver. I send him away unsatisfied. Such things are not for sale."

For several moments Volund was still, his eyes hooded in the shadows cast by his shaggy brows. When he finally looked up, his face was transformed into a tragic mask of sorrow and grief. "Bergelmir came again. In the night. We were taken unaware. My eldest son fought and died. I fought and was struck unconscious. They took the sword from my limp hand. They cut the ring from my wife's finger. My two young ones were trussed like calves for the slaughter."

Volund stopped again, his face going rigid, all emotion disappearing except for the hatred burning in his eyes. His voice was flat. "They left the village a smoking ruin. My two children and myself they tied on the backs of horses and carried to Utgard. There Bergelmir displayed his new sword, to the wonder of all. There he gave the ring to his wife.

"His wife did not like the fire in my eyes. She told Bergelmir I should be put to death and my children given to the gods, my son to please Nerthus, my daughter for the fire of Gymir.

"But Bergelmir was greedy. He wanted me to work my craft for him. He wanted many, many swords and arrowheads and spear tips so he could build a mighty army. His daughter wanted rings like her mother's, and his two sons wanted swords like their father's. Aye, their greed was endless.

"So it was decided. I would work for Bergelmir. My pay would be the lives of my children. The three of us were taken and left on Saevarstod, a tiny island off the tip of Nerthus's Grove in the Amsvartnir Sea.

"To make sure I didn't run away, they did this to me!" With a shout he stood, the bench tumbling backward. Every man in the hall watched breathlessly as the master smith lifted the legs of his breeches with trembling hands. A moan filled the air as they saw the scars. Hamstrung! The Jotun had hamstrung Volund! The moan turned to a growl of outrage. Buri himself came down from the High Seat and placed the bench upright.

When Volund was seated once more he began again. "So I became Bergelmir's smith. My son, Tror, who was ten, became my assistant. He stoked the fire, worked the bellows, carried the metal. My daughter, Thrud, only seven, kept the house and did the cooking. We survived. And I waited. For a year I worked and waited, hoping my time would come."

Lifting his empty drinking horn, Volund gestured to the man holding the pitcher. With his horn full once more, he drank deeply and continued. "I made many things, but the most beautiful I kept in a trunk. I let that be known, for I had a plan.

"Bergelmir's sons heard of the wonders I kept hidden. Their greed surpassed their father's, and one night they slipped undetected to my island. They threatened to kill my Thrud if I did not give them my treasures. I opened the chest. As they stood admiring the work, I struck them both down with my hammer, smashing it into the backs of their necks just below the skull. I had plans for the skulls.

"I dismantled the skin carraugh they had come in. Their bodies I stuffed beneath our outhouse. Shit and dead Jotun smell much alike, and they had come secretly, so no one realized where they had gone.

"From their skulls I made two cunning drinking bowls, edging the bone with finely incised silver inlaid with glimmering gold. Their teeth I fashioned into two necklaces of the most delicate workmanship. The bowls I gave to Bergelmir, the necklaces to his wife and daughter. To the daughter, Bodvild, I also hinted at even greater gifts hidden in my chest. When her eyes lit up with greed, my heart lit up with joy. My revenge was but half accomplished. Now the rest seemed possible.

"I made everything ready and waited. Bodvild came one night, alone and unseen. I opened the chest, and she gazed within, entranced.

"Then, while she feasted her eyes, I crept close and grabbed her. I raped her, as brutally as I could. First I attacked her between her legs, drawing blood and causing great pain. Then I turned her over and took her that way. Then I smashed her mouth, breaking her teeth, and violated her once more. I don't think I killed her." He shrugged. "I don't care."

The silence in the room was absolute. He drank again and went on. "We fled, paddling the carraugh she had come in. We passed so close to Utgard in the night that I could hear the damn Jotun snoring. Down the Sid we came, to where it joins the Iving to become the Gopul. There we left the skin boat and came overland, along the banks of the Iving. We hid by day, traveled by night. We made it to the ford just ahead of a group of Jotun warriors. For once, the gods were on my side," he said bitterly.

Volund stood, as straight and proud as his crippled body allowed. He raised his eyes and his two huge fists to the heavens. In a loud, passionate voice he called out, "Thus have I avenged my wife Jord and my eldest son Lorridi! Thus the mutilation of my own body! Thus the stealing of my treasures! I, Volund, have wreaked this vengeance on Bergelmir the Jotun, slaughtering and defiling his family even as he slaughtered and defiled mine! Hear me, O gods, and know that even now my hatred is not appeased! I would have the blood of the Sons of Ymir flow in rivers even as they let flow the blood of my people! I would expunge their cursed race from the face of Yggdrasil!" There were loud shouts of approval from all sides. Many thumped the benches with angry fists to show both their fury at the Jotun and their pleasure at the revenge taken by Volund.

"Now, I am nothing to the Aesir. I am not of your people, not of your blood. I have no kin here in whose hall I can seek refuge. Yet I know you hate the Jotun, and I do not believe you will turn me back to them." A thunderous protest rent the hall. Cries of "No!" "Never!" filled the air until the din was deafening.

Ignoring the noise, Volund went on. "I am nothing. I ask nothing for myself. Only refuge for my children do I ask of you, Buri of the Aesir. I will travel on if such be your wish."

Buri stood and came down from the High Seat. He put his hands on the master smith's broad shoulders and looked deeply into the strong sorrow-filled eyes. "Volund Smith," he began, his voice ringing through a suddenly silent hall, "you bring us no joy. A tale of horrible suffering, yes. Dread news of the rising up once more of our most relentless enemies, yes. Even greater hatred from the Jotun if we should harbor the killer of Bergelmir's sons and the defiler of his daughter, yes."

The leader of the Aesir raised his head and swept the waiting men with a burning glare. "Yet I'll be damned by the gods if I or any other Aesir will turn you or your children from our doors!"

As one, the Aesir in the Warrior's Hall rose to their feet and cheered, shouting and stamping their agreement. Buri looked at Volund and saw the hint of a tear in the man's gray eyes. Whether it was shed for his dead ones, himself, his children, or his newfound friends, Buri didn't know.

All he did know was that the Jotun were on the move again and something would have to be done. Something would have to be done soon.

IV

THE Jotun began to raid. Buri called the Allthing to consider what to do about the growing menace. From all over Asaheim the chieftains came to Asgard: from the Himinborg, the Idavoll, the Aesir, even from the far-off Valaskialf Plateau. Most brought their families and a few trusted retainers. On the plain around Asgard they set up their hide traveling tents.

The gathering quickly took on a festive air as the Aesir donned their finest clothes and wandered from tent to tent, renewing old friendships and swapping tales, gossip, and long pulls at jugs of frothy beer. Here and there the young danced to the sounds of tambour and bone flute. Skalds strolled about, strumming their harps, old and new songs on their lips. One of the most popular was about Borr's raid. It began:

> "To the south Borr strode,
>   the sword-feast making,
>
> leaving raven-joy
>   and ruin, he rode.
>
> The Serpent he slew,
>   sliced Jormungand's ear,
>
> dark magic smashing
>   with murderous ax."

The meeting of the chieftains in the Warrior's Hall was far more sober in character. Buri sat in the High Seat. The others sat on the benches along the walls of the hall.

"I say we strike at them now, before their strength becomes even greater," declared Ulf, a powerful man with huge hands and massive shoulders. He had been known to cleave a man in two with his sword. Several others muttered agreement with his words.

44

Borr frowned and stood. "We dare not turn our faces north and our backs south. Has Ulf forgotten the Vanir? Now they sneak about, darting from their dark forests on quick raids. If they know we're occupied elsewhere, they'll strike in force."

"Back-stabbing cowards, they are," growled Ulf. "Aye, you have the right of it, Borr. Now they only nip at our heels, but if we turn away, they'll throw themselves on our backs."

Gagnrad, a huge, shaggy warrior, stood glaring at them all from beneath bushy eyebrows. "Are the Aesir afraid of the slinking Vanir, then? For fear of the Forest People are we to let the bloody Jotun overrun our lands, burn our steads, rape our women, and take our sons and daughters to be sacrificed to Nerthus and Gymir? Do I stand in the Warrior's Hall or in the house where old women gather to mutter and remember past glories? Ulf was right the first time he spoke. Smash the Sons of Ymir, and if the Vanir dare rise behind us, turn and smash them too!"

There was a great deal of banging on the benches and stamping of the feet to show agreement with Gagnrad. Buri didn't like it. He rose from the High Seat to speak. The others quieted down.

"For days now we have argued back and forth," he began. "As we should. All men must be heard. But we have not reached agreement, and the more we talk, the further we seem to be from it." He looked sternly down at the two lines of men. "Gagnrad and those like him show the warlike soul of the Aesir. They are quick to anger, quick to pick up sword or ax and spring on the enemy. This is good. This is why the Aesir are mighty and dreaded by all their enemies." The banging and stamping showed general approval for his words.

"There are others, no less warlike than Gagnrad, no less ready to leap to the wolf-work, who yet hang back this time and counsel caution. Such a one is my own son, Borr. There is none who can call him sword-shy.

"I myself stand here in front of you, silver shining through my hair, and wonder. I have not grown this old by being weak and cowardly, but I have also not earned these silver hairs by being foolish. Many a strong man falls when beset from two sides at once.

"Aye, I hear my ax singing, calling out for Jotun blood, and I long to grasp and swing it, making red raven feast to the north of Iving once more, adding more bones to those left by the Sons of Ymir. Bergelmir fled last time. This time I would beg him stay, forever, to feed the grass!"

There was a roar of approval.

"Yet . . ." Buri paused for effect. "Yet while I hear my ax ring, there is another sound I hear. A rustling in the brush, a whispering in the trees behind my back. I know it is the sneaking Vanir, lurking, waiting with their short swords and sharp spears.

"I would go north, yes, but not without first securing my back." He saw Borr nodding and banging the bench as he sat down.

Gagnrad rose slowly to his feet. "Aye, Buri, though the silver is on your head, I know there is none on your warrior's spirit. At least, I would not wish to trade blows with you, Axhand." A general chuckle ran around the hall. "But can the silver have frosted your mind? 'I would go north,' you say. And then, 'I must face south.' I claim no great cleverness. My arm is my strength. Somehow you seem to me to be talking in circles. Have you a plan you've been waiting to spring on us these several days? I'd not put it past you."

Buri smiled. "A plan? I?" Laughter greeted his protest. They all knew him too well. Buri Axhand was one name he had earned. Buri the Clever was another. "Your plan," they called. "Let us hear your plan!"

He stood again. "Aye, then, a plan. One I did not bring out at first because I knew how ill it would set with men ready to run and do battle. Now that we have discussed the problems until we are weary of them, perhaps it will not seem as bad even to the most war-eager."

Squaring his shoulders, he drew himself to his full height and said in a loud voice, "I propose we try to reach an understanding with the Vanir. That we make truce with the people of the forest. That having made this truce, and with our backs secure, we cross the Iving and drive the Jotun back to the very Icerealm itself."

For a few moments there was silence in the Warrior's Hall as his words sank in. Then pandemonium broke loose. Gagnrad and the war party leaped to their feet roaring their anger. Borr and his followers also leaped up, clamoring agreement. The shouting, stamping, thumping, and fist-shaking continued until it became centered on two figures, Borr and Gagnrad. Buri winced. He had both dreaded and expected this.

A sudden quiet filled the room as everyone realized what was happening. Borr stood, fists clenched, his face drained of all color, eyes bulging in anger. Gagnrad stood across the hall, his face red, the veins in his neck standing out. There was on his visage the expression of a man who realizes he has spoken the wrong words and that it is too late to call them back.

Borr's voice slipped into the silence, soft and deadly. "What did you call me, Gagnrad?"

Gagnrad's eyes narrowed. "What's spoken is spoken. I called you coward."

Before anyone could even blink in astonishment, Borr threw himself across the hall and smashed a mighty blow into the center of the other man's face. Blood splattered in every direction as Gagnrad flew back against the wall and slumped down onto the bench. He sat for a second, stunned. Then, with a strangled bellow of rage, he launched himself at Borr.

Borr was the smaller of the two, but also the faster. As Gagnrad reached for him he stepped outside the other man's grasp and slammed his fist into the tender area just below the ribs. He could feel the bones give beneath the force of his punch. Gagnrad stumbled, going down on one knee, gasping for breath. Borr stepped around front again, ready to finish off the other man.

Gagnrad was far from finished. Quickly getting to his feet, he grabbed Borr in his embrace and began to squeeze. Several men had already died in his arms this way, earning him the name of Beargrasp. Borr strained back, trying to no avail to break the grip.

With a sudden sharp movement Borr drove his knee into Gagnrad's groin. The other man shrieked his agony and let go, stumbling back. Borr followed him, smashing his fists into the man's face and body again and again.

Gagnrad collapsed in a heap, his face a bloody mask of smashed nose and broken teeth. He groaned once and then was still. Borr glared about. His ribs hurt abominably; his fists ached. "Does anyone else call Borr Skullcracker coward?" he grunted between panting breaths. "I say we try Buri's plan. Do any question me?"

Silence hung heavily in the Warrior's Hall.

A messenger was sent to the Distingen, the council of nine women who ruled the Vanir. The Vanadis, or queen of the Forest People, headed this council. The eight Disir who made up the rest of the group were rumored to be sorceresses of great power who practiced the feared Seidar-magic.

The Vanir were an incredibly ancient race. Long before the Aesir had existed as a people, before even the Alfar or Dverg had appeared, the Vanir dwelt in Yggdrasil, the world that stretched from the Icerealm to the smoking fires of nether Muspellheim. They claimed to be descended directly from Audhumla, the Nourisher, who had been formed in the primeval mists of the vast and seemingly empty Ginnungagap. For countless aeons they had dwelt peacefully in the endless forests that covered the whole world.

There they had worshiped their gods, the Vettir. The Vanir believed the gods dwelt in everything. There were Landtvettir in the land, Nixvettir in the water, Ullvettir in the air. When the storm raged and lashed the forest, it was the Thrymvettir making their power felt. There were good Vettir, the Hollarvettir, and bad Vettir, the Uvvettir. The world of Yggdrasil was permeated by the Vettir, and everywhere the Vanir looked, they found something to worship and stand in awe of.

But the world had changed, slowly, inexorably. The deep forest had given way to tree-dotted plains, which in turn had fallen to wide-horizoned grasslands. The ice grew southward, the desert spread westward, the Smoking Lands reached for the sky, and gradually the forests of the Vanir had shrunk. Now the once numerous race lived squeezed between the plains of Asaheim on the north and the Smoking Lands on the south, between the realms of the Dverg and the Svartalfar to the west and the Valaskialf Plateau to the east.

The Vanir were smaller and slighter in build than the Aesir. Their hair was black, their skin an almost translucent white, and their large eyes a deep, catlike green. Not as strong or as warlike as the men of the plains, they were nonetheless dauntless fighters, quick, agile, and deadly with their short swords and javelins. Every man was a warrior, trained in the ways of forest warfare. But the deadliest fighters among the Children of Audhumla were the Valkyrja, the all-female guard of the Vanadis. Hand picked and rigorously trained, their equal was not to be found in the leafy realm of Vanaheim. Expert in the use of sword, javelin, bow, throwing knife, and ax, they could move like swift shadows, flitting along forest tracks even the deer didn't know. Mistresses of the art of ambuscade, they were familiar with the strategic value of every tree, bush, and rock in the land they defended. More silent than a light forest breeze, they could creep up on an enemy, strike a blow, and then melt into the shadows before one had a chance to strike back. They were especially adept at sneaking through the night to slit the throats of sentries or whole parties of invaders rolled up in their blankets. Many an Aesir had gone to fight the Vanir and woken to find the man next to him dead, with a ghastly second mouth grinning up at the morning light.

Buri knew the Forest People were dangerous in other ways too. They had deep minds with many unexpected twists. Sly and tricky, much given to plotting and scheming, they were difficult to deal with at the best of times. He remembered when he had built the Warrior's Hall in Asgard and had wanted one massive beam to hold up the roof. The only place such huge trees grew was in Vanaheim. Buri had two choices: fight his way in, cut down the right tree, and then fight his way back out again: or somehow strike a bargain with the Vanir.

Always cautious and known for his cleverness, he had chosen the latter tactic. With a small escort he had gone to the city of Folkvang to dicker over the cost of the help of the Forest People. Buri had finally achieved what he felt had been a modest victory: a promise to help find the tree, permission to cut it, and a guarantee of aid in moving it to the edge of the forest.

Even now Buri blushed to think how badly the Vanir had tricked him. The tree they found was far up in the hills, almost in the Smoking Lands. Vanir help in cutting it had consisted of advice and verbal encouragement. Aid in moving included supplying the traces and roller logs. Then, when the great trunk had reached the edge of the forest at the clearing around Folkvang, the Vanir had changed their minds and confiscated it. It was needed to build a new hall for the Vanadis! Buri and his party had barely managed to escape with their lives. Their gold and their honor were left behind.

Though that insult had been the start of the current round of raids between the two peoples, Buri still hoped that somehow a truce could be reached. There were many, many Jotun and nowhere near enough Aesir. If the Vanir were to join them, together the two nations could more than hold off the riders from the north.

We need them, Buri thought. What a pity we can't trust them.

Surprisingly, the Vanir agreed at once to come and confer with the Aesir. They sent Gullveig, eldest sister of the Vanadis,

Fiorgynn. Gullveig was one of the Disir and the second most important member of the Distingen. Buri had met her when he himself had been in Vanaheim and had once even dreamt he might match her with Borr by way of establishing a truce with the Vanir. But Vestla Ravenhair had ended all that. Vestla and a certain damn tree trunk!

Gullveig came with a guard of eighteen Valkyrja. They were dressed in soft ankle-high boots, leggings, and fringed shirts, all made of dark brown deerskin. The Disir had intricate patterns embroidered across the yoke and down the sleeves of her shirt, but other than that she was indistinguishable from the other members of her party.

She was every bit as beautiful as Buri remembered. Her long hair was midnight black and as shiny as Vestla's. Her white face was smooth and heart-shaped; her neck, long and gently curved. For one so slight she had a figure that was disturbingly lush. As she entered the Warrior's Hall every man's eyes burned brighter and his breechclout fit tighter. The looks she shot right and left from her green eyes were bold, appraising, and anything but maidenly or modest. When she sat in the High Seat beside Buri, even that grizzled old warrior, who had buried his lifelong wife only the season before, felt his heart race and his blood heat.

It was Borr who stood and spoke for the Aesir. He inclined his head slightly to the woman, then began. "The Aesir welcome you, Gullveig, sister of the Vanadis. You do us honor." A slight mocking smile played about the corners of Gullveig's mouth as she nodded acknowledgment of Borr's words. "The Disir Gullveig accepts your welcome, Borr Skullcracker. Well do we know of your prowess. In many things. It is a pleasure to see you at last with our own eyes. Yes. A pleasure." Her voice surprised them all. It was deep and throaty, a soft purr that filled the hall. It was the kind of voice women used when making love.

A slight flush rose up Borr's neck, but he kept on, his voice steady. "For many years our people have fought each other. Not in open warfare, with armies wheeling and clashing in the red work of sword and spear, but in little forays, night attacks, quick and deadly assaults. Both sides have lost. It is hard to see what either side has gained."

Gullveig nodded, her face serious. "This is so."

Borr continued. "Now the Jotun stir again. Years ago we smashed them at Bifrosti's Ford and hurled them back toward the Icerealm. They have grown strong once more and raid our steads, putting them to the torch and our people to the sword. Or worse."

"We have heard of this," murmured the Disir.

"Hearing of the Sons of Ymir and experiencing them are two very different things," Borr replied harshly. "The Aesir stand between the Vanir and the men of the grasslands. For this you should thank your Vettir."

Gullveig shrugged. "We have no dealings, either friendly or hostile, with the horsemen of the Jotun. Horses and forests do not mix. But the Dverg in Nidavellir trade with them, so they are not impossible to live with."

A murmur of surprise and concern rose from the Aesir. Borr chose to ignore it and press on. "The Jotun become a danger to us all. They will not stop in Asaheim. They will carry the raven feast with them into the forests of Vanaheim." He paused for effect. "If we let them."

The Disir looked at Borr more sharply now. "Speak plainly, man. If you have something to propose, propose it."

"Aye. The Aesir propose a truce with the Vanir to last as long as the youngest in this hall shall still live. We will not enter the forest, nor cut the trees, nor clear new lands to farm or graze. You will not raid our steads. This will free us to deal with the Jotun for the benefit of both our people. This the Aesir offer and agree to bind in blood. We will swear it by our gods and you by yours. He who breaks this truce will be turned over to the mercy of those injured to do with as they will."

Silence filled the hall. Borr sat down, and Gullveig stared off, unseeing, into the air. Finally Buri cleared his throat. "Umm. What says the Disir?"

The woman turned and stared at him, her face cold, neutral, and unreadable. "The Disir says nothing," she responded, "yet. This thing is a new idea. Never have the Vanir allied themselves with any of the New Races. This thing needs thinking on." The coldness left her face suddenly and was replaced by a look both sly and seductive. "While the Disir considers the idea proposed by the Aesir, she has a gift to share with them." She clapped her hands. The members of her party reached into the packs they had unslung from their backs and pulled out small corked earthenware amphorae. They brought them forward and placed them in front of the High Seat. There were at least forty of them.

The Aesir craned their necks and stared, a wondering mur-

mur rising from the benches. Gullveig smiled out over the
assembly. "This is a gift from the Vettir, particularly from
Beyla, the god who dwells with the bees. We call it mead. It
is the drink of the Vettir themselves, and we would share it
with the mighty Aesir." There was a rumble of pleasure from
the chieftains and a great licking of the lips. All had heard of
mead; none had been lucky enough to taste it. The Aesir brewed
a beer from the grain they grew, and they dearly loved to drink
it. But this . . . this was special.

Drinking cups were quickly produced as the Vanir went
around the hall, pouring out the golden liquid. The Disir was
the last to be served, and all waited until she raised her cup in
salute. Then they drank.

The murmurs of pleasure rapidly turned into a thundering
chorus of banging, stamping approval. Many drained their cups
in a second gulp, holding out their vessels for more as the Vanir
scurried about.

Borr drank slowly, carefully, sipping, not gulping. He
watched Gullveig from the corner of his eye so she could not
see where his attention was directed. Buri drained his cup and
the Disir was pouring a second, urging him to drink again. The
woman turned to view the scene in the hall, and the look on
her face made Borr freeze.

There was triumph there, and a malice so deep it stunned
him! He pretended to drink once more, to drain his cup, as her
eyes swept over him.

Something was wrong! He could sense it, see it in her eyes.
Borr looked about him. Many of the Aesir were on their third
cups. A few were already blinking stupidly, the effects of the
strong liquor becoming apparent. Here and there scuffles were
breaking out as men sought to have their cups filled before the
amphorae ran dry.

Suddenly Borr understood. The golden gift of the mead was
no gift at all! Only the Aesir drank, and unused to drink that
strong, they were rapidly becoming drunk! The Vanir, all nineteen of them, watched and waited, their long dirks thrust through
their belts, as the Aesir drank themselves into total vulnera-
bility!

Borr stood and flung his cup to the floor. In two steps he
reached the High Seat, dashing the cup from Buri's already
unsteady hand and grabbing Gullveig by the neck. He spun the
woman around, placing her between himself and the hall, his
own dagger pressed to her throat. With a bellow he brought

the whole room to a sudden standstill. Aesir stopped, cups outstretched. Vanir froze, amphorae extended.

"It's a trick, you fools!" he roared. "The Vanir have given a false gift, a gold worth nothing! See! They're not drinking, while you begin to stagger. And their knives are ready! Fools!"

Gullveig tried to speak, to call out to her guards, but Borr choked the sound before it could pass her lips. "You'll be silent, bitch. Only lies pass your lips." He looked up to see knives in the hands of the Vanir. Slowly, lightly, he drew the point of his dagger across Gullveig's throat, leaving behind a thin line that oozed a few drops of red. Borr laughed, his face twisted into a snarl. "One move, forest snakes, and your Disir wears a new smile." Slowly they put their dirks back in their belts, but their hands stayed close.

Most of the Aesir had recovered, shocked into instant sobriety. "Aesir," Borr commanded, "bind these vipers and take them from the hall. Give them to the old women to kill. Gagnrad, Ulf, Haakon, Sig, Vitar, Gorm, Hymir, stay." The men moved to do his bidding. A few of the Vanir struggled briefly, but in moments the hall was empty of all but Buri, Gullveig, and those Borr had asked to stay.

Borr slipped the woman's dagger from its place at her waist. "You," he growled, "we will not kill, though you may wish we had." His hand darted out and smashed into her face, knocking her from the High Seat to the floor of the hall. He followed, jerking her roughly from the ground. He grabbed the front of her shirt and ripped it in two, then he tore off her leggings. A second, smaller dirk was tied around her waist. Borr threw it across the room.

With a second slap he drove her to her knees, then hit her a third time so that she toppled, dazed and bleeding, onto her back. He took off his breechclout, and Gullveig moaned, knowing at last the fate Borr planned. The Aesir threw himself on her, brutally thrusting himself into her protesting body. "Treacherous bitch," he growled. While he raped her the others grinned and prepared for their turn.

When they had finished, they shoved her from the Warrior's Hall. The women and children waited outside with switches and stones. They drove her from Asgard, through the hide traveling tents that surrounded it, and out across the plain to the south.

Borr stood flanked by Buri and Gagnrad. He turned to the latter as the staggering figure of Gullveig disappeared across the plain. He held out his hand. "You were right, friend," he said gruffly. "The Aesir stand alone between two enemies. I wish it were not so. But it is." Gagnrad took his hand and shook it. "I would ride beside you, Borr, against Jotun or Vanir. Or both."

Buri looked at the two of them, then turned and began walking back toward the Warrior's Hall. He felt old and alone. Two enemies. Either way his people turned, one would always be at their backs. He felt a growing sense of doom.

V

THAT summer every man, woman, and child in Asaheim went armed at all times. Axes, swords, daggers, and spears were kept close at hand. Worried eyes constantly scanned the horizon, searching, yet fearing to find. The tension grew until it was almost unbearable.

It wasn't until the early fall, when the first touches of yellow and red colored the plain, that the Jotun struck. A group of some twenty or thirty swam their horses across the Iving just below its confluence with the broad Vid, then swooped southeast along the Vid, burning and killing as they went. The levies of the Aesir Plain rallied and met them, sending half of them racing back northward. The other half lay where they fell.

Buri decided it was time to gather the host to Asgard. He didn't like leaving his back uncovered, but he had no choice. However dangerous the Vanir might be, the Sons of Ymir were equally dangerous and far more numerous. Besides, the horsemen were clearly on the move.

The Aesir divided themselves into three groups. The left, under the command of Buri, covered the Iving from Bifrosti's Ford to the tumbled rocks of the Himinborg. Borr led the center, spread out to reach along the Iving to the River Fimbulthul. Between the Fimbulthul and the Bones of Ymir stood Gagnrad, ready to repulse any attack.

The only easy way to cross the deep, swift Iving was the ford. Just to the east of the ford the river fought its way through a turbulent area of rock-filled rapids. The water churned and splashed, sending a fine spray high into the air. If one crossed the ford at a certain time of day, when the sun was in the right position, a magnificent rainbow arched across the sky.

Buri stood now and watched it, the startling beauty of it affecting him in a way it never had before. The thought came to him that this was the last time he would ever see it, and somehow he knew it to be true. He shrugged. If it is written,

55

it is written. Because a man's doom was set down by the Nornir at his birth was no reason to sit at home and weep. Best to go out and meet it, ax in one's hand, song on one's lips.

Nevertheless, his mouth was dry and he found it hard to swallow as the scout rode up on his lathered horse. "They come," the man said breathlessly, "to force the ford." Buri nodded and turned to the messenger standing ready next to him. "Ride," he commanded. "Tell Borr and Gagnrad. We'll hold them until they arrive."

As the man vaulted onto his horse and sped off eastward, Buri looked to the north. There, sidelit by the morning sun, a column of dust was just becoming visible. The Horde was coming, and there were many of them. Come soon, Borr, he prayed silently. Come soon. I would see you one last time.

Borr and his men were in the saddle, pounding westward, within a few minutes of the arrival of the messenger. Old Axhand can hold them until we arrive, Borr told himself again and again. He can and he will. But he wondered anew what he had been wondering for some time now. Was Buri too old . . . ?

It was a good two hours at a steady gallop to the ford. From several miles away they caught sight of the cloud of dust that rose from the struggle. Skullcracker estimated its location. He didn't like the result. The Jotun had forced the ford!

The horses were lathered and badly winded by the time they crested a small rise and saw the battle spread out before them. The Jotun had indeed crossed the Iving, but Buri had managed to rally his forces to stop them before they had gained much more than a mile or so of territory to the south of the river. The leader of the Aesir, however, was in dire straits, surrounded by the howling horde of horsemen. His own horses had all been killed, and he and his surviving men fought the mounted enemy on foot from the top of a low hill. The dead were already piled deep around the defenders. Borr could see more than one arrow sticking out from Buri's body.

Skullcracker and his men had arrived barely in time, and luckily from exactly the right angle. With a roar loud enough to gladden the heart of Sigfod, God of Battle, and the flash of sword, ax, and spear, they struck the left flank of the Jotun from the rear, crumpling and flinging it before them in stunned disorder.

With a shock that nearly unseated him, Borr crashed into

his first adversary. The Jotun warrior howled at him, his teeth
bared in a feral grin, his curved sword whistling through the
air. Borr blocked with his shield, then sent the man's head
flying with a single stroke of his one-handed ax. Another enemy
attacked from the other side, thrusting at him with a spear. The
Aesir parried with his ax and slammed his shield into the man's
face, knocking him backward from his horse. Borr's own beast
trampled him into a bloody pulp.

Everything became a red whirl, swords flashing, axes
swinging, spears thrusting, blood and gore splattering over
everyone. The range was too close for the Jotun to use their
deadly bows, so it was man-to-man. Borr's horse went down,
a spear through its throat. He grabbed the leg of the man who
had delivered the death-thrust and threw him from his own
mount. Then he smashed his skull.

He looked up to the hill where his father still stood, ax in
hand, working bloody destruction, setting out the raven feast.
He saw Buri falter and drop to one knee. Three Jotun leapt at
him across the heap of corpses. The old man swept his ax up
from the ground to eviscerate one, but the other two struck at
him in unison with their swords and he pitched backward, chest
and left arm spouting blood. Borr's eyes met his father's across
the intervening yards of struggling, dying men for a brief second. Then, with the smile of one who knows he dies well,
Buri collapsed.

Borr gave a great cry of fury and anguish. He cursed Sigfod.
Jamming his small war ax into his belt, he unslung the mighty
two-handed battle-ax, Deathbringer, and shifted his shield around
to protect himself from behind. Then he began to roar and
stamp, yelling one word over and over. "Berserk! Berserk!
Berserk!" Foam began to fleck his lips; his breath came in great
sobbing shudders; his eyes became glassy and wildly burning.

With a sudden bellow he launched himself into the thickest
part of the fray, opening a red-spattered passage to the hill
where his father lay. Others seeing him took up the chant, and
the battle madness came over them too. Ripped and torn Jotun
flew from in front of them. Blows seemed to glance off them,
strikes that would have felled an ordinary man barely causing
them to pause. The Sons of Ymir began to fall back, awed by
the sheer ferocity of the attack.

Borr killed a horse and rider with one mighty sweep of his
ax. The blood of man and animal glinted redly on the blade and
ran down the haft in a river. He reached the still figure of his

father and stood astride the body, flinging back the broken bodies of the enemy with every move he made. He knew nothing, saw nothing, heard nothing beyond the constant sweep and smash of his ax.

Then suddenly there were no more Jotun to kill. Gagnrad had arrived, plowing into the horsemen with sword ready and eager to spill the enemy's guts out across the grass of the Himinborg Plain. This third assault was too much for the wild warriors from the grasslands. They turned and fled back across the Iving, leaving the dead to float sluggishly in the shallows of Bifrosti's Ford.

Gagnrad found Borr leaning wearily on his great ax, gazing sadly down at the still face of his father. The Skullcracker had carefully laid the silver-haired old man out, wiping the blood from his face and beard, pulling the edges of the slashed clothing together to hide the gaping wounds. The arrows he had either pulled out or broken off close to the punctured flesh.

"He died well," Borr said quietly. "Like a chieftain of the Aesir. He should sit high up on the benches in the Hall of the Gods." Gagnrad nodded.

Borr raised his gaze to the north and the Iving. "They've run back." Gagnrad nodded again. Skullcracker sighed. "This time we've been hurt too badly to follow and drive them the way Buri did before. We beat them, but that's all."

"Bergelmir fell," Gagnrad said. It was Borr's turn to nod. "And some two hundred or so broke past Buri's line on the left." He gestured with his head toward the towering rocks of the Himinborg. "Probably in there somewhere. We'll have to root them out."

For several moments Borr stared out across the plain toward the Himinborg, a considering look on his face. "No," he finally said softly. "No, I don't think so."

Gagnrad looked surprised. "But, they'll—" he began. Borr raised his hand to interrupt. "Take three hundred men, the freshest you can muster. Drive the Jotun southward toward the forest. We'll sent them as a gift to the Vanir." The other man looked puzzled but moved off to carry out the command. Borr watched him go, a hard, calculating smile twisting his lips.

Hours later a messenger staggered in from Asgard. The Vanir had attacked in force, sweeping north from the Gunnthro, burning steads and killing women, children, and old people

as they came. Those left in Asgard had defended it as best
they could. The Forest People had finally retreated, but not
before they had fired and destroyed most of the timber palisade
that surrounded the city.

The news hit bore Borr like a physical blow. Quickly he
dispatched as many men as he could spare to pursue the Vanir
and to protect the people of Asgard. But the enemy had several
hours head start, and Skullcracker knew that his exhausted men,
worn out by the battle with the Jotun, would never catch up.
It was just like the cursed Vanir. Hit and run. Damn them! He
was doubly glad now he had sent them his little present.

Buri was carried back to Asgard in state. Nine chieftains, Borr
leading, carried him on a litter draped with gold cloth. The old
leader of the Aesir was dressed in his best clothes, a golden
helmet on his head, golden torque around both his biceps, and
a heavy gold chain around his neck. His ax was laid across his
chest and his shield covered his lower body.

A great barrow was raised to the north of the city, and Buri
was laid to rest within it, seated and facing north. In death he
would guard his people from the Jotun even as he had in life.

A week later Borr was unanimously hailed as leader of the
Aesir. His first act was to begin the rebuilding of the wall
around Asgard.

It was more than a month before Gagnrad and his three
hundred finally returned. They had driven the Sons of Ymir
south, staying just out of range and avoiding any attempt to
join battle. Finally the horsemen had disappeared into the forests of Vanir. For two weeks Gagnrad patrolled the border
between the two nations, making sure the Jotun did not attempt
to slip back northward again. Nothing emerged from the deep,
still greenness except one or two wild-eyed and riderless horses.

The first snows of the season dusted the plains of Asaheim,
lightly covering the grisly remains of the great battle south of
the Iving. Wolf, fox, jackal, raven, eagle, and vulture had all
feasted on the Jotun dead for weeks. Maggots and swarms of
ants finished the job, leaving behind scattered piles of bleaching
bones. Next summer the grass would grow lush over this spot,
and Aesir cattle would fatten on the shattered hopes of the wild
horsemen from the north.

Winter would soon put an icy stop to Jotun raiding. The
Iving never froze, making the ford the only crossing even during

the Icetime. The Jotun never campaigned during the cold part of the year. They had all they could do to keep themselves and their herds alive and safe from the wrath of Gymir. The Aesir settled down to a few months of secure peace for the first time in recent memory, thanking Vindsval, God of Winter.

The messenger from the Vanir arrived quietly and alone. He was ushered into the Warrior's Hall where Borr and several of his key chieftains were discussing what should be done to handle the Jotun menace come spring. They had stopped the horsemen and wounded them gravely, but they all knew the Sons of Ymir would be back with warm weather, and they would be stronger than ever.

The slight man from the forest approached the High Seat cautiously, almost fearfully. He knew what had happened here only a few months before. Bowing low to Borr, he spoke: "I bear word from Fiorgynn, Vanadis of the Vanir, to Borr, chief of the Aesir."

Borr nodded for the man to continue. Licking his lips, he began. "The Vanadis thanks Borr for the gift and the lesson. It seems the Aesir have the right of it. Is mighty Borr still interested in a truce?"

A murmur rose from the men in the hall. Borr looked solemn. "What says the Disir Gullveig of this offer?"

The messenger looked surprised. "Gullveig? Gullveig says nothing. She is dead."

"Dead? How so?"

"She and three other Disir died, trampled to death, when they went out from the gates of Folkvang to greet the Jotun and offer them welcome."

"Ah." Borr nodded. "And Folkvang, how fares it?"

"It is mostly rebuilt."

"So. What are the terms the Vanadis wishes?"

"A truce between our people, to last as long as Yggdrasil exists. The Aesir will not encroach farther on the forests of the Vanir. The Vanir will not attack or harass your steads. We will pledge support whenever and wherever you find need to meet the Jotun in battle. Aesir and Vanir will exchange hostages as a guarantee for the truce. You will send your eldest son, Voden, to live with the Vanadis in Folkvang as one of her own children. One other may accompany him. We will send Niord and Frey, the Vanadis's own two sons, to live with the Aesir. Thus say the Vanadis and the Distingen." The man finished, bowed, and stepped back.

Borr sat, his left hand gently stroking his beard, his right fingers lightly drumming on the arm of the High Seat. He looked off into the distance for several moments, then focused his gaze and swung it to rest on Gagnrad. "What say you, Beargrasp, old friend?"

Huge and shaggy as always, the man rose and glanced about him. "Hmm. Now, none can say I have ever been much in favor of a truce with the Vanir." He laid a thick finger on his nose, broken and squashed by Borr's fists. "Not by a nose, I've not been." A chuckle went up from the assembled men.

"Still, I've seen what can happen when even warriors as mighty as the Aesir must face in two directions at the same time. We stopped the Jotun last time, barely. If the Vanir had truly wanted to destroy Asgard behind our backs, they could have. We all know that.

"The Sons of Ymir are far from smashed. They merely lick their wounds, waiting for the right moment, the right leader, to come roaring back across the Iving again. Bergelmir is dead, but it is rumored he has a nephew, a young lad called Hrod vitnir. Already the child is said to show signs of being a fierce warrior." He shrugged. "It is only hearsay, rumor, but that matters not. If it isn't Hrodvitnir, then some other will rise to lead and bring the Horde back across the Iving.

"When that happens, even I would rather have the Vanir by my side than behind my back." He sat down to a thumping and stamping of approval.

Another man rose, a chieftain from the Idavoll Plain. He doubted the wisdom of trusting the Vanir. Another stood. And another. In true Aesir fashion, every man would be heard.

Borr's attention began to drift. A truce with the Vanir! Buri's dream come true. It came just in time. As only Borr and a few others knew, the Aesir had been as badly cut up as the Jotun in that last battle. The Horde wouldn't be able to attack in force again for a few years. Raids, yes, probably constantly from now on, but a massive army like the one Bergelmir had put together was unlikely.

The problem wasn't only numbers. There were still enough of the Sons of Ymir left alive to make an army larger than anything the Aesir could field. The problem was leadership. The Jotun were a proud, contentious people and often fought bitter feuds among themselves. Uniting them wasn't easy.

Keeping them that way for any length of time was even harder. They had long memories and short tempers. Men who were riding together companionably one moment could be slashing at each other with their curved swords the next, determined to settle a score two generations old.

It took a strong, clever, ruthless leader to bring the Horde under control. The position of Warlord was won and maintained by the liberal use of both sword and dagger. All six Thrudgelmirs had risen that way. Bergelmir had had to murder his eldest brother and three cousins when he seized power.

Now Bergelmir was dead, and Volund had slain his sons. The direct line of Warlords that had begun with the first Thrudgelmir was broken. The leadership of the Horde was up for grabs.

Of course, it was always possible that it would be quite some time before anyone emerged the clear victor, or even that no one would be capable of establishing hegemony. Borr knew that in the past the Jotun had often gone for an entire generation without a Warlord. Somehow he doubted that would be the case this time. The Sons of Ymir seemed to bear a special hatred for the Aesir, which already halfway united them. Then there were the persistent rumors about Bergelmir's young nephew, Hrodvitnir. At best, he felt sure, they would only have a few years respite. Four or five at the outside. Then . . .

How many more battles like that last could they fight? One? Two? Three? No more, surely. Not alone, without allies. And who could they ally with? The Alfar were no help. There were too few of them, and they had not fought since the days of the First Dark Empire. They lived a strange, quiet life in their ancient forest, gathering from time to time in Vidblain, their "main place" (they had no towns in the usual sense), to talk and dance and remember the First Days. Gimle, the chief hall in Vidblain, didn't even have weapons or shields on its walls. No, the Alfar were of no help.

Who then? The Dverg? Not likely! The Dverg actually traded with the Jotun and seemed to get on fairly well with them. The Aesir had hardly ever dealt with the little men from Nidavellir, but the few meetings they had had were not likely to encourage thoughts of alliance.

The Vanir were the only ones left. Buri had seen this long ago, Borr realized, once again understanding how his father had earned the name The Clever. Certainly the man's own dealing with the Vanir had been far from successful, but his intentions had been correct, and his foresightedness remarkable.

Yet the price the Vanir asked! His own son! To be taken from him and Vestla to be raised by the Vanir in their dark forests. He shuddered. The very thought of the boy's growing up in such a place shriveled his soul. Never to see the sky arching from horizon to horizon. Never to ride across the plain, the wind blowing free in his hair . . .

Still, was it really so different from what would happen anyway? Voden was destined to go to be raised with Gagnrad's family in a few more years. It was customary. By having children raised in the families of other chieftains, the ties that bound the Aesir together were more firmly knotted. Borr himself had been raised that way.

More important yet, if Borr did not take advantage of the Vanir offer, would Voden have any chance of growing up at all? Or would the Jotun send them all to the Hall of the Gods?

Ah, Voden, Voden! Damn the gods that such a choice should have to be made! He thought of his son. The lad was soon to be eleven. Already he was showing great promise. Childhood fat had gone, leaving a lean, hard young body. Voden was somewhat solemn for one of so few years, but quick and alert, not afraid of a fight. He rough-and-tumbled with the best of them. About the only one of his own age he couldn't beat was young Tror. But then, no one could beat young Tror! In fact, no *two* could beat Volund's redheaded giant of a son!

Am I never to have the pleasure of showing my own son how to draw the bow, cast the spear, swing the ax? Damn! What will Vestla say? He winced to think of it. Her tears would be even harder to stand.

He sighed. And yet what choice do I have? The Vanadis is right, he realized. Only such important hostages will guarantee the truce, and only such a truce will guarantee our safety.

The Aesir must be kept safe. The Aesir are more important than any one man or child. I am no longer just a warrior or just a father, he reminded himself. I am the leader of my people. This fall, many Aesir gave much more than I am now called to sacrifice. There is no choice.

When the others had finished expressing their opinions, Borr stood and looked down at the messenger. His gaze was pensive. He raised his glance to the hall and swept the benches. Everywhere he looked, he could see that all had come to the same conclusion.

"Messenger," he began, "go tell your mistress the Aesir accept the offer of truce with the Vanir. It shall be as the Vanadis asks. On the first day of spring, let us meet at the place where the River Gunnthro leaves the land of the Vanir and enters that of the Aesir. There we will exchange hostages and pledges of peace and mutual support.

"And," he added softly as an afterthought, "tell your people to be prepared to begin their support once the summer sun warms the wagons of the Jotun."

The slight man nodded his understanding, bowed, and turned to go. As he left the hall, Gagnrad came to Borr's side, placing a friendly hand on his shoulder. "You give up a great deal for the safety of the Aesir. I only hope you're doing the right thing."

"So do I," came Borr's barely audible reply. "So do I."

VI

~~~

VODEN liked it by the forge. Especially on a day when Vindsval, God of Winter, drove the fine snow before him and hung icicles from every roof in Asgard.

He looked up as Tror shifted hands on the bellows. The big redheaded lad said it was important to shift so that you didn't get lopsided. For that reason he carefully counted the number of strokes he made, and every tenth time he reached ten, he switched.

"Want me to pump for a while?" Voden asked. Tror smiled and shook his head.

Volund chuckled. "Careful, young Voden, you'll make him lose his count. Then he'll end up all twisted like one of the Dverg."

Voden peered into the forge. "Looks ready. It's that red that's beyond red."

The smith looked. He nodded. "Aye. You've a good eye. Ready it is." He reached out and picked up his tongs "Get set, lads. Pray to whatever gods you honor most. This is something I've never tried before, to fix an iron head to an iron handle." He gripped his hammer.

Reaching out with the tongs, he pulled a massive chunk of iron from the forge and turned to place it on the anvil. Voden craned his neck to see, then stood to get a better view. An iron shaft about eighteen inches long lay next to the anvil. Volund placed the big chunk of glowing iron on the flat metal, then picked up the shaft and placed it over a hole that he had laboriously bored into the chunk. With several quick, mighty blows he drove the shaft into the chunk. "Have to work swiftly," he grunted between blows, "before the shaft heats and grows." He squinted down at his work, checking the angle the shaft made with the chunk. Satisfied, he began to work the chunk itself, forming and shaping it.

"That's the way with metal, lads. Heat it, it grows. Cool

it, it shrinks." Each time his hammer struck, sparks flew. "That's why we heat the metal before we work it. Hitting it takes away the heat, and it shrinks in the direction of the blow."

"It's a hammer," said Voden. "A giant hammer."

"Aye. That it is, but not for striking hot metals. It's all iron, head and handle. Heavy."

He stood back for a second, eyeing his work with a critical glance and wiping the sweat from his brow. Whatever he saw, he thrust the huge hammer back into the forge, the handle sticking out. "Pump, Tror," he commanded.

Voden frowned. "If it's not for striking metal, what's it for? It's too big for driving wood pegs."

Volund laughed. "So it is, so it is! No, it's not that, either. This"—he dropped his voice to a conspiratorial whisper and winked at the two boys—"this hammer is called Mjollnir, the Crusher. It's made in a special way. Eitri, one of the Dverg master smiths, told me of it years ago."

"Special? How?"

"Ah, Voden, always the curious one, aren't you? Always wanting to know. There are some things you're not ready for yet. Let it be enough to say I quench the iron in stallion's blood as I work it. The rest cannot be safely said." He looked solemn and grim.

"What's it for?" Voden demanded.

"It's Mjollnir, and it's for crushing."

"I know for crushing. For crushing what?"

"Heads," came the curt reply. Volund pulled the hammer from the forge once more and began to work the head with a flurry of blows. Occasionally he would stick the glowing iron into a wooden bucket filled with a dark liquid. A cloud of steam sizzled into the air when the metal met the fluid. Voden thought he could smell blood.

He stood back and watched, thinking. The hammer was clearly something special. Much too heavy to use as a tool, it could only be a weapon. Like Borr's big ax, but smaller and heavier. Voden couldn't even lift his father's battle ax over his head, much less swing it. If this hammer was even heavier, who in Yggdrasil could wield it?

The muscles on Volund's massive shoulders twisted and knotted as the hammer rose and fell. Ah, Voden thought, of course. The hammer Mjollnir was for Volund himself to use.

Which didn't make sense. The master smith was crippled.

Though he got around well enough, he'd never be able to move as swiftly as was necessary on a battlefield. Seeing the trouble the man was having just manipulating the hammer as he worked on it, the boy began to wonder if even he, with his incredible strength, would be able to swing the weapon as freely and quickly as would be required in a fight.

Who, then? Was the hammer just to be an offering to the gods? Perhaps to Sigfod, God of Battle? Possibly even to Fornjot the Destroyer, father of all gods? If so, what a waste!

The weapon that was rapidly emerging from beneath Volund's blows was magnificent. The head was basically rectangular, a good sixteen inches by seven, flaring at the ends and narrowing toward the middle. The shaft fit all the way through the head, a small bit sticking out above. The shaft itself was a rounded rectangle, tapering from about two by three inches at the grip to two by two where it entered the head.

How much did the whole thing weigh? Voden could only form a rough idea by watching the manner in which Volund handled it. Fifty pounds would be light, a hundred too much. Crusher indeed!

"Volund," the boy said in his most pleasant voice. The man grunted in response, his attention all on his work. "What mighty warrior is to carry Mjollnir into battle? Has someone commissioned you to make this wonderful weapon?"

The master smith looked up at Voden from under his shaggy brows. He shook his head slightly, then straightened and looked the boy directly in the eyes. "No, young Voden," he replied, "no Aesir warrior has commissioned Mjollnir." He laughed. "There are none who could swing it! The man who can use this weapon has yet to appear. When he does, he will be a great champion, a shield to protect the Aesir."

"Is he coming, this great champion?" the young man asked breathlessly.

"Aye," Volund answered with a quiet smile. "He is coming. In his own time, he is coming." A far-off look came into his eyes. Then his manner changed abruptly and he was all business again. "Now, you two," he ordered, fixing Voden and Tror with a commanding stare, "go off and find me old Groa. Mjollnir is nearing completion, and I have need of her." The two grumbled at leaving the warmth of the forge, but moved to do Volund's bidding. "And mind," he called as they reached the door, "don't come back once you find her! Things are to be done that are not for the likes of you to see!"

Outside, the fine snow was still driving down out of the north. On their way to Groa's they came across Honir, who had just finished an errand for his father. Together they went to the old witchwoman's hut.

Voden knocked cautiously. He pressed his ear to the door and heard a mumbling from within. He knocked again, more loudly. Suddenly the door flew inward and the two nearly tumbled into the dark, crowded room where Groa lived.

Groa had been old when Borr was a boy. Now she was ancient. Voden often wondered, seeing her shuffle around Asgard, what held her old body together. She seemed to be nothing more than an odd assortment of bones, skin, a few straggly hairs, and one burning, glaring eye. Children always avoided Groa, not because she was mean but because it seemed the right thing to do.

On seeing the two lads, Groa cackled. "Ah, hah, hah, yes, yes, it's the Nornir, it is. Come to tell old Groa Volund needs her."

Voden's eyes grew big with surprise. "Y-yes," he stammered, "th-that was our errand. How did you . . . ?"

"Ah, Groa has but one eye, but that eye sees more than both yours combined, young one." The old woman began to shuffle about the cluttered room, mumbling to herself as she gathered into a dirty skin pouch things she wanted to take. "Hmm. Wolfbane. Ah, ah, yes firewort. And newt, oh, yes, newt. Hmm."

Voden watched with interest. Tror wanted to leave now that the message had been delivered, but Voden shook off their hands. "Groa," he said, "why do you have but one eye?"

The woman turned in surprise. "What? Who's this has snuck up on old Groa? Ah, ah, young Voden. My, I thought you had left. Your friend wants you to badly enough. Run along now. Shoo, shoo." She waved them away and turned back to her rummaging.

"Come on," whispered Tror urgently, tugging at his sleeve so hard he almost pulled Voden over. Voden shook his head and stepped farther into the room, determined to get an answer. "Why only one eye?"

Groa turned slowly this time, a considering look in her eye. "Long has it been since I've seen such a hunger to know," she muttered. "What, young Voden, if you don't like the answer? What if it frightens you and haunts your dreams? What if it comes and sits on your chest in the night and stalks you even when the sun shines high? Eh? What then?"

The boy shrunk back, surprised at the old woman's vehemence. "I . . . I . . ." he stammered. Then he took hold of himself and straightened up. Looking Groa in the eye and putting every ounce of bravery he could muster into the words, he said, "Still, I would know."

A loud shrieking laugh gushed from the witchwoman's wrinkled mouth. Voden could see the blackened stumps of three teeth. "Ahhh, haaa, haaa," the old creature chortled, "ahhh, yes, yes! Such a one, such a one!

"So then, Voden, hear old Groa. This eye was plucked from my head by Mimir. Plucked raw and bloody it was by Mimir."

"W-why? Wh-what for?"

"For a drink, one little drink."

"O-of water?"

"Oh, aye, and nay. Water it was and water it wasn't. Once I drank and ever afterward I've been thirsty, so thirsty," she moaned. "'Twas no bargain, that drink. Yet I'd do it again."

"I don't understand."

Groa chuckled. "No. I hardly thought you would. Nor will you when I tell you more. Mimir lives to the north of the Amsvartnir Sea. There she tends a well. All who find it, and that is no easy task in itself, can drink from it, for a price. Oh, yes, a price! I paid with my eye. Others have left fingers, even whole hands behind. Mimir asks what she knows is hardest to give. For what you get in return is nothing less than Knowledge!"

Voden stood suddenly rigid. "Knowledge?" The old woman nodded solemnly. "What kind of knowledge?"

"That which most you need."

"What did you learn, Groa?"

The witchwoman stood and stared at him for several moments, then turned away and began rummaging again. "Enough," she muttered. "Volund calls. Enough. Go away, Voden."

Tror reached out and grabbed Voden by the arm. "Let's go," he commanded. And before he could protest, the young redheaded giant dragged him from the hut.

Groa turned as they left and watched the empty doorway for many minutes. Her mouth moved, but no words came out.

Finally she sighed. "Such a one," she muttered. "Such a one. The gods guard him. I fear he will tread in dark places. Such a one."

The wind had begun to die and the snow was falling more gently now. Voden, Tror, and Honir wandered around Asgard, looking for something interesting to do until Tror could return home. They passed Tyr's home and called him out to join them. Tyr, about a year younger than Voden, was a good companion, fearless, adventuresome, and always willing to dare or take a dare.

As they walked, their conversation drifted from topic to topic until finally it came to one every boy considered important: the gaining of their names. Shortly after birth every Aesir child was Namefastened by a close relative. This name was their given name and was generally the name they were called by in everyday conversation. As they grew older, however, the Aesir all strove to gain other names, their earned names. These generally related to strong personal characteristics or came from unusual exploits. Vestla, for example, was called Ravenhair because of the unusual color of her hair. Buri was known as Axhand for his prowess against the Jotun. Borr Skull-cracker's name had been earned in a similar manner. For the Aesir earning a name was one of the signs that adulthood had been reached.

For that reason name-earning was a constant topic of conversation among the children, especially the young boys. They loved to brag about their own future names and tease their friends by giving each other silly or foolish names.

Tyr began by looking slyly at Tror and saying, "I hear you've already earned your first name, Tror." The other boys pretended to take him seriously, demanding to hear the name Tror was supposedly being given. Tyr grinned mischievously, pausing for effect, then crowed out, "Tror Bellowsboy!"

The redheaded lad took a playful swipe at Tyr as Honir joined in. "No! No, that's not what I heard! I heard it was Tror Anvilthumper!" The smith's son howled in mock fury and began to chase Honir, but soon gave up the task as impossible since the long-legged youth could easily outdistance him.

"What do you want your first name to be?" Voden asked when the two came puffing back to join them.

Tror kicked thoughtfully at the snow for a moment, then

said softly, "I'd like Tror Ironarm, but it'll probably be Tror Smith." They all agreed that that seemed likely.

Now it was Tror's turn to gibe Tyr. "Word's out you've got a first name, too, Tyr. I believe it was Tyr Tremblelegs."

"'Tremblelegs'?" the young Aesir hollered. "I'll show you 'Tremblelegs,' you big red ox!" He leapt at Tror, swinging wildly. The young giant simply held the shorter youth at arm's length, allowing his fists to pummel empty air. Voden and Honir were laughing so hard they had to hold their sides.

Growling ferociously, Tyr finally stepped back. "Lucky for you I missed," he told Tror. Then he turned to them all and proudly declared, "My first name will be Fearless. I'll be known throughout all Asaheim as Tyr Fearless!" They all nodded and grinned. This was the name Tyr always chose.

"And you, Honir," Voden said, "what will you be called?"

"Ha!" Tror interjected. "Honir Storklegs, that's what!"

"No! No!" clamored Tyr. "He'll be Honir Tonguetie!"

Honir looked down at the ground and blushed, unable to answer their raillery.

"Hush," Voden demanded. "Let Honir speak for himself." Grumbling good-naturedly, the other two boys subsided.

Finally Honir looked up and said softly. "I'd be Honir Swift-foot."

"A perfect name!" Tror declared loudly. "Aye, it suits you, Honir!"

Grinning shyly, Honir looked over at Voden. "And you? What would you be called?"

A strange look came over Voden's face as he considered, a look that made the joke names the other boys had ready freeze in their throats even as they were about to shout them out. For several moments Voden stood and stared off into the snowstorm, his strangeness creating a circle of quiet in which the other boys stood mute and waiting.

"I think," he finally spoke in a dreamy, far-off voice, "I would be known as Voden Fjolsvid, Voden Verywise." The others took this name in silence, unsure precisely how to respond to such an odd choice.

They had walked wordlessly through the snow for perhaps a hundred paces when up ahead they saw a familiar figure turn into the street. Voden's serious face was split by a smile. It was his mother, Vestla Ravenhair, the most beautiful woman in all of Yggdrasil. He waved as she saw him, then gave his friends a quick good-bye and hurried to her.

When he reached her side, he was surprised by her expression. Her face was calm, as always, but there were fear and sorrow and pain in her eyes. Voden automatically put his arms around her and hugged her.

"Mother," he whispered, "what's the matter?"

She touched his head with a slightly quivering hand. "Nothing, nothing. Now go to the Warrior's Hall. Your father wants to see you."

VII

WHEN Voden opened the door of the Warrior's Hall, he was surprised by the total silence that greeted him. He peered in. The hall was empty, the benches along the walls without their usual load of rowdy occupants. Even the fires in the pit that ran down the center of the hall seemed to burn lower, subdued.

At the other end of the hall he could see his father, seated in the High Seat, chin resting on fist, eyes staring vacantly off into nothingness. Slowly, wondering what was going on, Voden walked up the long, still hall to Borr.

Borr noticed his son approaching. A strange expression swept across his face, an expression that increased Voden's sense of the oddness of it all. The boy reached the open space before the High Seat and dipped his head slightly in greeting to his father. Then he looked up into the eyes of the man who was leader of the Aesir.

Borr looked down and returned the gaze. He smiled slightly. "You have been out walking in the snow," he said with un accustomed gentleness. "There are still some unthawed flakes on your hair and shoulders. Were you with your friends?"

"Yes," Voden nodded, "with Tror, Honir, and Tyr."

"Ah," Borr responded sagely, "yes, good friends are important for an Aesir. Every warrior needs someone whom he can trust to guard his back and fight by his side." He paused, uncertain how to continue. By the gods, he thought, this is hard to say. My son, I'm sending you away, sacrificing you for my people. Easy to think, but so damn hard to say!

He cleared his throat. "Umm. Pull up a stool. We must talk, you and I. Umm. Yes." Where to begin? he wondered. Perhaps at the very beginning. He stared at the ceiling, unable to meet his son's expectant gaze, and began to speak in a far-off, musing tone.

"When Fornjot the Destroyer, father of all the gods, found Yggdrasil, it was beautiful beyond compare. The trees grew tall, the grasses lush. The sun shone bright and warm all year round. Berries and fruit were to be found everywhere. Game was plentiful and unafraid.

"Fornjot hated all he saw. He built his hall in the north. On either side of his High Seat he chained his two great wolves, Skoll and Hati. Skoll hopes to gobble up the sun someday. Hati hungers after the moon. From the slaver of their jaws a mighty river of ice flows, called the Elivagar. Its frozen waves even now pour southward to smash forests and cover ever more land in eternal winter.

"Three sons had Fornjot, and he called them Ler, Logi, and Kari. These were the first of the gods. Fornjot set Ler to rule over raging torrents, floods, deluges, and endless destructive rains. Logi was made lord of conflagrations, of searing flame, of forest fires, of the deadly blaze that sweeps uncontrolled across the plain. Kari took command of the wind, the devastating tornado, and all the bitter phenomena of winter. It is his son, Vindsval, God of Winter, who makes the Icetime so cruel.

"For a while Fornjot took great glee in destroying everything he could find. Soon the sport began to pale on him, for the only things to kill and torture were dumb animals and plants. No thinking, feeling creatures existed.

"The Destroyer thought long and hard. Then he took his ax and left his hall. He walked across the frozen waves of Elivagar until he found the shattered remains of two trees he had killed. From one he carved a man and called him Ask. From the other he carved a woman and Namefastened her Embla.

"Despite his skill in carving, they were still only inanimate pieces of wood. So he called his sons. Logi he commanded to provide Ask and Embla with the warmth of life and burning emotions. Kari gave them breath, the ability to speak, and swift-winged thought. Ler gifted them blood and set it flowing. He also gave them the patience of ever-lapping water. When his sons had finished, Fornjot pushed Ask and Embla out into the world. With a roar of mighty laughter he rejoiced that now he had thinking, feeling creatures to torture and destroy.

"Though Fornjot persecuted Ask and Embla, they were cleverer and stronger than he had foreseen. They not only managed to survive but had children, increasing their numbers. Though they suffered horribly, the two gave birth to a mighty race—the Aesir.

"When Fornjot saw that the spawn of Ask and Embla grew and prospered, he called Logi to him. He hacked off his son's

head and formed Sigfod, God of Battle. Logi grew a new head
as quickly as one flame replaces another when you try to fight
a fire.

"Then the Destroyer turned Sigfod loose among the Aesir.
Brother fell on brother, children on their parents. All Yggdrasil
reeked of blood and death. Fornjot rejoiced.

"Once more the Aesir were too clever for Fornjot. They
made peace with each other, realizing they were all children
of the same parents and that fighting amongst themselves was
foolish and self-destructive.

"Fornjot was furious. He cursed and raged. The earth shook
and the sky trembled. The sun and the moon hid behind clouds,
and the stars closed their eyes and disappeared. The Aesir were
afraid, but they clutched their weapons to them and waited to
see what would happen.

"For a long time Fornjot pondered. Finally he had an idea.
If the Aesir would not fight amongst themselves, he would
create other beings who were not Aesir to fight against them!
So the Destroyer made the other races of Yggdrasil to bedevil
and harm the children of Ask and Embla."

Borr paused for a moment and sighed. "At least that's what
our legends say. Surely it's true to the extent that the Aesir
have always found themselves surrounded by enemies who
howl after our blood. Ler, Logi, and Kari we have learned to
deal with pretty successfully. Sigfod, God of Battle, we've
succeeded in controlling amongst ourselves. It is Fornjot's third
sending that ever hounds us and threatens to overwhelm us.

"To the north the Sons of Ymir stand ready to strike as soon
as a new leader capable of uniting them arises. That will be
soon. To the south the Vanir lurk. Already they have burned
the walls of Asgard.

"Now we see a ray of hope. As we learned to live as brothers
with our fellow Aesir, there may be a way to live at peace with
the Vanir. Buri hoped for this. I, too, have dreamed of it. It
has happened. The Vanir have offered a truce. They will join
us to hold back the Jotun and once again frustrate the designs
of Fornjot.

"The price of the truce is high, Voden. Fiorgynn, the Vanadis
of the Vanir, asks two hostages. In turn she will send two. She
will send her sons, Niord and Frey. In exchange she asks for
my son and one other.

"I have decided to send you and Honir."

Voden sat quietly for a long time, his father's words echoing through his mind. A cold fear clutched at his heart, the shadows in the hall seemed to reach out for him.

I'm . . . I'm being sent away, he thought. Sent far away from Mother and my friends. Sent away. He couldn't come to grips with the immensity of the idea. Sent away to live with strange people in a place he'd never seen. He felt the tears struggling to break loose and concentrated on holding them back.

As he fought for control he noticed a strange thing. Part of his mind was cringing and cowering in fear and horror at the thought of being sent away, but another part was excited and consumed with curiosity at the idea of going someplace new, meeting new people, and learning new things. This was the part that asked so many questions of Volund, of old Groa, of his mother, of anyone who would listen and answer. The other part was the child, the ten-year-old Voden who feared what others his age feared and wanted what they wanted.

Which is the real me? he wondered for the first time. Is either one more real than the other? The very thought made his mind whirl and hurt. Only ten, a quiet voice reminded, only ten.

No, another voice denied. Not only ten. Older, infinitely older. Mind stretches endless through the universe, knowing neither age nor limit. Man shares in Mind and hence is likewise ageless and limitless. Only open to it, see it, realize it, become one with it.

A terrible longing enveloped Voden. To abandon the child and reach for that other . . . ah, how painful and how wonderful. Could it be done by one so young? (Not young, came the echo.) Did he really have any choice? He was being sent away. Away from his childhood, his family, his friends. Away.

Rather than going away, would it not be better to go toward? Toward that other part of him, that part that did not depend on childhood or parents or anything else? There would be joy in that. A different kind of joy, but joy nonetheless.

Did he have any choice? Wouldn't he do it sooner or later in any case? He remembered old Groa. She'd given an eye to drink at Mimir's well and been happy at the bargain. He didn't completely understand what she had meant, but he knew that the child in him never could. The other part would. Groa gave her eye. He would give his childhood. So be it.

A great shudder twisted through his body as though he were shrugging off an old skin. A terrible, deep calm settled over him. He looked up at his father.

What he saw was a middle-aged warrior burdened by both his own fate and the fate of his people. Borr hated what he was forced to do, but he would do it. It was written by the Nornir on the instant of his birth. Destiny could not be turned aside, would not be denied.

Voden felt a sudden welling of tenderness for his father. Borr was not a soft man. He was of the Aesir. Even his gods were his enemies. There was little place in his world for kindness and love. Yet Voden knew Borr loved Vestla, and himself, and his little brother. And all the Aesir. Because Borr was incapable of expressing that love didn't mean it wasn't there. It meant that Borr's personal tragedy was that much greater.

The boy rose from his bench and climbed the steps to the High Seat. He boosted himself up onto his father's lap and placed his arms around his thick neck. "I understand," he murmured into his father's beard, "I understand." Then he began to cry softly for the death of a ten-year-old.

Borr automatically put his arms around his son to comfort him, though he was too stunned by what he had seen in the boy's eyes to say anything.

It was dusk when Voden left the Warrior's Hall to return home. Borr had explained the arrangements to him carefully, asking his advice and trying to include him in the plan. They had decided on what clothes he would take, how much gift-gold to bring, which arm and neck torques would be appropriate for the son of the leader of the Aesir. They also discussed the making of a complete set of weapons in the Aesir style, suited to Voden's size and strength. Ax, sword, bow, and war spear, plus helmet and shield, so the young Aesir would have appropriate arms to practice with.

Asgard was quiet as Voden walked toward his parents' hall. Reaching it, he stood for a moment at the gate in the wattle fence that surrounded it. This is my home, he thought. Come spring, I'll be leaving it.

It was a simple building, much like all the rest in Asgard. About fifteen by thirty feet, the walls were of woven wattle plastered heavily with mud to make them windproof. The roof, which rose in a high peak fifteen feet from the ground, was covered with tightly tied bundles of the long grass that grew on the plain.

The inside was just as simple. The walls were lined with

rough planks and stood about eight feet high. Four feet in from them, and running from one end of the hall to the other on both sides, was a double row of pillars that held up the roof when the weight of the snow became great in the winter. Cross-beams spanned the width of the hall between the tops of each pair of pillars. Between the pillars and the wall were benches for sleeping and sitting. The center area was open, and much of the work of the household took place there. In the middle of the hall was the cooking pit, surrounded by large flat stones. Directly over it, hung from a long chain attached to the roof beam, was the huge bronze caldron in which meals were pre-pared.

At the end of the hall nearest Voden was the main entrance. Another smaller door at the other end was seldom used. At the far end, just beyond the table where they sat to eat, was the high seat. Beyond that, on the right side, was the closed cup-board where Borr and Vestla slept. Across from it was a smaller version where Voden and his little brother, Vethur, spent their nights huddled together for warmth. A hole at each gable end provided fresh air and allowed the smoke from the cook fire to escape.

The walls, posts, and cross-beams were hung with all man-ner of tools, weapons, cooking utensils, and decorations. Shaggy wolf and bear pelts were nailed here and there. A great chest behind the high seat held the treasure Borr had brought back from his raids. Other chests in the sleeping cupboards held the family's clothes. On the posts near the high seat hung Borr's great war ax and his battered shield.

When Voden entered, his mother was at the caldron, stirring something that filled the air with a delightful odor. Venison! The young man remembered that Thidrandi had gifted them with a fat doe only the week before. It had hung out back, aging, and now was ready.

Vestla looked up as he came through the door. Their eyes met and locked. Voden could tell she had been crying, but she was calm now and her gaze was steady. She called to Roskva, her serving maid, and told the girl to take her place. Then she gestured to Voden, beckoning him to the adults' sleeping cup-board.

Voden slid back the door of the cupboard and saw his mother sitting in the odd cross-legged position she preferred, the dark-ness of the sleeping place hiding her expression. He slid in and sat next to her, knees up to his chin, arms clasped around his legs. She reached over and shut the door.

For a moment the two of them sat in the dark; then Vestla began to speak. She spoke the common tongue perfectly now, but still had the strange accent, soft and lisping, that she had had at the beginning. Voden loved to listen to it. It reminded him of the sound the wind makes when it flows through a stand of pines.

"Voden," she began, "my firstborn, you leave." He nodded in the dark, even though he didn't think she could see. "Know, my son, that this grieves me greatly. But it must be. It is part of the Great Pattern. To oppose it would be fruitless. The Tao must flow.

"Now I would tell you part of the Pattern so you might glimpse some sense of its meaning. To comprehend it in its entirety is not given to mere mortals. Even the Yellow Robes from the Sunrise Empire cannot do that, and they are the wisest of all men." She paused for a moment and stirred lightly as if arranging her cloak.

"Once, my son, I, too, was called on to leave my home and my parents. I was about your age, ten seasons or so, when my mother and father heard that one of the Choosers from the Floating World was passing through our village. Every few years the Choosers journey through the dawn-lit land of Prin, seeking those qualified to enter the Sisterhood.

"I had always been accounted a pretty, charming child, so naturally my parents had high hopes. They were right. The Chooser nodded approval. My parents kissed me good-bye and left.

"To say I was bewildered and frightened would be an understatement. I was crushed. My parents had gone off without a backward look, leaving me with a total stranger! He was most kind, true, but still... It was only later that I learned what a great honor I had been to my parents and my village, and that I had made them wealthy to the end of their days. Yet, still, it hurt. It hurts yet. There is an empty place...

"So, to fill that empty place, I worked hard. Within a few years I had surpassed all those my age in skill. I was very proud and redoubled my efforts. My achievements and ability grew. By the time I reached seventeen seasons I was accounted one of the greatest the Floating World had ever trained. By twenty I was a legend. Even the Emperor of the Sunrise Empire made inquiry after me and my price.

"Beyond all expectation, the price set on me was met by

one of the Sons of Muspell, one of the seven rulers of the Dark Empire.

"My trainers wondered how such a thing could be. Never had one from the Floating World gone to Muspellheim, not even in the days of the First Dark Empire. I searched myself and found no explanation. I seemed to be moving with the Tao. We finally decided that the meaning must lie beyond our poor understanding in some purpose of the Great Pattern I was destined to serve.

"The rest you know. How Borr raided the caravan carrying me to Muspellheim, and how he fathered you in the midst of the reek of blood and battle."

She sighed and was silent for several moments. "Since that time I have meditated long into the nights, opening myself to the Tao, submerging myself in it, seeking, searching for the answer. When Borr first ripped the curtains from my wagon, I knew I was not destined to die in my own blood there on the Vigrid. I also understood that I could and would be his wife.

"But why?" Voden could sense the sweep of her arm in the dark as she gestured, including the hall, Asgard, all of Asaheim, in the move. "This is not what my trainers prepared me for. I was taught the arts of a courtesan. I can dance with such exquisite beauty that it brings tears to men's eyes, or with such voluptuous abandon that it brings fire to their groins. I can sing with a voice as clear and thrilling as the nightingale's. I know endless amusing tales, countless stories of amorous encounters. My fingers can evoke liquid beauty from the strings of a harp, or sighs and moans of pleasure from a man's body. I am mistress of the one thousand and one ways to give my master joy.

"My life was meant to be spent amidst luxury and beauty. I was to be covered with the finest, lightest silks, the most costly brocades. Jewels of unimaginable worth were to sparkle from my fingers, wrists, and neck. The rarest perfumes and oils were to have touched and smoothed my skin. I was to eat the daintiest foods, the most exotic cuisines, the most elegant concoctions of master chefs. Only the best vintages were to wet my mouth."

Again Vestla paused. There was no bitterness in her voice as she continued, just a calm and weary tone of acceptance and resignation. "Ah, but what was to have been is not. Instead I live in a smoky hall of mud-daubed walls and grass roof. I wear rough homespun. I make my lord's beer, cook his food, share his bed beneath a shaggy bear pelt. My hands grow rough with work, my beauty fades long before its time, my voice cracks, I have no harp, and none care to see me dance. My stories make no sense in this land."

Her voice grew in strength as she continued. "How can this be? Can there be some reason, some purpose to such a twisted fate? The need to know, to understand, burned like a flame in my mind. Yet search as I might within myself, I could find no answer.

"I am not practiced in the Seidar-magic, owe no allegiance to dark Svarthofdi, but some ability as a volva I have been granted by Vidolf. Yes, at times I can part the mists of the future just enough to glimpse what is meant to be. The price is heavy, and I fear to use my small skill.

"When, after years of seeking, I still found no answer, I turned at last to Vidolf and sought a vision. One was granted me." Voden could feel and hear the shudder that shook her body. "Ah, one was granted me," she whispered huskily, her voice loaded with remembered anguish.

"What . . . what was it, Mother?" the boy whispered back.

A long, empty silence followed. Finally Voden heard a soft murmuring of words he didn't know or understand. Gently, they rose and fell in a curious rhythm, wrapping around him, twisting through the dark. He listened with his whole being, trying to focus his mind and attention the way his mother had taught him. Almost, almost, the words began to make sense. He seemed to catch a glimmer of meaning that lay just beyond, just out of reach.

Then suddenly the words stopped. His concentration collapsed and the opening bud of understanding shriveled and died. He was back in the dark cupboard with his mother once more. He felt cold.

"No," she murmured, "no, such things are not for one of your age and understanding to know. The mere hearing might warp and blast your soul. In time, perhaps, but not now.

"Let it be enough, Voden, to say that at last I understood. The Tao is flowing as it must. My coming to Asaheim as Borr's wife is part of that flow. Your birthing was meant to be.

"This, too, this separation and journey to Vanaheim is meant to be. It will give pain to many, not least of all to you. But were it not to happen, even worse things would pass. Believe this to be true, my son."

Her voice became remote for a moment, taking on a singsong rhythm. "Know that one will come to you in your anguish, one sent from she who loves you most. From the sunrise will he come, bringing a light of understanding to you akin to the light that spills over the horizon when the sun climbs into the morning sky. Not all things will it illuminate. But enough, enough. The rest . . . the rest will remain hidden until another time."

"I . . . I don't understand, Mother."

He heard the sad smile in her voice. "No. Nor will you for many a season. Now you must accept and be satisfied with that. I know you, my son, and how you thirst to know. It will come. It will come all too soon. You may discover that the more you know, the more you wish to know, and the less happy your knowledge will make you.

"Enough. Know I love you. Know your father loves you, though he finds it hard to show. Know you are destined for great and dire things. And know that this trip to Vanaheim is the beginning of an adventure grander than any Yggdrasil has ever seen.

"Now it is time to eat."

Somehow the venison tasted less delicious than Voden had expected.

DARK EMPIRE

VIII

THE little man stood in the dark alley and shivered, though not from the cold. He could just make out a shape in the deeper blackness over by the wall.

His hand trembling, he reached inside his robe and pulled out the amulet that hung around his neck. Its cuneiform inscription glowed dully in the night. I'm protected, he told himself. My master, the Patesi Adad, one of the seven Sons of Muspell, is powerful, and I'm protected. In the distance he heard a sudden explosion of laughter and noise as someone either entered or left the tavern a few streets away. He longed for the light and warmth of the place and for the sounds and smells of human companionship. Here in this alley were only the darkness, the silence broken by the strange slithering sound of the thing that stalked him, the dank smell of rotting food, and a slightly acrid odor he couldn't place.

The thing slid closer. He backed farther down the narrow space between the faceless walls. Only a minor demon, he told himself. Nothing my amulet can't dispel. Nothing truly dangerous. Only something sent by my master's enemies to frighten and delay his messenger. But, oh, by the stealth of Rabisu, how I wish I'd not stopped for that wine! Had I gone straight as bidden, I'd be home now, warm in bed. Ay! Ay!

Why had they sent something from the netherworld after him? He, just a poor messenger and spy? Could it be the message? Perhaps it was more important than he'd thought! Wouldn't his master have sent anything really important by a fully Warded messenger, or even by one of the minor demons he controlled? On the other hand, the enemy might expect that. Sending a critical message with a mere spy, a man with no magic of his own, would be unexpected, might catch the enemy off guard. Ay! The thing moved closer!

Quickly he muttered the names of the seven demons his amulet covered: Alu, Irra, Ashakku, Gallu, Elimmu. Yes. And

Ahhazu and Labasu as well. Powerful demons, all of them.
He felt a bit more confidence. For who would send demons
greater than these against a simple messenger? Unless the message . . . He shivered.

And froze, a scream stifled in his suddenly constricted throat.
The thing that was stalking him stepped into the brighter dark
at the center of the alley. He moaned inwardly with utter terror.
Lamashtu, she who drinks men's blood and eats their flesh!
Lamashtu! He tried to think of her seven names and utter some
sort of prayer for protection.

With a whimper he stumbled backward. It was no use. His
mind wouldn't work. He couldn't remember more than three
names, and those so frightened him that he could barely stand.

The message! Yes, Lamashtu must want the message! He
fumbled in his pouch and drew forth the parchment packet
sealed with dire curses in arcane symbols. Falling to his knees,
he flung it toward the forward-gliding Lamashtu in a mute plea.

The demon stopped, her glowing eyes sweeping down to
look at the packet that lay between them. A hiss came from
her fanged, drooling mouth. Another shadow detached itself
from the walls of the alley and strode quickly to the monster's
side.

Ay! Ay! The little man almost cried out in relief. He knew
this one! Had seen him in the tavern just a short time ago!
Surely he would help. . . . Then his eyes caught the device on
the black giant's harness, and hope fled. The man was dedicated
to the service of Nergal! Someone very powerful had given his
name to Namtaru to carry down to Ereshkigal, Nergal's mate
and the dreaded queen of Aralu. He whimpered again and sank
in a heap, his body shaking and his teeth chattering in fear.

Bending down, the huge man looked at the packet. He took
a small vial from his harness and poured it over the seals. There
was a bright flash and a stench of rotted flesh. The little man
looked up. The black giant was grinning at the demon. In a
deep, hissing voice he muttered, "It is even as the Black One
said." Then he reached out and picked up the message, placing
it carefully in a pouch that hung from the left side of his harness.

The spy suddenly found his voice. "Please," he begged in
a piteous wail, "have mercy, O mighty one. Spare a poor
messenger. You have what you came for. Please let me go
home to my wife and children in peace."

Jormungand turned cold eyes on the trembling pile of dirty
rags and stringy flesh. "I have what I came for, swine, but

Lamashtu does not." With that he turned on his heel and strode away.

Behind he heard a nasty snicker, a thin scream, and then the ripping, slobbering sound of something unclean feasting on still quivering flesh.

The Serpent hurried through the empty streets of Maqam Nifl. There were many things loose tonight, some even he would not want to meet. Now that he had the damned message in his pouch, every creeping, sliding thing in the city would be converging on him. By the seven walls of Aralu, he'd best hurry! Thus far things had gone more smoothly than he'd thought possible.

He wondered briefly how the Black One had known that Bel Adad, the Patesi of Borsippa and Maqam Nifl, would send a message this important by a mere human. A truly bold plan, one that would surely have taken most by total surprise. Yet Surt had forseen it.

Jormungand had hidden himself in a pile of junk lumber close to Adad's palace. He'd been well Warded, but even then, there'd been a few close calls with prowling demons. By Namtaru, Bel Adad had incredible power!

At dusk the Serpent sensed several demonic messengers leaving the palace. Surt had not been interested in them, had told him to ignore them. Wait for the one who could *not* be carrying the message, he had said. Wait. So Jormungand waited in the woodpile while spiders and lizards crawled over him and patrolling monsters slid by.

Then, just after the last hour had rung, one came slinking down the alley. One whom no one would trust with a critical message. An ordinary spy, a mere worshiper of Rabisu, not even an adept. Yet there was an aura that clung to the man, an aura of deep magic. Jormungand followed.

In the tavern the huge, black man sat in a corner and watched. Yes, he told himself, this is the one Surt was waiting for. He muttered the words that drew Lamashtu as the little spy rose and went to the door, calling good night to the tavernkeeper. The rest had been easy.

Closer now. Almost, almost safe.

Abruptly he stopped, his ears and eyes probing the dark. He sniffed. There. That smell. The slightly metallic odor of serpent. Softly he drew his great blade from its scabbard.

It came at him from an alley just ahead and to his right. He recognized it immediately, Mushrussu, one of Tiamat's eleven, and an ally of Adad. Damn!

In a way the monster was almost beautiful. It had a long, sinuous body, clawed feet on six stubby legs, a tail with a scorpion's sting, a mouth full of fangs that dripped burning poison, and eyes that drove men mad. It was a creature of primeval chaos, a beast that hated order and life. Yet it glowed darkly with a strange, fascinating light of its own. He felt his gaze drifting toward its eyes, the desire to look deeply into them rising swiftly, almost overwhelming him.

"No!" he shouted out loud as he wrenched his gaze away. To look into those round orbs was to fall into endless insanity, to drop forever into the formless abyss where Tiamat dwelt. Keep your attention on the snout, he told himself. To ignore the head altogether was to invite death from the thing's fanged and poisonous mouth. But don't look at the eyes!

Mushrussu struck with a savage hiss. Jormungand leapt to the side and swung his sword at the thing's passing head. At the last moment he remembered the tail and its deadly barb. He threw himself back as the point slashed down and into the ground at exactly the place where he had been standing. Black ichor oozed from the sting, and the ground smoldered.

The head struck again, narrowly missing the giant warrior. Once more the barbed tail smashed downward, a split second too late.

As he whirled and twisted to avoid the serpent dragon, Jormungand realized that the thing's hide was incredibly thick and his sword simply wasn't biting deeply enough to kill it quickly. The monster could outlast him. He also realized that Mushrussu had a definite pattern of attack: first the head, then the tail. Dealing with both attacks made it almost impossible to get in a good enough stroke to penetrate that thick hide. He was too busy dodging to swing with his full strength. If he could only put the tail out of commission . . . But the armor around the tail was even thicker than that on the body, neck, and head.

An idea formed. It was insane, horribly risky, since it left him hopelessly trapped if it failed. But he knew as the tail sting grazed his harness that he had to do something, and do it quickly. He was tiring. The stench of the thing poisoned the air he breathed and was sapping his strength almost as rapidly as the effort he spent battling the monster.

Deciding, he twisted away from the snout and jumped back as the tail slashed at him. A quick look over his shoulder confirmed what his senses told him—he was only two steps from a wall. The head struck and he dodged, putting himself flat up against the wall. With a hiss of triumph Mushrussu shot its tail at him, coming in horizontally about stomach height. At the last instant Jormungand dropped flat to the ground and rolled, his sword cradled in his arms, under the beast's body, directly in front of its first pair of legs.

Mushrussu roared with pain as it smashed its tail into the solid bricks. Black poison splattered through the air, hissing as it fell. Jormungand caught a quick glimpse of the shattered barb as the monster jerked it back in a spasm of anguish. At that instant he struck upward with the point of his blade. The blow was true, and he felt it sink deep.

With a bellow the serpent dragon twisted and jumped back. The huge black warrior threw himself to one side, frantically rolling to escape the monster's slashing jaws. He scrambled to his feet, sword ready.

Mushrussu had had enough. Jormungand could sense the thing's eyes on him, measuring and remembering. Then he felt rather than heard Mushrussu's hissing voice. "Man," it said, "Mushrussu knows you. Tremble and be afraid, for you have no hope. I go now, but I will return for you when least you look for it. And I will crunch your bones between my teeth for all eternity."

Jormungand put a sneer on his face and spat at the creature in defiance. Inside he quailed and couldn't muster enough strength to speak. In a stench-filled flash it was gone, and he slumped to the ground, drained and sick. He vomited, heaving again and again until nothing was left in his stomach.

Finally on trembling legs he stood and staggered off. Nergal, he prayed, protect your servant, for right now I couldn't fight a child.

After what seemed like an eternity, he slumped against a strangely carved door frame in a featureless wall and knocked seven times in a special pattern. The door opened, and he crumpled forward to lie at Surt's feet.

When Jormungand finally returned to consciousness, it was to smell the bitter aroma of the Black One's magical fire and hear his muttered words of sorcery. Surt glanced up as the Serpent stirred. He nodded, completed the last words of the spell he was working on, and then leaned back, watching the black warrior as he sat up, holding his throbbing head in his hands.

"Look on your right forearm," he commanded.

Jormungand obediently pulled up his sleeve, then gasped as the livid mark came to view. He looked up at Surt. "Wha . . . what is it?"

"It's a serpent dragon biting its own barbed tail. The sign of Mushrussu. I take it you met the monster last night?" The giant warrior nodded grimly. "So. Yes. Although the creature didn't kill you, it marked you. Now it will stalk you. When you least expect it . . . snap! It will grab you and drag you down to its lair in Chaos where Tiamat and the other ten dwell. You are doomed, Serpent."

"Can mighty Nergal help me?"

Surt shrugged. "We do not control Bel Nergal. We only serve him. He rules the all-devouring, all-destructive fire. He reigns over the dead in Aralu. In war he stands supreme, the legions marching to his beck and call. He cannot be opposed. He revels in chaos, destruction, and death.

"Why should such a one do anything to frustrate Mushrussu? Rather expect him to help."

Jormungand's eyes burned with suppressed fury as he glared at the Black One. "I am your servant, Surt. I was on *your* dark errand. Protect me."

The slender, dark man smiled coldly. "You *were* my servant, Jormungand. Now Mushrussu has marked you. I have no power over the serpent dragon. It answers the call of Adad. My power grows, but to . . ." He paused, a thoughtful expression crossing his face. "Unless . . . hmm."

He looked down at the packet that lay unopened in front of him. Then with a calculating look he glanced up at Jormungand. "Serpent," he began, "there is one possibility. I think I know what lies within this folded parchment. If I am right, it will greatly increase my power. It might even allow me to Ward for a demon as powerful as Mushrussu. Not control it, mind you, but at least Ward myself and my servants against it.

"The packet was heavily guarded with dire spells. The vial I gave you canceled only those involved with touching it. All night I have worked to counteract those related to its opening. I think I've got them all. But . . . Ah, nothing is entirely sure when one deals with an enemy as devious as the Patesi Adad.

"So. I would open it and discover if my surmise about its

contents is correct. At the same time I hesitate, unsure if it is entirely safe. Now you are doomed in any case. Mushrussu could be on its way right now to claim you. You have nothing to lose. You could open the packet. If you die, the worst that happens is that the serpent dragon is cheated of its prey. But if the contents are as important as I suspect, I may be able to help you." Surt shrugged. "It's up to you. If you won't do it, I'll snatch some poor fool off the street to do it for me."

Jormungand gritted his teeth. His voice was tight with anger. "Since that time on the Vigrid, Surt, I have been your servant. I stood, then, on the nether bank of Hubur, my hand raised to knock at the first gate and summon Neti to open it. You snatched me from the seven-walled realm of Ereshkigal, Black One. Snatched me and made me your tool. For many years you have used me to help you gain power so you can work your rabid revenge on the blond warrior who sliced off my ear and sent me reeling to Aralu. Now, in my hour of need, you would use me one last time." His voice became a hissing growl as he stood unsteadily, his massive fists clenched, the muscles of his arms, neck, and shoulders bunched in fury.

Surt held up one thin hand, his forefinger pointing at Jormungand's face. "Know, Serpent, that I can blast you as easily as Mushrussu can snap off your head." The huge man froze in place. Surt chuckled deep in his throat. "Ah, yes, yes, I use you." He leaned forward, his palms flat on the tabletop on either side of the packet. "I brought you back from the edge of death to help me work my revenge against the Aesir swine who left both of us to the tender attentions of Sumul and her vulture brood. I need your great strength and warrior skills to overcome the many barriers that lie between me and my goal. Not everything can be accomplished by magic alone. Oh, no. Often a swift sliver of steel between the ribs is the best and most efficient method of dealing with an enemy."

The thin man's voice began to rise and his eyes to blaze as he went on. "Yes, I use you. You and anyone else who comes my way! My power grows, will grow, *must* grow! Yes! Yes! I gather dread forces to me! I rip apart the dark curtain and call dire things shambling to the light to do my bidding. They come, they come! To help me blast the bodies and wither the souls of my enemies!" Foam flecked his lips and spittle sprayed out as his excitement increased. "My power grows! Yes, and when it stands mighty and invincible I will strike northward, bringing flame and destruction to Borr. I will carry the Bane of Forests and bring dread and horror to all! To all!" His voice rose to a scream, and he stood shaking and panting. Jormungand shrank back, the madness in Surt's eyes searing his soul and making his mind quail.

"Now," the Black One continued, his voice back under control, "I have a key to greater power. Aid me, Serpent, once more. If I can, I will then aid you and Ward you against your dragon enemy. Do it! Now!"

Almost against his will Jormungand moved shakily toward the table and the packet that lay there. I have no choice, he told himself bitterly. Ever since that accursed battle on the Vigrid I have had no choice.

His fingers touched the parchment. "Open it," he heard Surt's emotion-hoarse voice command. "Open it." Carefully he broke the wax seal. He looked up at Surt. The little man was staring fixedly at the packet, his mouth moving slightly as he spoke unheard words, his forehead creased in worry. Jormungand wiped the sweat that suddenly ran down his forehead. If Surt was still worried about the magic that might guard this message . . .

The Serpent swallowed and reached out again with a slightly trembling hand. He slipped two fingers under the first flap and pushed it back, holding the packet down with the other three. Nothing happened. He folded back the second flap. Again nothing happened.

Only one more fold and the thing was open. One more. The giant warrior's teeth began to chatter. With one hand he held the corner of the packet. The fingers on the other reached out and began to bend back the flap.

A sudden shriek tore the tension in the room. Something launched itself at Jormungand's head from inside the packet. Only his battle-trained reflexes saved him. He jerked his head slightly to the side, and a small black thing struck his cheek. He staggered back in sudden pain, his hand reaching up to brush at the thing that he could feel eating its way into his flesh.

Surt sprang across the space between them, his hand outstretched, his finger pointing. A bright flame darted from his fingertip and seared Serpent's cheek. A flash filled the room with light, and a crash that sounded like thunder slammed into the walls and bounded back at them, making the two men's ears ring. In the middle of the roar the high shriek sounded again, but this time it was a cry of soul-withering agony.

Something small, furred, and smoldering fell from Jormungand's cheek to the floor. Eight legs twitched spasmodically, then were still. Surt reached down and picked the thing up. He held it out for the huge man to see.

"Looks like a spider," the Serpent grunted.

Surt nodded. "Yes and no," he said. "Actually it's a spider Zi, a spider's inner spirit, transformed into a minion of Bel Adad. You were fortunate. It was aiming for your eye. If it had hit, it would have penetrated your brain and then begun eating. Not a pretty death, and no amount of magic can save you from it once it's begun. It got you in the cheek and barely had time to burrow into the bone before I killed it."

Drained and dizzy, Jormungand shuffled back to the couch where he had awakened. He sat and held his head in his hands. "And what of Mushrussu? You said you'd help if I opened the packet."

Surt laughed darkly. "Yes, yes, so I said." The Serpent looked up, surprised by the laugh. The slender dark man was looking down at the open message, a gleam of triumph in his eyes. "Yes," he repeated, "so I said. And this," he repeated, stabbing the piece of parchment with a daggerlike finger, "gives me the power I need to help you, O faithful Serpent! The power to help you and to damn Borr to the blackest depths of my revenge!"

Surt threw back his head and shrieked with laughter. His whole body shook with the strength of his emotion. "Revenge," he howled like some animal gone mad. "Revenge! Against all my enemies! Soon they will cringe and whine about my feet!"

Jormungand huddled back against the wall of the little room and stared at his master. He didn't give a damn about the Sons of Muspell. If Surt destroyed them all in his hunger for greater and greater power, so much the better. But he couldn't help but feel a slight pang for the fate of Borr. By Nergal, the man was a magnificent warrior! He deserved a clean death on the battlefield, going down with his red-stained ax in hand. The death Surt planned for his ex-companion in raiding was anything but clean.

After a while the thin black man stopped laughing and began to rummage about on his table. Soon he was deep in some spell, working his dark and foul wizardry. Eventually the exhausted warrior fell asleep, wondering if he would awake alive or in the claws of Mushrussu.

VANAHEIM

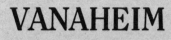

IX

~~~

THREE days before the vernal equinox, when night still held a slight but losing edge on day, Borr set off for the point on the Idavoll Plain where the River Gunnthro bursts forth from the leafy darkness of Vanaheim into the bright sunlight of Asaheim. Voden and Honir rode next to him. A party of twenty carefully chosen warriors accompanied them.

Voden was dressed like an Aesir chieftain. His feet were covered with soft leather riding boots made from the hide of a black bull. They came to a point and were stitched with intricate designs of serpents biting their tails. His breeches were loose fitting and open-bottomed, cut from soft, tightly woven fabric dyed a deep purple. A long-sleeved tunic of similar cloth dyed the same color reached to just below his hips. Around the waist was a black leather belt studded with silver and gold, the buckle crusted with sparkling jewels. From his left side a sword hung in a beautifully worked sheath. The pommel was a large jewel, deep blue in color, the guard inlaid with gold tracery in the serpent motif. Opposite the sword, a dagger was thrust through the belt. Plain and unadorned, it looked very old; in fact, it had come down through the family from Buri's grandfather, and it had an ancient, magical feel to it. A cloak of bright red cloth almost covered the sword on the left side, then rose at an angle to the right shoulder, where it was fastened by a large oval brooch crafted by Volund from some of the gold Borr had brought back from a raid. Its surface was covered with four intertwined beasts, each long and sinuous, each gripping the throat and limbs of the others with many twisting arms. Around both Voden's upper arms were torques of gold, their rounded surfaces covered with geometric designs in silver, their ends the heads of wolves with eyes of shining ruby. On Voden's head was a simple helmet, conical in shape, with a nosepiece that came down almost to his upper lip; the tip of the nosepiece was in the shape of a serpent's head. The edge of the helmet carried a repeating pattern of twining serpents worked in gold. Over his right shoulder a bearded ax hung, the beard helping to keep it in place. The blade of the ax was inlaid with a silver design of two wolves in combat, each biting the other's haunch. Voden's left hand held his horse's reins while in his right, its butt resting in a small pouch next to his stirrup, was a war spear, the spearhead damascened with silver and gold. On his back was slung a typical Aesir shield, round and made of hide-covered wood with a central iron boss to protect the arm and hand.

They arrived at the rendezvous point just as the sun cleared the horizon and day and night found themselves equal in strength. As they approached, the Vanir came slowly to meet them from the fastness of their forest.

First came nine female warriors of the special guard of the Vanadis. They were fierce and proud-looking, their black hair long and braided. All carried the short sword and javelin favored by the Vanir, and long, thin, wicked-looking daggers hung opposite their swords. It was said they could drop an enemy at fifty paces with one of these weapons. These Valkyrja also had axes, much smaller than those of the Aesir, which, like the daggers, could be thrown with deadly accuracy or used for desperate hand-to-hand combat. Each carried an oval, wickerwork shield slung on her back. They all wore the standard doeskin shirts and leggings of the Vanir, dyed a dark brown. The boots they wore were also brown.

Behind the Valkyrja came the eight Disir, dressed in black, their shirts embroidered with designs to show their office. Most were old and gray-haired.

Next came a small wagon drawn by two huge forest cats. The Aesir were startled to see these beasts of the night in broad daylight. The baleful glare in their yellow eyes made the horses nervous and skittish.

The wagon was incredible. It was made from a dark wood none of the Aesir had ever seen. A cover of bright green cloth hid its occupant from view. The wheels of the vehicle were made of thin wood bent around spokes that went to a hub. The front two wheels were attached to an axle that swiveled. The traces that bound the two forest cats to the wagon led back to the hubs of this set of wheels, so that the wagon would turn in the direction the cats turned.

The wooden body of the wagon was a half cylinder in shape. Every inch of the curved sides and flat ends were covered with

complex and interwoven carvings, with the main motif of vine
and leaf twisted and writhing. Here and there weird animals
with sinuous forms slipped among the vegetation.

Walking next to the wagon, wearing dark green shirts and
leggings, were two boys. They looked a great deal alike, though
it was plain the one on the left was the older and the one on
the right the more comely. Voden guessed they were Niord
and Frey.

Behind the wagon came another nine Valkyrja, armed as
were the others, but with short, straight bows carried across
their backs instead of shields, and quivers at their sides.

Borr motioned his party to dismount as the Vanir came up
to them. Four of the warriors took the horses and fell back
some ten paces, eyeing the great cats.

The Vanir stopped about two yards from Borr, who stood
in the center of the drawn-up Aesir, Voden and Honir flanking
him. The Valkyrja parted ranks, letting the Disir through to
stand in a group facing the Aesir. One, a twisted old crone
with straggly gray hair, raised her hand in greeting. "Hail,
Borr, chief of the Aesir," she croaked. "Hail and well met by
the Vanadis of the Vanir. Syr greets you in the name of she
who is daughter of Audhumla, and in the name of all the Vanir,
Children of the Nourisher, Siblings of the Vettir."

Borr raised his own hand in greeting. "Hail, Syr of the
Disir, valued adviser of the Vanadis. We come as agreed. Will
the Vanir still honor the agreement? I see you bring two boys
even as we do." He laid his hand on Voden's head. "This is
my son, Voden, who goes to live with the Vanadis as hostage.
This other is Honir, son of one of my chiefest men, a leader
of seventeen households on the Himinborg Plain surrounding
Asgard. Who vouches for the two you bring?"

A low, soft voice said from the wagon, "I do," and a hand
raised the covering from within. As one the Aesir caught their
breaths as a woman stepped from the wagon and jumped lightly
to the ground.

Dressed all in deep green doeskin, she stood five feet and
a few inches tall. She was slender of figure, with high, firm,
and full breasts. Her face was heart-shaped, with incredibly
large green eyes. Lush, slightly pouting lips opened just enough
to show small white teeth. Her chin was pointed, her nose
narrow and straight. Raven-black hair hung to her waist in soft
cascades. A necklace of forest cat claws hung around her neck,
and gloves of their fur covered her hands.

She motioned to the boys on either side of the wagon. They came to her, one on each side. Together the three walked toward Borr up an open aisle created by the other Vanir.

Borr stood as one stunned. Voden looked up and realized his father didn't know what to do. Instinctively, tugging at his father's hand, the boy bent his knee to the ground and bowed his head in homage to the Vanadis. With a start, his father and then all the other Aesir followed suit.

When they rose again, the Vanadis was looking straight at Voden, a slight smile playing about her lips. "This one," she said softly, as if speaking only to him, "is already half a son to me. It is good." She gestured the two boys flanking her to step slightly forward. "These are my sons. The elder is Niord. He is fifteen seasons. The younger, twelve seasons, is Frey."

"Fiorgynn," Borr said as he found his voice, "hail and well met. The Vanadis keeps her word."

"The Vanadis"—Fiorgynn laughed lightly—"*always* keeps her word. It is something to depend on. And to beware.

"Borr of the Aesir, hear me. Once a year would I have my sons by my side in Folkvang, in their places in many-seated Sessrymnyr. This will be for the eight days surrounding that when night holds greatest sway. Then will I send your own kin back to your halls, for there are ceremonies of such nature I would have none not sprung from Audhumla view. So shall it be." Borr silently nodded his agreement.

The woman clapped her glove-covered hands lightly. Two of the Valkyrja stepped forward, bearing large packs. "These are things my sons will need. I would have you train them in the ways of the Aesir, especially in the warrior's craft. Niord I think will prosper in such discipline. Frey will not do as well, so I would ask you to teach him the art of your skalds. And I would be greatly pleased if the lady Vestla might show him some of her skill with the harp. Though it is not to the Aesir taste, the sound of the Prin harp is one I long to hear."

Fiorgynn clapped her hands once again. Another of the Valkyrja stepped forward. From a pouch at her side she produced a massive arm ring of gold. There was easily as much of the yellow metal in it as in eight ordinary rings. Fiorgynn took it and held it up for all to see. "This," she said, "is the ring Draupnyr. Wear it every ninth night, O Borr, and it will bring you wealth and luck. It is inscribed with a charm in the runic script of the original tongue. There is much power in this ring. Anyone who swears an oath on it and then breaks that oath will be hunted out by Var, who wreaks horrible vengeance on those who slight their vows. Woe unto the oath-breaker when Var appears in all her majesty, for he shall be blasted and made mad!" She stepped up to Borr and handed him the arm ring.

The Aesir chieftain slipped the ring up his right arm. It fit perfectly. There was a murmur of approval from the men of the plains at this gift. Borr reached into a pouch slung over his left shoulder and lifted out something that made everyone in both groups gasp and stare. It was a necklace of golden filigree, light and heavy at the same time. In the middle was a representation of Yggdrasil, the World Tree, most cunningly conceived. At the base of the tree a baleful Nidhogg curled, gnawing at the root. His glaring eyes were smoky rubies. From there the trunk rose straight and strong, the bark clearly indicated with little flakes of gold. Nearer the top the branches spread with leaves of tiny emeralds. On one of the branches was a squirrel running up to pester and chatter at an eagle that sat, carved from a single onyx, on the very topmost branch. Four harts also leapt among the branches, nibbling at the leaves and tender young shoots. The topmost branches swept up and around to form the rest of the necklace. The clasp was a huge emerald mounted in gold. Borr held it out to Fiorgynn. "This is Brisingamen. It is made by Volund, the greatest smith in Yggdrasil. The technique is a closely guarded secret known only to him and four others: Alfrigg and Dvalin, Berling and Grerr. It has no magic but that of beauty."

"That," said Fiorgynn as she reached out and took the necklace, fastening it around her neck, "is the greatest magic of all. This gift pleases the Vanadis. It pleases her very much." She bowed her head slightly to Borr. "We have brought many delicacies and even some of Beyla's golden drink. We would share these with our allies and friends while the day is still fresh. Then we will talk about the details of this truce and alliance, and about what aid our warriors can give you in your fight against the Jotun."

The trip through the forest to Folkvang followed the right bank of the Gunnthro and took three days. As they went, Fiorgynn sat in the wagon with the cover raised and chatted gaily with Voden and Honir. Borr's son asked as many questions as the Vanadis seemed willing to answer. Honir remained mostly silent, staring with big eyes at the great cats pulling the wagon or off into the dark depths of the forest.

Late every afternoon they would arrive at a small cluster of dwellings nestled among the trees near a meadow or clearing. As they approached, one of the Valkyrja would blow a long, wavering note on a hunting horn. Before the sound had even a chance to echo out among the tree trunks, people would pour out from behind every bush, rock, and tree, laughing, singing, dancing, and calling out loudly, "Gefyn! Gefyn!" Voden asked one of the friendliest of the Disir what the word meant and was told it was one of the Vanadis's names and referred to her power to intercede with the Vettir and assure plentiful crops for all. It was the planting season, the Disir continued, and at this time the Vanadis always traveled about in her wagon, bringing the blessing of the Hollarvettir to her people and trying to calm and appease the evil Uvvettir so they wouldn't harm the young seedlings. The picking up and dropping off of hostages was just incidental to this year's grand tour. In the fall, around the time when day and night once again became equal and crops were about to be harvested, the Vanadis made another circuit to bless the harvest.

Voden watched the exuberant celebration with conflicting emotions. The Vanir hugged and kissed each other freely, man to woman, woman to woman, or man to man. Many of the kisses were anything but brotherly or sisterly. As the evening progressed, a large fire was lit and all danced around it, hand in hand, singing songs in a language he couldn't understand, but which he was told was the elder tongue, the everyday language of the Vanir. From time to time couples would leave the fire to disappear into the darkness. When they returned, they would drift apart and soon be off again with new partners.

The young Aesir didn't know what to think. It was all so strange and different! He tried to imagine his own people behaving in such a fashion. Impossible! Yes, the Aesir sang and danced, but never with such wild abandon. Songs were in one of the three skaldic measures, with a single person singing while the rest listened. Dancing was just as formal. The tambour and bone flute played to a certain measure, a certain beat, and the steps were known to all. There was none of this flinging oneself about, this shouting, this uproarious laughter! And to think of an Aesir woman going off with one man after another into the dark outside the fire . . . and doing it publicly! Even in the Warrior's Hall, during the long winter nights when the men

often drank too much of the dark Aesir beer and became rowdy
and disorderly, there was a greater sense of personal reticence
than here. There were rules in the hall. Here there seemed to
be only chaos.

Yet at the same time that it repelled him, it fascinated and
attracted him. Such freedom! To be able to do exactly what
one felt like doing, to be able to act without the hundreds of
restrictions that controlled and guided every action and movement among the Aesir. Ah!

Freedom was not the only thing that spoke to him from the
center of the Vanir bonfire. The twisting, writhing figures of
the dancers, spinning together, clasping each other, then whirling apart to find new partners, spoke to something deeper and
more primitive, something that was just stirring to life within
him. He didn't know what it was, couldn't define or come to
grips with it. It was something new, too new to be caught hold
of and studied. Yet when he saw the couples move off into the
dark, their hands groping feverishly at each other's bodies, he
felt it rise, hot and aching from somewhere near the very center
of his being.

Eventually, as the fire began to die down and the revelers
dropped in place from exhaustion, he fell into a fitful slumber
that was haunted by incomprehensible dreams.

Every morning when they left, it was the same. Voden wondered at the strangeness of it and finally worked up the courage
to ask old Syr, the Disir who was most willing to answer his
questions. "Syr," he began, as softly and sweetly as possible,
"where have all the men gone? There were nearly as many men
as women last night. Now only women are here to see us off."

Syr grinned, showing the gaps in her mouth where teeth no
longer were. "Ah, little Aesir male, you're used to a very
different world. Among the Vanir, women rule the hearth and
the hoe. Men help, oh, yes, in many ways. They rule the hunt,
and take part in war, but they live mostly in the forest, going
their own way, living their own lives. They come to us in
spring to help assure that all the ground both we and they furrow
will bear fruit." She chuckled. "Oh, yes, all the ground! In the
fall, they come again to help with the harvest. When the snow
lies deep on the forest floor and the sun slowly dies, they hide
in secret places and never let themselves be seen, though they
creep up and leave the choice catch of the hunt at our doors.

In summer, oh, yes, in the time of the sun's glory, they come and go as they please, proud and wild, taking what they wish, doing as they see fit. Then a king sits in Folkvang with the Vanadis. Only for a while, oh, yes, only for a while.

"You have much to learn, little Aesir. Much to learn."

They arrived at Folkvang on the afternoon of the third day. It stood at the point where the turbulent, fearsome River Slid and the roaring, storming River Hrid crashed together and formed the Gunnthro. The low growling of the two clashing rivers and the spray shot aloft from their meeting filled the air and were a constant presence.

Folkvang itself was larger and more impressive than Voden had expected. It was surrounded by a circular rampart with an inside diameter of at least two thousand feet. The rampart itself was made of earth and stood a good twelve feet high. The outer side was faced with tongue-and-groove planks of rough timber and sunk into the ground, rising vertically to about four feet above the top of the earthwork. About fifteen feet out beyond the wall was a ditch some twenty feet wide, filled with water from the rivers. The space between the wall and the ditch was open and bare to deny attackers any cover if they tried to storm and scale the rampart.

The earthwork was cut by four openings oriented to the cardinal points of the compass. Stout gates of massive planks strapped with brass stood open, surmounted by breastworks that ran across their tops. Narrow bridges led across the ditch to each of the gates. On the rampart sides of the bridges were small breastworks.

"Once," Fiorgynn said as they approached, "Folkvang stood unwalled. But Yggdrasil has changed, and the Jotun have paid us a visit. Much of this is new, Voden. The Vanir are an ancient people, but we learn quickly and act even more swiftly."

Inside the walls the roads that led to the gates became streets that divided the circle of the ramparts into four quadrants. All four led straight to the center of the circle where Fiorgynn's hall, Sessrymnyr, stood. Voden couldn't see it clearly yet, but it looked enormous.

As they passed through the north gate, surrounded by a singing, dancing crowd of jubilant Vanir, Voden noticed an open space some ten to twenty feet wide that ran around the inside of the rampart between it and the nearest houses. The houses themselves were set on either side of the north—south street in a square group of four. Two, at opposite ends of the square, ran north and south, the other two running east and west. In the center between them was an open court-yard.

They reached a cross-street running east and west just past the first set of houses. From what Voden could see, the street ran up to another group of four houses and then turned north—south in front of them. If it continued around on both sides, it must describe a square within the larger circle of the walls, Voden thought, which meant there was an outer ring of some eight groups of four houses each.

Beyond the cross-street were two more sets of four houses arranged in squares around open courtyards. In the courtyard on the right he could see a group of Valkyrja drilling with short swords. To the left, or east, a solemn group of children and adults, dressed in the same deep green as Fiorgynn, stood and watched the procession pass.

They had now reached the center of Folkvang and the great hall Sessrymnyr that stood there. Voden looked at it in awe. It was at least twice the size of the Warrior's Hall! Even more amazing, it appeared to be in the shape of a cross.

The building technique was totally new to the young Aesir. Two rows of great rafters had been sunk into the ground leaning toward each other at a sixty-degree angle. They met at a gigantic ridge pole at least one hundred feet long. Although he couldn't see them, he assumed there were cross-beams inside to help support the massive weight of the roof. The roof itself was shingled with rectangles of flat bark that extended down the angled rafters to about six feet above the ground. Some two feet farther in, vertical posts set in the soil rose up to the slanted rafters and formed the framework of a wall. On the inside of the posts were vertical planks that made up the wall proper. From wall to wall the width of the hall was about twenty feet.

Two buildings of the same size and shape had been built so that they crossed at their centers. Voden tried to picture what the inside would look like but failed. It would probably be spacious and airy and not at all like the narrow, post-filled halls of home. There was a double door at the end they were approaching, and Voden assumed similar ones would exist at the other three ends of the cross.

Fiorgynn's wagon stopped in the open area that surrounded the huge hall, and she got down. With a graceful gesture of her hand she indicated that Voden and Honir were to follow her inside.

As he entered, the young Aesir caught his breath. After a small anteroom the hall opened up and was every bit as spacious as he had imagined. The roof was a good twenty-five feet over his head. The walls of all four arms of the cross were lined with benches, justifying the description of the hall as "many-seated." In the center on a raised platform was the High Seat, wide enough to hold two. At each corner of the platform were two other seats, facing outward. Down the center of all four arms were long fire pits. There were indeed cross-beams, two sets of them, in fact, supporting the rafters.

As he walked down the long room toward the center of the hall, he gazed around in wonder at the rich, soft furs that covered every inch of the walls. Pelt after pelt of wolf and bear and other animals he couldn't identify were hung every-where he looked.

When they reached the High Seat, Fiorgynn mounted it, sat down, and smiled in a friendly manner at the two youths. Voden stood, trying to take it all in with his eyes, not knowing quite what to say or what to think.

He heard a light step behind him, and then a girl's voice, clear and strong, said, "So, these are the northern barbarians that've come to take my brothers' seats in Sessrymnyr. Huh! I think we should feed them to your forest cats, Mother!"

X

VODEN turned slowly to see a group of some six or seven children, ranging in age, he judged, from about twelve to no more than three. The biggest, a girl, stood glaring, her fists on her hips. The others hung back and clung together, peering at him with wondering eyes.

"Voden and Honir," came Fiorgynn's voice from behind him, "these are my children, led by my daughter Freyja, twin of my son, Frey, who is even now with your father in Asgard. Freyja, say hello to Voden and Honir."

"Hello, barbarians," sneered the girl.

"Hello," replied Voden mildly. Honir mumbled something and stood, shifting nervously from foot to foot.

"Freyja, dear, please take Voden and Honir and show them the family halls. Have their things brought to their sleeping places in the men's hall."

"Are you sure it's safe, Mother? I mean, have they been washed and deloused?"

"Freyja!"

The girl bowed grudgingly. "Yes, Vanadis." She looked up at Voden. "C'mon, barbarian, and bring your silent friend."

They trooped from Sessrymnyr by the north door and cut across the courtyard that surrounded the building to the group of four halls that stood to the northeast. As they walked, Voden studied Freyja. Like all the Vanir, she was short and slender, with dark hair, green eyes, and pale white skin. Alien to the Aesir as such coloring might be, Voden found it very attractive. The girl moved smoothly, like one of the forest cats that drew her mother's wagon. Freyja might be slender, the young Aesir decided, but there was a lithe strength about her that gave her an aura of barely restrained energy and power. He wondered if she were destined to be Vanadis after her mother.

There were four halls in the royal family complex, set in a square around the sides of an open courtyard. All were identical in structure: rectangular, but built the same way as Sessrymnyr. Each was eighty feet long by twenty wide. The south hall was for girls and women. The west hall held Fiorgynn's own apartments and those of the king, when one reigned with her. To the north was the hall where boys and men of the royal household lived. On the western side of the square was a hall dedicated to the many servants who cared for the Vanadis and her large family.

Voden asked Freyja what the other three complexes that lay to the northwest, southwest, and southeast of Sessrymnyr were for. She gave him a haughty look, then muttered that since he was too stupid to know, she guessed she'd have to tell him so he wouldn't blunder about and disrupt everything.

"The southeastern square contains kitchens, storerooms, and workrooms for weavers, leather workers, potters, and people like that. To the west of that is the square where the Disir live. Don't *ever* go in there. No man is allowed to. The northwestern square is for the Valkyrja. They have their own armory there, and a practice yard in the center as well as in one end of each barracks. They spend a lot of time drilling. I'd stay out of there, too, if I were you. They might decide to use you for target practice." She leered at him.

"What's in the rest of the city?" Voden asked, ignoring her smirk. "There seem to be a lot of halls inside the earthworks."

Freyja looked at him proudly. "Folkvang is the greatest city in all of Yggdrasil. There are forty-eight halls here, besides Sessrymnyr. Over ten hundreds of Vanir live within the Great Circle. Two hundred of them are Valkyrja, the fiercest warriors alive. Someday I will be a Valkyrja."

Voden walked along silently for a moment. Over ten hundreds! Almost twice as many as lived in Asgard. About as many warriors, though. He smiled secretly at Freyja's boast about the Valkyrja. Perhaps in the woods they might equal the Aesir. Perhaps. But man-to-man, or rather woman-to-man, they were no match for the men from the plains. The Aesir lived a harsher life than these Children of Audhumla. They had been surrounded by enemies ever since Fornjot had created them. Fighting was central to their very existence.

Freyja would be a warrior, eh? Perhaps it was time to teach this annoying girl a lesson. He was getting tired of her sneering condescension. I am Voden, son of Borr, he thought. I don't have to put up with her . . . her attitude!

"A warrior?" He laughed. "You'll have to grow a lot before

you can even hold a sword, much less swing one!"

Freyja stopped dead in her tracks, as did the rest of the children. They had reached the center of the courtyard surrounded by the halls of the royal complex. The girl turned slowly and looked Voden up and down with cold eyes. The other children just stared in stark surprise. Honir gulped and cleared his throat.

"What did you say, barbarian?" Freyja asked quietly.

"I said you're just a girl, not a warrior," Voden replied, a trifle too loudly.

"Maybe you'd like to fight me?"

Voden realized he'd made a mistake. By Sigfod, he silently cursed, I've gone and violated the first rule of a warrior: never fight on unknown ground. Too late to back out now, though, he thought. He decided to make an attempt anyway. "Fight a girl? Fagh!"

Freyja took a step toward him, lightly balanced on the balls of her feet. Her green eyes were tightly locked on his, her arms loose at her sides, fingers relaxed. "Are you afraid, barbarian? Afraid of a girl?" Her voice, though soft, lashed at him as if she were snarling out a curse.

The young Aesir had given all his weapons, except for the dagger, to a servant before entering Sessrymnyr. Now he drew the dagger and handed it to Honir. "Hold this," he said, forcing confidence into his voice, "while I teach this little forest cat a lesson."

He turned back to Freyja, and the two of them began to circle. The rest of the children gathered around, watching silently. Voden was surprised that Freyja hadn't come rushing in to attack. No, he thought, that's the way an Aesir would do it. This is Vanaheim. The Vanir fight differently. I only wish I knew more about how they fight!

He jumped forward, his arms shooting out to grab the slender girl. She leapt lightly out of his way, sticking out her foot in an attempt to trip him. He avoided it and spun around, making another grab. His fingers caught the fabric of her sleeve, and he stepped in closer to get a better grip. Her foot came up and smacked into his forearm, numbing it and breaking his grip.

In surprise he stepped back, cradling his arm. She stepped in immediately, her other foot flying toward his head. Voden ducked back, and the kick struck his shoulder, knocking him off balance. Instantly Freyja's first foot hooked around his ankle and swept up. He felt himself falling.

He hit but rolled and was on his feet in one move. The girl was ready. The young Aesir backed off, trying to get his wind and regain his sense of balance. Freyja kicked again, and he blocked with his forearm. The impact made them both wince. Another kick swept out toward his middle. He was getting the hang of it now and made a grab for the leg while stepping to the side to avoid the blow. He missed but could see that the attempt made Freyja more wary.

Holding his ground, he watched as she circled him, looking indeed like a forest cat stalking its prey. This time he was ready when she kicked. He blocked with his left arm and stepped swiftly in, making a grab for her with his right.

The next thing he knew, he was flying through the air. With a resounding thump he hit the ground. Dazed, he was not able to move swiftly enough to get up again. In a flash she was on his back, her finger moving across his throat as though drawing a dagger. "You're dead, barbarian," she crowed triumphantly. With a light jump she was off and standing in front of him offering him her hand to help him rise, her face split by a grin.

Voden looked up, surprised at the smile. She'd just slit his throat and now she was grinning and offering her hand! Then he realized how silly he must look, lying sprawled in the dust of the courtyard, his hair and clothes in total disarray. He couldn't help it. He smiled back and laughed.

Freyja chuckled as she helped him to his feet. "You're a mess," she said.

"And you're a warrior," he replied.

She looked up at him sharply, the smile suddenly warmer. "Thank you, Voden. You fought well for someone who's never had a chance to study with a Valkyrja mistress of the Thiodnuma."

"'Thiodnuma'?" he asked as he brushed the dust from his cloak and shirt.

"The 'sweeping people away,' the way the Valkyrja fight when they have no javelin or sword or bow. Don't you have something like it in Asaheim?"

"No. We learn to fight with spear, sword, ax, dagger, even with the shield. We learn to shoot the bow. Bare-handed . . . we just fight, that's all."

"Hmm." She considered. "I always thought everybody learned something like the Thiodnuma. I guess maybe you barbarians never expect to fight that way." She smiled to take the sting out of her words. "Maybe the Valkyrja will show you, Voden. You really should learn."

"Did Niord and Frey learn?"

"Oh, yes. Frey wasn't very good at it, but Niord was splendid."

"Do all men learn it?"

She put her fists on her hips and tilted her head to one side. "Do you ever stop asking questions?" She laughed. "No, all the men don't learn it. Only the men of the royal family. Since you are officially of the royal family now, you should be able to learn."

"When can I start?" He straightened up, having finished dusting off his breeches.

Exasperated, she shook her head and turned away, gesturing for him to follow. "Sometime *after* you've seen where you're going to stay."

He quickly came up beside her. "You'll ask your mother right away, won't you?"

"Yes," she said tartly. "Because the next time we fight, I want you to give a better accounting of yourself."

Voden was silent for the rest of the trip to the men's hall.

For the first week Voden saw almost nothing of Fiorgynn. Even Freyja was so busy with the training and classes she and the rest of the children in the Vanadis's household had to attend, she was unable to spend much time with the new arrivals. So the two Aesir lads set off on their own to explore Folkvang.

Everyone they met was friendly and seemed to know who they were. The women made much of them, commenting on their hair and eyes and exclaiming over how big they were for their age. The men were more reticent, acknowledging their presence with a nod, then going about their business without another look. Occasionally they would catch a glimpse of other children peeking out at them from doorways.

Folkvang seemed very strange to Voden and Honir. It was not at all what they had expected and certainly not at all like Asgard. The first thing that struck them was how quiet everything was. The Vanir simply weren't as . . . well, boisterous, Voden decided, as the Aesir. There was never any loud shouting, cursing, or plain rowdiness. Even the children, when they saw any, played quietly.

It wasn't that the Vanir weren't happy. On the contrary, they smiled a great deal, and Voden often heard them humming or singing soft songs in their liquid tongue while they worked.

Another thing that surprised him was the fact that the women seemed clearly to be in charge in Folkvang. Oh, there were plenty of men in the city, but when anything needed to be done, it was the women who came forward and organized the task. The men hung around, did what they were told, worked at minor jobs of their own, and appeared vaguely uneasy and out of place.

What a contrast to Asgard! There the men were definitely the ones who ran things. Well, Voden admitted, not everything. Women ruled the household and were in charge of gardening and the domestic animals. But in the things that counted—the council, warfare, herding, and farming—men were supreme. The young Aesir wondered if the men of Vanaheim even participated in the councils of the Vanadis.

There was another difference that struck him even more forcefully. No one, not even the men, ever wore weapons! He never saw even a dagger thrust through a belt. The Valkyrja went in and out of the gates with sword, javelin, and bow in hand, of course, and the guards on the walls were armed. But they alone bore arms.

At home even boys and girls had small knives. It was generally the first Tooth Gift received from grandparents. For a full-grown man to leave his hall without sword or ax strapped about his waist, well . . . it just wasn't done. To the Aesir, fighting and life were synonymous. A man without his weapons was a man without the means to fight, and hence without the means to stay alive. They lived by the code of Fornjot, in the world Fornjot had created through his malevolence. The Aesir were always ready for the worst.

Voden puzzled over these differences and others, many of which he couldn't even define. It was the way the Vanir walked and stood, the way they spoke, their elder tongue slipping smoothly and softly from their mouths, the looks they gave each other, the clothes, everything. There had to be a good reason behind it all. Whatever it was, he couldn't come to grips with it.

Asking Freyja didn't help any, either. At first she laughed and said he was silly. Then, when he persisted and started pointing out specific differences, she stared at him blankly and simply said that that was the way things had always been. Any attempts to push the questioning further had met with open hostility. How dared he question the ways of the Children of

the Nourisher, the Elder Race? she said coldly. A mere barbarian! Then she stalked off and avoided him for the rest of
the day.

Eventually, when all the spring planting and attendant ceremonies were completed, Fiorgynn recalled she had two guests
from Asaheim and called them to her in her own quarters.
Voden and Honir sat on the floor at her feet, along with Freyja
and several of the older children.

For a while the Vanadis told them of all the things she had
been doing, of the many villages visited, of the state of the
planting and the likelihood of a good harvest. This year, she
said, she had traveled far to the west, all the way to the scattered
hamlets along the banks of the mighty, forward-rushing River
Gopul.

"We were in a very small place, a tiny clearing in the woods
with three houses buried deep in the shadows, when a messenger came to tell us that a party of Dverg were coming across
the Gopul in a boat." Voden sat up, his interest excited by
mention of the Dverg. Fiorgynn noticed and smiled at him.
"They came from Nidavellir, Voden, the land that stretches
between the Gopul on the east, a north- and south-running spur
of the Smoking Lands on the west, and the River Sid to the
north. It's not an extensive land, but then, there aren't that
many Dverg."

"I've never seen any Dverg," Voden said.

"I have," sniffed Freyja importantly. "And Svartalfar, too."

Fiorgynn nodded. "Yes, dear. You've been fortunate. But
then, Voden's father has been all the way to the Twisted Lands
and fought by the side of men from the Dark Empire. We've
never done that."

The girl shivered. "Don't want to, either. Muspellheim's a
bad place."

"Bad? No, not bad. Just very, very different. As are the
Dverg." She looked at Voden. "They're not as tall as you. Not
even as big as Freyja. They're very broad and thick, with
strange gray skin, gray beards and hair, and gray eyes."

Voden's eyes opened wide. "Even the children have beards?"

Fiorgynn laughed merrily. "No, I don't suppose so, but then
I've never seen one of their children, or even one of their
women. Only men, with long gray beards and bushy eyebrows."

"Where did they come from?" Voden asked.

"Ah, well. They came out of the east many, many years

ago. Long, long before the Aesir were even a people. Probably long before Fornjot was even a god.

"You see, Voden, in those days the Smoking Lands were just beginning to rise. The Icerealm barely existed, and the Great Eastern Waste was a beautiful plain, dotted with groves of trees, veined with cool, frothing rivers. The Dverg dwelt there in a great city and were led by a brave and wise king named Alvis. Allied with the Alfar, they fought the First Dark Empire during its great period and won. At heavy cost, true, but it was still a victory.

"Then the rivers began to dry up, the trees to die, and the grass to wither. Many blamed it on the evil forces that broke loose when the First Dark Empire went crashing into ruin. Perhaps. I think it was just Yggdrasil growing and changing as all things must.

"In any case, the Dverg finally had to abandon the great city that Alvis had built for them. Homeless, they wandered westward. We took in all we could and helped them on their way. Two of their tribes settled in Nidavellir. The Earth Dverg built burrows in the forest while the Rock People sunk tunnels into the flanks of the Smoking Lands. A third group, led by Svarin, the son of Alvis, continued on westward and settled in Joruvellir, far, far toward the sunset, beyond Svartalfheim, at the very limits of the Western Forest. There they built a city called Aurvangar and gave birth eventually to a new tribe named the Lovar."

Voden sat thinking for several moments. "Yes, but where did they come from originally? I mean, Fornjot created the Aesir. Nerthus and Gymir gave birth to the Jotun. Audhumla the Nourisher brought the Vanir into Yggdrasil."

"Hmm. Yes, I see what you mean. Well, I can only tell you what they say of themselves, Voden. They claim to be descended from Blain, who was brother to Aurgelmir the Well-informed. Aurgelmir himself was one of the Original Beings that formed in Ginnungagap and was nourished by Audhumla. Does that help any? Like the Alfar, they worship the Huldre, the Hidden Ones, though I fear their version of the Huldre is quite different from that of the Children of Light.

"In any case, this group that crossed the Gopul to meet us was only five, led by the king of the Earth Dverg, Durin. Bold Thorin was there, and the pleasant Thekk. Wise old Radsvid brought his young nephew, Nyr. We had a fine visit. We traded, and I let them get the best of the bargain, as usual. Oh, what greedy things the Dverg are! Dour and silent until they smell gold or sense a profit; then their eyes light up, their mouths water, and they can barely contain themselves! I gave gold for good iron weapons, and nothing delights them more. When the trading was done, I gifted them with many amphorae of mead, and they sent each of you an ancient gold ring found beneath the forest mold. The gold is much diluted with baser metal and the workmanship is primitive, so they didn't much mind parting with them. I can't imagine where they came from or what race made them, but I found them charming in their simplicity and was pleased to accept them. I'll give them to you later.

"Oh, yes, and Voden, you'll be interested to know that they made much of Brisingamen, calling it the most wonderful necklace they had ever seen." She clapped her hands with remembered pleasure and laughed. "They were stunned when I told them a human smith had made it! 'Volund?' they cried. 'Who is this Volund?' Radsvid nodded sagely and said, 'Whoever he is, he has stolen the knowledge of Alfrigg and Dvalin, Berling and Grerr. Anyone who can steal anything from those tight fists has my respect!'" All of them laughed merrily at her gruff imitation of the Dverg, who, it was known, had trouble distinguishing between *t* and *d* when they spoke.

Once the children had all quieted down, Fiorgynn turned her attention to Voden and Honir again. "Now, how have you two been getting on in Folkvang? I hear you've been everywhere and met everybody."

Voden blushed slightly and Honir just sat quietly, tongue-tied as usual. "Uh, well, yes," Borr's son began, "we have looked around a bit, I guess."

"And asked a lot of questions, too!" Freyja added with a giggle. "'What's this?' 'Why's that?'" she parroted in a surprisingly good imitation of Voden's voice. "'Who? When? Where? Why? Which? What?' I didn't know there were so many different ways to ask questions, Mother!"

"If I don't ask questions, how will I ever find anything out?" Voden blurted, blushing even more deeply. When he realized what he'd just said, though, he burst out laughing. The others joined him.

"Ah, Voden, there is nothing wrong with asking questions, even a lot of questions, but don't be disappointed if you don't get many answers, or if the answers you do get don't seem to be very satisfying."

He looked up at Fiorgynn, blinking in surprise. "How . . . how did you know that? I mean, yes, that's right. But . . ."

"The most important questions don't even have answers, Voden. At least not any you can put into words."

"But if we don't know, how can we act? I mean, how do we know what to do if we don't know . . . I mean . . ."

"Sometimes knowing has to come from acting. Sometimes it must come from doing nothing but listening to the leaves growing. Wisdom is often found in silence, for words hide as much as they reveal.

"Ah, that's a bit much, even for young Voden. So you wish to learn, do you? Freyja tells me you would like to study the Thiodnuma. She says you have a 'special' need for it." Voden looked quickly out of the corner of his eye at the girl, but her face was calm and her look was bland and innocent. He nodded at Fiorgynn.

"Hmm. No Aesir has ever studied the Thiodnuma. In fact, to my knowledge, no one not of the Vanir has ever studied it." She paused as if deciding something. "Well, I guess since you are to be my son, it can't hurt to teach you. The more you understand the Vanir and our way of living, the better. You will act as a secure bridge between our peoples. You too, Honir," she added as an afterthought.

"Yes. You can begin tomorrow," she finished with a twinkle in her eye. "Although I'm not at all sure you won't be sorry you asked in a couple of days. Freyja, take him to see Geirahod right after breakfast. Eat lightly, Voden. It's best for the first few times, until you get used to it."

She stood and looked down at them with a warm smile. "Now, off with you, everyone! I've things to do before dinner, and you've got many lessons. Off with you!"

They all sprang to their feet and raced for the door. Freyja was in the lead by several lengths. As Voden came out into the courtyard she spun around and suddenly stepped to the side, sticking out her foot. He tried to avoid it, but tripped and went tumbling into the dust.

The young Aesir swallowed his anger and looked up calmly into Freyja's grinning face. "In a few weeks, little one, you'd better watch out," he said softly. "I owe you now, and I always pay my debts."   •

"Good." She chortled. "I'll be waiting to collect, mighty barbarian warrior!" She ran off, shouting over her shoulder, "Don't keep me waiting too long!"

XI

THE next few weeks were filled with a mixture of pain and exhilaration for Voden. The pain came from his lessons in the Thiodnuma. Geirahod was harsh taskmistress, especially so to a male not of Vanir blood. She drove him mercilessly, constantly pushing him beyond anything he had ever thought himself capable of. His dogged determination and willingness to drag his aching body up from the dirt of the practice yard for one more try soon won the Valkyrja's gruff respect. As the days grew longer and the summer solstice approached, she even began to be fond of the young blond barbarian who was showing such an unusual aptitude for the Thiodnuma. He actually seemed more interested and dedicated than the Vanir youths she taught!

If Voden's pain came from the Thiodnuma, so, in a more indirect way, did his exhilaration. For one thing, he was busy again, learning and doing something new, rather than wandering about aimlessly. For another, he was getting ready to surprise Freyja to get even with her. Finally, though he wouldn't even admit it to himself, working in the practice yard gave him the opportunity to see and talk to the slender girl every day. She teased him and was critical of his performance, but at least she was there.

When Voden wasn't in the practice yard going through the endless drills imposed by Geirahod, he continued to explore Folkvang with Honir. It was Honir, usually so quiet, who pointed out the change in the city.

At first Voden thought his long-legged fellow Aesir was imagining things. Once he began to look, he found that Honir was right. There *were* more men in the city than during the first few weeks of their stay, and their attitude was quite different.

Most of the newcomers were in their early twenties, dressed in rough, simply made clothes. They swaggered about in twos

118

and threes, talking loudly and staring openly and boldly at the young women. They didn't carry any weapons, but their actions were more like those Voden would have expected at home in Asgard. For some reason he found them mildly offensive.

Running across the old Disir Syr one day, he and Honir stopped to greet her. They both bowed respectfully and asked after her health. After some small talk over the weather and the state of the crops, Voden asked about the newcomers. Syr cackled and grinned. "Forest lads, strong and virile, yes, full of life and vigor. Oh, yes, full of life!" She laughed again, as if she had made a very clever joke.

"But what are they doing here?" Voden asked.

"Doing? Why they're getting ready to wrestle, that's what they're doing."

"Wrestle? What's 'wrestle'?"

Syr looked quizzically at Voden. "Doesn't know what wrestle is, he doesn't. Ah, ah, young Aesir, you've much to learn. Come, then, there's bound to be a match over in the northwest quadrant. That's where the first ones always start. Only three weeks left now, so they've begun. Yes, yes, come. I'm going that way in any case. Come, come." Exchanging a wondering look, the two Aesir boys followed the old Disir as she hobbled along, muttering to herself.

The northernmost of the two complexes in the northwest quadrant was usually devoted to those who tanned hides and cured pelts. Leather workers were also there, making boots, pouches, sword and dagger sheaths. Today, though, the complex was crowded with many people. In the central courtyard, which had been cleared of all equipment, four rough circles about twelve feet in diameter had been scratched out in the dust. Each was surrounded by groups of onlookers, both male and female.

In the center of each circle were two men, stripped to their loincloths. Their bodies glistened as though oiled. They hurled insults at each other, flexed their muscles, and bantered with the crowd, making lewd remarks to the younger, prettier women, who would answer back in kind.

Voden wormed his way to the front of the group around one of the circles. One of the young men in the ring saw him and made a comment to the crowd in the elder tongue. He walked over to the Aesir lad and stood in front of him, fists on his hips, legs spread wide. "Do you understand the language of true people, barbarian, or only your own uncouth tongue?"

Embarrassed, Voden could only stammer, "I—I'm trying to learn the elder tongue."

The other Vanir in the ring called out, "Tell him what you said in the common tongue. Even cattle understand that."

"I said, barbarian, that I wonder if it's true that you northern plainsmen have such big noses and such huge shaggy heads because your cocks and balls are small and hairless." The men in the crowd laughed heartily at the bright crimson flush that rushed up Voden's neck to his face. The women smiled. The young Aesir could not think of a reply. His tongue seemed stuck to the roof of his mouth. He wanted badly to disappear back into the anonymity of the crowd but was too confused to even move.

Apparently some in the crowd mistook his motionlessness for a willingness to face down his insulter. A woman's voice called out, "Ah, and leave the lad alone. If you're so big on cocks and balls, let's see the quality and quantity of yours, braggart. Fight and prove yourself! Enough of this strutting and jabbing at children with your tongue! If you want to jab at a woman, you'd best prove yourself!" The people around Voden roared their good-natured agreement.

The two young men went to the center of the circle and held their right palms over their heart. Then they reached out with their right hands and touched each other's hearts. That salutation completed, each grasped the other by the forearm, right hand on the outside, and spread their legs, leaning slightly in toward each other.

Suddenly the one nearest Voden, the one who had taunted him, lurched backward, trying to pull the other off balance. His opponent stepped in swiftly, though, attempting to push him off balance in turn. The first man twisted to his left, but the other pulled back and to his right. For several moments they circled warily, grasping arms. Occasionally one would feint, shifting his weight suddenly, pushing or pulling unexpectedly. Both remained as solid as rocks, feet widely and firmly planted in the dust of the circle.

Voden felt a presence beside him and looked up into the sparkling eyes of old Syr. "Force one foot outside the circle, crowd starts clapping, counting to nine. If the foot isn't back in, counts as a half fall. Two feet out at the same time, that's a half fall too. Force him to one knee, a half fall. Down to both knees, that's a full fall. To win clean, you get your man down, shoulders in the dirt, for a slow count of three. Otherwise three out of five falls wins. Watch, Aesir."

The young men's bodies were straining hard, the sweat beginning to roll down their skin. The muscles of the one who had insulted Voden were standing out. Voden could hear the noise of their breathing as they sucked in great breaths of air.

Without warning one of the men dropped to his knee. A ripple of surprise ran through the crowd and a look of triumph lit the face of his opponent. Then the one who had gone down shifted his grip, letting go the other's forearm with his right hand and grabbing his left leg just behind the knee. With a mighty upward heave he threw his opponent crashing into the dust.

As he fell the young man twisted and kicked out with his foot, breaking the grip of the other. He landed on his side rather than flat on his back. The attacker was on him instantly, trying for a choke hold.

For several moments they scrabbled around on the ground, each trying to gain a decisive hold on the other. Their bodies were covered with dust that sweat turned to mud. Livid marks showed where hands had gripped, and red scratches appeared where nails had slashed. The two were grunting with effort now, breathing in short, tortured gasps. Fingers groped and grasped, limbs bent in strange and unexpected configurations.

Suddenly the young man who had insulted Voden cried out in pain. The other combatant had managed to twist his arm up behind his back, hand almost to the nape of his neck. Despite his anguish he refused to yield. He gritted his teeth, dug in his toes, and gave a mighty shove.

Even Voden could hear the pop as his shoulder joint gave. The man gave a short, sharp yelp and passed out, falling face down in the dirt. The second man staggered to his feet and held both hands over his head in a sign of victory. Someone in the crowd called out, "Don't get too cocky, Aegyr. That's only your first, and this only the first day!" Several friends stepped into the ring and helped the victor from the scene of his triumph, making lusty jokes as they walked off.

The loser still lay in the dust, his arm twisted at an odd angle. Syr looked at him and muttered something to the man standing next to her. The two of them went and knelt down next to the unconscious young man, examining the dislocation. Syr reached out and grabbed the arm carefully, just above the elbow. With a swift jerk she snapped it back into place. The young man moaned but remained unconscious. Two friends picked him up and carried him off.

When Syr came back to stand with Voden, he asked, "Was it bad?" She looked down at him and scowled. "No worse than most," she replied. "Better than a lot. Nothing broken. It'll be sore for a week or two. He's out of it this year. Fool. That drop's one of the oldest tricks in the book."

Two new opponents were sizing each other up in the center of the ring. Voden watched them for a few moments, then turned and asked Syr, "What's it all for? I mean, why are they fighting?"

Her return look was long and considering. "Don't know, do you, little Aesir. So much to learn. So much. Old Syr could explain it all, yes, she could, but some things are best learned by yourself. Yes. Old Syr could explain, but she won't. Just keep your eyes and ears open, little plainsman. Try to forget who and what you are, where you came from, and the way you've been taught to live. Watch and try to see what's really there. Accept it for what it is, not what you think it should be. Try to understand without prejudging. If you can do that, young Voden, why, then maybe you really will be as important as the Vanadis thinks." She chuckled. "Yes. Maybe.

"Now I haven't more time to waste watching young bucks show their manliness. I must run the errands of a Disir, for an important time approaches and there is much to be done. So. Stay and watch, both of you. Pay attention. Learn."

The rest of the day Voden watched match after match. The more he saw, the more he realized there was to this strange method of fighting. Strength was important, to be sure, but endurance was just as critical. Some of the contestants fought as many as four bouts during the course of the day. Speed was also essential. Voden saw more than one man fall to an opponent weaker but quicker than he. A fourth necessity was cleverness. Some fought doggedly, almost stupidly, and by rote. Others invented and used wily stratagems. He saw one small man wear a bigger one out by dodging slickly every time the other tried to come to grips. Finally, totally frustrated, the big man attacked carelessly. The sloppiness of his assault combined with his fatigue landed him on his back. He hit so hard, he didn't come to for a good hour after the match was over.

Wrestling wasn't just random grappling, either, Voden quickly realized. There were many different techniques. He counted at least four separate ways to capture and lock an opponent's arm, and the legs were equally as important. This was a very carefully thought-out way of fighting. Small men would use holds that gave them the greatest advantage, while larger fighters might have an entirely different repertoire of attacks and escapes.

He noticed certain similarities to the Thiodnuma, at least in some of the trips and throws. Yet wrestling was not merely a form of the Thiodnuma. It was its own art, just as highly developed as the combat techniques of the Valkyrja.

The weakness of wrestling, he analyzed, lay in the fact that you had to come to grips with your opponent before you could use it. If he had a dagger, you'd likely die before you could throw an arm lock on him. What it needed was some way of attacking at a greater distance, say, like Thiodnuma had with its kicks. Geirahod had already shown him how a swift, accurate kick could effectively disarm a knife-wielding opponent and burden him with a broken wrist as well.

Yet, at the same time, the Thiodnuma had no good techniques for hand-to-hand grappling. Voden felt sure that once he was inside the "radius of defense," as Geirahod called it, he had an even chance against the Valkyrja's method of fighting. He grimaced, though, as he remembered the way Freyja had thrown him. That, he told himself, was only because I wasn't ready and didn't have my balance. If I were as firmly planted as one of these wrestlers . . . well, it might be a different story. The vision of grabbing Freyja and wrestling her down into the dirt excited and disturbed him. That would show her, he told himself, confused by his own sudden, unfamiliar emotions.

He turned back to the match he was watching. Could he learn to wrestle? he wondered. There certainly were plenty of men in Folkvang who knew how. Would any of them be willing to teach a boy, and an Aesir boy at that? He shrugged. There was only one way to find out.

The first four wrestlers he approached, all winners whose style he admired, sneered at him. The fifth sat and looked at him for so long that Voden began to wonder if the man had understood him.

"Yes, young barbarian, I understood. It's just that it's such a novel thought. You've no idea how to wrestle? That seems so strange. What's your name?"

"I'm Voden, sir."

"'Sir,' is it? Mark you, lad, I'm just a man, a simple man,

and a forester to boot. Not a 'sir' or anything so fine. I'm called Yngvi. So you want to learn to wrestle, eh? Why? You're not for trying to become king, are you?" he asked with a twinkle in his eye.

"King?" Voden answered blankly.

Yngvi stared unbelievingly at the young Aesir. "Then you don't know what this is all about?"

"Well . . . no. Syr said I should find out on my own."

The Vanir snorted. "That old sow. That's just the sort of thing she would say." He saw Voden's shocked and surprised look. "That's what Syr is, an old sow, and a bitch to boot. I'm not of the city men, barbarian, so I've not a city temperament. I say what I think, and the Uvvettir take whom they want.

"But the wrestling. You've really no idea? Well, then, for the next two weeks the wrestling will continue until each quadrant has produced a clear champion. I'll not last that long, nor would I want to. I'm not one of those as comes to be king. Not Yngvi. I come for the fun and the meeting of people. And a sweet little girl of seven!" He laughed happily. "Oh, and not to forget the mead as flows this time of the year. Yes, that's one thing in Folkvang that beats my home forest all hollow. Ah, that mead. And the girls that go with it. Umm." He licked his lips and rolled his eyes appreciatively.

"Well, as I was saying, the wrestling goes on till there be four champions. Then those four go to Sessrymnyr and have it out in the very presence of the Vanadis. Him as wins wins her and is king. Not for long," he muttered, "but a glorious time he has of it.

"That all happens on the day the sun is longest with us. For a few days after that, Folkvang is a lovely place. The mead flows and the girls try to see how many men they can take on. Oh, it's a wonderful time! Yes, and that's what we really all come for, winner or loser!" A smile spread across his face as he sat back, allowing his mind to wander.

He came back quickly, though, his voice suddenly sad, with just a slight edge of bitterness. "That's for a few days only. Then it's back to the woods again for the likes of poor Yngvi, until next year or until he's too old to wrestle anymore. It's back to the hunt until he drops some cold winter and sleeps to death in a bank of snow."

The Vanir looked strangely at Voden. "So why not," he said. "Why not teach a barbarian to wrestle? It's not done, but there's nothing as says it can't be, except *their* rules, and Yngvi gives not a bitter berry for *their* rules!

"By Beyla, my favorite Vettir, I'll do it! Can't do too much of a job, as I've only got two and a half weeks left before I'm back off to the woods again. I've a bit of drinking and screwing to do between now and then. Not to mention wrestling. But, why not? Serve the holy bitches right if you wrestled your way right up to the throne someday! Are you game to start right now? I'm done for the day, and drinking won't begin in earnest till sundown. I make it we've got a good three, four hours."

Voden grinned. "I'm ready! Thanks!"

Yngvi's answering grin was mocking. "Thank me later, lad, if you're not hurting too much to talk."

At the end of the first week Yngvi was finally knocked out of the running for the championship of the northwestern quadrant. From then on he and Voden spent the whole of each day together, watching the wrestling all morning and practicing all afternoon. Voden's regular classes with Geirahod were canceled as a festive atmosphere settled over Folkvang.

Toward the middle of the second week Voden noticed a change come over the people watching the matches. The loose, good-natured atmosphere gradually transformed into a more emotionally charged one. People began to shout and urge on the contestants. Injuries became more serious, and one man was killed when he broke his neck in a fall.

The strangest change, though, was in the women. They became shriller and more violent in their demands for action. When they watched the matches, they breathed heavily, their breasts rising and falling in swift jerks. If one of the opponents drew blood, their eyes shone, and many could be seen licking their lips. They mobbed the winners, clinging to them and running their hands over their dirt- and sweat-caked bodies. It all made Voden uneasy.

Some of the young boys, those about his own age, had begun to wrestle off to the side of the main events, and crowds often gathered to watch and cheer them on. There was one boy in particular who seemed a favorite. His name was Od, and he appeared to be two or three years older than Voden. The young Aesir took an instant dislike to him. When Yngvi teased him about it, Voden replied that Od fought sneakily, with more slyness than skill. "He fights dirty too," Voden accused after watching a match. "He hit that boy in the head with his elbow.

Dazed him, then threw him. That's not fair."

Yngvi shrugged. "Only thing as's not fair is eye-gouging and kneeing in the crotch. Yes, and punching. Out and out punching's not allowed. A slap with the elbow, or a clout with the open hand, that's not breaking any rules. Though I will admit it's not an elegant way to fight. I stay away from it myself because it's bad form. Still, a fall's a fall, barbarian."

Voden shook his head. "I'd rather win clean."

"Young Od'd rather win. Best not fight him yet, then."

The young Aesir looked at Yngvi in surprise. "I wasn't planning to. What made you say that?"

"Oh, just that a certain friend of yours seems to be taking great interest in Od's victories." He pointed across the circle of spectators. Voden saw Freyja standing there, watching the match.

The look on her face chilled him. Her lips were parted, her tongue sticking slightly out, touching the lower one. Her green eyes were large and misty-looking. Freyja's breast rose and fell swiftly, as though she were gasping for breath with the same effort as the two in the ring. Her whole body was tense with excitement.

At that moment Od tripped his opponent and threw him to the ground. The other lad was so stunned he lay there passively while the crowd chanted the count of three. Od stood and held his hands over his head, his eyes sweeping the circling watchers and meeting Freyja's. A strange, lazy smile passed between the two of them.

Voden found that his hands were trembling as he watched Od walk proudly around the circle. The Vanir dared every lad his own age to wrestle with him. One after the other, they looked away. Closer and closer Od came to where Voden stood next to Yngvi.

Finally Od reached him and stopped, looking him up and down with a cool, arrogant eye. "Barbarian," he said in a voice that carried across the circle, "you stand and watch. Do you dare come into the circle with me?"

Yngvi said "Ah, you're three years older than the Aesir, with three years more practice wrestling. Go pick on someone who's a more suitable match, Od."

Voden looked beyond Od and found Freyja watching him. There was a look of disdain on her face. The look struck deep into his soul, staggering him. He looked back at Od's arrogant visage, and something deep within him hardened.

Od was about to move on when Voden said softly, "Wait."
Surprised, the Vanir turned back to him. "It's true I'm younger
and not as practiced as you, but I'm not afraid. I'll fight you.
Only I wonder how brave you really are? Is the only reason
you pick me because you know I'm younger and not used to
fighting your way? I wonder."

The crowd murmured and Od flushed. "I'll fight you any
way you want, barbarian. And kick you all around the circle
while I'm at it. Name your terms."

Voden smiled. "In Asaheim we allow striking with the fist
above the waist. It's our way of fighting. My grandfather, Buri,
was known as Axhand since he once killed a Jotun chieftain
with a single blow from his fist. You strike in your wrestling,
but with the open hand, or the elbow. I would add just that to
our bout, Od, that we can strike with the fist."

Od looked uncertain. Yngvi laughed. "Not so sure now, are
you, Od? Well, well, make up your mind. The barbarian's
called your bluff. What do you say?"

The Vanir youth spat into the dust at Voden's feet. "I accept." He turned and walked back to the center of the circle.
"Let him strip down and let's get started. I want to beat him
swiftly so I can watch the evening's matches in the southeast
quadrant."

Yngvi helped Voden take off his shirt and breeches. "I hope
you're good at this closed-fist stuff," he whispered. "Have you
practiced it in Asgard? Od's angry. You'll need it."

Voden shrugged as he stood naked but for his loincloth. "I
made it up. We don't really study any kind of unarmed fighting
in Asaheim. We fight, yes, but there's no system or art to it.
I just wanted to throw him off guard."

"Oh, shit," said Yngvi, and showed him out into the ring.

XII

As Voden walked toward his opponent, touched his own heart with his right hand, and then reached out and touched Od's, his mind was working furiously. This is a seasoned fighter, he thought. He's got experience, speed, and age in his favor. We're about the same size, but I have a slight edge in weight and maybe strength.

What else do I have in my favor? Voden ran quickly down a rather short list. I've fought the rough-and-tumble Aesir way ever since I was old enough to walk. No science, no style, just fighting. I've studied the Thiodnuma with Geirahod for about two months and been wrestling with Yngvi for about a week and a half. Plus I *do* know how to punch.

What's the best strategy? he wondered as he gripped the Vanir's left forearm with his right hand and felt Od's right hand on his own left forearm. I've seen Od fight several times, so there's no need to circle around and feel him out. He, on the other hand, hasn't any idea how I fight. So he'll want to move around a little and get a sense of my strengths and weaknesses. Attack, then, swiftly and unexpectedly, he decided.

The two of them made sure their grips were secure and their feet firmly planted. Then Od grunted to indicate he was ready. Voden replied in kind.

Od began to circle slightly to his right, pushing on Voden's left arm to test his strength and balance. This was a classic, basic drill from the Thiodnuma, and the young Aesir put his plan of attack into effect instantly. He released Od's left arm, swung his right foot in and slightly to the right of the other boy's right, grabbed his right arm at the outside of the right shoulder with his own right, lowered his center of gravity by flexing his knees, and pulled sharply down and forward. With a squawk of surprise the Vanir fell over Voden's right leg and went crashing to the ground.

For a split second there was a stunned silence, then Yngvi

shouted with joy and several others joined him to cheer Voden on. Od rolled with the throw, getting as far from the Aesir as possible to avoid any attempt to pin him. He stood shakily and glared at Voden.

Slowly Od moved toward him, arms extended, ready to grapple again, but Voden wanted nothing to do with the usual rules of fighting. He felt wonderful and buoyant. I might lose this, he thought, but I'll show these damn Children of Audhumla that the Aesir are not to be trifled with.

Before Od could make contact, Voden stepped in suddenly and aimed a punch at the older boy's face. The Vanir managed to duck slightly, and the blow that would have hit him square in the mouth took him in the left eye instead. He staggered back. Voden waded in, his arms pumping, raining blows on Od. Two connected, one in the Vanir's stomach, the other on his nose. There was a roar from the crowd as Od's blood began to flow.

Od was far from finished, though. He was getting used to this crazy barbarian's wild style of fighting. Fending off a few more blows, he got ready for Voden to get close enough to grab. There! Instantly the young Vanir gripped his opponent's forearm and made a grab for his shoulder. In surprise the Aesir tried to step back. Od flowed right up to him and wound his right leg around Voden's left, pushing and throwing him backward.

Od stayed on top as Voden crashed to the ground. The boy from the plains wasn't a seasoned enough wrestler to remember to keep his head tucked in tightly, so the back of his head smashed into the hard earth of the courtyard. Dazed, his breath knocked out by Od's weight, Voden was barely aware of the lock the Vanir wove with his arms and legs. As he heard the crowd chanting "one . . . two . . ." he tried to wiggle free. Od's hold was unbreakable. "Three!" came the roar from the spectators.

Slowly, cautiously, as if unsure what his opponent would do, Od released his hold. Then he staggered up and back, watching warily as Voden sat and shook his head to clear it. The young Aesir looked at Od and said sarcastically, "Are you going to raise your arms in victory? Or aren't you sure you won?"

The Vanir flushed in anger, but stepped back as Voden stood. "Go on," Voden said. "You won. Raise your arms." Od looked at him, distrust flaring in his eyes. He took two quick steps back and raised his hands.

A silence greeted his gesture. Into the silence Voden said, "Congratulations, Vanir. Now wipe the blood from your face and tend to your eye. It's turning black already." With that, he turned and strode over to where Yngvi stood beaming. From the corner of his eye, he caught a glimpse of Freyja's face. The look that twisted it frightened him. He gripped Yngvi by the elbow and muttered, "Let's get out of here."

"I thought you had him, by damn. I really thought you had him. What in Beyla's lovely name happened, barbarian?" Yngvi and Voden were sitting up against the wooden palisade just outside the north gate. The Vanir woodsman had rounded up two amphorae of mead, and they were already half drunk.

"Knows mor'n me," Voden slurred. "Surprised 'im at first." He giggled. "Old Od'll have a beeeoootiful black eye to wear 'round for a while. He bleeds nice too."

Yngvi laughed. "Oh, that was wonderful! The look on his face was wonderful! As surprised a man as ever I've seen! I thought you said you didn't really know this fist fighting. Seems to me as you did all right for something you didn't know."

The young Aesir shrugged. "Tha's the Aesir way of fighting. Nothin' fancy. Just hit 'em where it hurts most. Since the balls are off-limits, go for the face and gut. No real style or system. Just hurt 'em. Tha's the Aesir way."

"Brawling." Yngvi nodded. "Bet you even gouge eyes when it's for real."

Voden shrugged again. "When it's real, only one person tells how the fight went. Whatever makes you that person is fine."

"Huh! Think as I like our way better. That thing you said about your grandfather, Clubhand or something. Was that true?"

The boy nodded. "True." He leaned back and closed his eyes. His voice took on a faraway, dreamlike tone, and he began to chant:

> "Buri gripped his ax tight,
>   glared across swift Iving,
>
> Smote the air all raging,
>   eyes ablaze with anger.

'Jotun skulls I'll smash now,
  spill their brains and blood out!

Let them learn my fury,
  leave no horseman living!'"

For a good half hour he went on, up and down, back and forth, weaving a glowing picture of that long-ago battle when Buri earned his name. When he'd finished, Yngvi sat silent for long minutes.

Finally the Vanir sighed. "Damn. That's some story, that is. Never heard anything like that. It...it almost seemed a song without music."

"Skalds have harps. They sing stories."

"By Beyla's golden balls, Voden, I almost think as I might like it in Asaheim. It...it must be so damn different. Oh, Vanaheim's fine, I guess. Couldn't live long without my forest and the hunt. Shit. Already getting a little anxious to be out of this town and away from these bossy women." He shuddered. "Make me nervous, they do, even now." He looked sharply at Voden. "Not afraid, mind you. Just...uneasy. Anyway, must be different in Asaheim. Damn different.

"That tale. You said Buri's your grandfather. Right?" Voden nodded. "Tha's strange, Voden, really strange. I mean, you knowing who your father's father is. Tha's weird, lad."

The Aesir looked up at him in surprise. "Wha's weird about that? Know my family back to Ask and Embla. Don't you?"

Yngvi shook his head. "Mother, yeah, grandmother. Uncles. But don' know who in Yggdrasil my father was, much less grandfather."

Voden sat upright and stared at his friend in dismay. "Don' know your father? Why...why, tha's impossible!"

"Don' know."

"Tha's crazy! You had to have a father! How could you not know who he is?"

The Vanir shrugged. "Could be almost anybody. Mos' kids are made 'tween the time when day and night are equal and when day begins to lose again. Women take anybody as comes along most of that time. Good fun for us. Makes it kind of hard to tell who the daddy is, though. Doesn't matter anyway. It's women as have the kids. Carry 'em around for nine months, they do. Then have 'em. Screaming and all. Even after that, kids stay with the women. Got to eat, got to. So what do men have to do with kids? One quick shot, tha's it. Mother's brothers closer in blood. Leas' he crawled out of the same place. Shit. Don't know who my own father was. You know your grandfather. Weird. Really weird," he mumbled. His voice ran down and he slumped over, falling asleep as the mead got the better of him.

Voden sat staring at Yngvi in horror. Not know who your father was? Not know? He felt suddenly sick. Standing, he stumbled a few steps and threw up. For several minutes he retched and retched. When he stopped, he could barely muster enough strength to walk back to where his friend lay, snoring loudly. Voden slumped down next to him. Not know your own father? His mind whirled and he closed his eyes. Not know?

The forest was very dark. Barely enough light to see where to put his feet as he crept slowly forward. Ahead he could make out a flickering glow. Fire in a clearing, he thought. He moved toward it.

Peering around one of the smooth, straight trees, he stared out into the round, open space. In the center was a fire. Around it women in black robes were dancing, hands linked. Before he could pull his head back, one of them saw him. Laughing and calling, they broke their dance and ran gaily toward him. Somewhere in the dark behind him he heard a snicker as he stepped into the light.

The women surrounded him, reaching out and touching his naked body, chattering excitedly, their eyes big and liquid, their mouths slightly parted, tongues rigidly pointing at him. Their hands fluttered over him like tiny white birds, landing here, there, everywhere, touching, stroking. He felt himself getting hard. In surprise he looked down. The women moaned happily and their hands flew more rapidly over his body, lightly stroking.

Suddenly they lifted him into the air and carried him toward the center of the circle. The fire was gone, and a woman sat there. He couldn't quite make out her face, because it kept shifting, but he knew it was Freyja—Vestla—Fiorgynn and many, many others.

She saw him and her breath began to come in hot little gasps. She reached out and the others pushed him toward her. She flickered, and the fire was there again. She flickered back,

*her mouth wide and smiling, her breasts thrust out, nipples
rigid, legs spread.*

*She held her arms out, her fingers reaching, clawlike, nails
long and red. The fire shone through her, hot and reaching,
reaching out for him with arms of red. Her mouth reached for
him, open, the teeth long and shining, tongue like red flame,
flickering. Her hands slipped around him, gently squeezing,
burning, red, hot, flickering.*

*He cried out hoarsely and tried to pull back. The women
holding him snickered like the thing in the dark and pushed
him toward the flames, the burning red mouth. He screamed
and struggled wildly, striking out. Ah, ah, the pain, the sweet
pain! He spasmed, hot fire pouring through him, the flames
licking, licking, reaching to devour him, hands holding and
stroking, stroking his naked body. Ah, ah, the warmth shot
from his body, hot and sticky. He screamed again, and the fire
flared up and overwhelmed him, burning everything to black,
black, black, soft warmth.*

Voden awoke with a start. It was night. The moon was in the
sky. He remembered the forest and sat up in terror. The fire.
The . . . the . . . Suddenly he felt it. Warm stickiness between
his legs. Trembling, he pulled out his loincloth to look. It was
white and thick and creamy

Yngvi opened one eye and peered at him sleepily. "Mmph,"
he grunted. "Now you're a man, barbarian." He rolled over
and went back to sleep.

For a long time Voden sat and stared off into the dark. There
is something wrong here. I'm missing something important
about Vanaheim, something I must know before I'm safe here.
He racked his brains, but the only idea he could come up with
was the realization that the mystery had something to do with
the way Freyja had looked after the wrestling match.

Her expression was that of a forest cat getting ready to
torture and kill its prey.

The finals for the championships of each quadrant took place
the next morning. There were four men left in the northwest.
Each had to wrestle all the others, two out of three falls winning,
the best overall record bringing victory.

Pushing the confusion of yesterday into the back of his mind, Voden watched the matches. People were unusually friendly toward him, especially the men. Several came up and clapped him on the shoulder, calling him "barbarian," yet somehow making it a compliment. Once he saw Od across the courtyard, but the older boy must have left almost immediately, because Voden was unable to find him when he went searching. Freyja was nowhere to be seen.

Voden studied the crowd as carefully as he did the wrestling. If anything, the smell of latent violence was stronger than ever. Both men and women were screaming during the matches now, their eyes wild with bloodlust. They wanted to see the loser hurt, not just beaten. Several women actually jumped one man who'd been thrown down with a body-jarring smash. They kicked and pummeled him, raking his bare skin with clawlike hands, leaving bloody tracks behind. Bleeding and battered, the man staggered off, his eyes wide with fear.

The sun was already a quarter of the way down toward the horizon when one of the combatants finally emerged triumphant. The crowd swept into the ring and lifted him to their shoulders, shouting and leaping about. In a body, they made for the street that ran toward the center of Folkvang. Voden, swept along in the press, had no choice but to follow.

The mob poured into Sessrymnyr at the same time that mobs carrying the other three quadrant champions arrived. The hall was filled with milling, howling people. In its center, calmly seated in the High Seat, Voden caught a glimpse of Fiorgynn, dressed in a filmy gown of pure white. The eight Disir were seated in their own chairs, wearing hooded robes of midnight black.

All four champions were carried to the head of the crowd and deposited on their feet in front of the Vanadis. She looked down at them and smiled. Then she rose and lifted her arms toward the ceiling. Silence fell throughout the hall.

"The day grows strong and virile," she chanted in a loud, high voice.

"Night waits," came the deep response from the eight cloaked Disir.

"The sun warms the land," she continued.

"Cold waits," they replied.

"Plants grow and flowers bloom."

"Death waits."

"It is the time of growing and life, of love and fecundity."

"Nothingness waits."

"I yearn. My body burns for a mate!"

"Burning devours."

"I long for lips to touch mine, for hands to feel the fullness of my breasts, for the thrusting pleasure of a mate!"

"Pleasure devours."

"Ah, ah, I seek a king. A king to lie with me and make me full of life!"

"Life devours."

"Is there one worthy of me? Is there one strong and virile enough to possess and satisfy me? Is there one?"

With a single voice the crowd roared back, "Yes!"

Fiorgynn stepped slowly and sinuously down from the High Seat to where the four men stood. She walked from one to the other, touching and stroking their bodies. The four quivered and moaned, barely able to contain themselves.

The Vanadis's eyes were wide and glowing now, her face flushed, her mouth open and round. She moved like a great cat, her full body almost visible through the soft, clinging gown. There was a sheen of sweat on her forehead and her upper lip.

Finishing her examination of the four, she stepped back up to the High Seat. Her glance smoldering, she looked down on them once again, her eyes caressing their limbs. "I would have all four of you," she purred, her voice husky with desire. "All four at the same time." She raised her eyes and swept the assembled mob. "But only the best, the most virile seed is good enough for the womb of the Vanadis!" she cried out in a great voice.

"Only the most virile!" howled the Disir in response.

"So," Fiorgynn continued, her voice quivering just slightly as she licked her lips, "you will come here, all four, tomorrow morning as the sun rises, and you will fight until it sets. He who wins"—her voice dropped into a deep growl—"will take me and be my king!"

The crowd roared their approval. Voden watched, stunned by the noise and the press of bodies. Everywhere he turned, the Vanir were touching each other, the women with their hands between the legs of the men, the men with their hands on the women's breasts. Faster than he could comprehend, they switched partners. Dizzy, faint with confusion, he wormed his way between them, making for the door. Several times wild-eyed women grabbed him and ran feverish hands over his body.

To his shame, he instantly responded, the hardness painful and cramped in his loincloth.

Finally he won his way clear. Leaving the noise and smell of human bodies behind, he walked swiftly up the north street and out the gate. He crossed the bridge over the moat and went on across the open area that surrounded Folkvang. Rather than enter the gathering dark that pooled within the forest, he turned to his left and made for the riverbank. There he stood for a long time, willing his heart to cease beating so wildly, gazing into the swirling, darkening waters of the Gunnthro.

Gradually his body calmed, but his thoughts refused to quiet down. They twisted and leaped, idea chasing idea, swooping in and out of his awareness. Fiorgynn's body, outlined by the white gown. The deep, menacing words of the black-robed Disir. The quivering bodies of the four champions. The writhing, blindly groping mob.

The sun set and darkness reached across the sky from behind him. He stood silent, willing the last remnant of the light to stay.

It left despite his prayers, and he found himself standing alone in the darkness.

XIII

THE sun was still a good hour and a half below the horizon when the servants woke Voden and Honir the next morning. Both boys were given clean white loincloths and told to put nothing else on. When they were ready, they left with the rest of the male members of Fiorgynn's household and entered Sessrymnyr by the northern door.

People were already beginning to fill the hall. The High Seat in the center of the cross was gone. In its place a circle was marked out with a thin chain of gold. Like those in the courtyards, the circle was about twelve feet in diameter. At eight points of the compass the eight chairs of the Disir were arranged. The Disir themselves, robed and hooded in black, were seated and waiting.

As Voden looked around, observing the growing crowd, he noticed that all the men were dressed the same as he and Honir were. The women wore sheer white gowns similar to the one Fiorgynn had appeared in the evening before.

The mood of the people was markedly different from the previous evening, however. They were quiet and subdued, for the most part sitting or walking with downcast eyes. No one touched or talked to his or her neighbor.

As usual for Folkvang, the women outnumbered the men. The ratio was better than usual, no more than two to one as opposed to the usual five or six to one, but the men were still a distinct minority. The newcomers who had swelled the ranks of the men were primarily young wrestlers from the forests. Voden recognized several he had seen fight. He looked everywhere but was unable to catch sight of Yngvi. Aside from the members of Fiorgynn's family, seated in privileged seats right up near the front, the young Aesir realized that no two men sat next to each other, or even behind or in front of each other. They were scattered throughout the crowd.

There was a stirring at each of the four doors, and the four champions entered. They too were dressed in white loincloths. Slowly, eyes down, heads humbly bowed, they walked toward the ring in the center of the hall.

Total silence fell over the multitude as the four reached the golden chair. The Disir stood, still facing inward. They raised their arms and chanted, "Enter now the magic circle. Enter now the eternal curve. Enter now the beginning with no end, the end with no beginning. Enter now the round of life and death and life."

The four crossed the line of gold and met in the exact center of the circle, the hall, the city. They turned outward, facing the cardinal points of the compass.

"This is the center," chanted the eight women in unison. "All comes from here, all returns. This is the womb of beginning, the tomb of ending. Tremble in fear and joy!"

A collective moan escaped the Vanir, and every man, woman, and child began to shake gently. Whether the moan was of pleasure or of fear, Voden couldn't decide.

The Disir began to chant again, the black-robed woman to the north beginning, answered by that on the south. The one on the northwest took up the response, and was followed by her sister at the southeast. Around and around the circle the litany ran.

"The sun is rising."
"The sun is setting."
"The sun grows mighty."
"The sun grows weaker."
"Warmth fills the air."
"Snow is coming."
"The earth is fertile."
"The earth lies frozen."

For several minutes the chant went on in the common tongue, then switched to the elder tongue. As near as Voden could tell, it was simply a repeat of what had already been said.

Then a strange thing happened. The chant stopped and a new sound filled the hall. At first it seemed like the sighing of the forest beneath the wind, or the sibilant rustlings of small creatures scurrying through underbrush. But as Voden listened he began to realize it was a language. It had an ancient feel, a sense of cities and temples long fallen and buried beneath forest mold, of people and places vanished into the mists of time. It sent shivers up and down his spine. He knew, somehow, that what he was hearing for the first time in his life was

nothing less than the original tongue, the first language ever
to fall from human lips. It was dark and deep, and his soul
quailed before its grim majesty.

The Disir returned to the common tongue and picked up a
different rhythm. Each spoke her part of the chant alone, beginning with the one on the north, then passing to the next one
counterclockwise.

> "In the beginning,
> nothing existed.
> There was no tree nor bush
> nor cooling stream;
> earth was unknown,
> and heaven above.
> Only Ginnungagap was.
> There was no grass.

> "Sun did not know her home,
> nor moon what strength she had,
> nor did stars know
> where they belonged.
> Vast and formless
> was the void.

> "Then Audhumla formed
> from swirling mist,
> the Nourisher took shape.
> And from her teats
> in frothing streams
> the milk of life began to flow."

The chant droned on, around and around the circle. It told
how Audhumla's breath condensed and formed solid land, how
drops of her milk then struck the land, giving rise to living
things. It went on to relate how the Nourisher, attracted by the
taste of salt, began to lick everything, implanting parts of her
own spirit in trees and bushes and rocks and animals, giving
birth to the Vettir, the gods that dwelled at the heart of every
object. Finally it revealed how, in licking two buds that had
fallen to the ground, Audhumla created the first Vanir.

Eventually this chant, too, came to an end. There was a
brief pause, as if everyone were gathering strength for what
was to follow. Then the eldest Disir threw her hands into the

air and cried out in a shrill, reedy old voice. "Rejoice, children of Audhumla, for your Vanadis will take a king!"

"Rejoice, rejoice!" they all cried back.

"Rejoice, Siblings of the Vettir, for he is mighty and virile and will fill her with life!"

"Rejoice, rejoice!"

Voden turned his attention to the crowd once more, letting the words of this new chant flow over and around him. A change was gradually taking place as the rite progressed. It was subtle at first, but with each phrase of the litany it grew and solidified.

The young Aesir had a difficult time identifying it. Not the same as the raw sexuality of the evening before, it still contained a strongly sensual undercurrent. More than that, there was a buoyant sense of joy that swooped and soared within it. Voden remembered the exhilaration he'd felt when he'd thrown Od in the ring. It was something like that, but much, much broader in scope. It seemed to encompass everything that lived and moved.

Joy and exuberant sensuality were only half of it. Grief and tears lay just beneath the surface, and deeper yet, despair and fear.

He shook his head, bewildered and overwhelmed. The currents, crosscurrents, and undercurrents of emotion that swept back and forth through Sessrymnyr were too much for an eleven-year-old boy to handle. Some, like hate and love, he recognized. Others he could only guess at or shrink back from as they stormed past.

The tension in the hall kept building and building until he thought his head would explode. His mind was wrenched first this way, then that, up, down, forward, backward. He felt his control slipping; his rational mind, exhausted, losing its grip. From deep within him forces began stirring, moving toward the light. Dark things, hidden, fettered, locked away, pushed down and back.

Dimly he heard the roar as the champions began to fight. Vaguely he realized he was on his feet, screaming and howling with the rest of the crowd; then even that awareness blinked out.

He shrieked and roared, frothed at the mouth, stamped his feet and raked the air with clawlike hands. One of the wrestlers smashed to the floor, blood spraying from his face as he hit. Voden almost choked with gleeful laughter. More! More! Blood!

Blood! The snap of an arm breaking brought paroxysms of joy. He bellowed and pounded on Honir's shoulder. Kill! Kill him!

Finally one man, his face bloody, stood alone and victorious in the center of the ring. His body was covered with a mixture of sweat, dirt, and blood. Wild-eyed, tongue lolling like that of a hunting wolf, he raised his hands and howled his triumph at the sky.

Suddenly Fiorgynn appeared inside the golden circle. A dead silence, heavy with fevered anticipation, fell on the mob as the champion saw her. A savage grin curved his lips, and he snarled. With one motion he ripped off his loincloth.

Fiorgynn cried out in a frantic voice, wordless yet filled with meaning. She tore the white robe from her body. For a second she stood naked before them, her breasts proud and heaving. Then, with a shriek that found instant response in the howl of the multitude, she flung herself into the champion's grasping arms. The two of them fell to the earth, making furious love with utter abandon.

Now the rest of the crowd began flinging off their clothes, grabbing the nearest partner, and falling to the floor of many-seated Sessrymnyr. Voden, the strip of white cloth in his hand, looked frantically for Freyja. He felt a hand on his shoulder and spun about.

It was Honir, his face a ghastly pale hue, his mouth twisted in fear, his eyes filled with terror. Voden stared at him blankly for a second, then began to turn away. The other boy grabbed him and slapped him hard across the face.

Like one awaking from a very deep sleep, the young Aesir blinked his eyes and shook his head. In a daze, he looked down at his own nakedness. With a gasp he took in the whole scene. A frightened moan, inaudible over the noise within the hall, escaped his lips.

Honir grabbed his elbow and began to pull him toward the door. Stepping over the writhing bodies of the Vanir, the two Aesir boys reached the north portal. Voden cast one last half-horrified, half-fascinated glance over his shoulder.

They ran then, ran until they reached the cool shade of the forest. They flung themselves down among the mossy roots of the trees and wept. Finally, drained of tears, they simply sat and stared at each other, not knowing what to say or do.

It was the usually silent Honir who eventually spoke. "What's going to happen to us, Voden?" he whispered. "What's going to happen?"

* * *

Dusk was settling over Folkvang before the two Aesir boys were brave and hungry enough to return to the city. As they walked through the north gate, everything seemed as it had always been. The Valkyrja on duty nodded to them, giving them the same vague, impersonal recognition the women warriors gave to everyone. People were going about their business as usual. Here and there the young wrestlers, once again dressed in normal Vanir attire, strutted about, chatting with friends and making eyes at the pretty girls who walked by. No one seemed to notice that the two were clad in nothing but their white loincloths.

Voden saw Yngvi down one of the cross-streets. The young forester waved but didn't come over, since he was busily engaged in a flirting match. The boy was just as happy. He wasn't sure he wanted to talk to any of the Vanir right now.

Relieved by the calm sense of normality that surrounded them, the two hurried to the men's hall. They put on their breeches and shirts, feeling more secure once their unaccustomed nakedness was covered.

Despite their original intention of not leaving the hall, curiosity soon got the better of them, and they ventured forth for a look around. They even managed to summon up enough courage to peep through one of the doors of Sessrymnyr. The High Seat was back in the center, and the golden circle had vanished. Things were neat and orderly, and there were no signs that anything out of the ordinary had taken place.

As always, they ate with the rest of the men in their own hall. Table conversation was about the weather, the state of the crops, and the usual trivia. No one mentioned the king, the rite, or anything the least bit atypical.

After finishing the meal Voden gestured to Honir, and the two of them left the hall. The night was warm and the moon cast a soft, misty light over everything. They found a dark corner at the northeastern edge of the men's hall and sat close together.

For a few moments Voden was as silent as Honir. Then he muttered, "I don't understand. They act like nothing happened. I mean, it was so big, so . . . so . . . How can they act like it didn't happen?" Honir shook his head in mute agreement.

"Something strange happened, Honir. I know it. Oh, I don't just mean the sex part. That was weird enough. Something else happened." His voice dropped to a hoarse whisper as he said, "Something magical. That's what took place. Magic."

"There was power loose," responded Honir, matching the other boy's whisper. Quickly the two looked around as if afraid someone or something was listening. "It was good power, the power of light, but it was dark too."

Voden nodded vigorously. "Yes, yes. You sensed it, then. It was odd. Like... like something huge in a bright light. Something that cast a very black shadow."

A thoughtful look came over Voden's face. "The Disir must be sorceresses, Honir. They must be deep in the Seidar-magic." His voice dropped to a frightened whisper again. "They must sacrifice to dark Svarthofdi! That was the original tongue they chanted in part of the time. I know it!"

Honir's eyes went wide with wonder. "The original tongue? You heard it? How do you know? How *could* you know?"

"I...I...can't say I just do. When they began to chant they used the common tongue, then they repeated the same thing in the elder tongue. The third time was different. They were saying something new, and they said it in the original tongue. I know it! I could *feel* it!"

The other boy looked long and silently at Voden. Finally he spoke, his voice so soft that his friend could barely catch the words. "I heard nothing, Voden. Only the common and elder tongues, and a sound like the forest makes in the evening when the wind blows softly from the east. It wasn't a language, only a sound. If... if you heard more, it can only mean one thing." His voice quavered slightly and dropped even lower, an undertone of fear weaving between his words. "It can only mean one thing." He paused as if gathering courage to speak, then uttered a single word. "Vilmeid."

A sudden chill ran up Voden's spine. He tried to speak, to say something to stop Honir from speaking, but the words froze in his throat. "Vilmeid," Honir repeated, more loudly this time. "Yes, I'll say it. Voden, you've been touched by Vilmeid, god of the Galdar-power!" He shuddered. "I...I fear you. And fear for you."

"Vilmeid." Voden spoke the name, the weight of it on his tongue almost choking him. "Vilmeid," he muttered again, finding it easier the second time. "Vil..." He felt Honir's hand on his arm and heard the boy's urgent whisper. "Don't, Voden! Don't invoke that name anymore!"

They sat without speaking for a long time, each wrapped

in his own thoughts. Honir finally broke the silence with a sigh. "If you heard the original tongue, if you recognized it as such, it can only mean that the Galdar-power is in you. It's probably always been there, way down deep, sleeping. Probably would have lain there forever if something hadn't disturbed it. Something has, and now there's nothing you can do. It'll grow. Especially here." He shook his head. "This place reeks of Seidar-magic. They stir dark things up. They're the ones that woke the Galdar-power in you. It was the Disir."

Voden stared at the ground, his expression suddenly bitter and angry. "We're a long way from home, Honir. A long way. In more than distance. Being here will change us." He looked up. There was a desperation in his glance. "Already I'm different. Different forever. I know I've always been a *little* different. Dark eyes instead of blue. The blood of Prin in my veins. A little different.

"Still, I always felt I was truly an Aesir. I lived and thought like an Aesir. How could I be anything else? Yet now I no longer live in the Aesir way, and how much longer will I be able to think like one? I learn the elder tongue. I study the Thiodnuma. I practice wrestling. Something new and dark and frightening is awake and stirring within me. Now this...this Galdar-power!

"I'm frightened, Honir," he said in a small, pleading voice. "What am I going to do?"

Honir sat up straight. "Do?" he said, his voice suddenly firm. "You *are* an Aesir, Voden. Whatever you say, whatever happens, deep inside at your very core, *you are an Aesir*. You're Borr's son, Buri's grandson. What'll you do? You'll do what any Aesir does. You'll fight. By Fornjot, *you'll fight*!"

"How, Honir? How can I fight myself?"

Neither boy had an answer. They sat, staring wordlessly up at the night sky. Eventually they fell asleep.

The next day Yngvi came looking for Voden. The young forester had a pack on his back. Voden could see that several amphorae of mead were stuffed into it.

"I've come to say good-bye, barbarian," Yngvi began. "I've already spent too much time in this city. I'm heading back to my woods." He shifted anxiously from foot to foot, as if he could hardly wait to be off.

"Look, Voden. Should you ever find the urge in you, come

visit Yngvi sometime. Can't offer you mead or women as is in Folkvang. What I can offer you is freedom of the hunt and the companionship of good forester lads. And no damn women to boss you around!"

The Aesir boy smiled and held out his hand. "Thanks, Yngvi. I might like that. And thanks for the wrestling lessons. I guess I wasn't the best student, losing like that to Od."

Yngvi gripped his hand firmly and held it for a moment, looking deep into Voden's eyes. "Aw, you did me proud, barbarian. By Beyla, with a few more lessons I think you really could have trounced him good!

"Listen. I talked to Frodar. He's a friend of mine for all that he lives in Folkvang and works in leather. He's old now, but once he was a great wrestler. The best. He likes the look of you, barbarian, and he has a score or two to settle with the Disir. So the long and short of it is, he's agreed to continue the lessons and make a real wrestler of you. Why, lad, by next year when I come back, you could end up king yourself!" Yngvi laughed heartily at his joke and at the look on Voden's face. He winked. "Not too keen on being king, eh? Nor is Yngvi. But wrestling — ah, that's worth doing for its own sake!

"Remember, now. If you get bored around all these beautiful women and all this fine mead, come look me up. South along the River Hrid to its second bend east. Then dead west. Ask anyone."

He dropped Voden's hand and turned to go. Suddenly he spun back and grabbed the young Aesir by the shoulders, peering intently into the boy's surprised eyes. "Be careful, barbarian. Tread softly. The ice is thinner and the water deeper than you know. It was a perilous thing to do, to send a boy to the Vanadis. Keep your balance and watch for trick throws." He gave Voden's shoulders a quick squeeze with his hands, then turned once more and began to walk swiftly in his long, forester's stride toward the south gate.

Voden stood and watched him go. As Yngvi reached the gate, he turned and raised a hand in final salute. The boy returned the gesture.

For a long time after the Vanir had disappeared, the young Aesir remained, gazing blankly off into the distance. He'd never felt so lonely in his whole life.

XIV

IN a few days most of the newcomers had left Folkvang. The only ones staying were those who had moved in to live with some woman. Things rapidly returned to normal. Every morning Voden was drilled by Geirahod in the techniques of the Thiodnuma. After the midday meal he spent several hours with a woman who was teaching Honir and him to speak the elder tongue. In the late afternoon when the others were resting, he stole away to visit Frodar, Yngvi's friend and his new wrestling instructor.

While most things were as they had been before, several things were markedly different. First of all, the attitude of the women toward the men was almost the reverse of what it had been. Now it was the men who seemed in charge. The women catered and deferred to them in almost everything. Even Freyja was meek and mild when she spoke to him.

The most amazing transformation, though, was in Fiorgynn. Most of the time she stayed in her own hall with her new king, shut away from the world. When she did venture forth, she was always in his company, clinging to his arm and gazing up into his face with adoring eyes. She generally looked disheveled, as if she had just risen from her bed.

The second big change was in the way the men acted. They were far louder and more boisterous than ever before, approaching the level common in Asgard. They were constantly demanding this or that from the fawning women, who rushed to satisfy their every whim. The king, whose name was Synyr, set the tone for the rest. Throughout the day Voden could hear him shouting his demands.

One thing that perplexed Voden was the fact that the Disir seemed to have vanished. Before, the eight women were always hurrying here and there about Folkvang, occupied with the business of the Distingen. Now they were gone. Voden hadn't caught even a passing glimpse of any of them since the proclaiming of the king in Sessrymnyr. He supposed they were simply keeping within the walls of their four halls. Though he was curious, he remembered Freyja's warning and decided it would be best not to go and check.

The young Aesir was happy they were absent, for he associated them with the awakening of his Galdar-power. The less he saw of the Disir, the better, he decided.

The summer passed that way. Long, warm, sunny days, as identical as beads on a string. The blandness of it lulled Voden and Honir, putting their worst fears to rest. The terror and bewilderment they had experienced at the summer solstice slowly faded into the background. Voden began to wonder if it had really all happened the way he remembered it. Only an occasional nightmare brought the experience back to haunt him. Even those were becoming fewer and further between. There was no sign of the Galdar-power stirring anymore. He began to hope it was all in the past, a fluke that could never happen again.

Then the days began to grow shorter and the nights longer and colder. Once again, things began to change.

It was a gradual change: so gradual, in fact, that neither of the two Aesir boys noticed it until a few days before the autumnal equinox, when, for the second time in the circle of the year, the light and dark divided the day evenly.

At first it was nothing but a tension in the air, something impalpable, impossible to define. The men were demanding less, the women responding more slowly, more grudgingly. On two occasions Voden saw Fiorgynn walking alone in the courtyard of the royal complex. She looked thoughtful and pensive. The boy feared to approach and break into her reverie.

Then on the equinox itself the Disir reappeared. In a body, the eight black-clad women shuffled through the streets of Folkvang, chanting softly in the elder tongue. From baskets woven of some dark reed they scattered dead flowers. Voden watched from a distance, the tone of the chant making his skin prickle.

The other men of Folkvang watched too. As the Disir passed they stopped whatever they were doing, came to the doors of the halls, and stared wordlessly at the chanting figures. For moments after the eight passed, the men stood with their faces wooden and expressionless, their eyes hooded. Then with a shake of the head and a softly muttered curse, they returned to their work, but not before the slightest look of fear flickered deep within their eyes.

The next day Voden could swear there were fewer men in the city. In the afternoon when he went to practice with Frodar, he noticed that one of the foresters was missing. The man had been living with a pretty young woman who was beginning to swell with child. He asked Frodar, but got only a sour look and a shrug for an answer.

By harvest time the women were clearly back in charge again. More men came from the forest to help get the crops in, but they were silent and unwilling to talk. There was a wild, almost trapped look in their eyes. As soon as the job was finished, they strode off into the green shadows, moving as quickly as if they feared pursuit.

Like all the rest of the women, Freyja had undergone another transformation. The meek and mild girl of the summer had been replaced by a haughty, sarcastic, hostile creature. She sneered at everything the Aesir lad said, calling him "barbarian" in a tone filled with contempt. She began to play pranks on him again, but they now took on a nasty character quite unlike those of the spring. Once he found a dog turd floating in his cup at dinner. Another time a rock barely missed his head as he rounded the corner of a hall.

Even Geirahod began to treat him more harshly. Nothing he did seemed to satisfy her any longer. He began to stumble through his drills, his confidence destroyed by her constant criticism.

The trees were a blaze of color, and the first frosts had killed the last flowers of summer, when it all came to a head. One evening after dinner Voden and Honir walked out of the men's hall to find Freyja and several of her friends waiting. Voden nodded a mildly polite greeting and began to walk on by. The girl stuck her foot out and tripped him, sending him sprawling.

Slowly Voden rose and dusted himself off. He refused to raise his eyes to Freyja's until he had completed what he was doing, despite the fact he knew she was waiting, glaring at him with barely repressed fury. Finally losing her temper she snarled, "Look at me, barbarian!"

The young Aesir looked up, his eyes locking with hers. A slight shock went through him. The hostility and anger in her gaze shook him to his core.

Freyja's lip curled with disdain. "You're filthy," she said.

"You smell, like all your kind. Why don't you go back home and sleep with the cattle where you belong? I can't stand the sight or stink of you!" She spat, hitting the leg of his breeches just above his boot.

Voden was too stunned to reply. He stood there, his face blank with surprise, his mind whirling in bewilderment. The girl took another step toward him. "I should throw you out of Folkvang myself," she said. Behind her, the other girls muttered their agreement. "You're not fit to walk our streets. Scum! Cow shit! Barbarian!"

Unexpectedly her foot came shooting up and out, hitting him square in the solar plexus. He staggered back, gasping and struggling for breath. Freyja pressed forward, her other foot swinging in an arc for his head. It caught him on the right side of the forehead, snapping his head back with an explosion of pain that blinded and dazed him. Before he could even think, a third kick smashed into his groin. With a cry of agony he crumpled to the ground and began to lose consciousness.

"Cattle shit," he heard her say as the darkness reached for him. "Barbarian cattle shit. He studied the Thiodnuma for a whole summer and doesn't know how to defend himself." Her voice droned on, reviling him. But he stopped listening as the blackness overwhelmed his mind.

They raised him up before them on a rock. He was wearing a golden robe, neatly worked with silver threads in a design of serpents biting their own tails.

One by one they approached on their hands and knees. They bowed again and again, then slowly, humbly rose and reached beneath his robe. When they touched him, they shivered with ecstasy, then fell to the ground, moaning and thrashing in pleasure.

One stepped out of the dark, hooded, silent. She flowed forward like a stalking forest cat, face and eyes hidden. No bowing, no crawling, she approached and reached him. Her hand shot out, parting his robe, stretching out to grasp him with strong fingers, pulling, squeezing.

He cried out in pain. The hooded one grew suddenly tall and dark. Green eyes glowed forth from deep within the hood. Her fingers squeezed, and he felt himself go limp. With a cry of victory she reached out with her other hand and ripped the golden robe from his body, exposing his nakedness to them all.

*They shrieked with laughter to see his boyish form, pointed
their skinny fingers at him and laughed, their mouths open,
moist and dark, deep, deep. He tried to pull back, tried to twist
away, but the hooded one held him fast, trapped in her scrawny,
clawlike hand. She jerked suddenly, trying to rip him apart.
He screamed and—*

Voden came to with a start. Honir was there, looking down,
fear and worry distorting his face. Another man also stood over
him, his eyes haunted, his face tense, his mouth both grim and
frightened.

The young Aesir sat up slowly. He could taste the vomit in
his mouth. The front of his shirt was covered with it. The kick
in the groin, he thought blearily. His head ached horribly.

Honir placed his hand behind Voden's back to steady his
friend. "Take it easy," he muttered. "Just sit until you're ready
to get up. No hurry."

"I saw it all," he heard the other say. "Saw everything. That
little bitch."

Voden looked up again. The speaker was Synyr, the king.
The man knelt next to him. "That bitch. She used the Thiodnuma against you," he said.

"Huh," the Aesir grunted. "Shoulda done better. I know
enough to fight her by now. Why didn't I do better? Arms and
legs felt like lead." His head was clearing now, the pain re-
ceding both there and in his groin. With the help of Honir and
Synyr he managed to stand. "Don't understand," he muttered
again. "I know enough to beat her. I'm sure of it. Why didn't
I use it?"

"Woman magic," Synyr responded. "Woman magic. They
can weaken you with a glance, shit, a word. Turn you from a
stud into a limp nothing." Holding him up on either side, Honir
and the king led Voden around the men's hall to the northeast
corner. Once there, they all sat.

"Thanks," Voden said to Synyr when they were settled. The
young man waved away his gratitude. "I . . . I've never met
you before. Not really. I'm Voden. This is Honir."

"I know." The king nodded. "The two Aesir hostages. Not
hard to tell you're not Vanir. They're getting to you, too, but
you still walk too tall for this time of the year to be Vanir."

"You . . . you're the king. The best wrestler in Vanaheim.
I . . . I saw you win. And . . ." The boy couldn't continue.

"And saw me take Fiorgynn," Synyr completed. "Yeah, her and about a dozen others that day. Been doin' it ever since too. Bet I've made a good ten babies, by the Vettir! Shit, that's all I've been doing for the last couple of months.

"Except not so much anymore," he continued, his voice beginning to sound worried. "Now I can't . . . I mean, sometimes I have trouble, you know, getting it up." His voice dropped to a whisper. "Sometimes lately, no matter what they do, it won't go up. Shit."

"Is . . . is that what you do in the hall all day?" Voden asked, his eyes wide with wonder.

Synyr shrugged. "What else is there for a king to do? I did 'em all. Fiorgynn and all the rest. All summer, as soon as I'd do one, the next one'd be at me. Shit, it was terrific! All day, all night. Damn, you need to be top wrestler in Vanaheim to last through that!"

His eyes grew clouded with worry again and he paused. "But since fall, you know, I've been having problems. Just little ones. Only now they're getting worse. Can't get it up as often. They keep demanding. I mean, they always want it, and shit, I can only do my best. What do they expect? The days are getting shorter, what do they expect?" His voice had dropped into a strange, whining mutter.

Voden stared at the king. "What happens when you can't do it?"

The man looked at him, a veiled fear deep in his eyes. "It's not my fault. I did 'em all summer. I made ten babies. At least ten. Not Fiorgynn. She doesn't have babies, except once in a while. Takes things. But the others, the other women. I made 'em all pregnant. What do they want?"

The young Aesir stared at Synyr, not knowing what to say. The fear in the king's eyes flared up suddenly. He leaned forward and grasped the boy's arm in a painful grip. His voice strained out of his mouth. "What do they want? I've given them everything. Every one of 'em, again and again." A whimper sounded deep in his throat. "Can't do any more. Won't get up like it used to. I'm trying. I'm trying!

"What if it goes completely limp?" he murmured as if talking to himself. "What then? What'll they do? There's so many of 'em and only one me. They have such sharp knives, such sharp knives."

"What . . . what do you mean?" Voden asked, his voice heavy with sudden dread.

Synyr leaned urgently forward. "I'm afraid, Aesir," he said in a hoarse whisper. "I'm afraid. They have such sharp knives. What'll they do if I can't get it up? What'll they do?"

Suddenly the young man stood and looked around wildly. "She'll be looking for me! Fiorgynn'll be looking for me. Wanting me to . . . Shit. What if I can't get it up? What'll they do? They've got such sharp knives," he moaned in terror. With a muffled groan he turned and ran off toward the hall where the Vanadis lived.

Voden and Honir sat in the dusk and looked at each other. Neither knew what to say. When it grew totally dark, the two Aesir boys rose without a word and went into the men's hall. They didn't sleep well that night.

As the days grew shorter and the winter solstice approached, the situation in Folkvang got worse. More men abandoned the city, including some of those who had been there in the spring when the two Aesir had arrived. The rest stayed indoors, out of sight.

One morning Voden was awoken by the sound of weeping. He and Honir slipped into their clothes and crept to the door of the hall. The other men of the Vanadis's household stayed in their beds, ignoring the sound, feigning sleep.

Voden opened the door a crack and peered out into the snow-filled courtyard. There, gathered in the predawn gloom, was a group of women. They were dressed in black, their faces smeared with ashes. Each was carrying a bundle of wheat stalks, the heads empty, the grain already threshed from them. All wept softly and piteously.

As the sun rose over the eastern treetops and shot its first light westward, the pitch and volume of the women's wailing rose until it filled the courtyard. The door to the Vanadis's hall was flung open, and Fiorgynn, followed by a worried-looking Synyr, came out to the crowd.

Fiorgynn, dressed in a plain shift of brown, her hair loose and tousled, raised her arms up to the sky and cried out in a loud voice, "Oh, what is this dismal sound I hear? Oh, what is this wailing I hear? Oh, what is this crying I hear? Oh, what is this sadness I hear?"

The volume of the weeping rose even higher. The women began to strike their bodies with their fists. Some clawed their own faces or arms, drawing thin lines of red on their skin.

"Is this the void that weeps?" Fiorgynn asked.

"Yes, yes, this is the void," moaned the massed women.

"Is this the Nourisher, Audhumla, that weeps?"

"Yes, yes, this is Audhumla," came the reply.

"Is this the earth, the sky, the waters, the world that weeps?"

"Yes, yes, this is the earth, the sky, the waters, the world that weeps."

"Are these the Children of Audhumla who weep?"

"Yes, yes, these are the Children of Audhumla who weep."

"Why do you weep, children of Audhumla?"

"We weep for the sun, the sun who is dying."

"Why do you weep, Children of Audhumla?"

"We weep for the warmth, the warmth that is dying."

"Why do you weep, Children of Audhumla?"

"We weep for the king, the king who is dying."

Synyr's head snapped up sharply on hearing that line, his expression stunned, his eyes frightened. Voden saw dark circles beneath the young man's eyes. The king's mouth worked, as if he were trying to force a denial past his lips. Nothing came out.

"Why do you weep, Children of Audhumla?" continued Fiorgynn.

"We weep for our men, our men who have left us."

"My sisters, my daughters, you weep for the sun, the warmth, the king, your men. What would you have me do?"

"Someone must pay for this loss. Someone must pay for our tears."

"My sisters, my daughters. Who must pay for this loss? Who must pay for your tears?"

"The king! The king! The king!" they all howled.

So swiftly that Synyr had no time to react, Fiorgynn shoved him, hard, propelling him into the midst of the crowd. He stumbled and nearly fell, catching himself at the last moment. One of the weeping women closest to him raised her bundle of wheat stalks and hit him with it. "The king must pay!" she cried as she struck. Others pushed forward with the same cry, hitting at Synyr with their bundles.

The women swarmed around the king. Synyr stood as if rooted to the spot. The beating he was taking from the wheat stalks couldn't have been very painful. The blows weren't even powerful enough to raise welts. Yet he winced and grimaced, groaned and whimpered, as if he were receiving a thorough drubbing. Once he turned his head to avoid a blow in the face and Voden caught a look at his eyes. They were strange and wild, both blank and frightened at the same time. The most overwhelming emotions the young Aesir could read in them were bewilderment and hopelessness. The great wrestler, the champion of all Vanaheim, the fighter who had killed two men in his rise to the top, stood helpless and defeated while a mob of weeping women struck him with wheat stalks. Then, unable to stand it any longer, he broke down and began to cry. He buried his face in his hands and stumbled, his body shaking with sobs, back into the Vanadis's hall.

The crowd of women let him go. Slowly their weeping stopped. For long moments complete silence reigned in the courtyard; then it was split by a muffled wail of lonely fear, torn from the throat of the hopeless man weeping alone within Fiorgynn's hall.

"The king has paid," Fiorgynn said quietly.

"The king has paid," the women answered.

"The king is dying," Fiorgynn continued.

"The king is dying," the crowd responded. "Soon, our Vanadis, it will be your turn to weep."

"Soon it will be my turn to weep."

"Who will pay then?" the women asked.

Without answering, Fiorgynn turned and walked slowly back into her hall. The crowd waited until she was out of sight, then began to disperse, shuffling out of the square in every direction.

When the square was once more empty, Voden slipped out of the men's hall. He walked to the center of the open space, to the place where Synyr had stood. Scattered everywhere were the little broken bundles of wheat stalks.

In the snow he saw the footprints of the king. This, he thought, is where he was when they struck him. He placed his own feet directly in the prints. Looking up, he saw the sun just clearing the rooftop of the easternmost building in the complex. The light of it shone direct and bright in his eyes. He looked away.

Gazing down at his fists, he realized they were tightly clenched. He loosened them, letting the fingers slowly unfold. Equally slowly he let the tension in his mind unfold, then looked carefully at what lay there.

During the ceremony, he had felt something stir deep within. It had been in response to the look on Synyr's face, the look of utter helplessness and hopelessness. Now the thing that had stirred hardened and took form. Perhaps it was a manifestation of the Galdar-power. Perhaps not. He didn't care. All he knew was that something had been decided. Not consciously by him, but by whatever it was that moved within him. He didn't understand the full extent of the decision. He knew only that it included an ironfast resolution never to let happen to him what had happened to Synyr.

It was only now that Voden realized that what had happened to the king *had* been happening to him. The atmosphere that pervaded Folkvang had begun to change him, make him act like the other men. He had cringed and slunk along, trying to avoid the glance or notice of the women. He had allowed himself to be so sapped of confidence and self-esteem that Freyja had beaten him easily. And when the women had wept in the square now and demanded that the king pay, he himself had felt the burden of guilt.

No more. The look in Synyr's eyes had snapped something in him, loosened some bond, let some tethered thing free. The Galdar-power? he wondered again. The gift of dread Vilmeid? It could well be. The Galdar-power was the other side of the Seidar-magic, the light to its dark, the noon to its midnight. Only men had it, though few enough wanted it. There was a price that had to be paid. . . . He shuddered. If it gave him strength against the all-pervasive might of the Seidar-magic here in Vanaheim, then perhaps that price was worth it. Perhaps.

He turned his mind from such dark thoughts. Best not dwell on it. It will come soon enough. For now, it had shored him up before he fell totally under the control of the women of Folkvang.

Realizing that he was ravenously hungry, he turned and strode back to the men's hall. Two pairs of eyes watched him as he went. One rejoiced to see him walk proudly, head held high as befit the son of Borr Skullcracker. The other worried and wondered just what had been brought into their midst.

A week and a half later Voden and Honir were called into the presence of the Vanadis. They went to see her in her hall. Synyr was there, sitting on a bench by the door, gazing dully at the morning sun. He nodded vaguely to them as they came in. They avoided his eyes.

Fiorgynn smiled down at them from her High Seat. "In three days," she said, her voice soft and friendly, "you will leave Folkvang to return to Asaheim for the eight days surrounding the winter solstice. This is as agreed with your father, Voden. My sons will return to Folkvang during that time."

Voden looked up at her. "Yes, Vanadis. I remember. At the end of the eight days we will return."

"That is correct." She paused for a moment, as if considering. "I will send gifts to Borr Skullcracker, Voden, and I will gift both you and Honir, for I am most pleased with the two of you. I have heard you both do well in your lessons, and that you, Voden, already speak the elder tongue with surprising facility. The blood of Prin is an advantage to you, my son."

The Aesir boy bowed his head at the compliment. "My mother, the lady Vestla, will be pleased to hear that you think so." As he looked up at her once more, he caught the slight flicker of doubt that passed deep within her eyes. Yes, damn you, he thought, Vestla is my mother, not you. I am her son, not yours! A bland smile hid his feelings.

The Vanadis nodded in dismissal. "I wish you a good, safe journey. I understand the snow is not deep, so it should be an easy one."

Both boys bowed to her and left.

Outside, as Voden had expected, Freyja and her friends were waiting. Honir froze as he saw them, but Voden kept walking, head down, as if he hadn't noticed them.

He was almost to Freyja when she spoke. "We're sending you packing, cattle shit. Back to pick up fresh lice in your foul hall." Voden kept walking, his head down, shoulders hunched. The girl was furious that he didn't respond. She stepped directly in his way.

Without hesitating or breaking his stride, he walked right into her right side. His right foot swept up and back, catching her behind the knee. At the same instant his right hand struck her left shoulder and his left grabbed her left sleeve and jerked down.

With a squawk of surprise, Freyja was slammed on her back into the snow. Voden was on her before she could move. He took a big wad of snow and stuffed it in her open mouth, smearing the excess around her face. "Here, little forest cat," he said softly, "have a nice taste of snow. Your mouth is always so sour, perhaps this will sweeten it."

Standing suddenly, he looked down at the sputtering girl, then up at her friends. "Won't one of you help her to her feet?

Nasty, smelly, cattle-shit barbarians lack the manners." None of them moved.

Freyja struggled up to her knees. Before she could rise any higher, Voden kicked her gently on the shoulder and sent her sprawling again. "Stay that way, Freyja, my dear. That's the way I want to remember my little forest cat while I'm home in Asgard among people."

Voden turned. With Honir following, he strode across the square to the men's hall.

DARK EMPIRE

XV

SURT slammed the ancient tome shut with a resounding thump. From where he sat sharpening his sword, Jormungand looked up in surprise. The slender man stood and began to pace the room, his eyes alight with excitement. The Serpent had never seen him like this.

"The key, Jormungand, the key! I think I've found it!"

The giant warrior looked blankly at his master.

"Yes, Serpent, I believe I've found what I've been looking for these many years!" Surt chuckled and rubbed his hands together with glee. "Soon, ah, ah, soon now the Sons of Muspell will bend their knees to me! To me, Surt, the Black One! The despised apprentice who was thrown out by his master! The common felon who stole to live, was caught, and contemptuously condemned to die! The raider who preyed on the caravans along the Great Route as it passed through the Twisted Lands! The wounded, dying castoff Borr left to perish on the Vigrid! The third-class wizard who practiced only the lowly Kishpu sorcery! Soon, soon they will quail before me! All of them! All!"

The slight man stopped and spun around to fix Jormungand with his wild glare. "For long years I have labored, learning minor spells, binding simple Gallas-demons to me, Warding against as many of the Utukku- and Saghulhaza-demons as possible. Slowly I have built my power. Always my ultimate goal seemed infinitely beyond me.

"For know, Serpent, that I seek nothing less than to be the Ellilutu, the Sovereign of Heaven, the Overlord of Muspellheim!"

Jormungand's head snapped up, his eyes staring in shocked amazement. "The . . . the . . . Ellilutu?" he stammered. "But . . . but . . . that's impossible! Bel Enlil is the Overlord. He holds the Tupsimati, the Tablets of Destiny. He is Patesi of Nippur, Lagash, and Ashur. By Nergal, Surt, you're insane! Enlil has

161

incredible power! He controls mighty demons and vast armies besides!" His voice dropped to a whisper. "Some even say he lays claim to the title of Nunamir."

Surt barked out a sudden sharp laugh. "I know all about Bel Enlil and his consort, Ninlil. I know of his castle, the mighty, mountainlike Ekur, that rises above the center of wide-spread Nippur. I know more about Enlil than does anyone in the world. I have studied him carefully, using many means, watching his every move as head of the Anunnaki, the council of seven Sons that rules Muspellheim. I have seen and noted the rivalries, the struggles, the unceasing battle for power among Enlil, Bel Marduk, and Bel Enki. I have observed how Bel Adad, our very own Patesi, plays all ends against the middle and hopes the three will destroy each other to leave him the victor. And, Serpent"—his voice dropped as Jormungand's had—"I can tell you that Enlil *is* the Nunamir!"

The huge warrior shuddered. "Yet you would match yourself against him? That's sheerest insanity!"

Surt nodded, a slight smile flickering across his thin lips. "Now, yes. It would be insane to attack now. I'm not ready yet. First I must become one of the Sons, become a member of the Anunnaki. Only from the inside may I achieve what I must."

Jormungand snorted in derision. "A Son? You? Best attack Enlil with a dirk and the smallest Gallas-demon you can summon. Get it over with."

The other man gave him a long, considering look. "Hmm. Perhaps it would seem that my ambitions are impossible. Perhaps. Only because you know so little." Surt paused, as if deciding. "Yes, yes, perhaps you should know more. It might make you a more effective servant. Yes.

"Very well, then," he continued as he pulled up one of the two chairs in the small, cramped room where they lived, "it is time I told you something of what I plan." He gestured with his hand, taking in their surroundings. "This," he said, "is far beneath us, even now. I am no mere novice wizard incapable of calling up more than a pathetic Gallas-demon. I have greater allies, Lamashtu for one, as you know. This room, this guise of weakness, is to misdirect my true enemy, Bel Adad."

The slender man chuckled to see Jormungand's surprise. "Yes, faithful Serpent, Adad is my chosen adversary, the first major step in my rise to power. I will defeat him and replace him to become the Patesi of Maqam Nifl and Borsippa; then I will hold his spot on the Anunnaki. His magical drum, the Lilissu, will be mine to use when I wish to call up the Storm Demons. Teshub will come at my command, and Resheph, and Pazuzu, and Rimmon. Ishkur, the chief of them all, will do my bidding. Ninurta of the stormy south wind will heed my every demand. Adad's magical ax will slaughter my enemies. You, faithful Serpent, you will be in command of the soldiers of Maqam Nifl and Borsippa to forge them into a mighty army fit to challenge that of any of the other Sons."

"They'll never accept an upstart," Jormungand protested. "You're not one of them."

Surt looked amused. "The Sons respect power, raw power. Anyone powerful enough to defeat one of the Patesi automatically becomes one himself. Bel Marduk is an example. Long before either of us was born, Marduk was a common soldier, the head of Enlil's personal guard. He was a mighty warrior, Serpent, one of the greatest ever. Enlil used him to defeat Kingu, who was then the Ellilutu and Patesi of Muspell. Through a masterful combination of dire magic and cold steel, Enlil prevailed. Marduk wrested the Tupsimati, the Tablets of Destiny, from Kingu's very hands and bore them in triumph to his master.

"In the process, something happened to Marduk. Perhaps some of the power that resides in the Tupsimati rubbed off on him, or perhaps he opened the Tablets and read some of the True Names inscribed there. No one knows. In any case, Marduk demanded that Enlil give him the lordship of Muspell as a reward for his invaluable service. At first Enlil demurred, but the other Sons were worried over the vast power Enlil had accumulated and feared he would add the armies of Muspell to his own forces and thus become invincible. So they backed Marduk's claim in the Anunnaki and forced Bel Enlil to agree. Thus Marduk rose to become Patesi and one of the Sons of Muspell. Now he competes on the same level with Enlil and Enki for the Ellilutu."

"Why pick Adad to fight, Surt? Surely Nannar, or better yet Utu, would be a weaker, easier foe. Or even ancient An, the eldest Son."

"Yes, yes, so it would seem. Take Utu, for example. Patesi of Sippar and of Larsa, the only city in all Muspellheim to survive the disaster of the First Dark Empire. Yes, Utu would *seem* the weakest of the Sons. He rules small cities, sparsely settled lands. Of all the demons of the netherworld, the dark

and fearful Kur, he controls only one, the fire demon Nusku.
On the Anunnaki he sides with no one, withdraws almost com-
pletely from the power struggle among Marduk, Enki, and
Enlil. None of the great books of magic are his.

"I admit, at first I thought of him. Yet, something bothered
me. I quake now to think how closely I escaped utter destruction!

"Utu, despite his seeming innocuousness, is perhaps the
most dangerous of all the Sons! The others don't ignore him,
they avoid him! They dread and fear him! Why? you ask. How
can this be? He seems so harmless. Ah, yes, *seems*.

"The fact is that Utu is the only Son who still deals directly
with the original gods, the Igigi! Nabu, the God of Wisdom,
answers his plea. Gira and Gibil protect him from sorcery.
Ninkarrak heals his wounds and guards his health. The others,
all three hundred of them, Mah, Mirsu, Ninki, Tagtug, Azag-
sug, all swarm around his altars when he burns sweet offerings
for them.

"No, Jormungand, Utu is not one to trifle with! I will give
him as wide a berth as possible. May he remain neutral and
inactive!

"Nannar, now, the Patesi of Ur, is a different matter. His
consort is lovely. Ah, yes, Ningal would grace my bed! His
necklace of lapis lazuli would give me the power to call forth
mighty Sedu, the winged bull. And I would give much to be
master of Bubbulu, the Evil Dark.

"The problem with Nannar is not Nannar; it is Enlil. Nannar
is the Ellilutu's faithful ally. Because of him, Enlil can stand
off both Marduk and Enki even should they combine. No, I
would not touch Nannar, for that would rouse Enlil long before
I am ready to face him.

"An, the eldest Son, he who once dwelled in Der but now
lives in strong-walled Uruk, would have been a possibility had
he not taken that bitch Innina as his consort. When Antu, his
original consort, died, the old man sought a new mate from
dawn-lit Prin. Had he bedded such a one, he would have been
my choice. Not even the fact that he holds the mighty *Maqlu*,
a book of great power, would have been enough to save an
aged fool dazzled by the charms of a woman from the Floating
World! But Innina, ah! I dread her power almost more than
that of Enlil himself. No, I stay away from An and his wife.

"Which leaves only Adad. Enki is too powerful, as is Marduk. Adad . . . ah, Adad. The Patesi is powerful, true, but hardly

invincible. Most important, though, he is isolated. The other Sons despise and distrust him. He is no man's ally, throwing his weight now here, now there, wherever it seems likely to do him the most good. The others, especially Enlil, Enki, and Marduk, know he hopes they will destroy each other and that he does everything in his power to promote just that situation. No, no one loves the man. All would be relieved, even pleased, were he destroyed, especially by someone they would feel was no threat. Someone, say, who seemed weak and unlearned in the arts necessary to a Patesi."

Jormungand shook his head impatiently. "That's all fine, but you're forgetting one thing. You're not powerful enough to challenge Adad and win. You may have a few demons at your call, but Lamashtu is no match for the likes of Pazuzu, not to mention Mushrussu! It's crazy, Surt!"

The Black One leaned back in his chair and fixed Jormungand with a triumphant look. "Again, you underestimate me. Well do I know that right now I am no match for Adad and his minions." Surt leaned forward, his face suddenly intense, his gaze burning. "I repeat, *right now* I am no match. Soon I will be. His match and much more!"

He stood without warning, leaping from his chair in his excitement. "Know, Serpent, that I have discovered a way to power vaster than anything Bel Adad, the pitiful Patesi of Maqam Nifl and Borsippa, can wield!" His voice dropped, becoming conspiratorial in tone. Jormungand had to listen carefully to catch every word that fell from the pacing man's lips.

"There is a book, a mighty book. A book whose name many fear even to pronounce. It is the dread *Utukki Limnuti*, the Book of Demons, that once belonged to the mighty Patesi Enmeenlu of Badtabira during the First Dark Empire. In it are the True Names of seven sevens of demons, copied from the Tupsimati itself! With those Names are the incantations necessary to raise those demons and gain control of them! The *Utukki Limnuti*, Serpent! A book as mighty as the *Maqlu*, which An holds, or the *Shurpu*, which Marduk possesses, or even the *Nimeqi* and *Shipti* of Enki!"

"But the *Utukki Limnuti* no longer exists, Surt," the huge warrior protested. "Everyone knows it was destroyed along with Enmeenlu, Badtabira, and everything for a hundred leagues around when the demons broke loose at the end of the First Dark Empire. It's gone, gone back to Kur where the demons dwell!"

Surt smiled slowly and evilly. "Yes, yes. Everyone *knows* that. Everyone. What if I told you everyone was wrong? What if I told you that the *Utukki Limnuti* still lies in a deep crypt beneath the ruins of Badtabira? What if I said that the demons were unable to carry it off, because the last thing Enmeenlu did was use his own blood to form a Ward not even the mightiest of those from dark Kur could broach? What if I said that I know how to pierce that Ward? What then?"

Jormungand swallowed, his throat and mouth dry with sudden fear. "You . . . you speak the truth, Master? The . . . Book of Demons yet exists on Earth?"

The thin man chuckled and nodded. "Yes, the truth, faithful Serpent. Ask not how I know. The finding out would blast your soul. It is enough to say I know. I know what none other in Muspellheim knows.

"I am going to the ruins of Badtabira to find the *Utukki Limnuti*. I am going to master it and all the demons named within its ancient pages. Then I am going to smash Bel Adad!

"I need your help, Jormungand, for the journey is a perilous one. No one knows the exact location of Badtabira, only that it lies somewhere beneath the sands of the Northern Waste, that once fruitful land ravaged by the demons at the end of the First Dark Empire. The Northern Waste itself lies beyond the Mashu Mountains, the mountains where the deadly Scorpion Men live. Even magic is not protection enough for such a journey. Cold steel, wielded by a mighty warrior, is necessary. Help me now, and soon you will command the armed might of Maqam Nifl and Borsippa! And someday you will be Warlord of all Muspellheim!"

Jormungand bowed his head in acceptance. Surely his master was mad. Still, what an adventure!

The journey was long and even more dangerous than Surt had promised. Many were the times Jormungand thought their end had come. When the Scorpion Men attacked in force, only he and Surt of their whole party escaped alive. The rest, hired in Kish, never left the Mashu Mountains. The Scorpion Men feasted on their poison-bloated bodies.

The desert that lay to the north of the Mashu was as deadly as the mountains. Living enemies were far fewer, but the heat, the sudden windstorms that filled the air with swirling sand, and the waterless, foodless waste itself were enemy enough for anyone. Surt needed every bit of the knowledge he had gained in the Twisted Lands to find the rare spring that trickled bitter water. Often they had nothing to eat but the stringy flesh of a snake foolish enough to attack them.

The Northern Waste was vast, and Surt had only a vague idea where the ruins of Badtabira lay. Once it had all been a land of lush greeness, flowing waters, and teeming cities. From the Mashu Mountains to the Smoking Lands, the heart of the First Dark Empire had stretched, rich and fruitful. Mighty Larak had been there, a great city on top of a mountain. Nunki had stood by the edge of the Western Sea, host to the trade of the world, and Badtabira, the queen of cities, had soared into a blue sky, her streets busy with traffic from every land.

The yellow-robed men of the Sunrise Empire had glided down her broad avenues, bringing trade and tribute. Stout Dverg from their own mighty city of Alvis plied their trade, selling tools, weapons, and wondrous jewelry crafted at their forges. The Alfar had come, slender and beautiful, and their dark cousins, the Svartalfar, had served the lords of the Empire. Kara Khitai had sent its children to gaze in wonder at the great towers that rose to meet the sky. Even the men of tiny, dawn-lit Prin, high in the towering Kunlun Mountains, wandered amid the glory of Badtabira.

Then the greed of the Sons of Muspell had grown boundless, and all the world rebelled against them. In their pride they gathered a mighty host and sent it north and east to crush all who would not bend the knee to them in abject surrender.

On the grassy plain that was now the Great Eastern Waste, the Sons of Muspell met the combined army of the Dverg and the Alfar, supported by detachments from Kara Khitai and the forests of the Vanir. The clash of the foes made the earth tremble and the sky darken. Rivers of blood sluiced across the plain; mounds of corpses piled up. The slaughter continued for two full days; then the Sons let loose their mightiest magic. The earth heaved, the streams leaped from their courses, the seas smashed across the land. Mountains fell and others rose, filling the sky with smoke and fire.

When the devastation was finished, the battered remnants of the mighty army of the First Dark Empire straggled back to Muspellheim. The Dverg, the Alfar, and their allies had won a costly victory. The Sons of Muspell had lost.

The loss soon became even greater. The calling of the demons had exhausted the Patesi, making them weaker than they had ever been. Without warning the demons rose up and struck back at the sorcerers who had held them in thrall. Alalgar of Nunki, Enmeenlu of Badtabira, Ensibzi of Larak, and Enmeendur of Sippar were their main targets. Larak was utterly destroyed when the Western Sea swallowed the land, roaring eastward in a towering wall of water. The ruins of Larak lay somewhere beneath the steaming waves of the Sea of Mists. Nunki was likewise inundated by the sea. Sippar was shaken until not one stone stood on another.

Badtabira, the home of Enmeenlu, owner of the *Utukki Limnuti*, was wasted as no city ever before had been wasted. The demons swarmed there. Every soul within the mighty walls was dragged screaming to the dread netherworld of Kur. The proud towers of the mightiest city on earth were pulled down and flung about in chaotic heaps. The countryside for a hundred leagues in every direction was blasted and scoured of life. When the demons had completed their work, nothing was left but sterile rock and sand. As far as eye could see, there was only the Northern Waste.

Only one of the Sons of Muspell survived that disaster. Ziusudra was his name, and like the present-day Patesi Utu, he had worshipped the Igigi, the three hundred gods of Muspell, rather than dealing with demons from Kur. In his city of Larsa, far to the south of Mashu Mountains, south even of Sippar, he waited out the seven days and seven nights of the demons' rampage. Then he gathered what was left of the people of Muspellheim and began to rebuild. Some said the Igigi had granted him immortality for his actions and that he still lived, far off on an island in the Southern Sea. Utu, who made his home in the rebuilt Sippar and ruled Larsa as well, was a direct descendant of Ziusudra, by blood as well as by his preference for the Igigi. If he knew of his forefather's whereabouts, he kept the secret to himself.

For weeks the two wandered the scorched and desolate face of the Northern Waste. Jormungand had long ago given up hope that his master knew where he was going. We will leave our bones on the sands, he thought dully. He only continued to place one foot in front of the other because his body refused to stop fighting.

One morning as the sun rose in bloated splendor and the endless hot breath of the wind blew from the west, the huge warrior knew he had reached his limit. His waterskin had been empty for two days now. His throat was swollen and as dry as the blowing sand. There was no strength in his legs. Dimly he wondered how Surt kept going. The slender man was so much thinner, so much weaker. How did he do it?

Surt staggered to his feet and gestured, his own mouth too dry to allow for speech. Besides, the effort was too much. There wasn't enough energy left to do anything but plod slowly north and west.

All morning they shuffled along, reeling with fatigue. About noon they struggled to the top of a slight rise. In the distance there was nothing but more distance. The land was as empty as always.

No, wait. There was something. Surt's eyes were incapable of seeing very far. The sun had half blinded him. Yet it wasn't anything he saw. No. It . . . was something . . . he felt. He sank to the ground concentrating all his energy, trying to open his mind.

There. A dark wing brushed his mind with horror. There again. To the north. An evil. An evil so old, so deep, he couldn't identify it.

Why would such a thing be there? His mind was slow and dim. It took all the strength he had left to think, but the conclusion he came to was inevitable. The evil he felt could only come from one place—Badtabira. It was the remnant, the slowly fading aura of the city and its fate.

Surt looked up to where Jormungand still stood. He knew that if the man sat, he would never rise again. Even the mighty Serpent has his limits, Surt thought. He is not driven the way I am. No thirst for revenge has he, a thirst that in me is stronger even than my thirst for water or life itself.

Slowly, weakly, the Black One rose and pointed to the north. "There," he croaked. "There." The Serpent's eyes followed his finger. The man nodded dull comprehension. When Surt began to plod down the rise, Jormungand followed.

The farther north they walked, the surer Surt was that they indeed approached their destination. The aura of lingering horror clung to the very stones that littered the ground. Soon it was so thick that even Jormungand began to pick it up. He looked at Surt, and the slender man nodded affirmation. Bad-tabira lay ahead.

They found a slow ooze of bitter water at the foot of a rock outcrop. Since the day was fading, and since it would take several hours to fill their waterskins, they decided to stay there for the night.

As dark covered the emptiness around them, a snake slid from a crack in the rock, drawn by the scent of possible prey. Jormungand killed it and they ate it raw, washed down by water so harsh it made them gag.

With the full coming of night, the sense of evil that hung over the landscape became even greater. Surt wove a simple Ward to enclose them. It wouldn't protect against a real demon, not against one of the Utukku or Saghulhaza, but against the aeon-old memory of such horrors, it was enough. They slept soundly.

In the morning sun the rock outcropping became an ancient piece of broken wall. Jormungand examined it closely. "From the thickness, I'd say it was part of the fortified wall that surrounded the city. We must be at the southern edge of Badtabira. Now what?"

Surt thought for a moment. "Assuming that the layout was generally the same as our own cities, the palace of Enmeenlu should be in the center. Hmm, yes. Let us go. Go carefully. The stench of evil is strong. Nergal knows what lurks here still. Keep your sword loose."

The two walked slowly through what at first glance appeared to be nothing more than an area dotted with many small mounds of rock. Closer examination, however, revealed that many of the rocks were chunks of larger pieces with dressed edges. The rubble that stretched as far as eye could see was ruin of a vast city. Jormungand was awed by its size, which was easily twice that of Muspell, he estimated. Maqam Nifl would have fit in a corner of this metropolis. The First Dark Empire must have been mighty indeed!

He spun around just in time. The feeling that they were being watched had been growing on his battle-trained senses for some time. The slight grit of one rock against another had been his only warning that his feeling was true.

As he jabbed out with his sword, the thing that had launched itself at them from behind a mound reared back and hissed. Jormungand was stunned. What by Namtaru's dread name was it? Never had he beheld such a hideous creature! It was a good twelve feet long, a pasty white, sinuous form propelled by a hundred legs. The pair nearest the head ended in large pincers with razor-sharp edges. Most horrible of all was the head itself. The face was a ghastly mockery of a human face. Great round eyes were set above a double hole of a nose; a tiny flap of flesh flopped about just over the two cavities. Beneath that was a wide, drooling mouth filled with yellow fangs. A bright red tongue lolled between the teeth. Huge ears stuck out to either side. Long, tangled black hair hung from the head.

The thing moaned as it reared, eyeing Jormungand's sword. "Uhhhhh," it slobbered, "uhhhhh, eat." The word was so unexpected, the Serpent almost dropped his weapon. By the seven walls of Aralu, the damn thing talked!

"Uhhhhh," it groaned again. "Eat, eat, hungry, hungry!" With that it launched itself at Jormungand. The warrior waited until the last possible moment, then twisted to the side, sweeping his blade down in a slashing blow that caught the monster just behind the left claw, which fell to the ground.

With a speed that surprised Jormungand, the creature wheeled its full twelve feet and charged again instantly. This time it was expecting his step to the side and nearly caught the warrior. Its slashing fangs ripped the stout leather of his harness with frightening ease.

Almost faster than the Serpent could follow, the monster spun and attacked once more. Jormungand planted his feet solidly and met the thing head-on. He held his sword high and brought it down on the fanged head in a swift blur, splitting it in two. The force of the thing's charge bowled him over and sent him sprawling.

As he picked himself up, the thrashing body spasmed one last time and lay still. He walked over and kicked at it with his foot. "What in the name of Nergal is this thing, Surt?" he asked. The slender dark man shrugged. "Well," Jormungand said. "I hope it was one of a kind. Do you think we'll find many such horrors in these ruins?"

"No man knows what these ruins hold. No man has been here in at least a handful of sars. Almost anything could be lurking, feeding on the evil that still abounds."

"A handful of sars? That's at least eighteen hundred years!"

"Yes. A sar is a cycle of three hundred and sixty years. The First Dark Empire lasted a hundred sars, so a mere handful is nothing by comparison."

Jormungand shook his head in amazement. "A hundred sars? It must have been mighty indeed! Yet in the end it all comes to this," he said, sweeping the ruins with a broad gesture of his arm. Deep in thought, he began to wipe the monster's blood from his sword.

As they moved on, the sense of horror became stronger and more palpable. Surt began to feel the pressure of gibbering evil sneaking around the edges of his mind. He looked at Jormungand. The man's face was rigid with control, his eyes haunted, darting about. There was a light sweat on his forehead and upper lip. Our Ward is in place, Surt told himself. We are safe from ordinary demons. Jormungand's sword is proof against most monsters. Despite that, he didn't feel safe. There was something . . . something he hadn't thought of . . . something that waited. . . . He shook his head. Enough. He couldn't let simple fear get the better of him. The evil that clung to Badtabira was ancient. It couldn't still be strong enough to—

Jormungand touched his arm. "There," the huge warrior said in a strained whisper. Surt followed his pointing finger to a mound of rubble higher than those surrounding it. The ceaseless west wind had scoured one edge of the mound. Just visible was the top of a bull's back and the bottom of a feathered wing. A statue of Sedu, the winged bull! Or at least a fragment of one. Such statues always guarded the entrance to the palace of Patesi. They had found the palace of Enmeenlu! Somewhere beneath it, in catacombs unwalked by human feet in over a thousand years, lay the *Utukki Limnuti*!

XVI

WHILE the light was still in the sky, they diligently searched the ruins, hoping to discover some sort of entrance to the catacombs. The only thing they found was a large, vicious lizard that became their dinner.

As darkness slowly pushed the light westward and below the horizon, Surt began to look over his shoulder again and again. At the same time Jormungand heard faint grating sounds coming from all around them. It sounded as if some huge creature were sliding through the rubble toward them from every direction. Or perhaps it was many smaller beasts. He listened again for a moment and shuddered. The sound wasn't natural, wasn't right. Nothing moved that way. Nothing.

Surt's over-the-shoulder looks, on the other hand, weren't a response to anything he heard. Rather it was something he felt, something that was lurking, waiting, just out of sight and sound. He probed it with his mind, trying to identify and locate it. It didn't seem to be any one place in particular. It pervaded the entire ruin, and it was ancient.

The Black One placed his Ward more carefully than ever that night, putting all the power he commanded into it. The difficulty was that it had to be a general Ward, one that would work against almost anything, since he hadn't the slightest idea what sort of thing might attack. If only he knew what to expect, he could make it more specific and a good deal stronger. As it was . . .

Their evening meal was a quiet one. Both men were listening, each in his own way, listening for signs of enemies that prowled the night. The rustling, sliding noises had nearly ceased, as if whatever had stalked them through the ruins had taken up position and now merely waited to spring. Jormungand stared into the blackness, his whole body tense, expecting that at any moment some fanged shape would launch itself at him.

His sword was drawn and lying across his crossed legs, his hand wrapped around the hilt.

A sense of dread was growing in Surt's heart. For the first time he found himself doubting the wisdom of having come to Badtabira. The evil that had destroyed this place was so immense! Back in the safety of Maqam Nifl it had seemed impossible that something that had flourished so long ago could still be dangerous. Now he wondered. He could feel it. Feel it stirring and waking, slithering toward him, oozing its way from deep within the very rocks. A chill of fear ran down his spine. He closed his eyes and tried to calm his mind. The mind must be still to work magic, he reminded himself, and magic may be our only hope.

Jormungand's urgent whisper startled him. Surt looked up. The giant warrior was standing, his sword ready, his body tense, a sheen of sweat glistening on his skin. The moon had risen, and the gleam of its full orb made the ruins glow with an eerie light. "Surt," Jormungand whispered again, "there are *things* out there."

The slight man swept the night with his eyes. At first he saw nothing but the age-old rubble of Badtabira stretching off in all directions. Then something moved where nothing should be moving. He strained, trying to see. "What is it?" he asked Jormungand.

"Nothing I've ever seen before," came the terse reply. "Can't get a good look in this light. Got a lot of legs. A lot of teeth. Stinks like dead flesh. Take a whiff, Surt."

Surt sniffed and instantly regretted it. How had he missed it before? The air was heavy with the stench of carrion. He almost gagged. "What . . . what are we going to do?" he mumbled.

Jormungand laughed quickly and grimly. "Probably die, unpleasantly. By Namtaru, the things look like some kind of mix of spider and wolf. Where in Nergal's name did they come from?"

"What are they waiting for? Why aren't they attacking?"

"Might be the Ward, Surt, or they might not be sure of just how dangerous we are. Near as I can make out, there are nineteen of them. Each about the size of a big dog. Furry. Sitting there, watching, waiting." He laughed again, the sound harsh in the quiet. "I figure I can kill maybe six or so before they pull me down. Nineteen is too many."

"Nineteen? Did you say nineteen? Yes, yes, that would fit!

Enmeenlu was served by a guard of nineteen demons, Serpent. They were the ones who led the attack against him and finally dragged him down to Kur. These things must be the remnants of the manifestations of their power. After eighteen hundred years they still hang on! The evil power that was unleashed here during the fall of the First Dark Empire was beyond imagining. Incredible!"

"Perhaps when you're finished admiring the power of Enmeenlu," Jormungand said sarcastically, "you could make some suggestions on how to get rid of these 'remnants' before they attack and chew us to pieces."

Surt concentrated. After a few moments he began to chant in a language Jormungand had never heard before. The words, if indeed words they were, slipped from between the little man's lips and skittered off into the night like tiny creatures trying desperately to find cover. As the Black One continued, the giant warrior noticed that the things that encircled them began to shift and move restlessly, as if uncertain of their prey. Surt finished and looked up.

"Still there," Jormungand informed him. "You didn't drive them away, but it seems like you've given them second thoughts about what to have for dinner. They look nervous now."

The thin man shrugged. "That's the most I can do. I think it should hold them, though." He sighed and sat back down again. "Might as well rest. It's a long night." The giant warrior didn't move and didn't reply. "Ah, well, then, suit yourself. Watch if you wish." He leaned back, the weariness that came from what he had just done rising up within him. Yes, he thought, guard against the things you see, if it makes you feel better. Are you aware, I wonder, of the real danger? The things you watch could rend our flesh and spill our blood, but the *other* thing, the thing I sense slowly growing in the dark, can drag our bodies and souls down to dreaded Kur to suffer endless torment. I am afraid, he admitted silently. If there was a way to back out now, I would take it. But there is no escape. We can only go forward. To what?

As dawn came the creatures left, but not before the two got a good look at them. They were waist high. Their heads were round, with a slight muzzle. Their faces were hairless and a dead-white in color. Two large bloodred eyes glared out, and a pair of slits functioned as a nose. Their mouths were slits, also, filled with yellow fangs, which dripped a thick, green, mucuslike fluid that was undoubtedly poisonous. Their bodies were oval, eight-legged, and covered with short black hair. The two legs nearest the head ended in crude four-fingered hands.

"Seem pretty solid for 'remnants,'" Jormungand muttered.

"Spider Zi, transformed and inhabited with demonic power," Surt explained. "They're very solid. I imagine they were a lot bigger once, but the power is slowly draining away. One day they'll just be ordinary spiders."

The huge warrior snorted. "Let's come back in a couple thousand years. I'm willing to wait."

Surt shook his head in denial. "There is no leaving. Something still dwells here in Badtabira, something far more powerful than degenerate demonic guards. We've disturbed its sleep, I'm afraid. It's not fully roused yet. If we flee, it will be awake long before we get far enough away to evade it. Our only hope now is to find the *Utukki Limnuti* before it comes completely to life. With power like that in our hands we might be able to escape."

"What is this thing we've disturbed, Surt?"

"I'm not certain. It could be some guardian the demons of Kur left behind to deny the *Utukki Limnuti* to any who might try to find it, or it could be the Ward placed on the book by Enmeenlu himself in his last moments. Neither will be pleasant to face."

Jormungand stared at Surt, his gaze heavy and grim. "Look around you, Black One. See the glory that was Badtabira, the mightiest city in the world. All its power, all its pride could not stop it from becoming just another pile of rubble. There is a lesson to be learned from the fate of Enmeenlu, Alalgar, Ensibzi, Enmeendur, and all the others of the First Dark Empire. I fear we are about to learn it." For a moment longer his unwavering gaze held that of his master.

Then he sighed and turned away. "It makes no difference. I've crossed the River Hubur once and stood before the seven gates of Aralu. It shouldn't be any harder this time."

It was mid-morning when Surt found what he was searching for. There was nothing visible to the eye to make the place any different from a thousand other spots within the ruin. Indeed, they had passed within a few feet of it several times.

The slender man had finally discovered it by going to the place he least wanted to, the place that made him feel the most fearful.

Jormungand pulled aside several blocks of stone and loose rubble to reveal a huge square stone with an iron ring in the middle set in the ground. He cleared the stone to its edges, then gripped the ring with both hands and heaved with all his might. It moved with unexpected ease to reveal a stairway leading down into stygian blackness. Stale air wafted up out of the hole, heavy with the smell of ancient dust.

The two men looked at each other. Surt spoke. "I will lead, Serpent, and make light with a certain spell I know. Follow close and keep a sharp eye behind. This will be a maze, with Nergal knows what lurking and slinking within." Jormungand nodded. He took a last look around as Surt started down the stone steps. It's only a lousy desert, he thought, but somehow I think I'm going to miss it. He put his feet upon the steps and disappeared from sight.

At the base of the steps Surt waited, a small green globe floating in the air about a foot over his head. It cast a strange light over the walls, floor, and ceiling of the tunnel where the stone steps ended. The walls of the tunnel were of dressed gray stone. The passage was about six feet wide by perhaps eight tall. Plenty of room to fight in, the warrior thought. With my back pressed to one of the walls I could hold off several opponents. Provided, he added, they were more or less human.

While Jormungand evaluated the defensive potential of the tunnel, Surt was staring fixedly at an inscription scrawled across the right-hand wall. The letters, unfamiliar to the warrior, had been written in a hasty scribble with some sort of material that was dark and flaking. Jormungand joined Surt.

"What is it?"

"A curse," Surt replied tersely. "Written in blood. I think I know whose."

"Enmeenlu's?"

Surt nodded. "Which means we're going the right way."

"Or the wrong way, depending how much you value your life."

The slender man grunted. With a gesture he turned and began to walk down the passage. They went slowly, cautiously. About thirty feet farther on, the corridor dead-ended in a cross-corridor. Surt paused, trying to decide which way to turn. Finally he nodded and turned right.

"How do you know to go right?" Jormungand asked.

"Because that's the way I don't want to go," came the answer.

The tunnel turned sharply downward and branched. At the point where the corridor split lay the remains of two warriors. Their skeletons were strangely twisted, as if they had been mauled by something huge and vicious. The sword of one was broken, and the other's was nowhere to be seen. Carefully the two intruders stepped over the bones and took the right-hand corridor again.

For some time they continued on and downward, always taking the right-hand choice. Here and there bodies lay sprawled in ancient death, all as if smashed by something monstrous. At one point Jormungand noticed marks on the corridor wall. For all the world they looked like claw marks. But they were incised into the solid stone a good two inches! The warrior wondered what sort of creature could do something like that to rock.

Eventually they came to a place where the passage widened to form a large circular room, perhaps thirty feet across and twenty feet high. Five dark openings led out of it. "Right again, Surt?" the warrior asked. The slight man concentrated, then shook his head. "No. The middle one. And we must go more cautiously than ever. The way begins to stink of evil."

They passed two more branchings of the tunnel. At the second Surt paused long, listening and looking intently. He moved slowly back and forth between the openings, as if he were a dog hunting for a scent. Finally, almost reluctantly, he chose the passageway on the right. "Neither is good," he explained. "This seems a bit less inviting."

The corridor turned and twisted like a serpent in agony. As they rounded one corner Jormungand stopped in his tracks and hissed to his companion to halt. Dead silence fell over them. Then barely at the edge of perception came the tiniest noise. They listened with all their might, trying to hear it well enough to identify it.

"Back the way we came," Jormungand whispered. "Something's following us."

His head cocked to one side, Surt nodded. "Yes. It sounds like something shuffling along. Could be one big thing or several smaller ones."

"Several smaller," judged the Serpent. "Should we keep going and try to outrun them, or stay here and surprise them?"

"What would be best for you?"

The warrior considered. "Guard the other direction, Surt. We'll wait here. Whatever's coming, it's coming fast. The noise is a lot louder now." He looked around. "Yes. Right here at this bend. We'll be just behind the corner when they come bursting around. Surprise."

They didn't have long to wait. Five creatures came shuffling around the corner in a tight formation. At first glance they seemed human. A second look showed that if they had been human, it was a long time ago. Their eyes were large and saucerlike, their noses flat and grotesquely wide. Instead of skin, they were covered with tiny scales that glistened wetly in the green light cast by Surt's globe. Their hands, which held sword or ax, were clawed. Their legs were short and bowed, making them of a size that fell between that of Surt and the giant warrior. When they saw the two, their long red tongues flicked out of narrow, lipless mouths, and a hiss of surprise filled the passage.

Jormungand didn't give them any chance to recover. With a cry he leapt forward, his sword flashing in a great arc, catching the one in the lead on the side of its neck and smashing through the thing's body to emerge below the opposite armpit. The Serpent pulled his blade down and back, then thrust forward, catching another of the creatures in the center of its face. Yellow ichor splattered in all directions as it reeled back into its three companions.

The warrior stepped back, preparing himself for their rush. With a combined hiss the three charged, their weapons reaching out to skewer him. He stepped quickly to the right, putting himself along the wall as he moved forward, sword sweeping out to catch the one nearest the wall in the stomach. The two survivors spun to face him, hoping to pin him to the wall. With a sudden lunge he flung himself to the side of the one on the left, knocking the creature's sword to the right. Then he reversed his sword's motion and slammed the blade into the thing's chest, burying it almost to the hilt. The creature twisted and fell, trapping his blade and pulling it from his grip.

Seeing him weaponless, the last creature leapt forward, its ax raised high. Jormungand threw himself to the right, hitting the floor and rolling. The ax smashed against the stone with a ringing clash and a shower of sparks. Recovering instantly, the thing whirled and struck again.

Jormungand managed to claw his dagger from where it was thrust through the belt of his harness. He flung it even as he dodged the ax. The creature raised its weapon to strike again, but suddenly stopped, staring in surprise at the hilt that protruded from its chest. With a hiss it crumpled to the stones.

The huge warrior stood and looked down at the five bodies, which began to heave and squirm. Jormungand stepped back, his eyes wide with horror. As he watched, the creatures rotted and turned into a mass of writhing maggots. Then the maggots putrefied, and all that was left were pools of stinking yellow fluid.

He turned away, gagging at the sight and smell. Surt stood calmly taking in the whole scene. "Reptile Zi, Serpent, inhabited by the Etimmu, ghosts, of Enmeenlu's guards. We near the *Utukki Limnuti*, for these are the servants the Patesi of Badtabira set to guard his treasure."

Bringing himself back under control, Jormungand retrieved both his sword and his dagger. He picked up one of the axes the creatures had carried. It was of a strange design, unlike anything he had ever seen. The haft was of ebony-colored wood, the blade bronze and double-headed. He felt the heft and balance of the weapon. Nodding silent approval, he thrust it through the belt of his harness.

They went forward again, down tunnel after tunnel, until the warrior lost all sense of time. Once they stopped briefly to sip a little water and eat the last few pieces of the lizard's flesh.

The farther they went, the greater became Jormungand's certainty that they were again being followed. Whenever they paused to choose direction, the warrior listened carefully. He heard nothing, yet the sense of being watched grew and grew. At the same time he found an unreasoning fear beginning to take root in his mind. Everything began to oppress him, and strange visions flashed through his consciousness. He imagined the weight of earth over them, realizing they were buried alive here deep beneath the Northern Waste. He found the dark that parted only briefly as they passed invading his thoughts as well. It was endless. Endless and full of horrors. Anything could be waiting just around the next corner. Drooling fangs and long claws, the stench of death and rotting corpses. Writhing maggots with grasping hands reaching out from the dark behind and all around, reaching and touching, pulling him down into lingering, screaming death. . . .

He cursed himself out loud. Surt stopped and turned to look back at him. The thin man's face was drained and tense, a slight dew of sweat on his forehead. His eyes were haunted by the same horror that Jormungand knew lurked in his own. The Black One's voice was hoarse and strained as he spoke. "Yes, Serpent, I feel it too. The Ward can't keep it out any longer. Prepare yourself. We must be getting very close."

The warrior nodded. With grim determination he thrust the fear that oozed through his mind back and down, bringing it under tenuous control.

The corridor suddenly ended in a massive wooden door bound with straps of iron and studded with nailheads of silver. There was no visible means of opening it. Surt paused and stood before it, chin in his hand, thinking carefully and deeply. After a few moments he stepped aside. "Try it." He gestured to Jormungand. "Push with your shoulder." The huge man leaned against the door and shoved with all his strength. It refused to budge. Surt did not seem surprised at this result. "Stand back, then," he commanded. "Shield your eyes."

Jormungand stepped back several paces, turned his back to the door, and gazed back along the corridor into the darkness. He heard the other man mumbling something in strange, unrecognizable words. There was a bright flash and a loud noise, followed by a shock wave that almost knocked the warrior off his feet. The light briefly revealed what waited just out of sight down the corridor. The Serpent spun about and grabbed Surt, leaping through the half-open door. Dropping his master, he spun about and slammed the heavy wooden door shut, leaning against it, gasping for breath and trying to control his trembling.

Surt looked at him in amazement. "What . . . what did you do that for?"

"The . . . thing . . . there was a thing . . . in the dark . . . following. . . . I . . ."

"What thing? What was it?"

"It . . . by Namtaru, Surt . . . I . . ." The man made an effort and brought himself back under control. He shook his head to clear it. "I . . . don't want . . . to . . . talk about it," he gritted out between tightly clenched teeth. "Don't want to remember." He shuddered. "But I won't go back that way. Won't."

The slender man touched his arm. "Calm, Serpent. We need not go back that way, but we do have to go forward." He gestured around the small room they were in. "This is only the antechamber. Beyond lies the main room. I think we'll find what we're looking for there." His voice dropped to a whisper. "We'll find the *Utukki Limnuti*!"

Jormungand pulled his sword from its scabbard and walked

slowly and cautiously with Surt to the door that lay at the opposite end of the chamber. The warrior reached out with the tip of the sword and pushed gently at the door. It swung open.

The two men looked at each other. "I'm going to expand the light," Surt whispered. "The next room is probably much larger, and we want to see everything. Be ready." Jormungand nodded and gripped his sword tighter.

Together they stepped quickly through the door. The light bloomed, bathing a vast chamber in its eerie green glow. What it revealed staggered the minds of the two. The room was easily two hundred feet square. Giant pillars in the form of serpent dragons soared upward to a ceiling that stood a good eighty feet over their heads. The vault itself was covered with deep blue lapis lazuli. Worked into its surface in brilliant jewels was a map of the heavens, every constellation in its proper place. The floor of the chamber was solid gold; the walls, silver inlaid with gold designs, again of serpent dragons.

In the exact center of the room was an enormous throne cut from a single, massive bloodstone. It glittered a sickly dark red in the greenish light, looking like a mound of clotted blood.

Seated on the throne was a giant man, dressed in cloth of gold. His face, as black as the corridors that filled the catacombs, was long and narrow, with thin lips, a pointed chin, and a high, narrow nose. Eyes, which glowed redly, were open and staring directly at them.

Surt gasped and pointed. On the man's lap lay an immense book bound in black leather. The *Utukki Limnuti*!

Before either of them could take a step forward, the mouth of the figure on the throne opened and a chilling laugh tumbled out, filling the hall and slamming into their ears. A voice followed the laugh, a voice so ringing it literally battered them to their knees. "Fools! You dare to enter the inner sanctum of Enmeenlu! You shall die eternally!" He raised a hand and gestured to the air. "Come, my pet, come and crunch their bones!"

"If you've any magic, Surt, you'd best use it now," muttered the dazed warrior. They watched in wonder as the air between them and the throne shimmered and thickened. A form began to appear. First the long, sinuous body, then the maned and fanged head, then the six strong, clawed legs.

Surt gasped again and began to tremble. "It's . . . it's Musirkeshda," he wailed in terror. "Musirkeshda, who sits next to Tiamat and gets second pick of prey."

Jormungand shook himself, trying to free his mind and limbs from the terror and hopelessness that seemed to grip them. This thing was sister to Mushrussu, his old enemy. He had fought the other to a standstill and he would fight this one, by Nergal! Namtaru might already be carrying his name to Ereshkigal in her seven-walled abode beyond the Hubur. But, by the Igigi, he was damned if he'd go peacefully! Let them all remember Jormungand, the mighty Serpent! With a roar that matched that of the creature he faced, he launched himself into the fight.

"Take this back to your sister, dragon bitch!" he screamed as he slashed at the monster's head. It hissed and reared back, barely evading the blow. The thing swiped at him, its claws flashing past his face. He stepped to the side and jabbed at its fanged mouth. Jormungand sensed the coming slash of the tail. He lunged back just as it slammed into the floor. He hacked at it, cutting a huge gash through the heavy scales. The bellow of the beast nearly deafened him.

It leapt at him, mouth agape. He twisted to the side, dodging the fangs and the first clawed foot. His sword jabbed forward, catching the monster behind the front left leg. The point sank deep. He turned and pulled, ripping the hole larger.

As he stepped back the second foot caught him in the side, claws raking him, tearing his clothes and ripping deep into his flesh. He gasped and staggered against one of the pillars, stunned by the force of the blow and the fiery pain that tore through his body. With a roar of triumph Musirkeshda reared up, its mouth drooling, its front claws pawing the air in anticipation of slashing his body to ribbons.

Jormungand realized he had only one chance. Without waiting, he threw himself forward, straining every last ounce of energy from his rapidly failing body. His sword gripped in both hands, he rammed into the dragon's chest directly below the first pair of legs, sinking the blade in to the hilt. Blood spewed out over him, burning hot and foul. Releasing his weapon, he flung himself to the right, rolling as he hit, trying to escape.

Musirkeshda shrieked in agony and dropped to its feet. It moaned, a bubbly sound coming from deep inside its scaly chest. The lionlike head swung around and saw the scrabbling form of Jormungand. The creature roared again and moved toward him, but the roar ended in a strangled gurgle. Musirkeshda stopped and shook its maned head. It opened its mouth as if to roar again, and a flood of steaming blood poured forth. The dragon looked down stupidly at the foul fluid that puddled on the floor, then, with a groan, crumpled to lie in its own blood.

Jormungand looked up to see Surt's pale face. Everything whirled about in confusion. He reached his hand to his side, trying to stop the pain. He pulled it away and saw that it was bright with his own blood.

The air around them vibrated with an ear-shattering roar. Light began to flash, and the walls of the room glowed. The figure on the throne had both hands extended in their direction. From his fingertips bolts of sheer energy streamed. Nergal, help me, Surt cried silently. Stand by your servant!

Reaching beneath his robe, he pulled out the talisman he had taken so many years ago from the corpse of the wizard on the Vigrid. He held it tightly with both hands and cleared his mind. Rapidly he began to chant. As he rolled out the spell a wall of darkness began to form between himself and the energy pouring from the fingers of the man on the throne. Surt's face broke into a heavy sweat. His whole body strained as if he were holding up the dark wall with his own strength.

There was an explosion, which knocked Surt flat by its power. Still he kept a firm grip on the talisman.

The room began to fill with darkness. Unlike the absence of light that had so haunted them in the tunnels, this darkness had substance and weight. It gibbered and snickered, full of evil, slinking presence. Surt knew instantly it was the Bubbulu, the Evil Dark. Bel Nannar controlled it in these times, but Enmeenlu had been the master of it during the days of the First Dark Empire. It returned now at his calling.

Jormungand struggled to his feet, his eyes wide with terror. "Do something, Surt! For the sake of Namtaru, do something! It's . . . it's eating my soul! Stop it!"

Surt whimpered and crawled across the floor to huddle against the wall. "Can't think," he moaned piteously. "Oh . . . oh . . . help! Too much power! My mind, my mind!"

The warrior staggered. Something slimy was trying to force its way into his mouth. Something else was wrapping itself around his leg, sliding upward with slow, dreadful purpose. There was another thing sitting on his head, slowly chewing its way into his brain. Ah! Ah! He screamed in agony.

He wrenched himself erect, lips clenched against the thing that attempted to push its way past. He looked up. Across the room, barely visible in the gloom, was the figure on the throne.

His eyes glowed brightly now, their red light shining like two beacons in the dark.

A sudden rage shook the huge warrior. Without thinking, he snatched the double-headed ax from his belt and flung it with all his might, aiming between the two red glows.

He heard a bellow of rage, saw a flash of light, felt the smashing force of an explosion. Then he felt nothing.

What happened next, Jormungand never knew and Surt would never tell. Once when the warrior asked him, the Black One turned haunted eyes on him, eyes sick with a memory he couldn't repress. The answer had been sufficient.

Somehow Surt had managed to wade through the magical chaos set loose when Jormungand's ax smashed the forehead of the creature on the throne. Surt was certain that the figure was nothing less than the corporeal remains of Enmeenlu himself. In any case, the double-headed bronze ax shattered the spells made fragile by the many years that had passed since their casting. Strange things had been loosed in the breaking. Surt managed to fend them off and win his way to the throne and the book on the knees of the destroyed figure.

He also managed to get the badly wounded Jormungand out of the catacombs. Then, supporting the warrior, he had staggered from the ruins of Badtabira ahead of a wave of demons sent from Kur to guard the palace.

The rest of the journey back to Maqam Nifl, impossible to most men, had seemed pleasant by comparison. Once back in the city of Bel Adad, the truly dangerous part of their quest began.

ASAHEIM

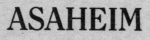

XVII

~~~

THE horsemen topped a swell in the snow-covered Himinborg Plain. They paused for a moment and gazed northward through the pale morning light. There, several miles off on the crest of a rise, stood Asgard. From this distance it appeared as a sprawl of dirty brown with tendrils of smoke twisting skyward toward the low gray clouds.

Voden sat silently on his horse and tried to come to grips with the emotions that surged through him. Joy, excitement, relief, even fear . . . yes, he could deal with them easily enough, but there was something else, something that disturbed him. Above and beyond his other feelings, detached in a way that made it seem as if it came from another place, another mind, was a vague sense of disappointment. Asgard looks so ugly there on its hill, a voice somewhere within him said. So small and crowded. So rough and crude.

He shook his head, suddenly angry. Such thoughts are unworthy of Voden, son of Borr, he told himself. I am Aesir, and Asgard is my home. I am returning to my people. Who are barbarians, came the soft, mocking reply.

With a sharp jerk he pulled up his horse's head and kicked it into motion. The others fell in line behind him. It seemed only right that Borr's eldest son should lead the procession as it entered Asgard.

After an official greeting at the gate from their fathers and several other chieftains, Voden and Honir separated and went to their own homes. Roskva and the other servants and bondmen and -women were gathered near the door of Voden's family hall to bid him welcome and make endless comments over how he had grown, what a fine warrior he would be, and so on. Working his way free of them as rapidly as politeness would allow, he stepped into the main part of the hall and looked to the other end where his mother sat smiling in the high seat. She gestured to him to approach.

As Voden drew near he noticed that she had changed. Her pregnancy was obvious, even at a distance, even seated. It wasn't until he got much closer, though, that he saw how tired and drawn she was. There were circles beneath her eyes and new lines across her forehead and at the corners of her mouth. The lines were smooth for the moment, but Voden knew they could twist into a grimace of pain at an instant's notice.

He took the hand she offered him and was surprised at how thin and light it was. The fingers seemed mere sticks, the veins stuck out on the back of the hand, and the palm was abnormally hot. He looked up and met her eyes. They held an amused look, and her mouth was curled in wry humor. "Yes, my son, soon you will have a little sister. She was conceived not long after you left. I doubt she will come while you are here. That would be a bit too soon. But it won't be long. No, not long."

They talked quietly for a while about Vanaheim and Voden's adventures there. Then Vestla seemed to tire suddenly and told him to go out and visit with his friends. "Tror," she said, "has been counting the days until you returned. Tyr, too. Go, before the two of them burst with curiosity."

Honir had already joined Tror and Tyr. The three of them were waiting outside the wattle fence that surrounded Voden's hall. Together the four friends wandered the streets of Asgard, chattering away, exchanging stories and telling of the exciting things that had happened since they had last seen each other.

To his surprise Voden found himself holding much back. By agreement he and Honir had decided to say nothing of the rites the Vanir held at the summer solstice. They had also agreed not to mention the first stirrings of the Galdar-power in Voden.

Even beyond that, Voden felt unable to share certain matters. He didn't mention his training in the Thiodnuma or wrestling. And though Honir told them of Freyja, Voden found himself incapable of saying anything about the girl or his feelings toward her.

As they walked and talked he found his mind drifting from the conversation. Things began to catch his eye, things he had known since he was old enough to walk. There was a patina of familiarity over them, a sense of rightness that made them suddenly stand out and demand his attention. Old Groa's hut with the still-unfixed leather hinge on the shutter that covered her only window summer and winter. The shed next to Tyr's family's hall where they had played many times. The large stone that stood in the middle of the open space at the center of Asgard where Mad Orni used to stand and babble his nonsense. The wattle fence that enclosed old Gangloti's pigs, though never for very long.

Everywhere he looked, everything he saw, seemed to shine with its own inner light. It was as if he were viewing all these things, all these totally familiar and ordinary things, for the first time. They were the same. Yet they were different.

The same, yet different. Some subtle but fundamental transformation had taken place in Asgard. Nothing had changed, yet it was all totally new, gleaming with freshness.

As swiftly as the feeling had come, it was gone. Voden blinked. He had been staring at a broken cart, a cart that had been lying in Thorir's yard ever since he could remember. A moment ago it had been special, full of meaning and possibilities he had never dreamed of. Now it was just an old broken cart, cast aside because it was worthless.

The other boys were standing and looking at him. Their gazes were perplexed, troubled. Voden returned their look, his face unreadable. Then he laughed and shrugged. They smiled, uncomfortable, but not quite knowing why.

Tror didn't know how to say it, or who to say it to. He was worried—no, not worried, concerned. Concerned for his friend.

Why? he asked himself as he lay in bed that night, burrowed beneath a bear pelt. Voden's fine. He's grown a good four fingers in height since he left. He seems healthy. If anything, he's quicker and faster than ever.

Then why? It wasn't anything definite. It was just . . . well, just that he seemed . . . different. Yes, that was it.

Take the way he tended to drift off and get lost in his own thoughts. Voden had always been a thinker. Tror's father had said he'd never known a lad with so many questions. But this was not the same. Voden wasn't asking questions. He was going somewhere inside, somewhere far away from his friends even as he walked with them.

Or what about the way he moved? No one else but Tror had noticed it. Voden moved differently now. Smoothly, gracefully. Next to him, the redheaded boy had felt like a stumbling ox.

You couldn't surprise him anymore, either. It seemed as if

he knew what you were going to do before you did yourself. He didn't have to be looking at you to know you were moving, as though he had eyes in the back of his head.

The strangeness didn't stop there. No, it went beyond physical things. Tror shivered slightly as he remembered what had happened the other day. They had been in Volund's workroom, helping the smith prepare sword blanks and spearheads. Voden had worked with them, cheerful, laughing, and as full of questions as he had always been.

Then his eyes fell on Mjollnir, the mighty hammer that Volund had made nearly a year ago. In an instant the smile and laugh vanished to be replaced by a strange brooding look and haunting silence.

When the work was completed, Voden drew Tror aside and spoke to him in an urgent whisper. "Tror," he said, "make me a promise."

Tror frowned, disturbed by the urgency and oddness of the request. "Promise?"

Voden nodded, his face serious, his eyes veiled and dark. "Yes. A promise about the hammer. Mjollnir."

"My father's hammer? The Crusher?"

"Yes."

Uneasy, the redheaded youth turned his head away. "It's my father's hammer. He made it for somebody. You remember, don't you?"

With surprisingly strong hands Voden grabbed Tror's chin and turned his head back until they were eye to eye. "I remember. Volund made that hammer for a great warrior, someone who will come along someday and be able to use it to protect the Aesir. It is destined to be."

Despite himself, Tror dropped his gaze from his friend's burning stare. "Wha-what do you want me to do? I'm only—"

"Something simple. I want you to promise me you'll try to lift it. Every day, you'll try. Just that. Nothing more."

Tror frowned again, a look of bafflement filling his face. "Lift it? I can't lift it. It's too heavy. My father can barely drag it along. How can I lift it?"

"Just *try* to lift it. Try every day."

The smith's son stared at the ground in silence for several moments, then muttered, "Well, all right. I guess it can't hurt anything. As long as all I have to do is *try* to lift it." He had raised his eyes and asked, "But why?"

It had happened then, and the shock of it still took away his breath when he remembered it. Voden had looked him full in the face and replied, his voice flat, hard, and commanding, "Don't ask. Do it."

Tror had been stunned, not so much by the words, or even the preemptive tone, as by the look that had transformed Voden's face into that of an utter stranger. A very old stranger, one with great and dark power, one who looked and judged and understood things no boy Voden's age should understand. Then, before Tror could even comprehend what had happened, the stranger was gone and the Voden he knew was back. But the friend that had returned was a bit more like the stranger than he had been before.

Tror shivered and burrowed deeper beneath the pelt. It was strange. And a little frightening.

Vestla watched her eldest son closely. He was growing so rapidly. In a few more months he would be twelve years old. Conceived amid the blood-soaked ruins of the caravan on the ninth day of the seventh month, he had been born nine months later on the seventh day, just as spring was softening the land.

From the very first she had known he was something special, precious, and unique. He was the reason she had left Prin, traveled the Great Route toward Muspellheim, been raped by Borr on the Vigrid. Voden was the point of it all, the manifestation that the Tao had been seeking to accomplish through her. It had taken her many years to understand, and even longer to accept.

Now, looking into his eyes as he sat in the hall and stared up at the rafters, she knew for certain. There was something in him that went beyond him, something that partook of the Tao. Wondrous are the ways of the Tao! Marvelous the twists and turns of the Great Pattern!

She felt both joy and pain. The brief glimpse she had once been given of the future had been frightening as well as enlightening. The Tao flowed on, yes, but it flowed through flames and death and destruction as well as through peace and prosperity. None of which mattered to the Tao. Those are our concerns, our petty human worries, she knew. Life and death, glory and ignominy, wealth and poverty, all are but swirls, swiftly forming and just as swiftly disappearing, in the driving flow of the Tao.

Vestla knew that, had known it since childhood. Her mother had told her many times when she had cried because there was not enough to eat. She had been taught it again in the Floating World. Let go of the self. Let go of desire and hope. Flow with the Tao and be. That is the only true happiness, the only escape from the grief that clings in gray veils to all of human endeavor.

She had tried, tried to give pleasure without concern for receiving any in return, tried to smother her own burning passions for the calm detachment the masters of the Floating World had demanded. She had succeeded, at times.

Total yielding, total dismissal of desire, though, had been beyond her. She burned at times, burned with a lust for life and the pleasures of the flesh. Even on the Vigrid, thrown to the blood-drenched ground, surrounded by the stink of death, she had felt surging passion when Borr had ripped off his breechclout. She had wanted him, even if it meant death. When he had thrust into her, she had nearly fainted with delight. How he filled her!

In the midst of her orgasm a light had broken over her mind and she had realized something. Joy and pain were inseparable. If one would have joy, one had to have pain. The openness to one automatically opened you to the other. The more intensely you could feel the one, the more intensely you could feel the other.

Yes, it was possible to kill desire, but only at the price of killing the force that drove men to greatness. True, the quelling of desire gave one a peacefulness no ordinary human could achieve. So did death.

She'd never been able to sort it out completely. She knew only that she wasn't willing to give up joy for peacefulness. She wasn't ready or able to cast aside desire or the pleasure of fleshly delights. If pain came with it, then she would have to live with the pain.

Since that time, she'd thrown herself into her own humanness. She'd been a wife and a mother, accepting both the grief and the happiness that went with her choice. She'd done nothing to fight the Tao, nothing to change the Great Pattern, nothing to alter or transform herself beyond what she immediately was.

The pleasures of seeing Voden grow had been offset by the pain of losing a child in birth. Vethur had been born, and there was joy in that. Anguish had come with the separation from

Voden, but there had been the satisfaction of knowing it was in keeping with the Tao.

Seeing him again was a bittersweet experience. He was the same, yet transformed. He was her son, yet belonged to something much greater than her. She had had him for almost twelve years. Now the Tao had him.

Her only despair came from the fact that she had no way of telling him what she knew. She had tried to teach him the techniques of mind control and meditation that she had learned in the Floating World. But he was young, and it was too soon to tell how well the lessons had been learned. She had spoken often of the Tao and the Great Pattern, hoping he would understand more than her feeble attempts at explanation could offer. She had done what she could.

There were only two more things to be done. She shuddered to think of them, a great surge of sadness welling up in her. Two things she had seen in her vision many years ago. The time for them was coming. Soon, all too soon. She touched her stomach tenderly, resting her hand lightly on its taut surface. The child stirred with life. You, she told it silently, are the first thing, my poor little daughter.

The second crossed her consciousness and her mind shied away from it. Tears blurred her vision and she blinked them away. I chose this life, she thought, chose to be totally and thoroughly immersed in it. Let me meet the pain and the grief with arms opened as wide as for the pleasure and joy.

Borr was quite pleased. The truce was working well. This summer the Vanir had sent several groups of foresters north to reinforce the Aesir raiding parties. The results had been very satisfying.

No new Warlord had emerged to unify the Jotun Horde, although individual Jotun chieftains had led war parties across the Iving. The Aesir had returned the favor, sending groups of battle-eager young men north to try their hand at the wolf-work. The Vanir, though fighting in an alien environment, had proved quite useful, especially in the task of silently cutting the throats of sentries. The men from the forest were incredibly adept at creeping up noiselessly in the dead of the night. More than one Jotun family had been slaughtered in their wagons before they could wake up to defend themselves.

As long as no Warlord managed to bring the Jotun together for another major invasion of Asaheim, the most they would have to worry about would be minor skirmishes. The only cloud on the horizon was young Hrodvitnir, the nephew of Bergelmir, the last Warlord. From all reports he was a fierce warrior, ruthless toward any who stood in his way. Those who had seen him in action described a short youth, fifteen years old, slender, with an amazing wiry strength and incredible speed. His horsemanship and bowmanship were beyond compare. He could hit a wand at fifty paces at a full gallop. Several times he had leaped from the saddle, run next to his horse for several yards, then catapulted himself back into place again. In battle he wore a wolf-pelt cloak and sported a wolf skull complete with fangs as a crest for his leather helmet. Clearly, he would bear watching.

Borr was also pleased with Voden. The boy had grown while in Folkvang. He was taller, stronger, faster. He had begun to look like a warrior. He had stopped the eternal chattering of questions about every conceivable thing. It was a pleasure to have him around. Borr let him come to the Warrior's Hall several times during the eight days he was in Asgard, and he behaved very well. He sat quietly on the benches, listening carefully and respectfully to the older men as they talked, relating stories of the summer's fighting. It was a good sign. Folkvang wasn't ruining him after all.

The two he'd taken in as his hostages had turned out better than he had hoped also. Young Frey wasn't worth much, true. He didn't rough-and-tumble like the other youths, preferring to sit with the women and make eyes at the girls. Niord was all right, though. A regular fellow, that one. Fit right in. Some day he might make a proper Aesir warrior.

Yes, yes. It had all worked out quite well. He still had one son at home. And soon Vestla would give him another child.

Next summer perhaps they would step up their raiding on the Jotun. Get more Vanir help. What would a raid on Utgard accomplish? He looked over to where his ax hung. Why not? Crack a few skulls in Utgard itself. It would teach the damned Sons of Ymir a good lesson. Yes.

The eight-day homecoming passed swiftly, and it was time for Voden and Honir to return to Folkvang. Tror and Tyr came to see them off. Just before Voden got into the saddle, Volund's son pulled him aside and whispered in his ear, "I'm doing what I promised."

Voden looked at him, his expression alert and interested. "Mjollnir," he responded. "The Crusher."

Tror nodded. "Every morning I get up before Father and go into the forge room to start the fire. Mjollnir's there. I try to lift it."

"And?" Voden asked intently.

"Can't budge it. I try twice. Nothing." He looked desolate. "I don't understand. It doesn't look that heavy. I should be able to move it at least. You don't suppose old Groa put a spell on it or something, do you? I don't know. Do you want me to keep trying? Even though I can't do it?"

Voden placed his hand on the other boy's shoulder and squeezed hard. "Yes. It's important. Keep trying."

"But why?" Tror asked in sudden exasperation. "Why is it so important?"

The answer was harsh and imperative. "Don't ask. I can't tell you. I just know it is."

Tror looked directly into Voden's eyes. The stranger was there, brooding. The redheaded boy felt chilled. It was Voden, but it wasn't. He looked away, unable to meet the gaze of the Voden-stranger. "All right," he mumbled. "All right."

They left soon after, and Tror followed them to the gate for a last good-bye. Then he watched as the small group disap peared across the snow-covered hills.

The dark line of the forest was just ahead when the messenger caught up with Voden and his party. The man had driven his horse so hard through the drifts that it had nearly foundered. He was equally as exhausted.

His message was short and alarming. Vestla's baby had come sooner than expected. It had been a long, hard labor, but the little girl was fine and healthy.

Vestla, however, was dying.

XVIII

"MOTHER."

Vestla opened her eyes. A vague, shadowy figure loomed over her. "Voden?" she whispered. "So dark. Can't see. Voden?"

Borr brought the lamp closer. "Yes," he mumbled, "yes, it's Voden, home from Folkvang." Voden shot a quick glance at his father's face. It was rigid with control. He was an Aesir chieftain, a warrior descendant of Ask and Embla. He would never show weakness, never let Fornjot see his grief, but what his face hid, his eyes showed. Voden felt a sudden surge of fondness for his father.

He looked down at his mother's ravaged face. Her eyes were sunken and glazed, surrounded by black rings of exhaustion. The skin was drawn tight across the cheekbones as if the flesh had melted away from beneath it. The full lips were dry and cracked.

Vestla raised a shaking hand in his direction. He took it, surprised to feel the coldness. Was life already withdrawing from her body? He closed his eyes against the tears that suddenly rose.

"Voden." He opened his eyes and squeezed her hand, unsure of his voice. "You came. Have you seen your sister? Isn't she beautiful?"

"Yes, Mother," he managed to say.

"I want you to Namefasten her, Voden. In Prin that's good luck. My older brother Namefastened me. Good luck. Call her Vili."

"I will."

"Ah, ah, it's so dark," she complained. Borr stood suddenly. "I'll...I'll get another lamp," he said, and turned quickly away.

Vestla smiled wanly. "Another lamp. The darkness isn't outside. It's in me. Growing. I'm dying, Voden. You know that."

"Yes . . . I . . ."

"Hush. Don't talk. Listen. My son, someone will come. I hoped he would be here by now. But the Tao . . . ah, ah . . . it still hurts . . . I live awhile longer."

"Rest, Mother. We can talk later when you're better. Rest."

"No. There is no 'later' any longer, my son. Not for Vestla. I return to the Tao from where I came. It hurts now, but soon the pain will be gone. Soon.

"Listen, now. One comes. One called Kao-Shir. He will be your guide. Trust him."

"Mother . . ."

"One last thing, Voden. One last thing, then I will rest. Yes. Then I will rest." She took a deep breath, let it out in a long shuddering sigh.

"Once I told you of a vision granted by Vidolf. I wanted to wait until you were older to tell you again. But : . . now I must give it to you. Don't try to understand it all, my son. Just open your mind the way I taught you. Let it enter and make a place for itself. It will return from time to time, and you can work toward understanding at your own pace."

She fell silent again, panting quickly, tired by her effort to speak. Borr had returned with another lamp and stood staring down at his wife, his face blank with incomprehension. He glanced at Voden, his look a question. The boy returned the look with impassive, hooded eyes.

Voden dropped his gaze to his mother's face. Her eyes were closed as if she were resting and gathering strength. He didn't know what she was going to say, and he both feared and desired her words. A vision from Vidolf. He remembered her mentioning it before he left for Folkvang, and now she was going to share it with him. Share the meaning and the burden.

As he sat trying to calm his mind and put it in the receptive mode she had taught him, he found a strange thing happening. At first his thoughts were like a roomful of chattering people. He forced himself to ignore them, one by one. They didn't cease talking, but they did fade into the background. Finally he was by himself in the midst of the room, silent, waiting.

No, not by himself. There was another there, standing just behind him. He turned in an attempt to identify the other, but it both was and wasn't there. Huge, amorphous, it permeated everything. It was wordless yet somehow full of meaning. It was disturbing, yet not frightening or threatening.

Vestla opened her eyes and began to speak. "I chewed the sacred leaves, and I chanted the invocation to Vidolf for hours. Then as I lay in a wondering daze the sky opened its belly and I saw through to the world that lies above the blue.

"Ah, ah, what glorious light! There grew the ash tree called Yggdrasil, tall and sacred, plastered with white clay, rising ever green above the spring of Urd. It suffers, it endures more pain than men can know. Four harts leap about its branches and eat the tender shoots, tearing holes in its living flesh. Their names are Dain, Dvalin, Duneyr, and Durathror. At its root, a greater danger yet! No tongue can count the serpents that coil and writhe there! They gnaw, they gnaw, they gnaw at the roots, seeking in their endless hunger to destroy the world! Nidhogg is their leader, great, sinuous, and ravenous. Goin and Moin are there. Ofnir and Svafir too. Grafvollud twists and chews as does the evil, gray-backed worm called Grabak.

"Wonder of wonders, above Yggdrasil hung all three phases of the moon waxing, full, and waning. They came down toward me and I could see that they were in truth women. The waxing moon was a crone, wrinkled and stooped. She called herself Urd. The full moon was a matron, rich with life. She was named Verdandi. The waning moon was a maid with long, shining hair. She answered to Skuld.

"They gathered round me and spoke. 'We are the Nornir,' they said. 'We are the three who rune-carve what was, what is, and what must be.' Ancient Urd croaked, 'I reveal the past, the necessity of what had to be.' She unveiled my own history from the day I was born, showing me how I came, by necessity, to be what I am. Then Verdandi spoke in a voice heavy with life. 'I know the present, the fullness of its being.' She plunged me into the midst of my own existence, my own pain and joy. Next Skuld, her lilting voice overflowing with promise and warning, whispered in my ear, 'I see the future, laden with hope, dire with danger.' She opened my eyes to what will be, far, far beyond even this day.

"Urd and Skuld took me by the hands and Verdandi led us to the spring. I helped them sprinkle Yggdrasil with the white, healing waters. As I worked they taught me this song to sing to you." Vestla paused, her tongue licking her lips. Sweat poured from her face, and her body trembled with the effort of retelling her vision. She began to sing in a thin, reedy voice that swiftly grew fuller and stronger:

"The white one comes of nine maids born
to guard the world with clam'rous horn.

The red one will the hammer wield
to serve the Aesir as a shield.

The bravest one will give his hand
to trap the great Wolf far from land.

The one-eyed one in time of need,
will grasp his spear and take the lead.

Beware the Wolf with gaping jaw,
beware the blood-tie with his kin.
Beware the Serpent's deadly jaw,
beware the web his master spins.

The Wolf will raise a mighty cry
and men of every race will die.

His kin with dark deceit will send
bright Aesir treasure to its end.

Bright flame will paint proud Asgard's wall
When Serpent makes his deadly call.

Behind them all, the direst threat,
the Black One's plot must still be met."

Vestla struggled to sit up, her gaze wild. Her voice had
risen until it filled the hall. Everyone had stopped, frozen in
the midst of what they were doing, riveted by the eerie power
of the dying woman's speech. For a moment she paused, gathering whatever reserves of energy still lay untapped within her
ruined body. Then she cried:

"An ax-age, a sword-age,
shields will be battered;
a wind-age, a wolf-age,
before the world is shattered!

The sun goes black,
Earth sinks from sight,
the heavens lack
their starry light!

Smoke billows high
by fire driven,

> flames lick the sky
> and heaven's riven!"

Suddenly Vestla reached up and grabbed Voden's face, thin hands clutching at his cheeks. "My son, my son! Twilight comes! Prepare yourself for what you must do! Learn what you are that you may do it! Look deep in Groa's other eye! Go to . . . go to . . ." The words died in her throat and she fell back against the bed, her hands falling limp and useless to her sides. Her lips moved, trying to form words. Voden leaned forward, his ear almost to her mouth. One last word whispered forth on a final, faint breath. "Seek . . ."

Voden jerked his head back as a sudden convulsion shook the fever-wasted form. Vestla's mouth flew open, her eyes rolled back, and her body arched like a tight-drawn bow. With a sigh her life fled, and the body collapsed in the limp sprawl of death.

Borr reached out, his hand shaking ever so slightly, and pulled the eyelids down with his forefinger. Gently he lifted the hands and crossed them over the still breast. He smoothed the disarranged hair, stroking it lovingly back into place.

Finally his eyes met Voden's. "She's dead," he said, his voice dull, his glance bleak and barren. "She's dead." A great shudder passed through his body. He lifted the fold of his cloak and covered his face. "Dead," came the muffled voice. Borr stood and stumbled blindly to the high seat. He slumped into it, silent, the cloak hiding his visage from view.

The tears came in such a hot rush that Voden had no time to stop or control them. With a wail of anguish that was echoed by everyone in the hall, he threw himself across Vestla's still corpse.

They opened up the eastern side of Buri's mound and placed Vestla in it, her dead eyes gazing toward the sunrise. Borr refused to show his face, even during the burial, and kept the cloak draped over his head. Voden had to lead him to the mound and back as though he were blind.

When he returned to his hall, Borr stumbled to the sleeping cupboard where he and Vestla had lain side by side throughout the years of their marriage. He crawled in, laid down, cloak over his head, and slid the door shut.

When Roskva came with meat and beer, he refused to speak or open the door. She left bowl and mug, a worried expression clouding her normally cheerful features. When she returned two hours later, they were untouched. Silently, her brow furrowed, she took them away.

Vethur was too young to truly grasp what had happened. After a day of the depressing silence of the hall he began to fidget, and Voden sent him out to play with his friends.

The wet nurse kept Vili quiet. The baby lay in her cradle, cooing softly and smiling at anyone who chanced to look down at her. Voden stood and stared at the tiny gurgling creature. I should hate you, he thought. You killed my mother. Yet I will Namefasten you Vili as she wished, and no one will dare utter the name you earned by your birthing. He clenched his fists. I should hate you, but by the icy beard of Fornjot, you have such sun-bright hair and raven-black eyes! Every time I look I see Vestla in you. The gods help me, he cried silently as he reached down and lifted the baby into his arms, holding it tight against his chest, I cannot help but love you! My little Vili, I pledge you my life, even as Mother did. She would wish it so, I know.

For two days Borr refused food or drink. Gagnrad came to see his old friend. Borr wouldn't open the sleeping cupboard door or say a word. For a time Gagnrad sat outside the cupboard and chatted about the things that were happening in the Warrior's Hall, about the plans for that summer's raids against the Sons of Ymir, about things in Asaheim in general. Eventually he stopped and fell as silent as the man on the other side of the closed door. He finally left, his look glum, shaking his head in despair.

By the third day the household was in a panic. In the late afternoon Roskva came to Voden, a pleading look in her eyes. "Please," she said quietly, "do something, or Borr will kill himself. I fear the loss has driven him mad. Save him for all of us."

Voden sat for some time after Roskva walked away, his face thoughtful. Then he rose and went to the cupboard. He knocked softly at the door. "Father," he said, his voice hoarse with sadness, "let me in. You are right. Life isn't worth living any longer. Taking food and drink is foolish. It would only prolong what is painful and useless. I want to die with you. Let me in."

· After a moment he heard a stir, and the door slid open partway. He crawled inside. Borr was crumpled in the far corner, the cloak still over his head. He lay unmoving. Voden closed the door. In the dark of the cupboard he could barely make out his father's shape.

Voden waited perhaps five minutes before he sighed and said, "The loss is too great. Dying is best. The Aesir will have to find a new chieftain. Perhaps Gagnrad. Once we are both in the mound with Mother, it will not matter. Perhaps Gagnrad will take in Vethur and Vili as well. But it doesn't matter."

"No," Borr replied, his voice empty, "it doesn't matter."

"From Prin to the Vigrid to Asaheim. What a journey Vestla took," Voden said. "It's without equal, I think. Now she's dead." The boy sighed hugely. "What a pity there's no one to sing of it, no skald to write a song in her memory and honor. What a tale it would make! They would sing it to the ends of time!

"But . . . well, there are none who know it as well as you, and you are determined to die with her. What a pity."

Borr stirred, shifting his weight slightly. "Yes. Yes, it is a pity. It would make a great song."

"I wish I were a skald such as you, Father. I've not had experience like yours. I'm too young. Besides, I'm determined to die with you. Though if I were writing a song about Mother, I'd start with something like this:

> "My mouth strains hard
> to move dead tongue
>
> to find and form my sorrow.
>
> No words are there
> to weigh or tell
>
> the deep despair my heart holds."

For several moments Borr continued to lie silent beneath his cloak. Then he spoke softly, saying, "Yes. That would be a good start. I would continue it thusly:

> "Dull is my mind
> all drear and sad
>
> the song-spring stopped with anguish.

No hope have I
  nor happiness

now love is laid in grave mound."

Voden nodded. "Ah, ah, yes, Father, yes. Then it would
go:

"From dawn-lit Prin
  with darkest hair

by traveled trail came Vestla.

In blood and smoke
  'midst battle dire

Borr finally found fair treasure."

The boy sighed again. "Yes. But it cannot be, for both of
us are determined to die."

Borr nodded beneath the cloak. "Determined to die."

"And Mother will go to the Hall of the Gods with no song
to honor her." Voden paused as if suddenly struck by an idea.
"Father," he said after a few moments, "Father, we are both
determined to die, but would it be so awful if we waited awhile
and composed a song for Mother first? I...I would hate to
think that she would pass not only from Yggdrasil but also
from the memory of the Aesir simply because we failed to
make her a song."

His father lowered the cloak and glanced at him, a considering look in his eyes. "You have a point, son. We do have a
duty. I don't know if I'm up to it, if I can even finish it. Still,
I do have a duty. Yes." He sat up and closed his eyes. "Have
some curds brought. I must have some food if I'm going to
compose a song."

Voden slipped from the cupboard and walked slowly to
where the house servants stood, watching and listening in mixed
fear and hope. He gestured to Roskva, and the woman quickly
poured some curds into a bowl. The boy carried it back to his
father. Borr opened his eyes and took the bowl from his son,
then lifted it to his lips and began to eat, scooping the soft
curds into his mouth with his fingers. He finished and handed
the bowl back to Voden.

"The next verse should tell of our ride back to Asaheim,"
he said, looking up thoughtfully at the ceiling of the cupboard.

"Yes, and how she came to be called Ravenhair." He gestured with his hand. "Come sit with me, son. Your verses weren't bad. You can be of help."

As the song progressed Borr's grief began to soften. He took simple food and water, sparingly but regularly. After three days he called Voden to the cupboard. "Son, go find the skald Ginnar. Bring him to me. That man could set a dog's whine to music, and he can entice more beauty from his harp than anyone in Yggdrasil. I would have him make my song to Vestla come alive."

All that day and most of the next the two men huddled in the cupboard and worked together. Occasionally a light touch of harp strings could be heard in the hall. The servants would stop in their work and gaze in wonder first at the cupboard and then at Voden, who sat and played with Vili.

On the evening of the second day Borr and Ginnar came from the cupboard. Borr went and sat in the high seat, and the skald sat on the edge of the platform by his feet, his harp in his hands. Borr gestured to Voden to come and sit next to him. The boy picked up Vili in one arm, took Vethur by the hand, and joined his father. The household servants gathered around and filled the benches.

"I've kept your verses, Voden, because they are good, and to honor you." Borr looked out at the expectant faces of the servants. His gaze softened and a half smile curved his lips. "I have made a song for Vestla," he said. "At first I lived only to complete the song. Now I live because I have written it. She would wish it so."

He nodded down at Ginnar. The skald's fingers flowed across the strings of his harp, and music poured forth. Borr began to sing, his voice heavy, full of tender meanings. As he sang of Vestla and all she had been, several of the women began to cry softly. Even the men's eyes glistened with unshed tears. A lump rose in Voden's throat. He swallowed several times, trying to control it.

The tears ran freely down Borr's face, but his voice stayed firm and strong. He sang the words he had created with a triumphant sadness, a celebration of both grief and love. He came to the last verse and his voice rose to meet the ending.

> "No purse can pay
>   the price of grief
>
> the dismal due of death loss.

But I must face
   my final days

with full man's heart, not mourning."

The final words faded out, the harp notes vibrated into the air of the hall. The silence was total, absolute. Ginnar stood and bowed to Borr. "Skullcracker, you have earned a new name today, and I will Namefasten it to you. I call you Wordwielder, for you wield words as deftly as you swing your great ax, and you crack the hearts of men with those words as surely as you crack their heads with your dread blade. I beg your permission to go and sing this song of Vestla in all the halls of Asaheim." Borr nodded, and Ginnar bowed. The skald turned and bowed also to the entire household. He strode from the hall, his fingers already picking the melody out on his harp, his lips forming around the words.

Borr looked over at Voden. He stretched out his hands, and Voden handed Vili to him. The man looked solemnly at the baby, his brow furrowed in concentration. "Yes," he murmured, "I see Vestla in her, blond hair or not. Yes, in every line she is her mother's daughter." His eyes sought Roskva. "It is time to hold a funeral feast for my wife. It is time to begin living again."

THE FOREST

XIX

"THE boy is dangerous."

Fiorgynn looked thoughtfully at Syr, then let her glance sweep across the faces of the other seven Disir. Their expressions were mixed. Gna and Eir looked interested in what Syr had just said. Syn and Hlin were carefully neutral. Lofyn and Syofyn appeared mildly shocked by the suggestion. Vor was unreadable, as always. The Vanadis sighed inwardly. Best let Syr continue, then. She nodded her consent.

The old woman leaned forward, her eyes hostile. "I never liked the whole scheme from the beginning. You all know that. Truce and alliance with one of the young races! Fagh! Allowing Aesir brats to come and live among us! Sending two of our own to crawl through the filth of their squalid huts! Letting our young forest lads go to fight by their sides against yet another of the young races! Insanity! It goes against the will of Audhumla! Who knows what evil will come of such things?"

The Vanadis sighed with exasperation. "We've been over all this long ago, Syr. The decision has already been made. Yggdrasil changes. It is the will of Audhumla, or it would not be so. We must change with it or we will perish as did the great beasts whose tread once shook the forest. The Jotun are a very real and present danger. Have you already forgotten how Gullveig, Fulla, and Bil died beneath the hooves of their horses and how grievously they wounded Folkvang? Surely we are strong enough and wise enough to control two Aesir boys and a few hot-blooded young foresters. If this is all you wish to bring up, Syr, I would as soon you remain silent."

"Nay, that is not all I wish to bring up. If Voden were an ordinary child, I would agree with you. There would be little to be said that has not been said before, though I think perhaps you underestimate the importance of those 'few hot-blooded young foresters.'

"But young Voden, ah, yes, young Voden is the key to it

211

all. For he is no ordinary child. No, not he."

Syofyn tossed her head, her long, black hair moving like liquid night. "He seems ordinary enough to me. If anything, he's more courteous and respectful toward the Disir and things Vanir than some of our own. I rather like him. He has nice eyes."

"Oh, he's likable enough. And courteous. And interested in learning things Vanir. Oh, yes. Vor can vouch for his learning. Already the Aesir speaks the elder tongue with greater fluency than many Vanir. Geirahod says he's one of her best students in the Thiodnuma. He is, also, I'm told, skilled in wrestling. Yes. But the mere fact that you like him, Syofyn, is hardly enough to put my mind at rest. I've yet to find the male, young or old, you don't like.

"No, sisters, it's not the courteous, studious, interested-in-things-Vanir Voden we see and deal with every day that worries me. No, no. That surface Voden is not dangerous. Ah, but the Voden that lurks below that fair surface, the one that hides behind the smiling face and friendly eyes, that one worries me."

Syofyn laughed. "You're imagining things, Syr! Jumping at shadows like a nervous doe. Vanadis, this is a waste of time. Syr is frightening herself with her own creations. We have more important things to attend to."

"Frightening myself, am I?" the old woman snarled. "You see a firm young body, a friendly smile, and think everything is fine. Bah! You think with your body, you young fool! I see deeper, and I see danger."

Before Syofyn could reply, Fiorgynn interrupted. "What thinks Vor of this? Vor, the oldest and wisest of us all?"

All eyes turned to the wrinkled, ancient crone who sat next to the Vanadis. "Vor says we'd be fools indeed not to listen to Syr. Since the two Aesir have come among us, Syr has watched them as closely as a sow watches her piglets. She has sharp eyes. She may have seen things the rest of us have missed. Not to hear her out would be as absurd as closing our eyes to the menace of the Jotun."

Fiorgynn nodded solemnly. "Vor speaks wisely. It cannot hurt to listen to what Syr has to say. Speak, then. The Distingen will hear you."

Syr smiled triumphantly. "Thank you, Vanadis. Vor is right. I have watched the Aesir boys closely. Honir is no problem.

Tongue-tied, a bit shy, not terribly bright, fleet as the wind when he runs, normal in every sense. He is no problem. We can control him as easily as we control our own.

"The son of Borr is another matter. When first he came I thought he was nothing but a curious child. The more I watched, though, the more I realized the mind behind that curiosity was anything but ordinary. He learns, that one, swiftly and well.

"Were that all, I would put him down as a bright young boy and have no worry. We have molded bright ones to our designs before. No, there is more here." She paused and frowned. "Something that goes beyond mere intelligence. The lad has a power and a strength that should not exist in one his age, Vanir or Aesir.

"Oh, yes, sisters, Voden is dangerous. Yes. He is dangerous because he has been touched by Vilmeid!"

Several of the Disir gasped in surprise. Hlin leaned forward and said, "Vilmeid? You mean . . ."

"Aye," Syr responded, her face grave, "I mean the boy has the Galdar-power in him."

"When did you first notice this?" Fiorgynn demanded. They all leaned forward to hear her reply.

"First? Well, I suspected something like it shortly after Synyr was made king. Voden changed. It was a small change. So small I wasn't sure I really saw it at first. But before he went back to Asgard at the winter solstice, it was stronger.

"And now, ah, now that he's come back after his mother's death, well, well, yes, now it is clear. Experiences like that tend to stir up the things that lie hidden in the dark parts of our minds. Yes, the Galdar-power is there, gaining in strength.

"It is weak yet, sisters, weak, but he is dangerous, and every day he grows more so."

Vor mused, her eyes distant with reverie. "Once there was another such among us. Do you remember him, Syr? It was before the time of most of you, but Syr and Eir should recall him. Do you, sisters?"

Eir nodded her gray head. "Yes. Sanngetall was his name, though we gave him a new one."

Vor hissed in merriment. "Ah, yes! We took something away and gave him a new name in return!"

"Jalk he became," Syr said. "I remember him well. Whatever happened to Sanngetall-Jalk, sister?"

Vor shrugged indifference. "Who knows? As Jalk, he left

part of himself behind and stumbled bleeding into the forest. Probably he bled to death or died of the shock. It makes no difference."

The Vanadis frowned. "I have heard this story. That was when Mardoll was Vanadis. It is not a pretty tale."

"That it isn't," agreed Vor. "But it is an instructive one. Sanngetall defied the will of Audhumla. He had the Galdarpower. He was dangerous. We stopped him."

"As we must stop Voden," added Syr.

Hlin shuddered. "We cannot harm the boy, especially that way. We have sworn to protect him as if he were one of our own. I, for one, will uphold that oath. He must not be harmed. Not that way."

Vor smiled a toothless grin. "You sound as softhearted as our loving Syofyn. Or like motherly Lofyn. If Syr is right, the boy is dangerous. Something must be done about him."

Fiorgynn held up her hand. "Hlin speaks well. Voden is a hostage. We may not harm him physically."

"Ah." Syr smirked. "'Physically.' Yes, Vanadis, you are right. Physically." She looked at Vor. "There are other ways to stop this danger from maturing, aren't there, wise one? Oh, yes. Ways that will barely leave a mark on his body. Yes. After all, it's not his body we fear."

The entire Distingen looked at Vor. The old crone sat with her eyes closed, a half smile curving her wrinkled lips. She sat unmoving for several moments, then opened one bright eye and said, "We would honor young Voden. His poor mother is dead. A tragedy. We would honor him. Yes. There is a rite, one that consecrates a man to Audhumla. A great honor. One no longer sought, true, for it requires a dangerous and often fatal ordeal. Sad, sad. So many have lost their senses undergoing it. That is why it was stopped when I was still as young and hot-bodied as Syofyn. Still, it is a great honor, especially appropriate for one whose mother has died, yes."

Fiorgynn's eyes narrowed. "I know this rite. Mardoll told me of it. She also told me it is forbidden."

"Forbidden? No, no, not forbidden. No longer used because of the danger. Sanngetall refused to undergo it, which was why we were forced to change him."

"What if Voden refuses?"

"Why should he refuse? Sanngetall knew what it meant. Voden knows nothing, and there are none to tell him. He will never suspect the danger until it is on him. Then it will be too late. One way or the other, our purpose will be accomplished."

Hlin looked uncomfortable. "What is this rite you speak of, Vor? Why is it so dangerous? How will it give us control over Voden? I'm not sure I like the sound of it."

Vor leaned back. Her eyes took on a faraway look. "In the First Age," she began, "just after Audhumla created the world, the Vettir and the Vanir lived together in total harmony. They were like children of the same mother, living in the same hall, sharing and mingling unself-consciously. There was no way to tell Vettir from Vanir, so much alike were they.

"The world was young then, and bountiful. The trees were always green and laden with ripe fruit. No one had to work, yet no one ever went hungry. The days were balmy and sun-filled, the nights warm and sensuous. Vettir and Vanir alike went naked, dancing, playing, and making love as they wished. All was joyful. No one ever grew old.

"In those days there was a woman of the Vettir named Glad, so beautiful that she glowed with an inner light. Her mother was Idun, and she loved her daughter very much.

"One day as Glad wandered through the forest she came upon a Vanir man bathing in a pool. As he stepped from the water, Glad saw the perfection of his body and instantly fell in love with him. She opened her arms and legs to him, and he fulfilled her every desire. His name was Oski.

"Glad and Oski became inseparable lovers. Wherever they went, whenever the urge came upon them, they fell into each other's arms and made love. They were insatiable. Neither could get enough of the other. Their joy was constant. Idun was greatly pleased for her daughter.

"Others were not so happy. Many women, both Vettir and Vanir, were jealous of Glad. They desired Oski for themselves. Many men, both Vettir and Vanir, were jealous of Oski. They desired Glad for themselves.

"Finally, Bolverk, a man of the Vanir, took counsel with Helblindi, a woman of the Vettir. Bolverk said, 'Since Glad will have no man but Oski, we must get rid of him.' Helblindi said, 'Since Oski will have no woman but Glad, we must get rid of her.' So they agreed to capture and kill them both.

"It wasn't hard to accomplish. Bolverk and Helblindi simply found the two lovers coupling ecstatically and fell on them, stabbing them to death. Then they carried the bodies to a cave and hid them, rolling great rocks in front of the cave's mouth.

"Idun missed her daughter. She missed hearing her laughter

and seeing her joy. For several days Idun assumed that Glad and Oski were simply off somewhere making love. When they failed to appear, however, she became worried and went searching for them. She asked every Vettir she met, 'Have you seen Glad and Oski?' The Vettir turned away without answering. She asked every Vanir she met, 'Have you seen Oski and Glad?' The Vanir turned away without answering.

"Finally Idun came to a place in the forest where a patch of bright red flowers bloomed. She had never seen such flowers before. She noticed there was a trail of them leading off in one direction. Fear clutching her heart, she followed the trail. It lead directly to the cave.

"Weeping, Idun rolled the rocks from the cave's mouth. Weeping, she carried Glad and Oski, still blended together in the embrace of their love, back to her home. There she buried them as they were, so that they might never be separated.

"Within three days a great tree began to grow on that spot. It grew and grew for six more days until it soared up out of sight into the heavens. Then Idun called all the Vettir and the Vanir to her. She called them to the base of the great tree.

"'Behold this great tree,' she told them. 'It is Glad and Oski. Its roots are as deep as their love. Its top reaches as high as their love. Its branches bear fruit as richly as their love.

"'As they died for their love, so shall this tree die. Its leaves shall turn red as blood and drop to the ground. Its fruit shall wither and rot. It shall stand as stark and empty as death itself.

"'This shall be so for all trees. Their leaves shall fall, their fruit rot, and they shall stand as though dead. Unless the Children of Audhumla work hard to harvest the fruit, they will go hungry. They will know fear and death.

"'But in the fullness of its time, the tree shall burst forth with life again. It shall be renewed. It shall bear green leaves and ripe fruit. It shall stand as rich and full as the love of Glad and Oski. So shall it be for all trees. And the Children of Audhumla will be joyous and celebrate the return of life and love. They shall be happy and full of food.

"'This shall happen each year, as long as the world the Nourisher created shall exist.'

"Then Idun looked out over the assembled Vettir and Vanir and frowned. 'Now I will leave you,' she said, 'and go to join Glad and Oski who dwell with Audhumla. Because you have caused this thing to happen, you can no longer live as before. The Vettir will enter everything, rocks, trees, animals, clouds,

flowers. There they will stay forever. The Vanir will keep their
own forms, but they must cover their bodies against the weather
and work hard to prepare for the time when all dies.

"'From this day on, all will know the pain of life and the
fear of death. All will know hunger and thirst, both the nodding
flower, the beast of the field, and the man and woman in their
hut. All will know cold and darkness.

"'Yet there will always be the chance for the joy of love
and the renewal of life. The love of Glad and Oski will not
disappear entirely from the world. It is too great to die.' With
those final words she ascended the great tree and was gone."

Vor looked at them all, her bright eyes moving slowly from
face to face. "The rite is that of Oski. It is the rite of death in
one form and rebirth and renewal in another. Through it a man
dies in his ordinary sense of being and becomes one with
Audhumla. He is reborn into a new being, part of the Nourisher." She smiled grimly. "Such a one loses much, as did
Oski, but he gains immeasurably more. To be with Audhumla
forever . . . ahh," she sighed, "that is much to be desired."

"It would also neutralize him completely," added Syr. "He
would no longer be a danger."

Vor snorted. "He would no longer be much of anything.
An eternal dreamer who would sit and stare off into vastness.
Once in a while we could trot him out and call up a vision
from him. He would be no problem. No problem at all."

Hlin shuddered. "Would he . . . would he be happy?"

Vor laughed shortly. "Happy? He would be Oski, constantly
loving the beautiful Glad, secure in the bosom of Audhumla.
He would know nothing but endless orgasmic ecstasy."

"He would be mindless," said Fiorgynn, her voice hard.

"Yes," Syr answered. "Mindless."

A silence fell over the Distingen. Each of the nine women
sat wrapped in her own thoughts. Fiorgynn finally looked up.
"Do we all agree then that Voden is dangerous, so dangerous
that we must act to control him?"

Syr, Vor, Gna, and Eir nodded firmly. Hlin, Syn, and Lofyn
agreed halfheartedly. Syofyn hesitated. "Is there no other
choice?"

"How else can we control him?" Syr demanded impatiently.

"Well . . ." the young Disir said thoughtfully, "there's Freyja."

Fiorgynn looked at her quizzically. "Freyja? What has my
daughter to do with this?"

Syofyn laughed lightly. "Syr has watched the two Aesir

closely, but there are some things she has missed. Perhaps she is too old to remember. Vanadis, though I doubt he realizes it himself, Voden is in love with Freyja!"

Realization dawned on Lofyn's face. "Yes, yes, of course! The way he looks at her! Yes, you're right."

Syr looked sourly at Syofyn. "I grant you precedence in matters of love, oh, yes, though I fail to see how that gives us a way to control Voden."

"How did Glad control Oski, sister? Surely you're not too old to understand that?"

The old woman grunted and looked away, disgusted. Syofyn's grin grew broader. "Wouldn't it be a better way to control the Aesir, sisters? It avoids the risk of damaging him and bringing down the wrath of his father on our heads, and it might even make him more than just a passive nonmenace. It could turn him into an active ally."

Vor returned the young woman's smile dryly. "You've forgotten one small thing, young one. You've forgotten Freyja. She is to be the Vanadis when Fiorgynn dies. She cannot be tied in marriage to some Aesir barbarian."

"There is another thing," Eir added. She nodded her head slightly in Fiorgynn's direction. "I pledged secrecy to your daughter, Vanadis, but I think this justifies the breach. She has come to me several times for contraceptive draughts. The cause for the need of such things is not Voden. It is Od. I doubt Freyja would be interested in Syofyn's little plan. The girl has a mind of her own."

Fiorgynn chuckled. "That she does. Syofyn, your idea is an interesting one, but I'm afraid I agree with Eir. It would take Freyja's complete cooperation, and I doubt very much we could get that." The young Disir bowed her head in acceptance. The Vanadis looked around the group one last time. "I take it we are agreed, then? Voden is a danger, one that must be met. We cannot allow the Galdar-power to grow to maturity in him. He will undergo the rite of Oski so that we can neutralize him."

"When shall it be?" Gna asked. "He will be twelve very soon. And the vernal equinox approaches. Though it is the time of the growing ascendancy of the sun and the male, it might be the right time anyway. Perhaps shortly after the journey and festivals of Gefyn. That is a very magical and potent time. How strong is the Galdar-power in him, Syr? Can we afford to wait until after the equinox?"

"As I said before, the power is weak yet, and he fears it, fights it, fails to understand what it is and what it means. The Aesir have little to do with Vilmeid. No, if anything, the boy is in a confused and weakened state. His mother's death but adds to the confusion. I believe the time you suggest would be fine, Gna, fine."

"There is something more too," Vor reminded them. "Holding the rite in the spring will give him plenty of time to recover before he has to return to Asgard for the winter solstice. With that much time we can bring him back to at least a semblance of normality."

Fiorgynn rose. "It is decided, then. Shortly after the vernal equinox, after Gefyn has toured Vanahcim in her wagon drawn by two forest cats, Voden will undergo the rite of Oski. He will become the lover of Glad and achieve oneness with Audhumla. It will be a great honor for him. We will honor both the boy, his father, and his people by doing such a thing. It will be tantamount to making him one of us, making him fully a Vanir. So shall it be."

The eight Disir bowed their heads and repeated in unison, "So shall it be." Syr and Vor traded a secret smile.

"Vor, Syr, and Hlin will be in charge of the ritual. Eir, you should be on hand in case your healing arts are needed. When it is over, we will hold a great feast in Sessrymnyr. Voden-Oski will sit in the High Seat next to me. It will be a great honor, second only to that given the king. A great honor. So shall it be."

"So shall it be," they responded. "As Audhumla would will it."

XX

HE fled through the dark forest. All around him he could hear the soft, insistent rustling made by his pursuers. There were so many of them!

Ahead the moon shone through the trees. A clearing. He staggered and almost fell. Must reach the clearing, he thought desperately. Must. He gulped great drafts of air and tried to force his weary legs to pump even faster. Must reach the light. Too much dark in the forest. Too much.

With a lurch he stumbled through the last underbrush onto the soft grass of the clearing. The sounds of pursuit were louder now and seemed to come from all directions. In panic he glanced around at the dark wall of the forest. With a shudder he moved toward the center of the moonlit openness.

In the middle of the clearing a rock stood. It was strangely shaped, rectangular and flat on the top. It was unnatural. He approached cautiously. The thing was lichen-covered. Beneath the lichen the side near him seemed to be carved with some sort of design. He leaned over, running his fingers across the surface, trying to make it out in the dim light. It seemed like writing. This line, this shape, seemed full of meaning. If only he could make it out, he might . . .

Something touched his shoulder. In sudden fear he spun around. The clearing was full. His pursuers had caught up. The ground swarmed and writhed with them. Creatures of every sort, their eyes were big with greed, their fangs and claws twitching with desire. They want to devour me, he realized. They want to tear me apart and eat me while I'm still alive.

With a shriek of horror and despair he leaped back against the rock, then scrambled to its top. The creatures closed in on him, their paws pulling him down to the flat stone surface and holding him tight no matter how hard he struggled.

The tall figure came then, robed in black. There seemed to be no face within the hood, only two glowing points that might have been eyes. The black one stood over him and gazed down. He felt suddenly cold and helpless. "Audhumla," he whimpered. The hood fell back and he saw the face. Half of it was beautiful, with soft skin; full, senuous lips; shining teeth; bright, loving eyes; proud nose; silky hair. The other half was putrid, with maggot-filled skin; shriveled lips; rotted teeth, pusy, oozing eyes; worm-eaten nose; straggly, dying hair. "Audhumla," he whimpered again, rigid with terror.

The figure raised its hands. One was soft and gentle, the other gnarled and clawlike. With both it held a long, wickedly gleaming knife. "We must feed my children," the figure whispered in a voice that came equally from the bed and the grave. The knife slashed down, and he screamed with the shock of pain. One of his fingers lay twitching in the moonlight. A creature grabbed it and began to gnaw on it. The knife slashed down again and again. The gibbering beasts crowded up, fighting and clawing to get a piece, then slobbering und drooling as they gobbled. He kept screaming.

He looked up and saw two ravens circling. "Come out of yourself," one of the ravens croaked.

"Come out of yourself," the other repeated.

The hot breath of two wolves played over his face. He looked to right and left. One stood on either side, paws on his chest, staring down into his eyes. "Come out of yourself," growled one, a huge gray

"Come out of yourself," repeated the large black one.

"Come out and we will take you away," the gray continued.

"You can ride on our backs," said the black.

"We are your brothers," the two finished.

The knife slashed down again and severed his left leg below the knee. He screamed. "I can't get out! I don't know how!"

"You can, you can!" the wolves and ravens cried in unison.

"No, no, no, no," he blubbered, the pain sweeping over him as the knife rose and fell. "I don't know how! I don't know how! Oh, Mother, Mother, help me!"

Audhumla snickered and cut off his ear. "I am the Mother. The Nourisher and Destroyer. There is no Mother but me to call on. I am all."

Hot anger filled him. "No! No! You're not Vestla! Not my mother! None of you are my mother! Damn you! Damn you all!" He gave a mighty jerk, using every ounce of strength left in his body.

He stood free. He looked down at the writhing thing on the

*stone, the thing Audhumla was slicing into pieces, the thing
the creatures were greedily eating. He looked at the two wolves
who sat, grins on their faces, waiting. He looked up at the two
ravens who circled. Stepping down from the stone, he put a
hand on each of the wolves' heads. "Come, brothers, let us
go from here."*

He woke with a start. It was dark. The stench of death was so
strong it made his head reel and his stomach heave. He threw
up, his whole body shaking with the force of his vomiting.

He tried to move and found that he was tied to something.
Suddenly full consciousness swept away the last fuzziness in
his mind and he knew. He was tied to the body of Glad. To
the dead body of Glad. The stench was the smell of rotting
flesh.

Unable to control himself, he spasmed once more, heaving
dryly. Spent, he lay limp and exhausted, feeling the cold flesh
of the dead body pressed against his own. His mind teetered
on the edge of madness.

From somewhere deep within he heard the growl of a wolf.
Then the hoarse voice of a raven said, "It's only a goat. Only
a goat." Yes, he realized. Yes. It's only a goat. Not really
Glad. And I'm not Oski. I'm Voden. Voden tied to the rotting
body of a dead she-goat and dumped into a cave by the Disir.
Yes.

Rotting body. Maggots. By the gods! Maggots! Fear slapped
him back into action. The maggots would eat the goat's flesh.
When they reached his, they would continue eating! He had
to get loose! Frantically he twisted and turned, trying to break
free. The bonds weren't that strong. He broke those binding
his wrists around the back of the goat. With trembling hands
he snapped the others that held him to the corpse.

Free at last, he rolled away. Thank Audhumla... *no!* Damn
it, no! Damn Audhumla! The rage rose in his breast like a
flame. Damn the... the... Disir! He couldn't think of a word
horrible enough to express his hatred and revulsion. Thank
Audhumla? Damn! Rather thank Fornjot. No, not that either.
The Destroyer hadn't come to his aid when he'd called on
him—how many times?—during the torture of the ritual.

His mind flashed back. They'd laid him out, drugged, a
Disir holding each arm, each leg. Syr had grabbed his foreskin
between her fingers, pulling it out as far as she could. Then

Vor had come with the razor-sharp flint knife and cut . . . cut . . . oh, sweet horror, the pain, the pain! They'd cut the skin and offered it to Audhumla! The Nourisher had taken it and placed it in her mouth and . . .

He pulled his mind back from the dark edge. Control, he told himself. Don't try to think of it all at once. Too much happened. Take it slow and easy, bit by bit. Otherwise it will overwhelm you.

Tentatively he reached down between his legs. There was a cloth wrapped around his groin. He felt what must be herbs within the binding. Only a dull ache. It must be mending. Carefully he probed. I'm still a man, he thought with relief. They only cut off a little bit of skin. That's all. A little bit. Slowly, take it slowly.

He ran his hands over his body. He was wet, probably from sweat and the slime from the dead body. Glad. They told him it was Glad and he was Oski. They made him copulate with the she-goat. Then they cut him. Drugged. All so foggy. Gods! I didn't know what I was doing! He shuddered and moaned.

Slowly he sat up. Hungry. Thirsty. Too dark to see anything. Must be food here somewhere. When did I last eat? he wondered. He groped around. His hand touched a pitcher. Ah, ah, water! He raised the pitcher to his lips, taking a long drink.

Instantly he knew it was wrong. He spit out the water. The bitter taste stayed in his mouth. Damn, damn, damn. Water was drugged. Should have thought of that. Oh, damn. Can feel it. Mind going again. Oh, help, help, please, no more visions! Can't take it!

The light grew and the figures came toward him. Two, three, more. He tried to lift his head, tried to flee from whatever new horrors the drug had brought him. A scream came out as a sigh. His mind teetered, teetered. Darkness closed around him.

"I say we should kill him and have done with it."

"You know that won't do. We'll have to wait till he gets here. He'll decide, he will. It's not for us."

"Aye, you've the right of it, Harbard. Remember them wolves as led us to him. That was a bit of strange, I say. I'd not want to kill such a one without knowing a bit more."

"All right," grumbled the first voice. "Have your own way, then, but I say kill the Vanadis's little toy and be done with it. Gives me the creeps, it does, what with that cave and the goat. What do you suppose they was doing with him, cutting him like that and all?"

"Magic," said the one called Harbard. "Seidar-magic as sure as you're born, Gylfi. And I say that if they was working magic on the lad, it can't be because they love him. You know we've one among us as they worked on long ago. For no reason other than that Jalk would want to talk with him, I'll not kill him."

"Huh. Someone's coming. That's Byggvir's call."

Voden opened his eyes. The moon gleamed through the treetops. He felt cold and numb. He closed his eyes again. As he lay there exhausted, he sensed someone approach and lean over him. He heard a voice say softly, "Ah, it's Voden." He opened his eyes slowly and looked up into the face of Yngvi.

For a moment he simply stared at his friend. Then, with a sudden surge of emotion, he sat up and flung his arms around the young forester's neck and began to cry hysterically. "There, there," Yngvi soothed. "It's all right now, lad. You're among friends now. Aye, among friends."

The rest of that night was a blur in Voden's overloaded mind. He kept passing out and waking up. Each time he became conscious, Yngvi was nearby. About dawn he vaguely remembered being carried over some rocks, behind a screen of bushes, and into a large, airy cave.

When he finally woke fully, he was lying on his back, covered with a heavy bear pelt. One of the gray stone walls of the cave was next to him. He reached out and touched it. Dry, real, comforting.

He turned his head and saw an incredibly old man sitting a few feet away, staring fixedly at him. Yngvi was standing behind the man.

The young forester nodded. "Awake now, are you? Been a full day you've been napping, barbarian. Are you feeling a bit better?"

Voden nodded. "Hungry. Thirsty," he managed to croak.

A third man came into view from the back of the cave with a steaming bowl of stew and a pottery mug of some dark liquid. "Here, lad. It'll make you feel right."

Greedily Voden gulped down the food and drink. The stew was filled with large chunks of meat. Whatever the mug held, it was bitter and invigorating. When he'd finished, he felt almost human again.

As he ate, the old man continued to stare. Voden put the bowl and mug aside and returned the stare. The old man snorted and looked up at Yngvi. "They scared him, and he bears more than a few raw wounds, but they didn't reach him. No, not they. Ha! They've not the strength to destroy those as Vilmeid has chosen for his own!" The old man cackled with glee and turned his stare back to Voden. "I'm Jalk, as once was Sanngetall."

"He's our leader," Yngvi added.

Voden looked in bewilderment from one to the other. Jalk laughed again. "Not a word does he understand! Ah, ah, a rare one you've brought me, Yngvi! Look at his eyes. See, see the power lurking there? Yes, yes! This is the one promised me by Vilmeid! This is the one!"

Jalk turned to his right and called out, "Harbard!" A tall man walked swiftly from the cave entrance and squatted next to Jalk. He looked over at Voden, nodded, and smiled. "Now," said the old man, "tell us again, Harbard, how you came on young Voden here."

"We was out hunting wolves. Been a pack pestering the deer in the area all winer. Wanted to get rid of 'em, we did. Trapped about seven over by the swamp. Of a sudden, two more showed up. What beasts they were! The gray stood as high as my chest at his shoulder. Grizzled he was, and powerful. Not a regular wolf, that one. The black was smaller, true, but such a look in his eyes! Froze a man to the spot, it did.

"Well, we just stopped and stared at 'em both. They looked us up and down and then began to run off. A few yards they went, then stopped and turned to stare back at us. Somehow it seemed they wanted us to follow, so I says, Let's for it.

"Led us quite a chase, they did. Right to the cave. The mouth was covered with boulders. There was fires still smoldering here and there. Aye. And some strange things lying around."

"Ravens?" Voden asked. "Were there any ravens?"

Harbard screwed up his face in concentration. "Aye, now that you mention it, I do recall seeing a pair hopping around. Big fellows, both."

Voden sighed and lay back. "Yes."

"Anyway," Harbard continued, giving him a strange look, "we rolled back the rocks and found the lad here. With a dead goat. He was a mess, the lad was, covered with dried blood and vomit. Strange writing on his body, too, and a bundle of herbs tied between his legs. A real mess. And the smell! I almost vomited myself, I did.

"So. We picked him up and sent Bragi out after Yngvi. The rest you know."

Jalk nodded and rubbed his hands. "Hamingjur. Familiar spirits. Yes, yes, the power runs deep in this one. Wolves and ravens. Not pleasant Hamingjur, no, but powerful. Ah, very, very powerful."

Voden felt strange. His mind was hazy, yet part of it seemed very alert. He found himself speaking, not knowing he was doing it. "Freki is gray and Geri is black. Hugin and Munin are the two winged ones."

A silence followed his words. Voden's mind drifted quietly. Those with him seemed to be holding their breaths, waiting for him to speak again. Moments passed, and when he remained silent, Jalk cleared his throat and muttered, "Aye, it's there. He doesn't know it fully himself, but it's there. Much work is to be done yet. So much. Still dangerous. It could all go bad, the lad could lose his mind or worse. Ah, ah, but what promise! What power! Clear out, the lot of you. Voden and I must talk."

Vaguely the young Aesir heard the others shuffling out of the cave. He felt Jalk pushing himself across the floor to sit close to him. He looked up into the old man's face.

"Open up, young one. Jalk would read your soul. Open up, I'll not hurt you. I must be sure. Much depends on it." Voden nodded and mumbled his assent, not certain exactly what he was agreeing to but somehow knowing there was little danger. His eyes drifted to Jalk's. The old man's opened wider and wider. Voden fell into them.

Jalk sat back with a sigh and gazed thoughtfully at the sleeping figure of the boy. He rubbed the bridge of his nose with tired fingers. By all the gods, he thought, the Disir have a good deal to answer for! They had nearly destroyed the lad. The rite and the drugs had twisted and warped the power that lay within the young Aesir, turning it back on itself, turning it into a swirling, chaotic, destructive force.

Yet somehow Voden had managed to survive the ordeal, had even managed to find his Hamingjur on his own! Jalk shook his head, his face grim. And what Hamingjur! Wolves and ravens. Symbols of war and death. Vilmeid had touched the boy, all right, but not lightly or pleasantly.

For a few moments he sat and stared vacantly at the wall of the cave. Things couldn't be left as they were, he realized. The Galdar-power had to be redirected. He only hoped it wasn't too late. So much damage had already been done. Damn the Disir!

He had to set things straight, or at least redo some of the damage in hopes Voden would heal naturally with time. Time, yes, that was the only sure cure. By himself, Jalk knew he couldn't do enough to bring the boy back to normal. Perhaps if he had a year or two to work with him. As it was . . .

As it was, he knew full well he didn't have much longer to live. His time wasn't measured in years or even months. The end was only days away. Days. And the lad needed years of help and guidance. Someone had to teach him the healing lore, and the names of all the spirits and demons, and the original tongue, and the runes. And the . . . ah, ah, it was endless, endless. So much to be learned to fully develop the Galdar-power. How will he learn it all? Who will teach him?

Voden stirred in his sleep, whimpering. Jalk muttered a curse. What a hideous mess the Disir had made of him! His mind on the edge of insanity, his system still full of the drugs they had stuffed into him, his body cut and mistreated . . . ah, what a damned mess!

What had to be done would have been difficult and dangerous even if the young Aesir had been totally sound of mind and body. This way . . . was it even possible? Would the added burden of new experiences, disturbing experiences, save the lad or utterly destroy him?

Do I have any choice? If I don't act now, I'll never have a chance to do anything for him. I'll be dead long before he's normal again, and then there'll be no one to help, no one to guide. That's the most I can hope for. A little help, a little guidance, put the Galdar-power right again, give him time to heal himself and discover his powers on his own, if such a thing were possible.

He rubbed the bridge of his nose again, weary and unsure. In hopes of doing him a little good, I risk killing him, he admitted. Except that it's more than that, more than a little good. He *will* go insane if I don't act. He *may* go insane because I act. It's hard to decide.

An unexpected thought entered his mind. Perhaps this was *precisely* the time to act. What the Disir had done to the lad had brought him to the edge of the most devastating crisis of mind, spirit, and body possible to a human being. Everything stood on the brink of utter dissolution and destruction. Literally, the universe was dissolving for Voden. It could dribble away completely, leaving nothing behind but a drooling, empty husk, or something new could be created from the disintegration of the old, something different and, Jalk hoped, better.

Jalk squared his thin shoulders and nodded his head firmly. Yes. Once he had been known as a man who always guessed right, a man who understood things that struck others dumb. He knew he had not lost that power when they had taken so much else from him. His guess was right. Now was the time, the very time, to act. This was the moment to transform what was and what is into what must be. The change wouldn't happen in an instant. It would take years to come to full fruition. No tree bore fruit until it was mature, and no trees became mature unless the seed was planted in the first place.

This would be the planting of the seed. Now if only it didn't kill the lad.

When he woke, Voden found Jalk sitting next to him, staring into space. The young Aesir stirred. The old man looked down, frowning. "Ah, lad," he said, "back again, are you? Hungry and thirsty, I'll wager. Yes. Here. Eat some stew and drink this. You'll be needing the energy."

Voden felt ravenously hungry. He gobbled the food. "How long did that take?" he wondered out loud between mouthfuls.

"Take? Ah, yes. A day."

The Aesir stopped eating and gawked in disbelief at the old man. "A day?"

Jalk shrugged. "A day and a half, actually. There's a lot in you, Voden, more than you can guess. And I only went a little way down. Too deep for me, most of it. Aye, too deep."

"I . . . What did you see?"

"Oh, many things, many things," Jalk answered. "Most of them a mystery." He frowned again. "You're what I thought you were. And more."

The old man's hand suddenly shot out and closed on Voden's shoulder. "Lad," he began, his voice urgent, "I've not many breaths left to draw on this earth. No, not I. For many seasons I've been waiting for one like you. You're not quite what I expected, you aren't at all, but I've waited too long and time's run out. So I'll have to trust. Aye," he muttered with a shake of his head, "I'll have to trust."

Jalk settled back and fixed Voden with a piercing glance. "Yggdrasil's changing, lad, faster than any of us know. The power of the Vanadis and the Disir is waning. Audhumla, aye, even Audhumla will pass away. Fornjot too. There's an evil brewing, an evil that will sweep all before it and bring everything crashing down in ruin. But in the destruction, there's a hope to destroy the evil as well. A hope, a thin hope.

"One is needed. One such as has never been before. One who both is and is not of Yggdrasil. One who both is and is not himself. One who sees clearly within as well as without, who's willing to march singing to his fate. One who's willing to lead a whole world to its destruction that it may be born again.

"Ah, ah, I've seen it all." He dropped his wrinkled head into his hands, hiding his face. "I've gone through the doorway, climbed the Tree, and looked down at what the Nornir have written. Now I must return to where I came from, return and leave this body for another, until I come back to march and fight in the final battle. Yes. The final battle."

He looked up, his eyes filled with tears. "There's so little I can say. You must do it all yourself. Let me guide you a bit. Seek what you are, Voden, for you aren't what others would have you be. Oh, no. Fiorgynn, Syr, and Vor would have you be Oski, their pawn. They fear the power in you. Others would have you lead and guide them. Not yet, not yet, not too soon. Until you know yourself, you can't lead others. No, no.

"You must open the doorway, climb the Tree, meet your fate. I'll teach you all I can in the time left me. The Disir'll be looking for you. They want you back. Soon they'll go to the cave to take you out. They'll expect to find a mindless creature, bloated on the flesh of a dead goat, mewling and puking and rolling in its own filth. They'll expect to find the Galdar-power turned against you and burnt out.

"Ah, ah, they'll roll back the rocks, for I've had them put in place once more, and they'll find . . . nothing! Ah, hah-hah! Yes, nothing!" The old man laughed in a high cackle.

"Then they'll know fear and come searching for you. You must be far from here when they find you, lad, or they'll kill us all, and we're the only hope the Vanir have. We're all that's left as their Seidar-magic crumbles and dies. We're destined to overcome them, to break their power and shatter their domination. Yes, yes. It must be so. Yggdrasil changes.

"I'll show you how to travel with your Hamingjur. I'll teach
you how to fly, to break through the plane to the other world.
Oh, they'd have dragged you down, smashed you into the mud.
I'll show you how to soar. Yes, soar!"

Jalk held out a small bit of what looked to Voden like a
mushroom. "Eat it. Chew it and swallow. Then follow me,
follow me, and I'll show you the way." The old man took a
similar piece, popped it into his mouth, and began chewing.
Voden followed his example.

The taste was bitter. Is it a drug? he wondered. If it is,
Jalk's taking it, too, so it can't be dangerous. A sense of warmth
began to spread outward from his center. He watched with a
strange, calm detachment as the old man reached behind and
produced a drum, about twelve inches across the head by eighteen inches deep. Both ends were covered with some kind of
animal hide stretched tight by laces that ran back and forth
between the two heads. The sides of the instrument were made
from wood. Odd runic symbols were carved into the wood and
painted on the hide. Jalk placed the drum on top of his crossed
legs. He picked up a drumstick made from a short piece of
wood capped with a piece of hide and slowly began to beat
the drum.

Gradually Jalk increased the tempo until Voden felt it invade
his body and his mind, moving in exact measure with the
pulsing of his blood. He felt his whole being begin to vibrate
with the rhythm of the drum. He abandoned himself to it and
let it carry him along effortlessly. Closing his eyes, he leaned
back against the wall of the cave.

XXI

For several moments Voden simply sat and relaxed. Then he felt Jalk's touch and opened his eyes. The old man was standing, beckoning to him. "Come. Don't be afraid. Come." Voden rose and walked with him to the mouth of the cave. Geri and Freki were standing there, their tongues lolling out, eyes bright and eager. "Come, little brother," they growled. "We will run on the wind. We will take you to our home beyond the sky." He jumped lightly onto Freki's back and Jalk climbed onto Geri's. A little forest bird landed on the old man's shoulder and whispered into his ear. Jalk laughed and smiled at Voden.

"They wait," he called out. "The Hamingjur are gathered and they wait. Come."

The two wolves began to run. They left the ground and bounded into the treetops, soaring higher and higher. Hugin and Munin joined them, croaking and flapping excitedly. Up and up they flew, up to where the sky opened and received them.

They swept along, twisting and turning through valleys made by mountainous piles of clouds. Finally they came to a hall built like those in Asgard and nestled snugly amid the towering white billows. Inside, the benches were lined with animals of all kinds. Hamingjur, Jalk told him, the ancestors of mankind, the familiar spirits that watched over and helped every human being.

Voden stood in their midst and sensed their eyes on him. Once before he had felt the eyes of many animals on him, there in the clearing when they had caught him. He shuddered briefly in grim memory. This was different, his mind told him, very different. This time the eyes were friendly and helping instead of hungry. "Are you ready?" they asked in unison.

"Yes," a confident voice said from somewhere within him. Several of the Hamingjur began to beat on drums. Others

231

took out rattles and began to shake them in time with the drums. The rest left the benches and began to dance around him, stepping slowly and precisely with the rhythm. Gradually the beat picked up until the hall was filled with whirling forms.

Without warning the drum stopped and they fell on him. With their teeth and claws they began to strip the flesh from his bones. He felt no fear, for Freki came and took his head and carried it to the High Seat. From there he calmly watched the whole proceeding.

They cleaned him to the bare bones, then took the bones and threw them into the fire. The flames leaped up and the bones began to glow. Jalk came to the High Seat and spoke to his head. "Thus you return to the primordial source of all life, the bone, so that you may be born again as an entirely new being. In the fire the bones are tempered and turned into a substance harder than the strongest iron."

When the bones were finished, the Hamingjur took them out of the fire and carefully arranged them on the floor. Jalk came and studied them. "Hmm," he said after a while, "you're short two bones, Voden. All are here but two." He looked up at the young Aesir's head, his expression grim and sad. "Two of your blood must die to provide those bones. I'm sorry. It must be so. Now listen closely, for I will name all your bones. These names you must know."

The naming finished, each Hamingjur approached the skeleton and vomited up the flesh it had swallowed. In their stomachs the flesh had been transformed. Now it glowed softly as it flowed back into place over the bones. Soon Voden's body was whole again. Geri came to the High Seat, picked up his head, and set it gently in place.

As Voden sat up and looked around, Jalk came and took him by the hand, raising him to his feet. "Now I will teach you a Power Song," the old man said.

"No," contradicted a mighty voice that halted them all. Its tones were laden with fell strength and the wild howling of all the winds of the world. It seemed to echo from the very ends of the sky. They looked up. On one of the rafters of the hall sat an immense eagle. "I am Raesvelg," the bird said, "Engulfer of Corpses, Messenger of Vilmeid. I will give Voden his Power Song." He fixed the young Aesir with a beady, glowing eye. "Learn this well, little one. It carries both your salvation and your doom.

"In days gone by I once was Ygg
Ere Voden they did name me.

And I was Har and Jafanhar
And also hailed to Thridi.

Bileyg I'll be and Vafudar
Till falls the mighty Ash Tree.

Then I'll be Ygg as once I was
Ere Voden they did name me."

A silence fell on all the Hamingjur in the hall. Voden stood, his eyes locked with those of Raesvelg. Jalk spoke into the quiet. "It's a dire song you teach, mighty one."

Raesvelg clashed his beak twice, the thunder of it rocking them back and nearly deafening them. "It is a dire song to raise dire power to meet a dire fate. Know, little one, that I am your Fylgjur, your tutelary spirit. Vilmeid has so willed it. Know this and quake with dread, for I am a mighty spirit, full of dark power and knowledge. It is I who have given you Geri and Freki, Hugin and Munin, as your Hamingjur. They are yours to command. You know the meaning of such helpers. It is not pleasant, but you will have much need of them.

"Three times will you see me, Voden. Once now, at your rebirth. Once again when you climb the Tree to where I sit surveying the world. Then will I give you what is mine to give. And one last time will you see me . . . as you die.

"Enough!" the giant eagle shrieked. "This grows wearisome! Enough!" With a mighty beat of wings that nearly bowled them over as it sent winds rushing in every direction, Raesvelg rose from the rafter. The roof of the hall fell back and the eagle soared swiftly out of sight.

Jalk stood looking after the great bird for a moment, his eyes troubled. He turned to Voden and said, "Go back now, lad. Go back with Freki to the world of Yngvi, Borr, Fiorgynn, Freyja, and the others. Your trials will be there. I must remain here, for my time to leave the other world is long overdue. I go now into a nest high in the Tree. There I will stay for a time so that I may be reborn to march in the last great battle."

Freki whined and nudged Voden. Jalk grasped him by the shoulders. "Good-bye, lad. Perhaps . . . perhaps we'll meet again. If only in dreams. Aye." Voden nodded and smiled tentatively.

Jalk smiled back. "Go now, lad. It won't be easy. That it won't. Remember Jalk and your friends, the Hamingjur. Aye, and even Raesvelg."

Voden placed his hands on Jalk's wrists, gave a little squeeze, then turned and climbed onto the great wolf's back. He twisted around to say good-bye to Jalk and the Hamingjur. There was nothing in sight but endless mounds of windswept clouds. Freki ran fast, swooping down to the treetops, then into the cave. Voden stepped off and went back to his place against the wall.

"Three days, Voden. Three days lying there in a trance. Like one dead you were. And Jalk, ah, Jalk, he was dead." Yngvi sat looking down at the ground, the firelight throwing flickering shadows across his face. "We buried him that third day." He sighed hugely and looked up, his eyes dark with unpleasant memory. "You had us worried awhile there, lad. When you finally opened your eyes there was a wild look in them. You couldn't speak a word, only grunt and howl like some beast. You didn't know a one of us, not even me. We thought you'd gone mad for sure. You'd clean forgotten how to walk, or even feed yourself!" Yngvi chuckled ruefully. "For six days now I've been a mother to you! Taught you everything you know, I have!"

"I'm . . . I'm all right now," Voden responded hesitantly.

"That you're not, barbarian. Oh, aye, you're back with us again in mind. You're talking and eating and walking on your own, thank Beyla. But you're still weak as a kitten, and confused too. I see how you drift off now and then. It's no use trying to fool an old friend like Yngvi, lad. No, you're far from all right."

Voden shook his head, as much to clear it as to contradict the forester. "No. I've got to be all right. Yngvi, I can't stay. They'll be looking for me, and I can't let them find me here."

"They're already looking. Started yesterday. Valkyrja everywhere, combing the forest like they lost their best throwing axes."

The young Aesir struggled to his feet. "Can't stay. Got to get away from here."

Yngvi stood and caught him by the elbow. "You're in no condition to be traveling. Rest a few days. Besides, it's night right now. Where would you be going anyway?"

Voden sat back down. "Night. So it is. Yes. Going? Where

would I be going? Back to Folkvang. You've got to take me, Yngvi. If they find me here they'll kill all of you. Jalk said so."

"By Beyla, Voden! I was wrong! Your mind's not back with us, it's as cracked as an old pot! Take you back to Folkvang! Deliver you right into their hands! That's as crazed as anything I've ever heard. Why, they'll just rope you to another she-goat! No, I'll not hear of it."

The young Aesir took a deep breath to help focus his attention and clear the haze from his mind. "Listen, Yngvi. Take me back. Take me or I swear on Jalk's grave that I'll go on my own. They want me back in Folkvang, and they won't stop searching until they find me and bring me, trussed to a pole like a slaughtered deer, right into Sessrymnyr. If I return on my own, though, they'll never know exactly what happened. That will worry them and give me a little power over them. They'll fear and avoid what they can't understand, and they'll never understand how or why I came back. Their confusion will give me time, time to recover from all this. I've got to have time to get well. Do it, Yngvi. It's my only hope."

The forester looked at Voden in surprise. The tone of the young man's voice was strong and commanding. It brooked no refusal. There was something in his eyes, too, that was even more powerful, more demanding, something that reminded Yngvi vaguely of Jalk. He couldn't face it. He lowered his glance. "Aye, lad, aye. As you wish, then. It's back to Folkvang for you. Now you've got to eat. You'll need all the strength you can get for the trip. We'll be traveling light and without any fire. Nothing but cold, dry rations. We'll take Harbard and Byggvir. A bigger party'll just be harder to hide. Eat. We'll leave when the moon goes down. Travel at night. Sleep by day. Aye, that's the way of it."

The Valkyrja on duty at the south gate recognized him before he had covered half the space between the forest edge and the moat. There was a quick flurry of activity around the portal, but by the time he reached the bridge, everything was back to normal and the guard merely gave him a nod of recognition as he passed into the city.

He walked up the straight north–south avenue directly toward Sessrymnyr. His mind was still numb and dazed, and his body felt as if it were somewhere far away. He was still feeling the effect of the drugs given to him by the Disir and Jalk. Although he had eaten and slept during the trip back to Folkvang, he was exhausted to the point of faintness. He walked slowly, as though in a dream, his feet heavy and shuffling. He could dimly feel the eyes of the city on him, watching and wondering.

When he reached the cross-shaped hall in the middle of Folkvang, he paused for a moment, leaning against the wall by the south door, getting his breath, gathering his small reserve of strength. Softly he sang the Power Song Raesvelg had taught him. Let it work, he prayed. I need all the power I can get.

Pulling himself upright, squaring his shoulders, he stepped through the open door into the small anteroom. I must do this, he told himself, must do this last thing to get the time I need. Unless I confront them now, all will be lost. I must do it. Taking a deep breath, he stepped through the anteroom door, into the main hall.

At the center of the hall Fiorgynn sat in the High Seat. The Disir were all in place around her. Voden walked slowly and deliberately down the long hall, his eyes locked on those of the Vanadis. He could feel the stares of the other eight, probing, weighing, trying to decide. Fiorgynn's eyes held a question. Beyond the question was a doubt. Behind the doubt was fear.

Fiorgynn smiled in a tight way. She nodded toward Voden. "Welcome home, Oski, welcome home."

Suddenly, as though a gray veil had been torn from before his eyes, the world clicked into sharp focus for the young Aesir. His weariness and uncertainty dropped away like a traveler's cloak thrown off as the sun comes from behind the clouds to warm the land. He felt the power course through his body. His head rose higher, prouder; his eyes burned with a strange light. He knew he would pay dearly for it later on. At the moment, though, he enjoyed the feeling of exhilaration.

"I am no lover of she-goats," he said, his voice soft but grim. "If you wish to greet me, Vanadis, use my proper name. It is Voden, son of Borr, son of Vestla, child of the Aesir."

A sigh that was almost a gasp rose from the Disir. Fiorgynn's eyes widened ever so slightly. "Voden," she said. "Welcome home, Voden."

The young Aesir made a show of looking around him, his expression bitter. "Home?" he finally said. "This is not home. This is Sessrymnyr in Folkvang where I am hostage. I stay here because I must, not because I wish to.

"I am tired, Vanadis. I wish to rest. I will go to the men's hall now." He turned and without another word walked down the hall and out the door. He held himself up, stiff and proud, all the way to the men's hall. Walking to his sleeping bench, he nodded to Honir, who gazed at him with wondering eyes. Then he crumpled onto the bench and was instantly asleep.

In Sessrymnyr a long silence followed his departure. It was finally broken by Vor's sigh. "Ah," the old woman said softly. "We have failed."

"Completely," responded Gna gloomily. "It looks much as if we awakened the very thing we sought to put to rest."

"Perhaps, perhaps," countered Vor. "That merely means we will have to find another way. A more direct way."

"If there is no way?" Fiorgynn questioned grimly.

"Nonsense," Syr growled. "The lad's but twelve. The Galdar-power's just begun to stir in him. It's hardly fulfilled its potential. That takes years; oh, yes, many years. So much can happen to a young barbarian as he grows up. So much."

Vor sighed again. "Yes, yes, it's true. Sad but true. Accidents have a way of happening."

Hlin frowned. "Tread carefully, old one. We have his father to deal with. Any 'accident' that happens to young Voden better be damn convincing." She looked to Fiorgynn. "For one, I'm sick of this. Let the lad be. We run more danger with schemes like this than we do from his someday power."

"Yes," Syofyn agreed with a smile. "Enough of this kind of plotting. I still think my idea is best. Freyja might be more willing to help than any of you think. You're all underestimating her. Vanadis, I wish you'd let me talk with the girl."

Fiorgynn gazed at the young Disir thoughtfully. "Voden is only twelve. That seems a bit young for what you propose."

Syofyn laughed. "'Tis old enough! Certainly, though, it would work better in a year or two. We could use that time to enlist Freyja's help. It would be best if both parties were ready and willing. In the meantime we could treat Voden with friendliness and affection. Ready him for what is to come, so to speak. Besides, danger will only speed up the development of the Galdar-power. A peaceful environment will cause it to grow more slowly."

Vor looked musingly at Syofyn. "Hmm. Could it be that

Vor has misjudged you, dear?"

"Fagh!" Syr exploded scornfully. "She thinks with her heart and her body!"

"But she thinks," replied Vor. "Possibly she thinks more deeply, more subtly, than any of us is aware. Let us discuss this plan of Syofyn's, Vanadis. Yes. There may be much to it."

As they talked Syofyn sat back, a half smile on her lips. She saw Fiorgynn's expression turn thoughtful. Hlin, Syn, and Gna were doubtful but willing to consider something that seemed so gentle in comparison with the rite of Oski. Vor was in favor of the plan. Eir and Lofyn were neutral. Only Syr scowled sourly.

Take a care, Syr, Syofyn thought. Take a care. Your days of power on the Distingen have been long. Now it is time for younger blood to take the lead. She smiled sweetly at Syr, then joined in the discussion.

Honir sat in the dark of the men's hall and stared at Voden's dim form. A chill ran up his spine. He's doing it again, he thought. He's singing in his sleep. Softly, he pleaded word-lessly, sing softly. Don't wake up the rest of them. They all think things are odd enough as it is. If they knew you sing in your sleep, too . . .

He moved closer and listened intently. Not a word that made sense. Was it even a language? It was always like that. Sounds that were not quite words.

Voden turned suddenly, and Honir jerked back, startled. So restless now. He always tossed and turned, sometimes thrashing about. In the mornings he was always last to rise, with dark circles beneath dull, weary eyes.

He's so different since he came back out of the forest, so strange. He'll walk around in a fog for hours, hardly remem-bering when it's time to eat. There are times when he's so absentminded, he even forgets the names of his closest friends. He'll stare blankly at them when they greet him, as if he'd never seen them before in his life.

Then there are days when he disappears completely. Walks out the gate, into the forest, and disappears. Honir had followed him once. Voden had gone through the woods to a small clear-ing. He'd simply sat at the edge of the clearing, all alone, staring toward its center. He always seemed happy when he came back from his lonely walks in the forest, so Honir had learned to accept it. If his friend loved solitude, why, then he should have solitude.

Yet it hurt him that Voden no longer shared any of his secrets with him. True, they had slowly been drifting apart, but they had always shared a certain intimacy that went beyond what either had with other friends. After all, they were the only two Aesir in the city, the only two hostages. It was hard enough being this far from home. When your friend, your tie to that home, became distant and aloof . . .

Honir realized Voden was awake and looking at him. He drew back slightly, but the other boy's hand shot out and grabbed his wrist with an iron grip. Voden raised his free hand to his lips in an appeal for silence. He rose, still gripping Honir's wrist, and motioned the other to follow.

They went out of the men's hall and around to the side farthest from the courtyard. They sat facing each other. For long minutes Voden stared at Honir's face as if searching for something. Finally he nodded as if satisfied. "Yes," he said huskily, "you're really Honir."

His voice puzzled, Honir replied, "Of course I'm Honir. Who else would I be?"

"Not only who else. What else. They last so long, the dreams do. Right through the day at times. I'm . . . I'm never too sure if what I'm seeing is real or from the dreams. At times I'm not even sure there's any boundary anymore. My life seems nothing but a dream. And the dreams themselves but dreams within a deeper dream."

"Sometimes . . . sometimes you sing in your sleep, Voden. I . . . I . . . can't understand. . . . I . . ."

Voden reached out suddenly and touched his arm above the elbow. "Understand? Don't even hope for understanding, Honir. You're on the outside looking in. I'm on the inside. *I* don't understand. Don't *you* even hope to."

"The . . . the . . . Galdar-power?"

Voden nodded slowly. "Yes. It's all confused. The Disir, Jalk, Raesvelg . . . It swirls about so wildly I feel like I'm about to fall down."

"You . . . you already have. Twice."

"Gods! In public?"

"Yes. Once while we were eating in the men's hall. Once right in the courtyard. Eir came and looked at you both times. She just muttered that you were fine, a little weak, but fine.

You always woke up afterward as if nothing had happened. I didn't mention it to you. I was afraid to. Besides, I thought you knew. I thought..."

Voden held up his hand to stop his friend. "It's all right, Honir. Twice. Lately?"

"No. That was shortly after you got back. In the first month or so. You don't do that anymore, but you—"

"I know," Voden interrupted. "I wander off by myself, forget things, act strange. Yes, yes, I know." He was silent for several moments, his gaze fixed on the ground. When he finally looked up, his eyes were bleak. "Honir, I don't completely understand what's happening to me. I know it has to do with the Galdar-power and what those damned Disir tried to do to me. It also has to do with my journey with Jalk to the hall of the Hamingjur. And with Raesvelg, my Fylgjur... Ah, I'm talking a foreign language to you. I'm sorry.

"I'm sick, Honir, very sick. There's no one to cure me. No one. I have to do it myself. Without anyone to guide or help me. It's... it's an enormous task. I'm not sure if I'll make it. Or when. But I'm trying, believe that, I'm trying as hard as I can. Support me, Honir. Watch me and protect me. Keep the Disir from me, especially if I have a seizure again. Please."

Honir nodded, unable to speak. Voden continued, "I'm not fighting merely for my own life. I don't know how I know that, but it's true. Raesvelg said I had a dire fate to meet. Jalk said something about Yggdrasil changing. It's beyond me, but somehow I'm all mixed up in it. I'm not making much sense. It gets all confused in my head. Things get fuzzy and dim, and I seem to drift off. Stay by me, Honir. I may not act like it, but I need you now very much. The dreams come and go, and I can't tell dream from reality or reality from..." His voice trailed off and his gaze became vacant. He stood slowly, languidly. A dreamy look settled over his face. Honir rose with him, staring. Voden turned and walked back into the men's hall, lay down, and fell asleep.

Honir sat in the dark of the men's hall and stared at Voden's dim form. He felt frightened for himself. And for his friend.

THE IVING

XXII

WINTER came early that year, the first snow falling a good month before its usual time. Cold gripped the land more harshly than any then alive could remember. Below the rapids where the Slid and the Hrid met, the Gunnthro froze solid. The Vanir from Folkvang went out to look at the river and stood staring in amazement at such a thing. Travelers who managed to fight their weary way through the deep drifts that blanketed the forest floor said that the Svol and the Fimbulthul were frozen all the way to the Iving. The Iving, chunks of ice floating down its length, remained open. The Vegsvin, Non, Thyn, Geirvimul, and Vid were so far off across the frozen land that no word of their condition came to Folkvang.

By the time of the winter solstice, when Voden and Honir were due to return to Asgard for their yearly visit, the snow was so deep, horses could barely manage to plow their way through. Travel on foot was virtually impossible. The boys left three days sooner than ordinary and the trip took six days instead of the usual three. The two of them were exhausted and half frozen by the time they rode through the gates of the chief city of the Aesir.

Gagnrad looked at Borr in surprise and shook his head. "Now I'm sure you've had too much of this damn mead. By Fornjot, Borr, the lad's only twelve."

Borr growled low in his throat and wagged an unsteady finger at his friend. "Can hold my mead. 'M not drunk. Not crazy, either. Boy's nearly thirteen. Big for his age too. An' he's got the blood of Buri and Borr in his veins, by Sigfod!"

The other man looked skyward in mute appeal. "He's raving. Don't listen to a thing he says, Fornjot. Dammit, Borr, I know whose blood runs in his veins. I just don't want to see it running over the ground. It isn't only taking Voden along that bothers me, either. It's the whole idea of a winter raid."

"Never been done, ha? Tha's what bothers you, ha? Bah! Tha' jus' proves how good an idea it is. If no one's ever done it, no one'll be 'specting it! Ha!"

Gagnrad sat back and stared silently at his friend. Borr raised his mug and drank again. Drinks too damn much of that mead, Gagnrad thought. Since Vestla died, the Vanadis had been sending regular gifts of mead to the chief of the Aesir, and the chief of the Aesir had been drinking most of the gifts himself.

What was worse, Borr wasn't a cheerful, roistering drunk anymore. Instead of bellowing out bawdy songs or joining in a friendly bout of rough and tumble fighting, he'd sit in his seat, thinking and scowling. Then, sooner or later, he'd say something nasty or insulting to someone. If it came to a fight, he'd fight dirty, going for the eyes or groin with an unwarranted viciousness.

There was another change that bothered Gagnrad, too, one he hadn't noticed at first. Last summer the Jotun had been unusually active. Hrodvitnir had managed to stir up the young men, and the number of raiding parties had increased dramatically. The Aesir had responded in kind, supported by their allies from Vanaheim. Borr had taken the lead in the fighting.

Nothing unusual about that, of course. Borr was always in the thick of things when the wolf-work was done. In the past, though, Borr had always fought with coolness and detachment. He had killed quickly and efficiently.

Since Vestla's death, Gagnrad remembered with a slight shudder, Borr had begun to fight in a new way. He wounded and maimed, making death as painful and lingering as possible. The light in his eyes had been that of bloodlust rather than battle-lust. He had slaughtered, not fought.

Oh it was subtle, Gagnrad admitted. At first he'd doubted that he saw right. But the time at that camp, when they set the Jotun wagons afire and the warriors had tried to send the women and children out and Borr had . . . It hadn't been pretty. Killing armed men was one thing, but women and children . . . And to do *that* to them while their husbands and fathers were burned alive . . .

He shuddered again. No, that wasn't the Borr of old, the glory-hungry, ax-wielding carver of the raven feast. What could have changed him so? Vestla's death? Gagnrad knew his friend had loved the strange woman from Prin. Could the dead so change the living? Did she have some power that extended beyond the grave? Nonsense! Foolishness! Yet he knew that Borr had had no woman, not one, since he had buried Vestla in the mound.

Or was it the damned mead? The gods knew he drank too much of the stuff. A sudden suspicion flashed across his mind. Why was the Vanadis sending so much of the golden liquor nowadays? Did she know what it would do? Was it part of some dark Vanir plot, as it had been with Gullveig?

Gagnrad shook his head in dismay and turned his mind back to the present. Now, he thought, he isn't satisfied with slaughtering the Jotun during the summer. Now he wants to lead us in a winter raid as well! Is there to be no time of peace?

He had to admit, though, that the idea was tactically sound. The snow was deep and travel was hard for the Jotun. Their horses had shorter legs than those of the Aesir. In the open they tended to be faster and have greater endurance, but in deep snow like they had this year, the Aesir horses had a definite edge.

What's more, he admitted, he's right in saying no one would expect a raid this time of year. They could catch the Sons of Ymir sleeping in their wagons.

Borr was watching him, his glance sly. "Ahhh. I see you've thought it out. Had a little mead, but 'm not drunk or crazy." His eyes glittered strangely. "Sev'ral camps just the other side of the Iving. Slip across just after dusk. Hit 'em hard. Burn 'em down. Be back by dawn. Those camps're awful damn close. Bes' to hit 'em 'fore they hit us."

Gagnrad thought for another few minutes. "Damn cold and uncomfortable raid," he muttered, almost half agreeing with the idea. "Bringing along Voden, though, that's not wise."

"Aw, look, Beargrasp, 's not a stupid idea. Look, he can hol' the horses. He's almost thirteen. Doesn't have to swing an ax. Though'll bet he could, by Sigfod. Jus' hol' the horses, tha's all. Someday he'll be an Aesir warrior, maybe even chief in Asgard, like me an' Buri. He's been there with those damn women for years now. Little raid'd do 'im good. See his father and the Aesir fight. Learn a little."

"Well . . ." Gagnrad began to weaken. "If all he does is hold the horses . . ."

"Done! Good! Boy's been home two days now. Rested up from the trip here. Get a group of hot-bloods, Beargrasp, and we'll do it night after tomorrow night. I've got the camp all picked out. Been planning it for weeks. Weeks." Borr rose unsteadily. "Need some rest, then. See you." He walked slowly and carefully to the door of the hall and left.

For several minutes Gagnrad sat and stared at the closed door. Something's wrong, he thought. With him, with me, with this idea, with Yggdrasil. I wish I knew what in Fornjot's name it is.

Low swift-moving clouds covered the sky the whole day long and made the night blacker than usual. The wind blew steadily from the west and carried more than a hint of snow.

They crossed the Iving at Bifrosti's Ford, confident that in weather like this the Jotun wouldn't be guarding it. On the other side they turned east, their horses plowing a path through the deep snow that drifted on the banks of the darkly murmuring river.

It was nearly midnight when they reached the Jotun camp that they planned to attack. The wagons were drawn up in a circle around a small herd of cattle and sheep. No lights shone. No sound could be heard except the hissing of the wind as it drove loose snow across the plain.

They passed to the south, between the wagons and the Iving, then doubled back to approach the enemy from downwind so as not to alert the dogs. Two men went forward to scout, to get an idea of the number of Jotun in the camp.

Voden stood next to his horse, using the animal as a wind-break. The other men either huddled behind their horses for warmth as he did or stamped about, trying to get blood flowing in numb feet and hands. There were ten Aesir warriors, with Voden making the total eleven. Every one of the ten was a seasoned fighter, personally chosen by Borr and Gagnrad. Nikar was there, the blade of his long battle spear honed to razor sharpness. Biflidi stood next to him, his face grim, his eyes sparkling. Across from them was the short warrior Eikinskialdi, with his oaken shield and long sword, quietly talking with the massively muscled Sinar. The others Voden knew by sight only.

When the two scouts returned, it was Vak, the eldest, who gave the report. "Nine wagons in total. Figure at least one man per wagon. Minimum of nine warriors, probably no more than fifteen. We're outnumbered, most likely, but we have surprise on our side. Nobody seems to be stirring."

Borr nodded and turned to Baleyg, a warrior from the Idavoll

Plain, whom Voden had never met. "Keep the fire ready. As soon as we attack, you and Vak torch two or three of the wagons. It'll confuse them and give us some light to see by." He looked slowly around the group. "This is a raid. We kill swiftly and then leave just as swiftly. There are two other camps in this area, to the north and the east. They'll be swarming around here in no time. If we hit hard and fast, everything will work out well, and we'll have plenty of time to escape. Our horses are faster in this snow, but they're also tired from the trip here. Best to go back the way we came since a trail already exists through the drifts. All right, get ready."

The Aesir chieftain turned to his son. "We'll walk the horses closer to the camp then leave them with you. After we attack, approach close to the wagon ring with the animals and have them ready in case we need to get away in a hurry. Keep a sharp lookout to the north and east. If you see or hear anything, yell out. And stay outside the ring, hear? You've only that ax and a knife and too little experience using either. You're here to hold the horses and watch. See you do that and nothing else." Voden nodded his understanding. Borr looked deeply into his son's eyes for a moment, then turned and said, "Let's go."

Muffling their weapons in their cloaks, they crept slowly forward. Voden's heart was racing with excitement, yet he felt a strange calm settling over his mind. The whole thing had been confusing and more than a bit frightening up to this point. He'd been surprised and disturbed when Borr had told him the plan and said he was to come along and hold the horses. An honor, everyone had said, for a lad not quite thirteen to accompany seasoned warriors on a raid. All that day Voden's mind had been in a turmoil. He'd pictured the scene to come a thousand times. Warriors slicing and hacking, blood spurting, shrieks and curses filling the air. Battle. Death. It frightened him, repelled him, fascinated him. His first battle. Not just a wrestling match; a battle in which men's lives would be spilled warm and steaming onto the snow. Perhaps Borr's. He'd shuddered and rejected the vision, turning his mind to something else, but it had slunk back again and again. The night before, his dreams had been full of twisted, looming dread.

The ride through the dark and cold had been numbing. It had left him bewildered, shivering, with a feeling of emptiness. They were almost on the enemy, almost within striking distance of the wagons of the Sons of Ymir. Now he felt calm and detached as if it were all happening a long distance away, happening to someone else.

The Aesir handed him the reins of their horses, and he stopped as they stalked the last few paces forward to the ring of wagons. Suddenly a dog began to bark, and Borr shouted, and they all lunged up and between the wagons, screaming their war cries.

Light flared up as two of the wagons began to burn, and Voden could see the Jotun tumbling from their homes, half dressed, with weapons in their hands. He saw Borr swing his ax at one and watched as the man sprawled backward, his chest spouting gore.

Voden tried to count the enemy. As near as he could tell, there were more than ten, possibly as many as fifteen. Two had died almost immediately, their blood staining the snow in steaming streaks. Every one of the Aesir was engaged now, trading blows with the Jotun. Voden could see the frightened faces of women and children peering from the wagons, watching their husbands, sons, brothers, fight and die. One child, a boy of no more than eight or nine, leaped from a wagon and raced to the side of the man Borr had slain. The child flung himself on the cooling, stiffening body, his face twisted with horror and anguish. The tears that poured from his eyes mingled with his father's blood. He looked up, hatred transforming his visage into that of a snarling animal. He grabbed his father's short curved sword and sprang at one of the Aesir. The warrior saw him coming from the corner of his eye and cut him down with a backhanded sweep of his sword. The boy slumped in the snow, a bloody bundle of rags.

The Jotun withdrew in good order against the northernmost wagons. They formed a line of bristling iron and flashing death. Twice the Aesir hit them, and twice the Sons of Ymir repulsed their enemies. One of their number, a tall man with long, drooping mustaches, cried out in a loud voice, "Cowards! Dogs! Night-killers! Is there one among you brave enough to fight Skrymir man to man? Pah! Cowards all!"

Borr, his ax bloody, his eyes wild, roared back, "Ha! A brave Jotun! Eater of dogs and children! You'd fight one of us alone, eh? I am Borr, son of Buri, known as Skullcracker, and more than one dead Jotun swine has known it to be a well-earned name!"

"Is Borr brave enough to fight Skrymir? Let our battle decide the issue! If I win, you will ride back to Asaheim in disgrace, all except Borr, whose blood and body will feed the spot in Jotunheim where he falls. If you win, the Sons of Ymir will down their weapons and you may slaughter us. The women and children must not be harmed. Agreed, Borr?"

Gagnrad whispered furiously to Borr, casting glances to the north and east as he did so. Borr shook him off with a curse and hefted his ax. "Agreed!" he shouted at Skrymir. "Let the duel begin!"

The giant Jotun sprang toward the Aesir, and the two men met with a clash of iron. The short sword of the Jotun was light and swift and moved in a blur. Borr caught it on his shield and struck back at his opponent with his ax. Skrymir took the blow on his own shield.

For several moments the two men traded blows, hacking at each other, blocking with their shields. Without realizing it, Voden moved inside the ring of wagons where he could watch the battle between the two men in the flickering light of the burning wagons. Everyone stood silent, intent on the duel, except Gagnrad, who constantly looked north and eastward, a worried expression on his face.

Skrymir smashed his shield against Borr's and aimed a low cut for his opponent's stomach. Borr stepped back, and the sweeping blade barely missed him. His ax came smashing down and cracked the Jotun's shield. Again they met in a flurry of blows, any one of which would have been enough to flatten an ordinary man. The crack in the Jotun's shield widened. At the same time Skrymir managed to slice a good-sized chunk off Borr's shield.

The two men circled, their breaths coming in short gasps, the sweat pouring from their bodies. Each was bleeding from nicks and slashes where the other had briefly got through the guard of his opponent. The Jotun had given Borr a nasty gash on his left shoulder. For his own part, Borr had opened a hole in Skrymir's side with a blow from his ax. The only thing that had saved the Son of Ymir was the leather armor in which he had been sleeping.

Borr connected with a shattering blow that broke Skrymir's shield in two. The Jotun flung the remnants aside and threw himself at Borr, his sword flashing and whirling in an incredible rain of blows. Borr's own shield cracked but didn't split. He fended off the attack and hit the Jotun in the shoulder with his ax. The blade glanced off without biting. Again he struck, with the same result. Borr cursed Sigfod. The ax had been dulled on the Jotun's shield. It refused to bite!

In sudden rage he threw down both shield and ax and launched himself at Skrymir. The Jotun was so surprised, he failed to strike. Borr grappled with him and threw him to the ground. Then he sank his teeth into Skrymir's neck, and, with a savage twist, ripped out his throat. The Jotun's shriek ended in a gurgle of bloody froth. He spasmed twice, then went limp. Borr lifted his bloody muzzle and howled insanely at the sky. He leaped to his feet, grabbed Skrymir's sword, and threw himself on the nearest Jotun.

For a second the other Aesir stood in horror and dismay. The Jotun were stunned into immobility. Then everything dissolved into a mad, screaming, murdering riot. The Aesir, overcome by battle madness, went berserk and began slaughtering everything that came to hand—man, woman, child, animal. Baleyg ran from wagon to wagon, firing each one, slashing at anyone who tried to escape.

Voden was rooted to the spot, his mind reeling with anguish and despair. A child ran past him, screaming in terror. Nikar followed and thrust his spear through the tiny back. The point came out the front, flicked, and then withdrew. The child, a girl, crumpled into the dirty, bloody snow. Voden saw her face. Her glazing eyes met his. She held out one hand in trembling appeal, as though asking why, and died. Voden's stomach spasmed and he retched again and again until he was weak. He staggered back against the horses and sat down. Hot tears poured down his face and his body heaved with soundless sobs.

Gagnrad grabbed Borr, screaming at him. The light of animal fury left the Aesir chieftain's eyes like a candle snuffing out. He looked in the direction his friend pointed, then nodded. Gagnrad turned and bellowed to the Aesir, "Let's ride! By Fornjot, they're coming from the other camps! Let's ride!"

Six men rushed past Voden and grabbed the reins of their horses. Six. Borr flung Voden on his mount. "Ride, damn you! Back the way we came!" He leaped onto his own horse and kicked the animal into a gallop.

In a group they swept from the burning camp. Behind, to the east, they could hear the yipping of approaching horsemen. Gagnrad thanked the gods for the terrible weather and dark night. If the Jotun had been able to use their bows . . . He looked around him. Borr was in the lead. Voden and Eikinskialdi right behind. Nikar and Vak were right behind him. Baleyg, bleeding badly from a wound in his side, was bringing up the rear.

The sound of their pursuers became louder. Damn, Gagnrad thought, we're following our old trail and so are they! So much for the advantage of our long-legged horses. He called to Borr. "Split up! Head for deeper snow! It's our only hope!" Borr called back his agreement.

Gagnrad looked back and saw that Baleyg had reined in. He raised his sword in salute to Gagnrad, then turned and rode back toward the enemy. Damn, Gagnrad realized, the man knows his wound is fatal! He's going back to delay them! By Fornjot, there's a true Aesir!

Voden found himself alone in the night, his horse plunging westward through virgin snow. West for a while, he thought dully, then south to Iving. Head for the ford. No. Better yet, try to swim it up higher. They won't expect that. He turned south.

He heard the noise of someone pursuing him. It was too dark to see much, but the sound was clear. A chill of fear went through his body. A Jotun was after him, enraged, thirsty for his blood, his curved blade longing to slash his life and tumble it to the ground. His hand went to the battle-ax at his waist. Panic hit him like a punch in the stomach. I don't know how to use an ax! I know how to wrestle and I know the Thiodnuma, but I've hardly practiced with an ax!

Death opened its eyes and gazed into his. Deep in the abyss of those grim orbs he saw a body sprawled in the snow, its face covered with its own gore. Horror clutched his mind, and he whimpered. He was so frightened, he could barely keep his seat on the plunging horse.

Then something solidified within him and he stopped shaking. His mind went cold and hard. Death still grinned at him, but its eyes were closed. Carefully he listened to the sounds of pursuit. Whoever it was, they were coming closer. He concentrated. Not more than two, by the sound of it. Maybe only one! Sigfod, he silently pleaded, let it be only one.

In a few more moments he was sure. It was one man, and he was gaining rapidly. It wouldn't be long now, Voden estimated. He looked forward. The Iving had to be somewhere in that direction. He knew he'd never reach it in time.

He made a decision and pulled his horse up, then turned it in a tight circle and headed the way he'd come. He pulled the ax from his belt and swung the shield on his back around to his left arm.

The Jotun loomed up suddenly out of the night, a look of surprise on his face. He tried to rein in his horse, but Voden was on him too swiftly. The horses crashed together with a bone-jarring impact, and Voden slashed at the man's face with his ax. The blow went true, and the Jotun flung himself backward with a shriek, his face blossoming red with a gout of blood and shattered bone.

The force of the collision threw Voden forward and to one side. He heard his horse scream in agony and felt a hot stab of pain in his right shoulder. The ground came up and slammed the consciousness out of him.

He woke to numbing cold and a driving snow. It was lighter, probably morning, but he could barely see more than five feet in any direction. He moved and a throbbing pain in his shoulder took away his breath. Afraid to look, he reached up his hand and touched a cold piece of metal. The Jotun's sword! It was stuck in his shoulder! The man must have delivered the thrust as he fell. Voden felt along the blade. Yes. It entered his shoulder there and... he felt over the top of the shoulder... yes, came out there. He could feel the blood trickling down across his chest.

Got to pull it out, he thought. If it stays in, I'll bleed to death. By the gods, how much blood have I already lost? Gritting his teeth, he gripped the blade as firmly as he could and pulled hard. The sword slid out and he fainted.

He woke again, covered with snow, number, colder, and weaker than he'd ever felt in his life. Geri and Freki sat looking at him, their tongues lolling out, their muzzles red with blood. "You work the feast well, little brother," Geri snarled.

"Come, now," Freki growled, "you cannot stay here. We will take you back to the Iving and see you across. Up now, little brother. Up. To linger is to die."

Painfully Voden lurched to a sitting position. The wound had stopped bleeding. He couldn't feel his hands or feet. Looking around at the driving snow, he moaned. "Don't know where to go. Don't know the way."

"Come," said Geri, rising and moving close to him. "Come grip my fur and rise. We will lead you."

Slowly Voden struggled to a standing posture. When he was

up, Geri began to move off slowly. The Aesir boy stumbled
along next to the wolf. Freki moved close to him on the other
side. "Good, little brother, good. Keep putting one foot in front
of the other."

"The Iving," he murmured, "how will I ever cross the
Iving?"

Damn that cow, Ai cursed. To pick such a day to wander off.
A day when Vindsval and his kin are doing their best to make
life miserable. I've got to find her. Damn cow. He headed
north toward the river.

He almost stumbled over the figure that lay unmoving in
the snow. In astonishment he bent over and looked. A boy! A
wounded boy! By the gods! And wolf tracks all around! He
hefted his spear nervously and peered into the swirling snow.

Hmm. Boy was well dressed. Still alive, too. Hmm. Well
dressed, like the son of a chieftain. Hmm. Rescue him, might
be a nice reward in it. Might be.

But the cow. Have to find the cow. Might be a very nice
reward. Maybe a cow. Maybe two cows! He stood, trying to
decide. If I take the boy back to my hut, I give up a chance
of finding that damn cow. If I go for the cow, the boy dies.
No one would know. Couldn't blame me. But he's well dressed.
Maybe a chieftain's son. Could be a reward. Two cows.

With a sigh he picked up the limp form and began to trudge
back home. No weather to look for a cow in, anyway.

XXIII

"LUCKY, that's what he is. Lucky. Yes, yes, only lost one little toe and the tips of three fingers, he did. Ah, yes, a regular favorite of Vindsval he must be, this one." Old Groa muttered constantly under her breath as she puttered about Voden's bed. They had set up a special place for him in the center of the hall, near the fire.

The drone of the old woman's voice almost lulled Voden back to sleep, but he'd slept enough. For a while they'd thought he'd never wake again. Then they'd worried that the fever and delirium wouldn't break. Finally, though, after a week and a half, he'd opened his eyes, and Groa had grinned her toothless grin and declared he would live.

"Five cows!" Groa's voice exploded with indignation. "Five cows Borr gives that fool Ai for carrying him in. What will he give old Groa for bringing his frozen body back to life? Ah, ah, yes, yes. More than five! By the eyes of Svarthofdi, yes, more than five!" She stopped talking and fixed Voden with her single eye. Her gaze was bright, intelligent, and penetrating. For several moments she stared at him, weighing and measuring what she saw in his face.

"Why is he so glum and silent then? Saved from Vindsval he was. Turned from an icicle back into a boy he was. Yet he sits and stares into space." She laughed a swift cackle. "Ah, hah, hah. Thinks old Groa doesn't know what's bothering him. She knows, young Voden, she knows." Her voice dropped to a hoarse, confidential whisper. "He wants to know so much, so much. Such a hunger he has. But it's not that that bothers him right now, oh, no. It's not hunger, but rather having swallowed too much. For he knows things now that he never knew, never even suspected before. Ah, ah, yes, yes, and what he knows stalks him down the dark ways of his mind, and he fears it. Old Groa knows, Voden, aye, she knows." One skinny finger pointed to her empty eye socket. "She paid her own price at Mimir's well. You've paid yours in another place. Yet only a little have you paid. There's more to come. Yes, yes, much more to come. You're going to . . ."

The door opened and Borr came in. Groa stopped talking, returning to her mumble as she turned away and began to rummage about in a sack she had placed near the foot of the bed.

The Aesir chieftain walked slowly over to his son and stood looking down at him. His eyes were bloodshot, his face flushed, and his breath smelled of mead. "Well," he began, trying to force jolliness into his voice, "looking better and better, Voden. Just came from the Warrior's Hall, and they were asking for you. Eikinskialdi, Nikar, Vak, and Gagnrad, they were asking for you. Told them you were mending fine, fine."

He backed up and sat on the bench that ran down the side of the hall nearest Voden's bed. For a few moments the only noise that broke the silence was the old woman's puttering and mumbling. "Ah, Voden, that was bravely done," Borr began abruptly. "Yes, that with the ax was bravely done. We're all proud of you. First blood and only twelve. Didn't mean it to turn out that way, you know. Sorry about it. But that was bravely done."

Borr stopped again, looked down at the floor for a while, then at his silent son. Voden's gaze was unfocused, unseeing. Borr couldn't tell whether the boy was listening or not. It was unnerving.

"Yes. Well. We were stunned when you disappeared like that. Of a sudden you weren't with the rest of us. I mean, we scattered, but we all headed in more or less the same direction, to meet at the ford. Waited as long as we dared. When you didn't come, I was for going back after you. You can ask Gagnrad. It's true. The others made me come back to Asgard. Almost carried me.

"We . . . we gave you up for lost or dead. Then Ai showed up with this body. It was you." The Aesir chieftain paused once more, a wondering look coming over his features. "It was you, more dead than alive, but it was you. Ai had found you on *this* side of the Iving. Without your horse. None of us can . . . I mean, it can't be swum and . . . ah, well, let it be.

"You slept like the dead for two days. Old Groa worked on you constantly, tending your wound, rubbing oils into your limbs, massaging you, pouring herb drinks into you. Then you began to rave . . . you said many strange things, Voden. None of us could understand most of them. A lot was in some other language. You . . . you mentioned Geri and Freki. You told about the Jotun and how you killed him, and something about a goat and Oski and Jalk and . . ." His voice trailed off in confusion.

"Well. Now Groa says you're getting better, mending. Lost the first joint on the first three fingers of your left hand to frostbite. Little toe on that foot too. Looked like you were going to lose an ear for a while, but no, she saved that. Thank Fornjot for Groa, Voden. Yes, well, I . . ." Borr stood and looked down at his son. The boy continued to stare off vacantly. Borr shifted from foot to foot, uncomfortable and unsure of what to say or do next. "Well, then . . . guess I'll tell them at the Warrior's Hall you sent your regards. They'll be glad to hear you're doing well. Yes," he continued, turning away and shuffling off down the hall toward the door, "yes, I'll go back to the hall and leave you to Groa." At the door he hesitated and then turned halfway around.

"Ah, Voden. I . . . I want you to know I'm proud of you. We're all proud of you. You acted like a real Aesir warrior. If . . . if your mother were still alive . . . I know she'd be proud too. She'd . . ." His voice ran down to a mutter. He turned and left the hall.

Proud? Voden thought. Proud of a killer? I smashed the ax into his face. It shattered the bone, and the blood splattered through the air with bits of flesh flying after it. I killed him.

What am I? What are we, we Aesir? Fornjot's creations, carved by the Destroyer from death itself. We bring devastation and slaughter wherever we go.

A little girl runs crying, afraid, fleeing. The spear flicks out. She crumples and looks up, surprised, her eyes accusing, glazing with death. Innocent. Dead. Murdered. Senseless. Destructive.

Falling. Grappling on the ground. Teeth sinking into the throat, bright blood welling up, the wrench and twist of the head, the tearing of the flesh, the choking, gurgling scream. A bloody face raised to the sky, howling, twisted, bestial. My father.

I am Aesir. I've been telling myself that for years. Every time I realized how horrible the Vanir are beneath that calm, beautiful surface, every time I saw the seething evil that dwells at the center of their existence, I told myself I am Aesir, I am not like them. I am better. I am Aesir.

Barbarians. Animals. Murderers of defenseless women and children. Rapists. Yes. I was conceived of rape. My father raped my mother. She was his prize, his booty. Only later did she become his wife. I've heard it sung a hundred times.

What am I? I killed that Jotun. I turned and killed him. Could I have outrun him? Could I have escaped without killing him? I never tried. I turned and smashed my ax into his face, and showered the white snow with blood and bone and gobbets of slaughtered flesh.

I. I did that. What am I? An Aesir. Yes. As vicious and bestial as the rest. A killer created by the arch-killer of them all, Fornjot the Destroyer.

But am I an Aesir? Am I really? Or am I part Vanir too? Doesn't the darkness that lurks, the black, hungry evil they call Audhumla the Nourisher, doesn't that lie in me too? Haven't they released it? They tried to make me Oski, mated me to a she-goat, defiled and used me in ways I can't even think of. I know the Thiodnuma, the elder tongue, the wrestling. I am Vanir as well as Aesir.

Or am I something altogether different? Vilmeid has touched me, and the Galdar-power is awake and prowling through my mind. I don't understand it, I can't control it, but I can feel it, slowly growing stronger.

At times I think I'm going crazy. I see and hear things that aren't there for other people. Geri and Freki. Hugin and Munin. Sometimes other Hamingjur come to me while I'm walking alone in the forest and talk to me. Sometimes I go to other places, places so strange I can't describe them to myself. And then there are the dreams. Dreams that keep right on even after I open my eyes in the morning.

He shuddered and moaned softly. What's happening to me? What have they done to me? I feel so sick all the time. I can't eat or sleep well. I hurt, both my body and my mind. What have they done to me? Damn them! Damn them all! They poke and pry, push me this way and that, try to make me what I'm not, Oski, an Aesir warrior, I don't know what.

Anger flooded his mind, bringing tears of frustration and rage. His whole body trembled with suppressed fury. He clenched his fists against it, holding it back, keeping it in, sensing that if he lost control even slightly, he would lose it completely. He bit his lip hard and tasted blood.

His head hurt horribly. The blood pounded in surges that matched the tempo of the chaotic ideas that swirled around in a formless, directionless maelstrom. Murdered children, rotting she-goats, gigantic eagles, black-robed Disir, dancing Hamingjur, all rolled and twisted through his mind, tumbled together in meaningless confusion. He shut his eyes against them, pressing the heels of his palms over his eyelids until everything turned red, split by blinding white flashes of pain.

Is that what I am? he wondered with anguish. This chaos? Am I mad? If not, then what am I?

What am I? By all the gods, *what am I?*

Pushed beyond the point of endurance, he slipped into unconsciousness. As he fell into the dark, his last question echoed after him, leaving uncertainty behind as it faded.

Voden recovered slowly, almost grudgingly. Tror came to see him every day once old Groa decided he could have visitors. The red-haired youth was as tall as a man now and heavily muscled from the work he performed with his father. Bluff and generally good-humored, he was nevertheless clearly not one to be trifled with. His strength, though still not fully realized, had already earned him a reputation. Strangely, however, he refused offers to join the other youths his age in training to be a warrior. Working at the forge with his father, he said with a quiet smile, was challenge enough for anyone. He had plenty to do and no need to raid in Jotunheim. Volund let his son do as he wished without making his own opinion known. No one cared to question Tror's decision or call him coward.

With a puzzled expression on his face, he told Voden how he still tried twice a day to lift Mjollnir—without success. "It can't be that heavy. It just can't. Why, I can lift a hundred pounds without any strain. Yet that hammer, ah, I can't so much as budge it. I remember my father said it was destined for a special warrior. He said that the day he made it. Remember? Well...maybe no one can lift it. Except that special warrior, I mean. I don't know. Oh, I'll keep on trying, don't worry about that. It's a habit now. I get out of bed, blow up the fire in the forge, try to lift Mjollnir, then help Thrud get breakfast ready. I won't stop. I promised. Don't understand it, though. Can't be that heavy."

Voden enjoyed speaking with Tror. He found his old friend's gruff gentleness soothing. Tyr's visits were more trying. The

fierce young lad wanted to hear all about the raid and how
Voden had killed the Jotun. Tyr could hardly wait to be allowed
to do battle. He practiced every day with every weapon. Even
Borr admitted that the youngster would make an uncommonly
brave and surpassingly good warrior one of these days. But
after the experience with Voden, the Aesir leader hesitated to
take anyone too young on new raids. Besides, Borr had agreed
with the others that there would be no more raiding that winter.
Tyr could barely repress his anger and jealousy.

Gagnrad and the others dropped by occasionally to praise
Voden and tell him he was a true Aesir warrior. His father
often sat by his side and told him rambling, pointless tales
about when he himself had been a boy.

Honir went back to Folkvang alone since Voden was unable
to travel. The Vanadis was understanding and sent a message
hoping for his speedy recovery. Even Freyja sent a little note,
complimenting him on his kill and telling him to hurry back
so he could tell her all about it.

By his thirteenth birthday, on the seventh day of the fourth
month, he was well enough to travel. Borr gave him a new
ax, larger and heavier than the one he had left in the face of
the Jotun. He accepted it with downcast eyes, so that no one
could see his feelings, and thanked his father quietly. As he
rode from Asgard, the ax hung by its beard over his shoulder.

VANAHEIM

XXIV

THE greeting he received in Folkvang was surprisingly cordial. Fiorgynn herself, with Freyja next to her, met him at the north gate. The Vanadis gave him a warm hug. Freyja planted a slightly embarrassed kiss on his cheek. The look in her eyes disturbed him. It was the same hot, hungry look that he had seen so often in people's eyes during the summer wrestling. He blushed, and they all laughed. The Disir came forward, and each one praised him. Syofyn took his horse by the bridle, put one arm around his shoulder, and walked him back to the men's hall. She chattered gaily, telling him of the things that had happened while he had been raiding and convalescing.

The men and boys in the hall were formally courteous and correct, but they seemed a little afraid of him, a little in awe. This one, their actions seemed to proclaim, had killed a man, a full-grown Jotun warrior. He had done it with an ax, like that which hung over his shoulder. Voden ignored their looks and whispers. He went to his bed, unpacked his things, and then lay down, staring sightlessly up at the ceiling. Honir saw the look in his eyes and left him alone. There was nothing he could do for his friend. Nothing anyone could do. He was sick, and as he had said, he would have to cure himself.

Spring came slowly and grudgingly. Summer followed, cool and rainy. Voden walked through life in a thoughtful daze. He frowned constantly as if he suffered from a mild headache or was thinking through some difficult riddle. He spent most of his time alone, wandering about in the forest to the east of Folkvang. Sometimes he would be gone for two or three days at a time, making his bed beneath a bush or on a convenient pile of leaves. For a while Fiorgynn had him followed by the Valkyrja, but he never went anywhere, met anyone, or did anything, so she stopped the surveillance.

Voden's primary feeling was one of exhaustion and numbness. He found it difficult to concentrate long enough to hold a conversation. He stopped his lessons in the elder tongue, the Thiodnuma, and wrestling. His appetite disappeared, and he had to force himself to eat when he began to lose too much weight. The food tasted like dust, but he gagged it down. At times he found himself talking or singing out loud without realizing it. The line between fantasy and reality vanished almost entirely. The horses crashed together with a bone-jarring impact and Voden slashed at the man's face with his ax. The blow went true and the Jotun flung himself backward with a shriek, his face blossoming red with a gout of blood and shattered bone. Geri picked the little girl up and turned her over so he could see the look in her eyes. Someone had torn out her throat. Raesvelg flapped his mighty wings and called him Ygg, but the pain in his shoulder was too great, and he sank back in the snow. The she-goat looked at him with accusing eyes as the spear flicked in and out of Jalk as he tumbled toward the drum and Audhumla raised the knife high to plunge down from the sky with Hugin flapping by his side as Freyja looked with hungry eyes while he slashed at the man's face with his ax. The blow went true and the creatures closed in on him, their paws pulling him down to the flat stone surface. He leaned over, running his fingers across the surface, trying to make it out in the dim light. It seemed like writing. It almost seemed like . . .

Fall came and the harvest was poor. Winter struck with fury. He returned home at the solstice. There was hunger everywhere. No one had the energy to wade through the snow to raid Jotun camps and kill children.

Spring arrived late and heavy with rain. A cold, dreary day marked Voden's fourteenth year. Summer followed, but the clouds and dampness stayed.

Slowly the young Aesir seemed to recover. At least to all outward appearances, he became more normal. He smiled occasionally, and even laughed now and then. Yet those who knew him best wondered, for something strange and unsettling lurked deep in his eyes and around the corners of his mouth. Both Syr and Syofyn watched closely. Neither one could decide exactly what she saw.

Freyja didn't know exactly what it was, either, but whatever it was, she liked it. When Voden looked at her, his eyes hooded and mysterious, she felt a strange warmth growing inside. Od was nice, yes, very nice. So...so energetic and strong and satisfying. But Voden promised something else, something that went beyond the physical. He did unexpected things to her mind, things she didn't understand, things that excited her a great deal.

She'd tried to get his attention in a hundred different little ways that only women know. She'd sat near him whenever possible. Smiled at him. Was nice to him. Asked his advice. Laughed at things he said. Shared. Talked. Walked. Sat.

There'd been a response. Sometimes. A wan smile. A pale, halfhearted laugh. A nod. A quick flicker of interest deep in his dark eyes. Nothing more than that. He remained distant, aloof, cautious, mysterious, unreachable...fascinating. He was so tall now, and his body was so light-skinned, covered with blond hair. She wondered what it would be like to...

Fiorgynn watched both Voden and her daughter with a growing sense of mystification. She did everything she could, subtly, to throw the two of them in each other's way. She'd seen Freyja's growing interest, noticed the occasional flashes of reciprocal interest from Voden. Yet the boy's reserve never seemed to break down. Despite everything that could be done, he remained detached and dreamy. She wondered if there were any way to reach him, to pull aside that veil of indifference, to pierce that armor of vagueness. If Syofyn's plan was ever going to work, something would have to be done. Perhaps Eir knew of a way. Yes, perhaps there was an herb or something. A potion. She watched with puzzled eyes and wondered.

When the two Aesir boys went home for the solstice, she called the Distingen together and asked their advice. Syr was unusually silent. Syofyn, on the other hand, was voluble and took over the meeting. "Voden," she declared, "is ripe for the picking! All Freyja has to do is reach out, and he'll fall into her hands. And into ours! I told you, Vanadis, this is the way to do it. It can't fail!"

"Except," Syr grumped in a hostile tone, "sweet Syofyn, you forget two things. First, Voden seems to be dedicated to dreaming and not doing. Second, no one has really consulted Freyja on this whole thing."

"Freyja is interested," Fiorgynn interjected. "I've watched her carefully, and she's definitely intrigued by Voden."

"Intrigued," muttered Syr. "Intrigued isn't enough."

Syofyn smiled. "I think something can be arranged." The others turned to look at her. "Voden approaches his fifteenth birthday. At the same time the vernal equinox approaches. We all know what that means. Now, for the past few years, Freyja has spent the festivities with Od, which has left no opportunity for Voden. Suppose Od were not here. Suppose he were sent off with some of the young foresters to aid the Aesir against the Jotun. Earlier than usual to send them off, but given the state of tension between the Aesir and the Sons of Ymir, I'm sure the arrangement wouldn't seem strange."

Hlin complained, "Od's a bit younger than those we usually send. Not quite eighteen, if I remember."

Syofyn shrugged. "Voden killed his first man before he was thirteen. I rather imagine Od will be eager to catch up. They've had a rivalry going for some time now. Od will cooperate if the matter is put correctly. He doesn't lack strength or bravery, Audhumla knows."

Vor scowled. "Fine. With Od out of the way, Freyja will be free to choose another for the vernal festivities. What makes you so sure she'll pick Voden?"

"She'll pick Voden," Syofyn said firmly. "He's the only other one that interests her. We can help the matter along by seeing to it that the two of them go to the bonfire together. We control the festivities. It won't be hard to arrange."

The ancient woman nodded grudgingly. "It might work. How do you intend to overcome Voden's indifference? For two years now the lad's been walking around as though he were a million miles from here."

Syofyn looked at Eir. "Our expert on potions has given me assurances that that will be no problem."

Eir shrugged. "Nothing is easier. White mandragora for him, black mandragora for her. It must be dug carefully. Draw three circles around it with a copper sword, then face west while digging with a copper trowel. An assistant, preferably a woman with much sexual experience, must dance windershins around the outer circle while it's being dug, whispering lascivious and erotic suggestions. As it is plucked from the ground it will shriek, and prayers must be immediately offered to Frigg, the Vettir concerned with such things. There are many ways to administer mandragora, in food or drink. It should be no problem."

"The results?" Fiorgynn inquired with a slightly bemused smile.

"Ah, if I mark the black and the white roots with the names of two people and let them lie together before preparing them, then administer the potion to those to whom the roots have been consecrated, why, the results will be uncontrollable lust."

"Uncontrollable lust," Syofyn repeated, grinning widely. "Mandragora is a very powerful aphrodisiac. Best of all, Eir assures me the effects will be long in wearing off. Isn't that so?"

Eir agreed. "Indeed. The effects will last for two or three days. They won't be able to stop. They'll fall down exhausted, but as soon as they get their breath back, they'll start again. Smaller doses can be administered on an occasional basis to keep things that way until they both die of fatigue. Though I imagine we will be more moderate."

"In any case," Syofyn crowed triumphantly, "Freyja and Voden would do as we wished, and the young Aesir would be in our power! It can be done, Vanadis! It must be done!"

Fiorgynn looked thoughtfully at Eir. "Is there any danger of side effects?"

The healer nodded reluctantly. "Naturally. If the dosage is too high they'll literally kill themselves with lovemaking. Mandragora is very powerful, one of the sovereign plants, Vanadis. But I don't think it will be too hard to control the amount they receive. Still, there is danger. It could destroy their minds. I'm willing to take that chance. I know my craft well, Vanadis. I'll not make a mistake."

Lofyn frowned. "I don't like it. It . . . it seems unclean somehow. I suppose it's better than the last thing we tried." She shuddered in memory. "That was horrid. At least this time he'll be getting something he really seems to want. Not a she-goat. Yet it doesn't seem right. It just doesn't."

Fiorgynn looked at the others. Hlin gazed at the floor, bit her lip, and nodded unhappily. Syr sneered and nodded. Vor, Gna, Syn, and Eir nodded firmly. Syofyn's smile was triumphant. "So," Fiorgynn said softly, "it's decided. We'll try Syofyn's plan at the vernal equinox. We'll use Freyja and the root of lust to put our reins firmly on young Voden. So shall it be."

"So shall it be," they repeated.

And Syofyn added, "As Audhumla would will it."

XXV

A warm softness smoothed the harsh edges of the winter winds. Day slowly pulled itself free from the long night and the sun spent more and more time gazing fondly at the earth. Life began to flow within the trees and plants, and their buds swelled with the fullness of it.

Even Voden responded to the onrush of spring. The warmth of the sun seemed to melt the winter that had gripped his mind and soul for so long. With a sudden exuberance he rejoined in the training for the Thiodnuma and took up wrestling lessons once more. To the astonishment of both Geirahod and Frodar, the young Aesir was more adept than ever. Honir watched with cautious optimism and wondered how long it would last.

At the third hour of the night of the day ruled by Frigg, the Vettir of love, Eir dug the mandragora roots. Carefully, muttering prayers to the goddess and making obscene suggestions to the roots, she incised the white one with the runes of Voden's name and the black with Freyja's. At the tenth hour of the night she bound the two roots together with sinew of sparrow gut and gently swathed them in dove down.

For a week they lay together until Frigg's day came again. At the first hour of daylight Eir unbound and crushed the roots together in a copper mortar with a copper pestle. She added bits of swan egg, rose leaves, and myrtle berries to the mixture. Completing the process with solemn invocations to the Vettir of love, she placed the mixture between an emerald and a turquoise, allowing it to rest until the eighth hour of the same day. Then she took the dry, powderlike substance that remained at the bottom of the mortar and placed it in a container made from the bone of an Iynx, the beast sacred to Frigg.

* * *

The contingent of Vanir foresters was sent early to Asgard that year. Raiding across the Iving had already begun, and the Aesir were delighted by the timely arrival of their allies. They were somewhat surprised that the Vanadis had sent along someone as young as Od. Usually the lads from Vanaheim were in their twenties. But since Aesir often joined in the raiding at fifteen or sixteen, they didn't see anything too out of line in a Vanir of almost eighteen taking part in the wolf-work.

Freyja was dismayed by her mother's decision to send Od. After a few days of sulking, however, she realized it meant she would be able to pick a new partner or partners for the vernal equinox. About that same time Geirahod matched her and Voden in the practice yard. The contact with his hard young body gave her a thrill, and she made a decision. She would batter down his defenses, overcome his reserve. She would have him for the equinox.

Voden couldn't help but notice Freyja's interest. When they practiced the various throws and holds of the Thiodnuma, she would press her body against his in a way that disturbed and tantalized him. Often in the middle of a match he would suddenly find himself hard, almost bulging out of his loincloth. At first he was horribly embarrassed. Then when he saw Freyja's lazy smile and the admiring look in her eyes, he lost his self-consciousness and began to enjoy the feeling of the cloth rubbing against him as he moved, or the firm pressure of her body against his as they grappled. More than once he was positive he felt her fingers gently touch him. Furtively he passed fleeting hands across her breasts.

By the time of the vernal equinox they were both ready. There was no question in either of their minds as to what would happen. As the bonfire was lit in the open to the south of the city, they walked hand in hand toward it across the small bridge. Fiorgynn had provided them with a flask of special mead by way of showing her approval. She had also given Voden a copper ring set with an emerald and Freyja a similar one with a turquoise. Syofyn had made wreaths of myrtle for them to wear.

The heat from the fire felt good. Voden offered Freyja a drink of mead and then took a long swallow himself. It burned slightly going down, but started a small fire glowing in his stomach once it settled into place.

The crowd around the fire grew, and some started dancing. Others began to chant, clapping their hands to provide rhythm for the dancers. From somewhere on the other side of the fire came the shrill notes of a bone flute.

Voden and Freyja both took another sip of the mead and then joined the dancers. At first Voden tried to remain aware of what was happening around him. Swiftly his attention narrowed and focused entirely on the swaying, twisting body of Freyja. As she moved and writhed, her breasts pressed against the fabric of the light robe she wore. Her mouth was slightly parted, her tongue just touching her upper lip. As they danced she began to sweat, and the moisture added a sheen to her already glowing skin.

They danced together, isolated from the others, their attention totally focused on each other. Freyja moved close to Voden and began to rub her body up and down against his. His legs began to tremble and feel weak. The warm glow in his stomach moved lower.

With a sudden sweep Freyja lifted the robe that covered her and threw it off. Gasping, the young Aesir gazed at her body, covered now by nothing other than a loincloth similar to his own. Her skin glistened with the exertions of her dancing. Her breasts, small, high, and hard, moved as she continued writhing to the rhythm. The muscles of her thighs rippled as she twisted and leaped into the air.

His hands shaking, his fingers numb, Voden stripped off the shirt and leggings he wore. Freyja's eyes ran over his body, then her fingers lightly followed as she drew him to her. Touching, chest to chest, thigh to thigh, they danced slowly.

Voden could barely breathe. He panted for air, his mind reeling. Thought was impossible. Only one thing dominated his consciousness. He gasped and nearly fell as he felt Freyja's hands thrust into his loincloth. He dimly heard her sob as she felt the size and heat of him. Then, barely knowing what he was doing, he was half carrying, half dragging her away from the fire into the darkness.

They were hardly out of the lighted area before Freyja pulled the loincloth from him and sank to her knees, enveloping him with her mouth. He moaned and nearly crumpled as her tongue ran over him. Then he was on the ground, tearing the cloth from her waist, whimpering and groaning with his lust.

She spread her legs wide, and he thrust himself into her. With a hiss of pleasure she wrapped her legs around the small of his back so he could thrust deeper. Pumping as hard and fast as he could, Voden felt the warmth flowing from her. He sought her mouth and thrust his tongue deep into it.

Freyja felt him in her. She arched her back to let him penetrate even deeper. Ahhh, ahhh, by Audhumla, how he filled her. He was Od, he was Oski, he was the male principle of the universe, the thrusting, demanding, hardness . . . and it felt so good, so good. So . . . good . . . she was . . . coming . . . wave on wave of . . . pleasure and . . . oh . . . oh . . . *ohhhhhh!*

Voden couldn't help himself. With a feeling halfway between pain and ecstasy, he came in a flood. He bucked and jerked, thrusting wildly, crying in a high-pitched wail.

For a moment the two of them lay exhausted, staring into each other's eyes. Freyja expected he would lose his hardness and roll off, his passion sated for the moment. Later he might be interested again. That was later, and she wanted so much more right now!

But he didn't leave her. Instead he began to move again. In a mixture of wonder and delight she responded, pulling her legs up tight against her chest, hooking them over his shoulders. *Ahhh,* he went so deep that way! She felt her whole body rippling with sensation. She came, suddenly and viciously, with an intensity that almost made her lose consciousness. She felt him swell abruptly, his size almost unbelievable in her. Then the flood broke, going deep, deep into her, deeper than any ever before.

Still he stayed in her. In a delirium of passion she pushed him back and up. Without letting him slip out, she clung to him as he went over on his back. Astride him, on her knees, she began to move up and down. After a moment he joined in, thrusting hard and fast from beneath. She held on, riding him, feeling him in her. She raised herself slightly in the air, crushed her breasts against his chest and came in a long, sobbing orgasm.

Like a wild animal out of control, Voden rolled her over on her back once more. Then, with a low growl that sounded only half-human, he withdrew, turned her on her belly, lifted her, and slid into her from behind. Whimpering and sobbing, she buried her face in her hands, biting her thumb. She screamed as she came, a cry that came out of the dark mists of time, a primitive howl like those that had echoed in the forest since life had walked the earth.

The last vestiges of their humanity stripped away, the two of them lost themselves in pure bestial lust. She scratched and tore at his body, biting his neck and lips. He bit her, too, marking and bruising her skin in a dozen places.

How long it went on, neither knew. Finally they fell into an exhausted sleep.

Freyja came back to consciousness in response to a resumption of Voden's thrusting movement. Slowly, gently, he woke her. She came and felt him doing the same. Their eyes wondering, they looked at each other and murmured senseless words of love. He withdrew, stood, and lifted her to stand beside him. They both felt weak and dizzy. For a time they remained there, clinging together in the dim light of dawn. Dazed, they looked around as if aware for the first time there was a world outside each other's arms.

Other eyes, much sharper, much clearer, watched them as well. Syofyn gloated. It had worked! Voden was theirs! The Galdar-power was nothing compared to the power of sex! The young Disir had known it would be so and knew that she would now be the most powerful member of the Distingen after Fiorgynn. Perhaps when Fiorgynn died, she would become Vanadis, especially if Freyja was nothing but a love slave to Voden. And who knew when Fiorgynn would die? She wasn't ancient like Vor, but things happened. And if Syofyn was the most powerful, the one who controlled Voden and hence the Aesir alliance . . . well . . .

Syr watched and muttered curses. Yes, yes, Syofyn had won this round, but how long could such a thing last? Voden had the Galdar-power in him. The mandragora would keep it at bay for a while, confused and dissipated in sexual frenzy. But how long? Would the lad die of exhaustion first? Or would the Galdar-power somehow break the power of the drug? Surely that must have been what happened during the rite of Oski. Somehow the cursed Galdar-power had helped him fight free of the drugs they had given him, perhaps protecting him from their full effects. Would it do the same thing now? How long could Syofyn's plan work? And what would happen once it failed? Ah, ah, then it was back to old Syr. Then the Vanadis would see the validity of her plans. Yes, yes, there were ways to control the lad's mind. Potions could be mixed. Oh, yes. There were ways.

Honir crept back into the shadow of the forest and felt ill. He had seen the whole thing. Watched over the two of them all night long as they made love and then slept. He had sniffed

the mead and tasted a drop of it with the tip of his tongue.
Bitter. Strange. Drugged. He knew his friend was in danger,
but he didn't know what to do about it. Best to watch and wait.
He shuddered. As much as he dreaded it, perhaps the Galdar-
power was the only thing that could save Voden. If only he
knew what to do!

Weeks passed. The intensity of their lust faded a little, but for
Voden, Freyja was still the center of his world. He rose every
morning with but one thought in mind: I must see her, I must
be in her. At night when he crept into his bed in the men's
hall, his last thought was of new ways to please her.

Yet at times, at the edge of consciousness as he was falling
asleep, he felt a strange stirring deep within, as if something
were slumbering restlessly and turning over. It was brief and
vague, passing quickly, instantly suppressed. Yet it was there.
Somewhere.

During the day his mind was totally taken up with Freyja.
He spent every possible moment with her. The two of them
would steal off to the forest together whenever they could and
make fevered love. Every night they would meet outside the
walls and repeat the acts of the day until both were tired and
sorely in need of sleep.

Voden wrestled poorly that summer. His heart simply wasn't
in it, and he lacked energy as well as concentration. Yngvi
scowled when he saw his young friend clinging to Freyja at
every moment. He and Honir held long, deep discussions, from
which he emerged frowning and shaking his head. If only Jalk
were still alive, he thought, *he* would know what to do. He
agreed with Honir that there was something strange in all this,
but he couldn't guess what it was any more than could Honir.
Perhaps if he could get Voden away from Folkvang for a while.
But how? On what pretext? The Disir seemed to shadow the
boy everywhere, especially that young one, Syofyn.

After the choosing of the king, Yngvi stayed on in Folkvang for the first time in his life. He had tried and tried to
convince himself that everything was all right with Voden and
that in just a little while the young Aesir would return to his
usual self. Try as he might, he couldn't believe it was true.
Something was deeply and gravely wrong with his friend. The
situation wasn't normal, and he realized that time alone wouldn't
solve it.

Together he and Honir observed Voden carefully, following his every move. The more they watched, the surer they became that somehow the Disir, and especially Syofyn and Eir, had something to do with the Aesir youth's condition.

Yngvi became worried. Jalk had made it very clear that Voden was someone special, someone he had been told about in that other land he visited, someone who was crucial to the future of the Vanir and all of Yggdrasil. If Voden was now in trouble—and Yngvi was convinced he was in very serious danger indeed—then everything for which he and Jalk had struggled for so long was likely also in jeopardy.

What should I do? he asked himself for the hundredth time as he saw Freyja take Voden by the hand and lead him off into the forest like a tame fawn. What would Jalk have done? An idea began to form in his mind. The only hope was to take Voden away from Folkvang, away from Freyja, away from whatever it was the Disir were doing to him. Yes, he decided, the lad had to be rescued.

The only difficulty was that Voden didn't want to leave Folkvang, let alone Freyja. When Yngvi mentioned the idea late one afternoon toward the end of the summer, the Aesir lad looked at him with a blank expression that swiftly turned hostile. "Leave?" he muttered. "Why? Freyja doesn't want to go anywhere. Why should I leave?"

"Well, I supposed you might be wanting to see Jalk's grave is all," Yngvi said lamely. "He's been dead years now, and you've never come to see his grave. I just thought as it might be of interest to..."

"No," Voden interrupted flatly. "I don't want to see Jalk's grave. I...I hardly remember him. There used to be dreams, but those are gone now. Thank Audhumla, those are gone. I'm at peace, Yngvi. At peace. Leave me that way. I've...I've got to go find Freyja now. She needs me." He turned and ran off.

The forester stood thoughtfully and watched him go. For an instant he had seen something in Voden's eyes. A quick flash, like the sudden shine of a fish's scales deep in cloudy water. It had come when he'd mentioned the dreams. There had been longing in it, and fear.

Certain now that he was right, Yngvi approached Honir and laid out a plan to him. At first the young Aesir rejected the idea outright. Gradually, as his own concern and dismay over

Voden's behavior became deeper, he began to soften. Finally, reluctantly, he agreed.

They decided to act during the first snowstorm of the early winter. After finalizing their arrangements, Yngvi left Folkvang to make his own preparations. If he was right about the role of the Disir in his friend's problem, he would have to plan with care. They would be furious at his meddling and wouldn't hesitate to use the Valkyrja against him and his men. Even more he feared their possible use of the Seidar-magic. He had to cover his tracks carefully and completely.

As it happened, the first snow of the year came later than usual, but it was that much greater as if to make up for it. For five days the wind howled out of the northwest, driving the swirling whiteness before it. Drifts piled up several feet in depth. After the third day everyone in Folkvang stayed indoors to wait it out.

It was only by the fifth day, when the wind had abated and the snow stopped falling, that they discovered Voden was missing. Freyja became hysterical and Eir had to give her special potions to calm her down. The Vanadis questioned Honir, but the normally silent lad had even less than usual to say. Voden's disappearance remained a mystery. The Valkyrja were sent out to search, but not one trace of him, alive or dead, was discovered. Fiorgynn began to wonder what she would tell the messengers from Borr when they came to bring the hostages back to Asgard for the winter solstice.

XXVI

~~~~~~~~~~

EIR looked down at the unconscious, sweat-drenched form of Freyja. The Disir's eyes were hooded and unreadable. She held the limp wrist in her hand and felt the pulse. "Deep, now. Asleep," she murmured to Fiorgynn.

"But when it wears off, what then, healer?" The Vanadis hit the last word with angry emphasis, and Eir winced. She looked up, her eyes meeting Fiorgynn's. "Then we find out if it's cleared her system yet. If so, fine. If not"—she shrugged unhappily—"then we must make her sleep again."

"What happened, Eir?" Fiorgynn asked wearily, no longer the Vanadis but simply a worried mother. "I thought you said you knew what you were doing."

Eir bowed her head. "I thought so, too, but no one has ever been on mandragora this long before. We started slipping small doses into their food a month before the equinox, to help develop their interest in each other. Then I had to keep on increasing the amount, because they began to develop a tolerance to it. I . . . I never thought it would come to this. Believe me, Fiorgynn, I never thought this would happen."

For a moment Fiorgynn looked silently at the restless form of her daughter. "A week now. An entire week." She looked up at Eir and said softly, plaintively, "Will she live?"

The healer dropped her gaze. "I honestly don't know. I think the chances are good. But . . ."

"But what?"

"But . . . there are some things worse than dying, Vanadis. I'm not too sure what she'll be like if she does live. Her mind . . ."

There was a silence then between the two of them, a silence filled with tension that stretched out and out until Eir wanted to scream. Fiorgynn finally broke it by murmuring, "Sweet Audhumla. I allowed this to happen to my own daughter. I listened to Syofyn and you and the others, and I allowed this

276

to happen. What have I done? What have we all done?

"And the boy? What about Voden, Eir? What are his chances? He doesn't have you to watch over him. Wherever he is, if he's still alive, he doesn't have you."

Eir let out a long breath. "I, for one, hope he lies frozen in a snowbank, that he wandered off into that storm and finally fell asleep, gently and forever. If he's still alive in some forester's hovel . . . without proper potions, the pain of withdrawal from the mandragora will drive him insane. If he doesn't kill himself, he'll end up a drooling idiot."

Fiorgynn's eyes met hers once again. They were haunted and full of fear. "What have we done?"

"I don't know, Vanadis. I honestly don't know."

"For the sake of Beyla, hold him down!"

"Owww! Dammit, he bit me! Drew blood he did! Dammit, watch out there, or he'll get loose!"

"Gods! I can't stand the howling! Sounds like the father of all wolves, he does! Sweet Glad, I wish he'd stop!"

Yngvi shook his head, his face drawn and fearful. "I think he's gone mad. I've never seen anything like it. Hold him there, by Beyla! Get that rope back around his arms! That's it! Good. Now hold his jaws open, Harbard. Bragi, pour that slop down his throat. Gangleri says it'll calm him. Yes. That's it."

As they tightened the ropes that bound the howling, struggling figure, Yngvi stood back and wiped his brow. He shivered as he watched the panting, writhing creature that had once been his friend. Not human now, he thought dismally. No. Mad. Wild. An animal. An animal in horrible torment. Spoke only one word. Wailed, howled, screeched it. Freyja. Ffffrrree-eyyyjjjaaaaa! Ah, ah, how it echoed in his ears and in his dreams. For days now the Aesir had been like this. Frothing at the mouth, wild in the eyes, screaming and fighting, trying to break free and run into the forest in search of Ffffrrree-eyyyjjjaaaaa.

Not human anymore. Not Voden, not the bright, inquisitive young barbarian from the Himinborg Plain. A crazy thing that groveled in its own shit and howled. All the Vettir forgive me. What have I done? He caught a half-formed sob in his throat and swallowed it. The drink was taking effect. Voden was calming down, falling into a stupor. By Beyla, he thought, I wish I'd never kidnapped the boy from Folkvang. It seemed the right thing to do. I only meant to save him from the Disir. What have I done?

Freki nudged him. "We heard you calling, little brother. Your howl rings through the nine worlds, and we came."

"Yes," Geri growled from the other side of the rude bed where Voden lay, "come with us and stop this noise. Come. You remember how."

Voden rose and looked down at his body. Yngvi and the other foresters were doing the same. The expressions on their faces were frightened and worried. Geri whined, and Voden turned to follow the two Hamingjur out the cave.

Outside he mounted Freki's back, and the pair began to run swiftly across the snow. As the forest flashed by more and more quickly, they began to mount to the sky. "Where are we going?" Voden called out, the wind whipping the words from his mouth even as he spoke them.

"To the center of the world," Geri howled. "To the place where all nine meet, the axis, the Great Tree that holds all together. We go to Yggdrasil itself!"

A mountain loomed ahead of them, towering into the sky, clouds hiding its peak. They climbed higher and higher, but still the mountain rose above them. Hugin and Munin joined them, flapping and croaking. "This is the Great Mountain," they told him. "We will enter it and dive to its very core. There we will come to the Great Tree, the World Tree, Yggdrasil, the Mount of Ygg, the steed the Terrible One rides."

Voden began to chant, his voice rising shrill and piercing, the words flung like arrows into the teeth of the rushing air:

> "In days gone by I once was Ygg
> Ere Voden they did name me.
>
> And I was Har and Jafanhar
> And also hailed to Thridi.
>
> Bileyg I'll be and Vafudar
> Till falls the mighty Ash Tree.
>
> Then I'll be Ygg as once I was
> Ere Voden they did name me.

"Geri, Freki, Hugin, Munin, am I Ygg? Is the World Tree my mount? What does it mean? I don't understand."

"Nor will you until the time is right and your power is ripe," Freki growled deep in his throat. "We know little more than you, little brother. If you once were Ygg, then we did not know you, for that was in the First Age when men and gods were one and all the nine worlds blended unmixed and without barriers. If you will be Ygg, we cannot see, for that is beyond the power of mere Hamingjur. We are here to help and cannot do more."

Voden thought for a moment as the wind whipped through his hair. "Geri and Freki, I know what you do. You carry me and protect me. You came to me in the snow in Jotunheim and brought me across the wide Iving. But what do you do, Hugin and Munin?"

Hugin settled on his left shoulder and croaked, "Swift as thought am I. Through me your mind can fly the world over."

From his right shoulder Munin spoke. "Nothing do I forget. What I see is forever at your command."

The young Aesir nodded. "Then I'll send you out each day to fly over the world so that I can know what's happening." He paused in sudden concern. "You must always be sure to come back. It worries me that you might get lost, Hugin, in the vastness of the nine worlds. And should you fail to return, Munin...ah...should you fail..." The ravens bobbed their heads up and down, but had no answer to offer.

The clouds parted and the cliff opened in a wide cave. Without pausing the five of them plunged into its mouth and began to fall rapidly through the dark. Down, down they went, faster and faster, until talk was impossible and thought had to be suspended.

Abruptly they broke into a new world of light. Vast and endless, the brightness filled the sky. It had no apparent source It was everywhere, permeating everything. In the midst of the light rose the soaring Ash Tree, the axis of all the worlds, the source and being of Yggdrasil, Yggdrasil itself. They made for a broad branch and landed.

Voden got off Freki's back and looked around, his eyes dazzled by the light. Several other beings were on the branch, waiting. One was a wizened old bear, his face kind and filled with wisdom. Another was a twisted thing with bulging eyes and drooling lips, warped and horrible. The third was his mother, dressed in a shining robe, embroidered with an infinite tumult of animal shapes. In the background, against the trunk of the Tree, was a vague, frightening shadow, a presence of power, an absence of everything.

The bear came forward and placed its grizzled paw on Voden's heart. "How will you use your power, my son? Will you heal or hurt? Be destroyer or mender? Be black or white?"

Without thinking Voden spoke. "I would do all. Both warrior and healer would I be. Both black and white."

"Ahhh," the bear responded, his shaggy head shaking slowly back and forth. "Ahhh." The twisted thing sucked in its breath and moaned a single word that sounded like "Ygg." Vestla's face became still and thoughtful. The bear turned and spoke to the shadow. "Master, the power you gave him has spoken. It is as you willed."

The darkness stirred, and Voden felt sudden horror. His mind flared with fear, and he shrank back against Geri. A mere whisper of sound came from the shadow and set them all quivering. "It is as I willed." Then the shadow melted and disappeared.

With a sigh of relief the bear murmured, "The Master is gone."

Voden stepped toward Vestla. "Mother," he began, "please, why am I here?"

"You are in grave danger, my son, in danger of dying or going mad. Your life is once more at a critical point where you may or may not survive. Your Hamingjur brought you here at the request of the Master. The Master also called Father Bear, also myself and this twisted one that dwells in the realm of Niflheim at the root of Yggdrasil where Nidhogg lurks."

"Why?"

"The Master placed the Galdar-power in you. The Disir sought to destroy it in their fear. Jalk set it right, but he could only begin the process, and there is much you must learn before you can use it properly. Now the Disir have tried again to divert it, this time with the mandragora."

"Mandragora?"

"The root of lust."

Voden's jaw dropped, and he stared at his mother. "Lust? Do you mean . . . ?"

Vestla nodded sadly. "Yes, Voden. The Disir put mandragora in your food to waken your lust. They sought to bury the

Galdar-power beneath an avalanche of passion, to put the reins of control on your mind."

"Freyja? Did she . . ."

"Freyja too. They prepared the black root for her; fed it, mixed with yours, to her. In her food, in her drink, everywhere."

Stunned, Voden sat down on the branch. "Then . . . then she didn't love me. It was . . . it was just a drug. Something they made her do. Not . . . not something she wanted. I . . . I . . ." He leaped to his feet, sudden rage filling him. He clenched his fists and shook them at the light that filled the world. "Damn them! Damn them all! Can't they leave me alone? Can't they leave me anything to believe in? I curse them! All of them!" Tears began to pour down his face, his words cut off by sobs that broke, uncontrollable, from deep inside. "Oh, Freyja," he moaned, "all a lie! All a lie!"

For several moments he cried while the rest stood by and watched. Finally his sobs died and he stood, shoulders slumped in despair, his eyes dull. He looked at them all. "And none comfort me," he said softly. "Even my mother stands and watches my grief."

Father Bear shuffled forward. "Your grief and your sickness are yours alone, Voden. We cannot interfere. The Master has so willed it. That is true of all who have the Galdar-power. They must heal themselves. We can only instruct, and even that is limited to telling or showing. We cannot help you do. The power is in you. You must learn to call on it. Only thus can you survive."

"Why should I want to survive? I'm nothing. I have nothing. My past is filled with empty longing. My present is a twisting body wracked with intolerable pain. My future appears one long, endless struggle. I'm not Aesir. I'm not Vanir. I'm not—"

"Yessss," hissed the twisted thing, hopping up and down in vile excitement, "yesss, yield, manling; die, oh, die so Nidhogg can gnaw your corpse and we may suck your soul; oh, yesss, give up, the struggle is too hard; yesss, die." The thing humped forward, its claws stretched out, reaching for him.

Voden jerked upright, startled and repulsed by the greed and odor of the creature. "What are you? Why are you here?"

The hideous monster smirked and moved closer. "I? Young master, no name have I, nooo, but many names do I know, oh, yesss; come, Master, yesss, come, the mandragora is strong;

yield, die, I will take you to Niflheim, to the root of the Tree; come, yesss."

A cold dampness radiated from the creature. It touched Voden and wrapped around him, draining the energy from his limbs. He began to slump. "Yesss," the thing hissed as it slid forward. "Yesss, sssooo tired, sssooo weary, nothing to live for, no reason to struggle, and all the pain, yesss, end all the pain, yield, let the mandragora have its way, come with me, come." Slowly it reached out its hand to take his.

"No!" With a shout he stepped back, the power suddenly flowing through his body. "No, I won't yield! Who are you? I demand you tell me! I, Voden, demand it." He swept them all with commanding eyes. "Yes, I demand that you tell me who and what you are. You were sent by the Master, you say. Then, why? What have you to do with me?

"We'll begin with you, twisted one."

The thing writhed back from him with a wail. "Oh, don't strike me, Master! I have no name, except Despair, but I know many, I can teach you the names of all the demons who steal men's souls and make them sick, yesss, that is why the Master ordered me here, I swear it!"

The bear shuffled forward and bowed. "I am Father Bear. I will speak the First Names of many things, and teach you the original tongue so you may call them. This knowledge you must have."

Vestla stepped up and bowed. She smiled radiantly. "My son, I am the Mother of Animals. I will take you to your place on the Tree, the place you may return to whenever you wish. I will part the mists of the future to let you see what you must do. A glimpse. A quick glimpse. One you will forget, but which will ever guide you. Your journey has only begun. What started in the spontaneity of a vision granted by Vilmeid can only come to be through a long and dangerous search by you. The Galdar-power will protect you, but you must save yourself."

She paused and smiled again. "As you just did, for the moment. But you are not safe yet. Listen, and we three will teach you what you must know to survive the mandragora and the things that will threaten you in the near future. Beyond that, you will be on your own. Learn well, or else you will fail at the first step of the journey. You must seek the place where you may gaze into Groa's other eye. The way is long and perilous. Yet it too is a mere beginning."

"Beginnings, endings," Father Bear chanted in a singsong voice, "all are one and return to the Tree. Endings, beginnings, neither can be until the other exists. Listen now, Voden, and listen well. I will sing to you the First Names. Learn now, Voden, and learn well."

"For failure," the twisted thing hissed, "is death."

THE FIRST NAME

XXVII

~

BORR shot a quick sidelong glanced at Gagnrad, then turned his eyes once more to the scene in front of him. There, at the edge of the Idavoll Plain, near where the mighty Gunnthro swept from the forests of the Vanir, Fiorgynn sat in her wagon, the cover off. The eight Disir flanked her, four on each side. Behind them in three ranks of nine were heavily armed Valkryja.

But there was only one Aesir youth with the Vanadis. One. Honir. Borr took stock of his own retinue. Himself, Gagnrad, sixteen warriors, all mounted and armed, Niord, Frey, and two new hostages. He would have expected the Vanadis to bring an equal number. Yet she brought twenty-seven warriors, one Aesir, and no new hostages.

He cursed himself silently. Should have known something was wrong when they didn't send Voden home for the solstice. I should have guessed. Said he was sick, couldn't travel. A lie. Should have known.

Now it's too late. They outnumber us. If it comes to a fight, we could lose. Damn! How should I play this? Be open, friendly, and understanding? Or tough and demanding? Buri would have been all smiles, lulled them into a false sense of security, then hit them when they were relaxed. That's why they called him The Clever. But I'm known as Skullcracker. Best behave as I really am.

"Where is my son?"

"He is not here," Fiorgynn said softly.

Borr snorted. "I'm not so old that my eyes are failing. I can see that he's not here. I asked where he is. I expect an answer."

Fiorgynn looked down, then up at Borr. Her eyes were sad. The Aesir chieftain couldn't help but notice the circles beneath and the many new wrinkles around them. She's getting old, he thought in wonderment. So am I, he realized in turn. All the more reason to want my son by my side in Asgard.

"Voden is dead." The words were spoken softly, gently, yet they hit Borr with brutal force. He gasped. Dead? Voden dead? "As we told you, he fell ill around the solstice. He was too sick to travel. Eir... Eir did everything she could. Freyja was sick too. She almost died. She still hasn't recovered completely. Voden... Voden died about two weeks ago. I'm... we're sorry. We..."

"Dead?" Borr turned stunned eyes to Gagnrad. "Dead? My son is dead?"

Gagnrad's face was hard. "The body, Vanadis? We would have the body so we can place it in the mound with his mother and grandfather, as is fitting for an Aesir. That way, when he goes to the Hall of the Gods, he will be seated next to them and won't be lonely."

Fiorgynn shot a quick glance at Eir. "The body? We... we didn't bring it. We buried it weeks ago. It's probably rotted by now."

"Then the remains. The bones and skull. We must have them and place them in the grave mound. It is our way, Vanadis," Gagnrad said firmly.

"Well, yes, the remains. Of course, we will send them to you. Of course."

Borr had recovered sufficiently to wonder at Gagnrad's actions. His lifelong friend was cold and controlled, but Borr could sense the seething anger just beneath the surface. He decided to follow the man's lead. Something was amiss.

Gagnrad continued, "And where, Vanadis, are the new hostages? You bring only Honir. We bring Niord and Frey. You know we sent messages indicating that we wished to have Voden and Honir back, that it was time they returned to their people and took their place in the Warrior's Hall. Likewise we thought Niord and Frey might want to return to many-seated Sessrymnyr. You see them here, and you see two new hostages to renew the truce. Yet I see none among your large number.

"Why such a large number, Vanadis? Surely you don't fear Jotun raiding parties? Since the truce, not one has penetrated this far toward the forests of Vanaheim. What do you fear that you have so many armed Valkyrja? Not us. We come with the usual number."

Fiorgynn looked uncomfortable. "We were unsure how you would respond to the death of Voden."

"Death is not unknown among the Aesir, Vanadis," Borr responded. "I have lost my wife, a child at birth, and now a son. I still have my son, Vethur, and my daughter, Vili. Life is possible. We do not slaughter our allies, even if our son falls sick among them and dies."

"If indeed that is how he died," said Gagnrad harshly.

Everyone gasped. "What . . . what do you mean?" Fiorgynn asked.

"Honir, to me!" commanded Gagnrad. The boy leaped from among the Disir and raced swiftly to stand next to the Aesir warrior. He was pale and trembling. It happened so quickly, no one had a chance to stop him.

"Calm, lad, calm," the huge Aesir advised. "Honir, how did Voden die?"

Honir looked back at the frozen faces of Fiorgynn and the Disir. "He . . . no one knows if he's dead or not. They . . . they never found his body."

"Was he sick?"

"Not in the usual sense, no. It was a lie at the solstice. I was afraid to say anything, because I didn't know what they'd do to him if they found him. We helped him escape, Yngvi and I, took him where they couldn't do anything more to him. They . . . they . . . I . . . " Emotion overcame the Aesir lad, and he was unable to continue.

For a short time the only sound was Honir's sobbing and the soft whisper of the wind in the grass. Even the horses stood as if shocked into motionlessness. Borr looked from Honir to Gagnrad to Fiorgynn. He clenched his fist and took one step in her direction. "Where is my son, Vanadis?" he demanded, his voice hoarse and angry.

Fiorgynn sighed, and her shoulders slumped. "I don't know," she replied, her voice small and hopeless. "I don't know. He disappeared in the early winter during the first big snowstorm. We searched and searched. We're still searching. We've found nothing."

"Who is Yngvi?"

The Vanadis looked puzzled. "Yngvi?" She looked at her Disir. "Yngvi? I don't know. Honir mentioned him. Do any of you know?"

"Aye," said Syr. "Aye, I know. A forester. Wrestles in Folkvang every summer. Better than most, but never wins. Not he. Busy talking with all the other lads, he is. Lives somewhere to the west of the Hrid."

"Yngvi," muttered Vor thoughtfully. "Yngvi. Yes. I remember. Jalk had a brother named Yngvi. Left Folkvang shortly after Jalk did. Too old to be a young forester, though. This Yngvi could be his son. If Jalk lived . . ." She let the thought hang in the air.

Borr turned to Honir. "You mentioned that you and Yngvi helped Voden escape. What did you mean, lad?"

Honir looked worried. "I . . . I didn't think it would hurt him. I only wanted to help. We were worried about how he was acting. Ever since the vernal equinox, he and Freyja were . . ." He paused and gulped, his face flaming red. "I mean, he was acting strange. We . . . we were . . . afraid there was something wrong. I mean . . ."

"What happened, lad?" Gagnrad said softly but firmly. "No one's going to hurt you now. Tell us what happened."

"Well, during the storm I got Voden to go with me outside the south gate. Told him Freyja was there. He . . . he . . . was half wild because he hadn't been with her for two days and . . . Well, Yngvi and two others were waiting. They grabbed him and tied him. He wouldn't have gone any other way. He started raving and screaming. We . . . we . . . tied him and they . . . they . . . took him. . . . I don't know what happened then. That's all I know."

"By Audhumla," muttered Fiorgynn, her gaze fixed on Honir. "Who would have thought that Honir, silent Honir, would be the one? We questioned him, but he said he didn't know anything. He was the one."

"Honir," Borr asked, gaining the lad's attention, "do you know where he is? Is he alive?"

Honir shook his head miserably. "I don't know. He's with Yngvi, but I don't know where that is, or if he's alive. I don't know."

Gagnrad and Borr exchanged glances. Their faces were hard and determined. "Vanadis," Borr began, "this is a breach of the truce between us."

"That Honir and a forester kidnapped your son? How can that be a breach on our part?"

"They felt it necessary to kidnap him to protect him from something you were doing to him. What that something was, I can't quite fathom yet, but it must have been serious to prompt someone like Honir to action. *That* is a breach, Vanadis, and a very serious one."

Fiorgynn was silent. Finally she lifted her eyes and stared hard at Borr. "There are twenty-seven seasoned warriors in my train, Aesir. Twenty-seven."

Borr nodded. "There are. I have sixteen Aesir, all men who have fought many battles against the Jotun and come away alive. Twenty-seven you have, trained and ready, but not battle-hardened. I think the odds are about even, Vanir."

Gagnrad touched his shoulder. "Not any longer," he muttered, gesturing toward the south with his head. Emerging from the trees was a group of foresters on foot.

"You come well attended to truce meetings, Vanadis," Borr commented bitterly.

The Vanadis shifted worriedly in her wagon. "They are not part of my train," she responded.

Honir came to sudden attention, his eyes riveted on the approaching figures. "Yngvi. And Voden! Voden!" In great excitement he broke from Gagnrad's side and sprinted across the plain, calling out to his friend.

Everyone remained silent and still as the band of foresters approached. Voden was indeed among them, dressed as they were. Soft brown doeskin leggings and a hunting shirt covered his tall, slender form. From beneath the leather cap on his head his blond hair fell almost to his shoulders. His face was stern and drawn; the evidence of great suffering and grave sickness recently past were clearly written there. His eyes were dark and cold.

The band formed a circle between the two groups. The young foresters, bows slung across their backs, hands on the axes at their waists, facing outward, surrounded Yngvi, Voden, and Honir.

Voden bowed first to his father, then turned and bowed slightly to Fiorgynn. "Greetings, Vanadis." The depth and resonance of his voice surprised them all. "I would have been here sooner, but we kept running into Valkyrja patrols." There was mockery in his words. "We let them all pass in peace, though I doubt they were aware of their luck." Yngvi smiled, as did the other foresters. Voden turned back to his father. "Father. I see you have Frey and Niord. Honir tells me you wish to exchange them for the two of us so that we might come back to Asgard and take our rightful places in the Warrior's Hall."

Borr grinned proudly. "Yes. I would have my son by my side."

Voden's lips curved upward at the ends, but his eyes stayed cold and flat. The result looked more like a snarl than a smile. "No, Father. I will not return to Asgard to be at your side."

Syofyn looked triumphantly at Voden. "So, you will come back to Folkvang with us, Voden? Freyja is there waiting for you."

The strange expression on the young man's face turned into a true snarl as he whirled to face the Disir. "Ah, Syofyn. Of course. You would be here. And Syr too. And dear, dear Eir, the healer."

He looked over the group as if searching for someone. "Where is Freyja? My sweet, loving Freyja? Did she survive the potions you gave us, Eir, or did her mind snap, as mine nearly did?" His voice rose in pitch and took on a hysterical edge. "Did she writhe and thrash about in pain? Did she know the horror, the sweating agony, I knew? Does she live? Is she a drooling, broken shell?"

"She . . . she lives, thank Audhumla," Fiorgynn murmured, her voice choked with emotion. "She almost died, but she lives and is sane."

Voden took the news silently. The bitterness in his expression softened slightly. "Then I send her my regards, Vanadis. Tell her . . . tell her I wish it had been real. And tell her that although we may not have shared true love, at least we have shared pain. I . . . won't forget her."

His voice broke slightly on the last word. The fact seemed to fill him with renewed anger. He spun back to face his father and Gagnrad. "I will not return to Folkvang or to Asgard."

"You are Aesir," Borr protested. "You belong in Asgard. You . . ."

"Aesir?" Voden's voice was heavy with sarcasm. "No. At best, half Aesir. The other half of my blood flows from dawn-lit Prin. Vestla was never Aesir."

"You belong with us, Voden," Gagnrad said.

"Then why have I spent the last six years of my life among the Vanir? I speak the elder tongue, Beargrasp. I know the Thiodnuma. I wrestle." He looked down at the doeskin clothes he wore. "I even dress like a Vanir forester. Surely I am as much Vanir as Aesir."

"Yes," Fiorgynn said swiftly. "Yes, Voden, you are Vanir. You are my son as surely as Niord and Frey are. More so. You . . . may not believe it, but I love you. I was heartsick when you disappeared. I . . ."

Voden laughed harshly. "How well you lie even now, Fiorgynn! I am a son to you. Yes, I almost do believe you mean it. After the way I've seen you use your own daughter, I almost believe it. Being your son is hardly something to be proud of. Besides, I have a mother."

"You are Aesir," Borr stated firmly.

"Why? Because I killed a Jotun? Because I'm as vicious as the next man? I've seen what it is to be Aesir. I've seen the blood flow, heard the death screams of little children. Gods! Every time I close my eyes I see and hear it all.

"Fornjot is the perfect god for the Aesir, father. Fornjot the Destroyer. Yes. Perfect." He spat disgustedly on the ground.

"Voden, enough of this. You will come home with me," Borr demanded, his voice short and angry.

Voden stared at his father for a few moments, then answered, his voice flat and unyielding. "I will go nowhere with anyone unless I wish it. Get used to that idea, Father."

"Don't make me force you, son."

Voden barked out a harsh laugh as each forester loosened the ax in his belt. He pulled his own out and held it lightly in his hand. "Try and one of us dies, Father. Remember the wizard from Muspellheim you killed on the Vigrid? The skalds say that you hurled your ax at him and hit, from—what?—fifteen feet? I can split a reed from thirty. Or your head. It's all the same.

"No, Father, you won't force me. Neither will the Vanadis. All Yggdrasil cannot force me any longer. All my life I've been pushed from one thing to another. Sent to Folkvang so that you might sate your hatred against the Jotun with the help of new allies. Drugged, cut, and tied to a goat to appease the hunger of the Disir for control and their fear of the Galdarpower. Fed mandragora to shackle me with lust. No longer."

Everyone stood and stared at the young man, wonder and fear on their faces. He seemed larger than life. Larger and stronger, strangely dark and glowing at the same time. A power radiated from him, a power that cowed and frightened them. His gaze, fierce and wild like that of a hunting wolf, swept over them as he talked, and they cringed. "I am not going to Asgard to learn the craft of killing Jotun women and children just to please my father and Fornjot. I am not returning to Folkvang to be used by the Disir.

"I am on a different journey now, one I did not start on my own, but which I must finish that way." He fixed Syr with a burning glance. "The power, old sow, the Galdar-power that Vilmeid gave me and you so feared and tried to destroy, it grows. My foot is on the path and I must follow it.

"My mother told me of it as she was dying. I didn't understand it then, but I remembered. Her words have echoed anew in my mind for months now: 'My son, my son! Twilight comes! Prepare yourself for what you must do! Learn what you are that you may do it! Look deep in Groa's other eye! Go to . . . go to . . . seek . . .'" He paused for a moment and glared at them all.

"'Learn what you are . . .' What am I now? Nothing. What have I been? A tool bent to the will and use of others.

"No longer. The power grows within me. My foot is on the path. I cannot, will not, turn back. I will follow it to its end, no matter what the price."

"We will go with you," Yngvi cried out. "By Beyla, Voden, we'll go with you to Nidhogg's realm itself!" The other foresters joined with shouts of affirmation.

Voden looked at Yngvi, his face soft and filled with love. "Ah, my friend, my friend. I owe you so much. You and Jalk. Without you . . ." He shuddered. "Yes," he mused, "it would be wonderful to have you all with me, but it cannot be. No. I must walk the way alone, must heal my own sickness. Thank you. But . . ."

"Where will you go, Voden?" Honir asked, his voice small and filled with anxiety.

The young Aesir gazed fondly at his fellow hostage. "Where my mother suggested. I'll go to look in Groa's other eye."

"But . . . but she has only one."

"And where is the other?"

Honir looked puzzled. "I don't know."

"Years ago, when her husband Aurvandil disappeared, she went searching for him. That was before the Jotun lived north of the Iving. She wandered north until she came to Mimir's well. There she left her other eye in payment for a sip. That is where I go, Honir. To Mimir's well."

"But . . ." his father sputtered, "that's just an old wives' tale! A story the old hag made up! There's no such thing as Mimir's well. You're mad. You're—"

"I'll go with you, Voden," Honir interrupted. "We've gone through so much together. I'm not afraid."

"Ah, my long-legged friend." Voden laughed softly. "I know you'd stand by me through anything. You already have. But this time you cannot come. No one can. I meant what I said. I must go alone."

"It's dangerous. One man alone on such a long trip. You'll need help."

Voden smiled mysteriously. "I have help. Freki and Geri will guard over me at night. At dawn Hugin and Munin will fly out and report back what they see. No, I won't be without help."

"You are mad," his father muttered, shaking his head in dismay. "Come back with us. I . . . Please, Voden."

"Father. All of you. Try to understand. I do what I must. There are forces involved that I can't comprehend. Yggdrasil is changing. Dark things are shambling toward the light. A time of dread is coming. I must prepare. I must.

"What . . . what you have all done to me is done. It is part of something greater than any of us can understand. But I must know. I must go forward. To stand still while Yggdrasil changes is to die. None of you can control me any longer. Something much vaster has swept me up, and I will follow it. With my eyes and my mind and my heart open, I will follow it."

Voden gazed at his father with a sad but unwavering gaze. "I will take my first name, Father, like a true Aesir, but I will take it on my own. I am Vafudar, the Wanderer."

"Alone?" muttered Borr. "You'll wander alone?"

"I've been alone for years. More alone than any of you could ever know." Voden stepped slowly from the circle of the foresters. His throwing ax was back in its place in his belt. A bow was slung over one shoulder, paralleled by a quiver of arrows. A small pack hung in the center of his back. Opposite his ax, thrust through the belt, was the ancient dagger Buri had given him as his Tooth Gift.

He stopped and silently regarded the three groups. Then he smiled almost shyly. "This is an ending and a beginning. I've traveled long and hard to reach this point of departure. Now Voden Vafudar, the Wanderer, bids you all good-bye." Turning away, he walked off across the plain toward the west and the River Gunnthro.

Soundlessly they watched him until he was out of sight. Then without exchanging another word, they left.

Slowly the grass of the Idavoll sprang back up where they had trampled it. Within a few days there was nothing to mark the spot where they had stood.

Glossary of Names and Places

Adad—Patesi of Maqam Nifl and Borsippa.

Aesir—a race of farmer-herders living south of the River Iving and north of the forests of Vanaheim.

Alfar—an ancient race, now few in number, who dwell in the forests of Alfheim.

Alfheim—the land of the Alfar. It lies north of Asaheim in the forests to the south of the Bones of Ymir.

Amsvartnir Sea—a freshwater inland sea to the northwest of Asaheim.

An—the eldest Son of Muspell. He is the Patesi of Uruk and Der.

Aralu—the land of the dead in the religion of Muspellheim. It has seven gates, tended by the gatekeeper Neti, and seven walls. It lies across the River Hubur. It is ruled by Nergal and Ereshkigal.

Asaheim—the land of the Aesir. It is composed of three plains: the Himinborg, the Idavoll, and the Aesir; plus the Valaskialf Plateau. It is bounded on the north by the River Iving and on the south by the forests of Vanaheim.

Asgard—the principal city of the Aesir and home of Voden, Borr, and Buri.

Ask—the first man of the Aesir, created from a tree trunk by Fornjot.

Audhumla—the Nourisher, chief deity of the Vanir; created the world and everything in it.

Badtabira—the major city of the First Dark Empire. It was destroyed by demons at the fall of the Empire.

Baru—the book of foretelling, owned by Utu.

Bel—an honorific title similar to "Lord."

Bergelmir—second son of the sixth Thrudgelmir. The only Jotun warlord to escape the debacle of the first assault on Asaheim. Becomes Warlord of the Horde for the second assault.

Beyla—Vettir, or god, of the bees; giver of mead.

Bifrosti's Ford—the only good crossing over the River Iving. To the north of Asgard and just east of the Himinborg.

Bones of Ymir—a range of rugged hills to the south of the River Iving.

Borr Skullcracker—chieftain of the Aesir after Buri. Father of Voden. Husband of Vestla Ravenhair.

Borsippa—city of Muspellheim. To the south of Maqam Nifl. Ruled by Adad.

Buri Axhand—chieftain of the Aesir. Father of Borr Skullcracker. Grandfather of Voden.

Cuthah—temple of Nergal. Powerful during the First Dark Empire. Destroyed by the Sons of Muspell during the Second Dark Empire.

Der—city in Muspellheim, ruled by the eldest Son, An. It is situated athwart the only opening in the Great Wall, directly on the Great Route to the east.

Disir—a group of eight women who rule Vanaheim with the Vanadis: Eir, Gna, (Gullveig), Hlin, Lofyn, Syn, Syofyn, Syr, Vor.

Distingen—ruling council of the Vanir. It is composed of nine members: the Vanadis and the eight Disir.

Dverg—a race of short men who dwell in the mountains and forests of Nidavellir. They are known for their skill in metalsmithing.

Eir—one of the Disir. A healer, deeply versed in Seidar-magic and herb lore.

Elivagar—the river of ice that runs from Fornjot's Hall. It is formed by the slaver from the jaws of his two wolves, Skoll and Hati.

Embla—the first woman of the Aesir, created from a tree trunk by Fornjot.

Enki—Patesi of Eridu and Kish.

Enlil—the Ellilutu of Muspellheim. Patesi of Nippur, Lagash, and Ashur. Head of the Anunnaki. Holder of the Tupsimati, the Tablets of Destiny.

Enmeenlu—one of the Sons of Muspell from the First Dark Empire. He was Patesi of Badtabira.

Ereshkigal—consort of Nergal and queen of Aralu.

Fiorgynn—queen, or Vanadis, of the Vanir. Mother of Niord, Frey, and Freyja.

Folkvang—the principal city of the Vanir, in Vanaheim. Home of Fiorgynn, the Vanadis.

Fornjot—the Destroyer, chief god of the Aesir.

Freki—one of Voden's Hamingjur, a gray wolf.

Frey—son of Fiorgynn. Sent along with his brother, Niord, as hostage to the Aesir to guarantee the treaty.

Freyja—daughter of Fiorgynn. Sister of Frey and Niord.

Frigg—Vettir, or goddess, of sexual love.

Fylgjur—tutelary spirit of those who practice the Galdar-power.

Gagnrad Beargrasp—Aesir chieftain, friend of Borr Skull-cracker.

Galdar-power—type of magical power granted by Vilmeid.

Gallas-demons—category of minor demons controlled by the simplest spells.

Geirahod—the Valkyrja who taught Thiodnuma to Voden.

Gerl—one of Voden's Hamingjur, a black wolf.

Glad—legendary lover of Oski.

Gna—one of the Disir.

Groa—witchwoman of the Aesir.

Gullveig—one of the Disir and sister of Fiorgynn. Heads the first delegation to the Aesir. Raped and beaten by Borr. Dies during Jotun raid on Vanaheim.

Gymir—the sky god of the Jotun. The sun is his eye. Sacrifices to him are burned on a pyre. Father of Ymir.

Hamingjur—helping guardian spirits. Animal familiars of those who practice the Galdar power.

Himinborg—an area of huge, tumbled boulders to the south and east of the confluence of the River Iving and the River Sid. Also the name of the plain in that general area.

Hlin—one of the Disir.

Honir—boyhood friend of Voden. Accompanies him to Folkvang as a hostage to guarantee the treaty with the Vanir.

Hrodvitnir—nephew of Bergelmir. A promising young Jotun warrior.

Hugin—one of Voden's Hamingjur, a raven.

Idun—mother of Glad.

Igigi—the original gods of Muspellheim. There are three hundred of them.

Innina—consort of the Patesi An. A powerful sorceress.

Jalk—practitioner of the Galdar-power. Befriends Voden and helps teach him. Leader of the foresters. Originally called Sanngetall.

Jormungand—a huge warrior, guard of the caravan attacked by Borr. Servant of Surt.

Jotun—a race of seminomadic herdsmen who inhabit the grasslands north of the River Iving.

Jotunheim—the land of the Jotun. It is a vast grassland that stretches north from the River Iving all the way to the Icerealm. On the west it is bounded by the Amsvartnir Sea and the Western Forest, on the east by the Great Eastern Waste.

Kara Khitai—a country that lies on the eastern side of the Great Eastern Waste, on the western slopes of the Kunlun Mountains. It is known for its fierce warrior-monks.

Kari—one of the three sons of Fornjot. He rules the wind. Vindsval, the God of Winter, was created from his body by Fornjot.

Kur—the nether regions according to the religion of Muspellheim. It is the dwelling place of demons and of Tiamat and her serpent-dragon brood. Aralu is located in the Kur.

Lamashtu—a she-demon who drinks men's blood and eats their flesh. An ally of Surt.

Ler—one of the three sons of Fornjot. He rules the water.

Lofyn—one of the Disir.

Logi—one of the three sons of Fornjot. He rules fire. Sigfod, the God of Battle, was created from his body by Fornjot.

mandragora—mandrake root, a powerful herb often used as an aphrodisiac.

Maqam Nifl—city of Muspellheim. At the southern end of the Niflsea. Home of Surt. Ruled by Adad.

Maqlu—one of the most important books of magic in Muspellheim. It controls the Utukku-demons and contains protective counter-spells. It is owned by An.

Marduk—Patesi of Muspell.

Mashu Mountains—range of mountains that stretches across northern Muspellheim from east to west. Just south of the Northern Waste.

Mjollnir—hammer made by Volund.

Mount Hela—a volcanic mountain that lies in the center of the Niflsea.

Munin—one of Voden's Hamingjur, a raven.

Mushrussu—a serpent-dragon. One of Taimat's brood and a personal enemy of Jormungand.

Musirkeshda—a serpent-dragon. One of Tiamat's brood, allied with Enmeenlu and guardian of the *Utukki Limnuti*.

Muspell—one of chief cities of Muspellheim. Ruled by Marduk.

Muspellheim—the land where the Sons of Muspell dwell. It is to the south of the Sea of Mists and the Twisted Lands. It was the site of the First Dark Empire.

Namtaru—a demon servant of Nergal. Messenger of the land of the dead, Aralu. He carries the names of those about to die to Ereshkigal.

Nannar—Patesi of Ur.

Nergal—Lord of Aralu, the netherworld of the dead. Also God of War.

Nerthus—Earth goddess of the Jotun. She "inhabits" a wagon, drawn by bulls with golden horns, and goes everywhere with the Jotun. The wagon is kept in a sacred grove. Sacrifices are hung on her sacred tree, an ash. Mother of Ymir.

Nidavellir—the land of the Dverg. It lies in the forests and mountain slopes to the west of the River Gopul, south of the River Sid.

Niflsea—a misty sea about one hundred miles long and thirty-five miles wide. It lies in eastern Muspellheim, just south of the Mashu Mountains.

Nimeqi—one of the most important books of magic in Muspellheim. It contains secret magical knowledge and is owned by Enki.

Niord—son of Fiorgynn. Sent along with his brother, Frey, as hostage to the Aesir to guarantee the treaty.

Nornir—the three who determine the fate of every Aesir at birth. They are Urd, Verdandi, and Skuld.

Northern Waste—a vast desert that covers the entire northern part of Muspellheim. Once a fertile plain. In the far west it is known as the Great Sandy Desert. In the far east it is called the Bitter Quarter.

Nunamir—title applied to Enlil. There is no direct translation. It refers to his evil, magical powers and ability to talk directly with the dead, using their spirits to do his bidding. Considered one of the most feared and dreaded titles in Muspellheim.

Od—Vanir boy wrestler, opponent of Voden.

Oski—legendary lover of Glad.

Patesi—Priest-king. The title of the seven Sons of Muspell: Adad, An, Enki, Enlil, Marduk, Nannar, Utu.

Prin—a small country that lies high on the eastern slopes of the Kunlun Mountains, far to the east across the Great Eastern Waste.

Rabisu—a demon also known as the Croucher or the Spy. Rabisu is worshipped by thieves and spies.

Raesvelg—Voden's Fylgjur, a giant eagle.

rivers—the major rivers of Yggdrasil are the Iving, Sid, Gopul, Hrid, Gunnthro, Fimbulthul, Slid, Svol, Thyn, Vegsvin, Non, Geirvimul, Leipt, Vid, Gomul, and Gjoll.

Roskva—servingwoman in Borr's household.

Saghulhaza-demons—category of major demons controlled by the spells of the *Shurpu*.

Seidar-magic—a form of magic practiced mainly by women.

Sessrymnyr—Fiorgynn's hall in Folkvang.

Shipti—one of the most important books of magic in Muspellheim. It is a book of incantations and is owned by Enki.

Shurpu—one of the most important books of magic in Muspellheim. It controls the Saghulhaza-demons and contains many Wardspells. It is owned by Marduk.

Skald—an Aesir poet-singer gifted in composing and singing verses about the exploits of prominent Aesir.

Skuld—one of the Nornir. Identified with the waning moon. Shows the future. A maid.

Smoking Lands—range of volcanic mountains to the south of Vanaheim.

Sumal—goddess/mother of vultures.

Sunrise Empire—a vast empire that lies to the east of the Kunlun Mountains. It stretches all the way to the Eastern Sea.

Surt—companion of Borr during his raids in the Twisted Lands. Master of Jormungand. Servant of Nergal.

Svartalfar—a race related to the Alfar, but of mixed blood because of their long servitude to the Sons of Muspell during the First Dark Empire. They dwell to the west of the Dverg.

Svartalfheim—the land of the Svartalfar. It lies west of Nidavellir and south of the Amsvartnir Sea.

Svarthofdi—the goddess who gives the Seidar-magic. Common to all the races of Yggdrasil.

Syn—one of the Disir.

Synyr—one-time "king" of Vanaheim from the summer solstice to the winter solstice.

Syofyn—one of the Disir.

Syr—one of the Disir.

Thiodnuma—the "sweeping people away." A fighting technique of the Valkyrja, akin to jujitsu.

Tiamat—leader and most powerful of the serpent-dragons that dwell in the Kur. Tiamat is the personification of primeval chaos.

Tiamat's Eleven—the brood of serpent-dragons that dwell in the Kur at the edge of Apsu, the abyss. Tiamat is the leader. Mushrussu and Musirkeshda are two of the other ten.

Tror—Son of Volund the master smith. Boyhood friend and companion of Voden.

Tupsimati—the Tablets of Destiny. The most powerful book of magic in Muspellheim. It dates from long before the First Dark Empire. It contains the original names of all beings and gives one the power to call up any demon or god.

Tyr—boyhood friend of Voden.

Urd—one of the Nornir. Identified with the waxing moon. Shows the past. A crone.

Uruk—city of Muspellheim near the Niflsea. Ruled by An. Home of his consort, the sorceress Innina.

Utgard—the chief city of the Jotun, composed of wagons.

Utu—Patesi of Sippar and Larsa. Worshiper of the Igigi, the original gods of Muspellheim.

Utukki-Limnuti—potent book of magic from the First Dark Empire. Originally owned by Enmeenlu. Contains the original names of seven sevens of demons, copied directly from the Tupsimati. Thought to have disappeared during the destruction of Badtabira at the fall of the First Empire.

Utukku-demons—category of major demons controlled by the spells of the *Maqlu*.

Valkyrja—female warriors of the Vanir. They form a special guard for the Vanadis.

Vanadis—title equivalent to queen of the Vanir, in Vanaheim.

Vanaheim—the land of the Vanir. It consists of a vast tract of forest stretching from the River Gopul in the west to the Valaskialf Plateau in the east; from the plains of Asaheim in the north to the Smoking Lands in the south.

Vanir—a race of forest dwellers who live in the forest south of the plains of the Aesir and north of the Smoking Lands.

Verdandi—one of the Nornir. Identified with the full moon. Shows the present. A woman.

Vestla Ravenhair—wife of Borr. Mother of Voden. A trained courtesan from the Floating World of Prin. Captured by Borr in a raid on a caravan.

Vettir—gods of the Vanir. They are omnipresent in all things. The Vanir see themselves as siblings of the Vettir.

Vidolf—the goddess who gives visions of the future. Common to all the races of Yggdrasil.

Vigrid Plain—a salt desert in the Twisted Lands.

Vili—younger sister of Voden.

Vilmeid—the god who gives the Galdar-power. Common to all the races of Yggdrasil.

Vindsval—Aesir God of Winter. Son of Kari.

Voden—son of Borr Skullcracker and Vestla Ravenhair.

Volund—a master smith from a people who live far to the north and west of Asaheim. His son is Tror. His daughter is Thrud.

Volva—a seeress.

Vor—the oldest of the Disir. Known for her wisdom.

Yggdrasil—the world. It consists of the Icerealm in the north and Jotunheim, Alfheim, Nidavellir, Svartalfheim, Asaheim, Vanaheim, and Muspellheim in the south. To the east Kara Khitai,

Prin, and the Sunrise Empire. To the west is the Western Forest, which eventually ends at the Sunset Sea. The image of Yggdrasil is a great ash tree.

Ymir—the first Jotun, conceived by Nerthus and Gymir in a violent storm. One of his legs fathered children on the other to create the whole race of the Jotun, the Sons of Ymir.

Yngvi—young forester and wrestler from Vanaheim, a friend of Voden.

Zi—the inner life-spirit of a thing. Often used in the magic of Muspellheim.

Stories

~of~

Swords and Sorcery

MURDER, MAYHEM, SKULLDUGGERY...
AND A CAST OF CHARACTERS YOU'LL NEVER FORGET!

THIEVES' WORLD ™

EDITED BY
ROBERT LYNN ASPRIN and LYNN ABBEY

FANTASTICAL ADVENTURES

One Thumb, the crooked bartender at the Vulgar Unicorn...*Enas Yorl*, magician and shape changer ...Jubal, ex-gladiator and crime lord...*Lythande the Star-browed*, master swordsman and would-be wizard...these are just a few of the players you will meet in a mystical place called Sanctuary. This is *Thieves' World*. Enter with care.

__80583-3	THIEVES' WORLD	**$2.95**
__79579-X	TALES FROM THE	**$2.95**
	VULGAR UNICORN	
__76031-7	SHADOWS OF SANCTUARY	**$2.95**
__78712-6	STORM SEASON	**$2.95**
__22550-0	THE FACE OF CHAOS	**$2.95**
__80593-0	WINGS OF OMEN	**$2.95**

Prices may be slightly higher in Canada.
